MANIPULATION
A LAND FORCE WARRIOR CHRONICLE

R.C. SCOTT

Copyright © 2007 Alfred Fasola
All rights reserved.

ISBN: 1-4196-7556-7
ISBN-13: 978-1419675560

Visit www.booksurge.com to order additional copies.

A F Fasola Associates
2755 Magnolia Woods Drive
Mt. Pleasant, SC 29464

This book is a work of fiction. Names, characters, places and incidents either are products of the author's imagination or are used fictitiously. Any resemblance to actual events or locales or persons living or dead is entirely coincidental.

All rights reserved, including the right to reproduce this book or portions thereof in any form whatsoever. For information address and information about special discounts for bulk purchases, please contact: A F Fasola Associates, 2755 Magnolia Woods Drive, Mt. Pleasant, SC 29464.

Manufactured in the United States of America

Library of Congress
Cataloging-in-Publication Data

**Dedicated to the brave men and
women of our Armed Services
. . . especially**

Alfred F. Fasola Ph.d, M.D.
Captain, U.S. Army
World War II

and

Ross W. Scott (deceased)
Staff Sergeant, U.S. Army
World War II

PROLOGUE

*TUESDAY
JANUARY 12, 2009
WASHINGTON, D.C.*

The nation's capital was simultaneously the most dangerous yet most secure place on the planet as the 44th President of the United States was sworn into office.

Nobody alive could ever remember its snowing and blowing so hard on an Inaugural Tuesday in Washington D.C. Rumor had it that it had snowed like a bastard the day George Washington was sworn into office in New York, but there were no records to substantiate that fact. The snow was already a foot-and-a-half deep around the swept steps of the Pentagon and that portion of the grounds that served as the reviewing stands, dais, and VIP seating. While the media filled air time speculating about the weather, there was no doubt that this was the first Inaugural held on the grounds of the Pentagon, and never before had there been remotely the same level of military presence. One entire armored battalion provided ground security forming an outer ring almost three miles in diameter. The no-fly zone extended deep into Virginia and Maryland with F-18's and Apache gun-ships scrambled and alert. The grounds themselves were managed by the Secret Service and a Special Operations Task Force.

Against this military backdrop the entire country was focused on the issue of national security and the global war on terror. Fifty-five percent of the voters believed the man being sworn into office today could do a better job than the woman he ran against, at leading the country in the most vital arena of national security. Recent events served to unequivocally convince Americans that our basic way of life was under attack, and we were most definitely at war. The President-elect had made it abundantly clear during the hard-fought campaign that he would not support a military draft. He would, however, initiate major changes in the manner in which the U. S. Armed Services conducted war. "It is," he said, "the twenty-first century, and we will adapt twenty-first century science and technology to the process of protecting our vital interests". A spokesperson for the new President announced at the morning's press briefing that much more would be said about this issue during the Inaugural Address.

"I want to conclude this address with a brief but important message to those who planned and executed the recent attacks on American citizens at home and abroad. We heard you loudly and clearly. And now I want you to hear me with the same clarity. As my first act as President I am signing Executive Order 911 effective immediately. By this authority, the Armed Forces of the United States are ordered to proceed with the rapid deployment of a new program to retool our military to bring state-of-the-art technologies to bear on the global war on terrorism. I intend to utilize the Land Force Warrior Program to restore order in the Middle East, then as a vehicle to negotiations that will result in a lasting peace. I am now speaking directly to the Muslim World. To those of you who seek to live in peace and participate fully in the global commu-

nity, *I extend my hand and commit to you the support of my entire administration. To those of you who make an abomination of the Word of God and who seek to spread chaos and death, I also give you a commitment. We will take the battle to you wherever you are. We will bring the full force of civilization to bear against you and we will eradicate you from the face of the earth. May God have mercy on your souls".*

"Well, Mr. Brady," said General Cadman, "that about sums it up. You heard the President this morning invoke a new Executive Order specifically referring to the Land Force Warrior Program. The Joint Chiefs are ready to go to contract with your company if you can deliver the three new weapons systems within the allotted time frame. Oh, and I can't overemphasize that you must deliver an Artificial Intelligence capability as well as the basic weapons systems specifications."

Patrick Brady's face was frozen in a mask as indecipherable as the machinations of his psychotic mind as he was offered entree into the upper echelon of defense contractors feasting at the public trough. Twenty-five years of busting balls and kissing ass were finally paying off. He remained emotionless in front of the General and his adjutant, Colonel Norman Franks, as he processed the information, but inside he was wearing a billion dollar smile that could have illuminated the dark alleyways of the most crime-infested city in America, doubling tonight as our hopeful nation's capital.

The three men were huddled together in an alcove off the lobby of the Hay Adams Hotel, site of one of the many Inaugural events occurring that evening to usher in the new administration. Patrick Brady cut a formidable figure in his traditional Armani tux. Standing three inches over six feet he had the rugged good looks of a middle-aged leading man with piercing grey eyes and the physical presence of a retired athlete who still spent every day in the gym. He transitioned from his sphinx-like concentration to unaffected bonhomie as he put his arm around General Cadman's bear-like shoulders and looked him directly in the eyes saying, "Yes sir, I can deliver everything that you need to implement Land Force Warrior with a brand of firepower that will restore order to the region decisively. The Zybercor Command and Control System can assimilate all your individualized weaponry into a real-time integrated network. Our new miniaturized laser technology is ready for point-and-shoot application and our wearable computers can easily be adapted to Land Force Warrior specs. And, yes, General, I will have an Artificial Intelligence capability in my pocket.....as if you and your colleagues could ever make up your minds about using it." A picture of virtue and sincerity Brady bowed theatrically, confident that he had just told the two high-ranking military men exactly what they wanted to hear. An experienced and disciplined negotiator, Brady never showed his hand until he knew exactly what the other party wanted and, most importantly, well understood their fears. He appreciated the kind of pressure the Joint Chiefs were under but, nonetheless, needed confirmation before he pressed for his final set of demands.

"Now that we are in bed together," said Brady with a conspiratorial wink, "what are the chances we can buy some more time to get all these systems up and working?"

Colonel Franks smiled at Brady, and with a confirming nod from his boss and old friend, the General, fielded the question. "Patrick, my friend, when the Man calls you into the Oval Office and directs you to do something important for your country and tells you it must be done in such and such a time.....well, it's like an eight-hundred-pound gorilla screwing a chicken....the chicken wants to say 'No' but can't catch its breath".

"That's pretty graphic," said Brady. "I assume that if said Man was seated in the Oval Office, he must have met with you gentlemen right after he was sworn in as President." Brady fully realized now that the President was "hands-on" in this matter and would apply the kind of mind-numbing pressure that could make even studs like Franks and Cadman sweat through their lapels.

Cadman was watching the exchange between Brady and Franks and felt compelled to add some explanatory remarks in support of his new Commander in Chief. "This President is a very smart man. He is all too aware that his options are severely limited as a result of the drastic cutback in Iraq last year. The civil war has spread throughout the Middle East and into North Africa, and thanks to that bastard, Putin, the mullahs have the bomb. With Iran calling the shots, the President is afraid they'll re-direct our crude oil supply to provide for China's growing demand. Hell, we'll be over $6.00 at the pump by year end as it is. He believes that the Land Force Warrior Program would give him the big stick he needs to bring the parties to the negotiating table. He committed to the American people that he would not implement a draft. Hell, that's probably what got him elected. He's betting that the Land Force Warrior Program would reinvigorate the whole process, get the job done in the Middle East, and drive a new generation of recruits into the volunteer Army. Capice?"

Brady realized that Cadman and Franks were well and truly screwed. It was too late for them to change horses now. He had them by the balls.

"I understand exactly where we are," said Brady, "however, if we're going to meet these time frames we're going to have to rewrite the rule book. Let me tell you what I have in mind."

Under normal circumstances Franks and Cadman would scrupulously follow regulations to the letter. **But these were not normal circumstances so they swallowed the hook at exactly the same time and leaned forward, giving Patrick Brady their undivided attention as the Marine Corps Band struck up "*Hail to the Chief*" and a phalanx of Secret Service agents preceded the President and First Lady into the lobby.**

CHAPTER ONE

SEPTEMBER 18, 2009
WHITE SANDS, NM
1400 MOUNTAIN STANDARD TIME

In the history of the world there had never been a soldier like Terrel Macklin.

At six-feet, three-inches tall and two-hundred pounds, "Mack" could travel at fifteen miles per hour for an indefinite period of time. According to the technical manual he could sprint up to thirty miles per hour; however, he still had difficulty maintaining his balance at the higher speeds. Several of the new applications had arrived only two weeks ago so he was going to have to rely upon the Basic Package for today's live-fire exercise. The technical team that developed the Land Force Warrior Program was brilliant but they had never been in combat. It took time to integrate new systems and applications. You can't read a user manual when the other people are trying to take your head off.

His boots were desert brown and went halfway up his calves. The soles were four inches thick with a pad-like bottom that had a lip uniformly three inches wider than the sole, creating a horseshoe-like effect. The intricate electronic mechanism located in the heel fired a network of interconnected "bones", creating a virtual skeleton that simulated the neural and muscular pathways of the foot. As Mack pushed off with the balls of his feet the power pack literally exploded him forward at approximately five times the normal rate of speed; whether walking, jogging, or sprinting.

MANIPULATION

The 'smart' body armor started at the kneecaps and went up the torso to the neck and down the arms to the wrists. The woven fabric technology allowed for a cooling mechanism that kept body temperature at a perfect 98.6 degrees Fahrenheit in spite of the outside temperature of 106. The Basic Package of the new Land Force Warrior Program consisted of an exoskeleton that was lightweight and incredibly strong. Body armor had progressed from ceramic plating to advanced titanium discs linked together to absorb the force of impact while neutralizing the penetration capability of even the most devastating of modern ammunition, such as the new version of armor-piercing rounds. The integration of the newer-class, lighter-weight armor, with the patented Zybercor exoskeleton, was 90% complete. Computer chips were embedded every half inch throughout the meshed outerwear. Any impact was dispersed over the entire fabric and a message was transmitted instantaneously to a UH60 Black Hawk Medevac chopper that was as well equipped as a Johns Hopkins surgical suite.

White Sands was over 5,500 square miles of government-owned land. The live-fire exercise scheduled to commence at 1500 Mountain Standard Time would pit a Land Force Warrior Tiger Team against radical Islamic terrorists recruited from the general population at Guantanamo Bay. The designated battlefield was 50 square miles. An armored battalion and two squads of F-18s were on hand to ensure that the prisoners of war adhered to the rules of engagement and stayed within the established boundaries. Those were the only restraints......beyond that it was 'kill or be killed'.

Terrel Macklin was not there by accident. Not since the Apollo Space Program had the U.S. government conducted such a thorough recruitment and evaluation process to identify the best and brightest from its Armed Services. The Land Force Warrior Program reported directly to the Joint Chiefs of Staff. Four-Star General Walter T. Cadman, U.S. Army, was the sponsor. Colonel Norman A. Franks, U.S.M.C., was the point man and oversaw the selection process. After months of debate, the personnel committee determined that the Land Force Warriors would be recruited from the ranks of Sergeant in the Marines and Army Infantry. The backbone of the Armed Forces of the United States since World War One, Sergeants trained the troops, led the troops, and were uniquely skilled at separating the pepper from the flyshit, particularly when the feces was being scattered by the wind propulsion machines.

Selection of the top twenty candidates was initiated after screening a pool of more than a thousand volunteers. Candidates understood that they were buying into a career decision anchored by a ten-year employment agreement. They would undergo the most comprehensive training program ever implemented by the Armed Forces. Millions would be spent on each man. The initial training and development program for the top twenty candidates was six months. The objective was not only the creation of an elite new warrior class, but also the ranking of the top twenty and, specifically, the selection of the best of the best to "prototype" and beta-test the Land Force Warrior Program.

Macklin was the first among equals. A product of Chicago's public schools Terrel was on the fast track of the professional soldier. A two-letter man at the University of Illinois majoring in electrical engineering, he had an easy smile and was wicked smart. Macklin volunteered for the Land Force Warrior Program the morning the specs were posted. The first three months consisted of round-the-clock exercises that were mentally ruthless and physically grueling, yet seemingly irrelevant to the Program's stated objectives. It was during the last three months of the evaluation, however, when Macklin separated himself from the other candidates. He had a 'gift' that the others didn't have. It was hard to describe. They all had similar physical, psychological, and emotional attributes and they represented the *crème de la crème* of America's young warriors. Macklin was just different. What distinguished him from the rest was his.......judgment. He seemed to consistently process information better than the rest. Abstract and mechanical reasoning, scenario interpretation, linear programming...... his gift cut through all the disciplines. A surefire way to screw up a good idea is to appoint a committee. In this case, however, the committee got it right. Judgment, the committee spokesperson reasoned, was the single most important factor for Land Force Warrior success. If the Joint Chiefs were betting heavily on LFW as the linchpin in the war on global terror....well then the committee's job was to provide the men who would make the best decision at the sharp edge of the program.

Macklin wasn't the smartest of the candidates. There were several 150+ IQ's. He was simply the most effective at processing information and coming up consistently with the full range of available options....then making the best choice and moving forward with confidence.

One of the most challenging aspects of the evaluation process was called Leadership Dynamics and Organization Effectiveness (LDOE). A three-week session held at the Marine Training Center at Quantico the LDOE Assessment took into consideration a wide variety of exercises including individual physical competition, team competition focused on problem-solving, consensus building, oral presentation, abstract and mechanical reasoning, and logic. All exercises were carefully administered and monitored by a team of a dozen experts representing the military branches, psychological fields, and a variety of technical areas. The candidates were subjected to conditions that tested their physical, emotional, and psychological limits. Sleep deprivation combined with a lack of food and water tested their abilities to reason and communicate effectively under relentless pressure. Many of the problems posed to the candidate teams were without discernible solutions. The exercises were designed to maximize frustration and create discord and confusion within teams.

It was during this phase of the process that Macklin began to separate from the pack. His unique ability to reason was apparent to all, in combination with his skill of obtaining 'buy in' from his other team members regardless of the composition of the team or the magnitude of difficulty contained in the exercise. He received the highest grade, by far, in Leadership Dynamics and Organization Effectiveness and overnight became the man to watch. Macklin was a time compression machine. He was processing solutions by the time the median range was still struggling with identifying the problem. Even the number two and three in the class scored significantly lower in this all-important exercise.

The last phase of the evaluation was Colonel Franks, one on one, with the top three candidates: Terrel Macklin, Sgt. Roy T. Rottenger (75th Infantry Battalion, U.S. Army), and another Marine, First Sgt. William "Billy" Poole.

Franks wished he was twenty years younger, and a candidate for this Program himself, as he stared across the conference table at Macklin. When Franks looked you in the eye it appeared that he didn't have the capacity to blink. Mack held his gaze, however, sitting erect yet relaxed, and waiting for the kind of grilling you can only get from a decorated Marine Corps Colonel.

"Sergeant, you are one of three remaining candidates. One of you will strap on a new technology and go to war for your country. The Joint Chiefs are putting billions of dollars behind this program. Son, I believe Land Force Warrior will change the complexion of warfare. Why should we select you?"

"Colonel Franks, with all due respect, we both know that all of the men selected for this evaluation will be strapping on the technology. I am getting the impression that you are looking for something more specific in this selection process. May I ask what that is before I respond?"

Shit, he is smart, thought Franks as he pondered the query.

"In truth, Sergeant, everyone in the Pentagon is not 100% behind LFW. There are other competing programs looking for dough. We're going to have to prove this in the field. Do you understand me?"

"Yes, sir. You cannot go wrong with any of the three of us. Rottenger and Poole are good men. I'd trust either of them with my life."

"I agree with you. However, you scored considerably higher in some important areas and I need to understand why. The evaluation teams, specifically the psychologists, believe that you have an advanced template in your head that serves as a framework for interpreting and processing information. The physiological data taken from the EEG and EKG machines during the battle simulations suggested that your body and brain chemistry was functioning more efficiently than the other guys.... you know, producing a higher level of concentration and intensity. Are they correct? What are you thinking about out there?"

"Colonel, growing up on the south side of Chicago, I learned early to hit 'em as hard as you can, as fast as you can, where it hurts 'em the most, when they ain't lookin'. You can sort the rest of the issues out while they're on the ground, Sir."

Franks was dissatisfied. Not because it was a wrong answer; it just failed to explain Macklin's unique gift. So the Colonel remained determined to drill down with his customary doggedness. "Son, I've read and forgotten more about military history than you'll ever know. That is about the tritest answer that I have ever heard and I certainly expected more out of you than this silly sound-bite shit. Would you like to take one more shot at answering my question before I throw your ass out of here?"

"What is it that you want to know, Sir? I have been with the program all the way. I hope that I have demonstrated my mental toughness and leadership skills. If you find that I am lacking in any way, I believe I'm entitled to know." Macklin leaned forward as he counter punched and waited for the inevitable verbal attack to follow.

"I want to know what's in your gut. Why are you here?" Franks watched closely as Macklin's eyes narrowed and he became very still. Mack bit his lip as he massaged the soft flesh between his thumb and forefinger. The shrinks reported that he resorted to that reflex when he was under pressure. It was an effective relaxation technique.

Macklin kept his voice low and steady. He looked Franks in the eye as his pupils dilated and turned an odd shade of yellow. "Those people killed my baby sister and I promised my Grandma I would prove that our God was more righteous than theirs. I want to kill the motherfuckers."

Norm Franks was a man first and a Marine second. Norm and June Franks had lost their only son in Desert Storm. A Special Ops Marine, Sgt. Robert Franks had been liaison to the Scots' Black Watch, assigned to take out the Scuds aimed at Haifa and Tel Aviv. He was killed covering his unit's escape and received the regiment's highest award in a private ceremony in Edinburgh Castle. Norm reached across the table, took Macklin's hand and said, "Son, I feel your pain. Now you and I are beginning to understand each other. Come with me. I want to buy you a beer."

* * *

SAME DAY
1430 MOUNTAIN STANDARD TIME
WHITE SANDS, N.M.

Cadman and Franks had decided that the Land Force Warrior Program would be comprised of semi-independent, multi-disciplinary forces dubbed "Tiger Team", in deference to nature's most efficient hunter. Each Tiger Team would have the hitting power of a division but with infinitely more speed, as well as the flexibility to seal off borders and to isolate and eradicate hostiles.

Whereas Macklin was the 'tip of the sword' in the Land Force Warrior Program, Lester Grossman was the sword's hilt, providing direction and stability. As overall tactical coordinator of Land Force Warrior (LFW) Tiger Team One, Grossman was conducting pre-battle protocol in a specially-adapted AWAC, high above the battlefield.

"Mack, how they hangin, my man?" said Grossman as he worked the keyboard attached to the massive array of interactive screens and satellite displays. "We have exactly thirty minutes to show time...on my...mark" as all Tiger Team members synched watches. Lester felt the adrenaline kick into high gear and knew that everybody on his team was experiencing the same rush as they prepared for a real-time, full-fire battle fought on American soil against a well-armed and highly dangerous enemy.

"I am on-line and ready to rock down here, little brother", said Macklin. Mack dropped the durable flat panel screen from his breastplate and activated the satellite telemetry, displaying a ten square mile image. The Land Force Warrior body armor had a built-in computer screen that was attached to the exoskeleton with brackets at the bottom that held the flat panel screen in place against the breastplate. With the push of a button, two mechanical arms lowered the screen and held it firmly in place so that Macklin had a clear view of the battlefield, leaving both hands available for other tasks. With a twist of his head, an eyepiece dropped over his acrylic high tech helmet activating the network communications system linking his Tiger Team to the AWAC flying a circular pattern five miles above the valley floor. While Macklin implemented his readiness protocol, Grossman shifted his attention to a last-minute review of his vast array of weapons options. The Tiger Team consisted of two fast-moving Apache attack helicopters as well as a Medevac chopper, a half-dozen thirty-foot drones, and an artillery battery six miles behind the engagement area. In theory there were dozens of additional weapons options, but the purpose of today's live-fire exercise was to test the efficacy of the Basic Package.

"Gents," said Grossman, "for the next eight minutes I will be reviewing all your weapons systems and will require a confirming acknowledgment at 1445 ....do you copy?" After receiving immediate acknowledgment, Lester concentrated on his offensive assets.

Two of the drones were equipped with the new generation of sensor-fused weapons that expanded the theory of cluster bombs using the satellite imaging technology to identify multiple enemy targets for simultaneous detonation of up to twenty 'smart' bomblets. The CBU-101 carried by the drones was a smaller version of the CBU-97 customized for the

Land Force Warrior Program.

The new generation of drones was capable of carrying a variety of delivery systems including maximum impact thermo-baric bombs for deployment in Afghanistan and other mountainous terrains where enemy assets were inaccessible. The thermo-baric bomb created an intense fireball able to penetrate deep underground targets through the release of mono-propellant fuel combined with highly combustible energy particles.

The artillery component of Tiger Team consisted of the German-made Panzer Howitzer 2000, the world's most advanced cannon artillery system. Only 55 tons, the mobile artillery had a maximum speed of 40 mph with armor protection and outstanding capability over rough terrain. Ideal for Tiger Team, the Howitzer combined speed and mobility with unparalleled punch from its quick-firing 155 mm gun, capable of 10 round barrages in twenty-second intervals. The system was fully automated from priming to loading to clearing, and had a range of approximately 40 miles. Its rounds were capable of self-correction through 'smart' linkage with the satellite.

Within eighteen months the technical team had reported they would adapt the new class of "Precision Guided Extended Range Artillery Projectiles," the XM982 Excalibur, to the Land Force Warrior artillery capability. The projectiles would carry a range of payloads including anti-armor and dual purpose munitions. Their plan included transferring the sensor-fused munitions to the artillery freeing up the drones for expanded high altitude roles.

The new generation of Apache gun-ships

(AH69A) had increased its horsepower to 2,100 for each of its turbo shaft engines. As the main rotor spun it exerted a rotation force on the entire body of the helicopter; the rear blades reacted against this force pushing the tail boom in the opposite direction. Thus, the pilot could rotate the helicopter in either direction or hover simply by changing the pitch of the rear blades. This simple yet effective mechanical system made the Apache ideal for the Land Force Warrior Program as it became a highly mobile or stationary platform for its chain gun and Hellfire missiles and rockets. Grossman had pushed Cadman and Franks to have access to the new Comanche Series, arguing that its greater firepower, mobility, and stealth features would trump the Apache, but got a 'thumbs down'.

The Hellfire missiles had their own guidance systems with a payload of copper-lined warheads capable of burning through the heaviest tank armor in existence. Each missile was equipped with its own steering control and propulsion system utilizing laser pulses in a variety of coded patterns; therefore targeting could be controlled from the AWAC, the Apaches, or the Land Force Warrior on the ground. Each Apache carried twenty-four missiles on four firing rails attached to pylons mounted to its undercarriage. As a result of the satellite telemetry and integrated command and control systems, the new generation of warheads could overcome the obstacles of cloud cover which historically blocked the laser beam, thus losing sight of its target. The version adapted for Land Force Warrior made the Apache far less vulnerable to attack as the laser targeting could be 'handed-off' to the AWAC or ground force. In addition, a radar-seeking mode could be instantaneously deployed in the event of sand storms.

The new Apache model was equipped with four Hydra rocket launchers carrying twenty-five folding-tin 2.75 inch aerial rockets in launching tubes ignited by automated triggers that were instructed to launch singly or in clusters with a variety of warhead designs. The Land Force Warrior applications included high-powered explosives as well as smoke-producing materials to cloak the Land Force Warrior while the M330-50mm automatic cannon eliminated threatening close-range targets. Mounted on the turret under the helicopter's nose, the integrated command and control system drove the hydraulics that swung the turret from side to side as well as up and down. An electric motor rotated the chain gun design which slid the bolt assembly back and forth to load, fire, extract, and eject cartridges far more efficiently and effectively than ordinary machine guns which merely used the force of the cartridge explosion to move the bolt. The magazine held up to 2,000 rounds and could fire up to 800 rounds a minute.

Satisfied that his weapons systems were combat-ready, Grossman brought the satellite on-line and synched up the space telemetry with Macklin's ground-eye view. "We are now linked up Mack," said Lester. "You have the eyes in the sky and I am seeing your world as well. I think I like it better up here."

Macklin chuckled and said " I feel sorry for you up there missing out on all the fun. Just make sure you have my ass covered. I want to assist our Islamic brothers along their journey to join Allah."

The satellite imagery was now shared with all of

MANIPULATION

the Tiger Team members. Instantaneously the state of play on the battlefield became crystal clear, three heavily armed enemy forces with ground and air mobility were strategically deployed in and around the valley. The Rx Lightyear stationary satellite had been launched four months prior. Its high-resolution capability allowed for excruciating detail as well as fixed and mobile analysis of the entire battlefield. The Lightyear capability was supplemented by Mack's eyepiece giving all parties the real-time perspective of space and ground views simultaneously.

With the flat-paneled screen in place, Mack was hands-free. His left arm was encased in a lightweight apparatus that housed a pulse cannon with the capacity to disable most types of electrical systems. Unlike the large footprint effect of a nuclear or non-nuclear electro magnetic pulse (EMP), the Land Force Warrior variation compressed the pulse and focused the effect in a target-specific environment with a range up to two miles. The ability to disable vital electronic systems selectively allowed for flexibility in border protection as well as urban situations. On his right arm running down to his hand was a highly experimental laser gun. The Widowmaker AS2 had a devastating impact on light armored vehicles incinerating anything in its path up to one and a half miles distant. Its effectiveness against enemy ground personnel was......well.....fucking unbelievable.

Macklin had no use for Patrick Brady, whom he had met on several occasions during the selection and training process. He believed Brady was just like all the other greedy bastards building piles of money on top of the dead bodies of real soldiers.

However, at the moment, he was grateful for the technology that made him the baddest ass in this Valley of Death.

Zybercor Corporation had built its reputation as a defense contractor ever since its Chief Executive Officer and founder, Patrick Fortune Brady, developed the first wearable computers in the mid-nineties. The company developed an early generation weapons division after 9/11/2001 and had been at the leading edge of laser technology since 2005. The patents were heavily protected and built around a formula that created a powerful chemical oxygen iodine laser. Recent enhancements had resulted in the capability to fire a continuous stream of energy; a great improvement over earlier three-to-five-second bursts. The Zybercor technology was a solid-state design making the system infrastructure far more compact and efficient than the traditional Tactical High Energy Chemical Laser that had to operate off the engine of a Humvee or Apache helicopter. The miniaturized 'point and shoot' technology developed by Zybercor cracked the code eliminating dependency upon a large mass of chemicals to convert to laser capability. The Widowmaker possessed instant targeting and incredible striking power, using 800 pulses of light in two seconds to drill through five inches of steel. The unique features of the Zybercor power pack redefined the cost-effectiveness and efficiency of the diode arrays to allow high quality beams to propagate with great precision over long distances with a narrow, intense, and well-shaped beam. Macklin completed his check list and notified Grossman on-line with his call sign that all systems were 'go'.

The Land Force Warrior Program operating

manual was highly specific. Protocol compliance was zero tolerance.......absolutely no exceptions.

Unbeknownst to the civilian contractors and heavy brass reviewing the exercise from the safety of Command and Control, Mack removed a photograph of a beautiful young girl from his gloved left hand and slid it under the webbing of his helmet. This was more than a real-time exercise for him. His younger sister had died in Iraq 18 months before in an ambush in the city of Basra. She was part of a medical unit helping treat civilians caught in the middle of a firefight. After her death Terrel dropped out of college and enlisted in the Marines. He chose to forego Officer Training and get straight into the action. At the funeral on the south side of Chicago, Macklin had to hold up his mom and grandmother. Shareen had been the apple of their eyes. She was the youngest of four. He was the older brother. Her death made things very, very personal.

* * *

Muhammed Kalil was a forty-two year old devout Muslim. His family had been killed in an Israeli missile attack in Gaza City in 1997 while he was at work at a construction site several miles away. From that day forward he had committed his life to Jihad. He was wounded in the fourth month of Allied occupation in Afghanistan, losing his right arm above the elbow. Kalil was a gifted leader. The distinction he had earned as a senior Al Qaeda operative in the field carried over to the 400+ prisoners-of-war in the highest security facility at Guantanamo Bay.

He was uniquely respected among both Sunni and Shiite.

Kalil had been approached three months earlier by a nondescript American in a Brooks Brothers suit. He was offered a deal he could not refuse. He was told that he could hand pick 60 men to coordinate and lead in a pitched battle against a U.S. military force. A planning and staging facility had been built at White Sands consisting of a cluster of Quonset huts, an airline hangar and a com center with an attached kitchen. Kalil and his team, under heavy guard, would have 10 days to select armaments. The sitrep was theoretical; his mission was the destruction of a U.S. border protection force deployed on the Syria-Iraq border. The exercise, however, would be anything but theoretical. The deal was simple. Win and go free. Lose and return to your cages at Guantanamo. In other words, a fight to the death.

1430 MOUNTAIN STANDARD TIME
WHITE SANDS, N.M.

Kalil had divided his force into three self-contained units, each led by seasoned operatives, comprised of a virtual All-Star team of radical Islamic terrorists from all corners of the world: Iraq, Syria, Afghanistan, Sudan, Indonesia, and Saudi Arabia. The three teams were strategically deployed in a triangular configuration dominating the valley that cut through the center of the designated battlefield.

Team Alpha was deployed in the foothills to the north at an elevation of 1600 feet above the valley floor with excellent cover and a commanding view of the entire area. They were dug in. Two mortar teams were set at 60 degree angles to the valley floor creating a cone of fire that could easily adjust based upon the size and make-up of the U.S. ground force. The mortar teams were supported by a 50-caliber machine gun and a dozen riflemen with AK47 assault rifles and traditional body armor. A lone sniper was stationed behind the most westerly mortar team so that the sun's movement would make him virtually invisible as the afternoon progressed. He was equipped with the Barrett M107 rifle capable of incredible knockdown power, using .50-caliber ammunition, with an effective range of 1,500 meters. The 10X telescope and bipod coupled with its 10-round semi-automatic action greatly enhanced its effectiveness against a single target through multiple trigger pulls. He could consistently hit a tin can up to a mile away.

Team Beta was deployed directly opposite Alpha Team approximately a quarter mile from the southern lip of a ridge overlooking the valley. They had excellent cover behind a sea of sand dunes. Team Beta was mobile. A two-man command and control team directed half a dozen three-man dune buggies. Each mobile unit was equipped with an Asimov S46 swivel machine gun and a Godunov cannon capable of firing 20 rounds per minute from a canister mounted on the base of an eight inch barrel. One load had the equivalent punch of three grenades. All drivers were hard-wired to command and control. Instead of a steering wheel and floor pedals, the vehicles were fitted with handlebars for steering and speed, freeing up the feet to operate two thirty-caliber machine guns mounted on the front chassis. Top speed was seventy miles per hour.

Kalil was coordinating the battle from Charlie Team which was deployed at the far western edge of the valley approximately eight miles from the point at which Master Gunnery Sergeant First Class Terrel Macklin was to enter the killing field at 1500 Mountain Standard Time, thereby commencing the exercise. Charlie was loaded. A Howitzer battery was located east of a dry streambed where three German attack helicopters with four-man commando teams were located. Kalil's command tent was positioned thirty yards behind the helicopters. He sat over a laptop with a view of the easternmost entrance to the valley approximately eight miles away. His eyes and ears were concentrated on Team Alpha. A sighter transmitted real-time images from a state of the art telescope linked to Kalil's laptop. Kalil prayed to Allah for strength and wisdom. Let vengeance be mine, he implored. 'But Your will be done'.

1430 MOUNTAIN STANDARD TIME
WHITE SANDS COMMAND AND CONTROL CENTER
WHITE SANDS, N.M.

Seated around the high-tech conference table at the command and control center, Patrick Brady and Tony DiStefano, Zybercor Director of Security, studied their briefing packages as General Cadman and Colonel Franks debriefed the executive staff who had planned today's battle scenario. Brady was eavesdropping, as usual. In spite of the calm, professional demeanor of the senior military staff, Brady was well aware that there was grave concern that the quality of weapons made available to the enemy force from Guantanamo could do some real damage to the Land Force Warrior Tiger Team. He knew that Colonel Franks, in particular, felt that they were rushing the implementation of the new systems despite the strategy that had been agreed upon in the lobby of the Hay Adams on Inaugural Tuesday in January. The entire team had been at it twenty-four/seven for the last six months but there was still much to be done. The situation in the Middle East had continued to deteriorate and Congress had become as committed as the President to a spring redeployment to protect American interests.

The Pentagon was made to understand that long-term strategic advantage resided in our ability to restrict the flow of men and material across national borders without committing tens of thousands of additional troops.....troops that we didn't have. The country would not support a draft. Already stretched to the breaking point, our armed forces would be unable to develop the leverage to drive the various parties to the negotiating table without a technological breakthrough. Technology-rich, the Land Force Warrior Program aligned perfectly with the military, diplomatic and political goals of the new administration. The President realized that there would be strong public support for additional military funding as long as we weren't filling body bags with American sons and daughters.

Cadman and Franks finished the debriefing and dismissed all but the essential few necessary to transfer video and communications elements to the command and control center. Cadman wanted to restrict knowledge of today's events to the smallest circle possible. Brady knew that both Cadman and Franks had their asses on the line. In the long history of the U.S. military, never before had there been a real-time, live-fire exercise of this magnitude. In Brady's mind there was no option. The fine print of the 250 page contract with the Pentagon called for a Joint Armed Services Review on the fifteenth of November and Zybercor was going to be subject to a high degree of scrutiny. The lucrative production phase of the agreement would not go into effect until the efficacy of the weapons systems had been validated. He rationalized that the risks were far outweighed by the benefits and, besides, soldiers were paid to take risks. He needed to test the functionality of his systems under the most extreme conditions imaginable. Patrick Brady never let someone else's agony get in the way of opportunity and he realized only too well that his contract with the Pentagon would fulfill his life's ambition. Nothing was going to stop him now. "Are we all set?" asked Brady as the four members of the Task Force took their seats.

"We're as ready as we're going to be," replied Franks, answering for his boss. He was already on the record as objecting to the exercise and was doing all he could to maintain a professional demeanor and not strangle Brady on the spot. He tried one last time. "Is there any way we could delay this for a couple of days?" he asked.

"We've been through this a dozen times," replied Brady. He knew that he had Cadman's support for his plan, so that ultimately Franks would have to come around. "The White House is in a big hurry and that means we cut corners everywhere we can. We agreed that a live-fire, uncontrolled exercise is necessary if we are going to meet these deadlines. Can we just get on with this Norm? Norm?"

MANIPULATION

Franks stared Brady down. He knew Brady was a businessman, first and always and would never understand the loyalty that a commander had for his troops in the field. "O.K." said Franks, "If you would each open your briefing package, I'll walk you through the prep phase. We go live in thirty minutes."

* * *

1500 MOUNTAIN STANDARD TIME

At exactly 1500 Mountain Standard Time, as Kalil fired up his laptop, Terrel Macklin entered the valley and went 'Red', commencing real-time communications with Lester and all elements of the Tiger Team. As the parties came on-line, Mack ordered Lester to advance Phase I Battle Plan with an initial threat assessment and asset maximization scenario.

While Macklin was undergoing the trials associated with the Land Force Warrior training and development program, Lester Grossman had been busily adapting the Air Force Augmented Cognition (AugCog) technology to the patented Zybercor Communications and Network Command System (CNCS). The AugCog technology represented a significant leap forward in the interpretation of various cognitive states allowing devices to be used more efficiently and effectively in high stress situations. Through the optimization of information transfer, storage, recognition, and filtering, Lester could obtain much more specific information regarding the state of enemy targets. Empirical data was then supplemented by the spatial resolution system of the Lightyear Satellite and loaded into the LFW decision support mechanism used to assist Lester in the selection of appropriate weaponry. The combination of these systems completed the transformation of the U.S. military from classic 'platform centric' warfare to 'network centric' warfare in the blink of an eye. Once Grossman decided upon an initial battle plan, he would provide targeting information to all Tiger Team members who would then execute an integrated multi-pronged attack. Grossman would carefully monitor the engagement and shift assets as required from commencement to conclusion.

Zybercor's advanced computing technology was patented in 2008 protecting a hybrid computing architecture using a unique blend of bio-mechanics in combination with traditional materials. Powerful and fast, the Zybercor system incorporated data storage/retrieval and processing mechanisms with density and performance metrics far beyond state of the art silicon technologies. In addition to processing efficiencies, the Zybercor patented architecture would be able to acquire new attributes enabling the evolution toward faster and more intelligent systems. Today, however, machines served man......not the other way around. And Lester was "the Man".

Lester had purposely been excluded from the exercise planning and staging and his intel, while sketchy, was the same as Sergeant Macklin's. However, he had participated in thousands of simulations and was considered to be a war game genius. But today was different. Today was the real thing. Lester, though, was neither nervous nor concerned. He had been preparing for today his entire life.

* * *

Head of Neurology at Saint Barnabas Hospital in Livingston, New Jersey, Dr. Martin Grossman had big plans for his firstborn, Lester. He and his wife, Ruth, nurtured him lovingly through his early years and marveled at his progress both in and out of the classroom. Convinced that they had sired a son who would one day accomplish great things, they had two more children, were active in the synagogue, and counted their blessings, completely unaware that Lester had developed a serious addiction that was in full bloom by age eleven. Lester was addicted to video games. He couldn't get enough. In order not to alarm his parents he was careful to maintain straight A's in school and hide his obsession as good addicts do. He was 'on the box' every weekday for his requisite limit of one hour but logged another three to four while his family slept. Lester's drugs of choice were the military and science fiction games in which success was a function of hand-eye coordination, multi-tasking capability and relentless focus. Lester knew how to play the game of life as well. As long as he gave his parents what they wanted....their illusion....he would be allowed to compete in the endless variety of weekend video game tournaments which he won with regularity as he quietly established himself as the best of the best.

Addiction is a lonely endeavor and as a teenager, Lester began to show symptoms of withdrawal and isolation, spending more time in his room and choosing weekend tournaments over social functions. His only friends were fellow 'gamers' and he showed only a marginal interest in the opposite sex. Concerned with what they mistook as a change in behavior, his parents insisted that Lester see a psychologist who was also a colleague and friend of the good doctor.

The Grossmans waited patiently for the requisite four sessions to take place so that they could be reassured by Dr. Feingold that Lester was going through a rather typical teenage phase. That reassurance never came. Dr. Grossman and Ruth attended the fifth session with Lester and Dr. Feingold and were informed that their soon-to-be-sixteen-year-old son would be exchanging video games for the real thing; he was committed to joining the Army immediately after high school. That night Dr. Grossman asked his wife if she had had an affair with a goy because no Jewish boy with his genes would forego medical school for a life in the military. She laughed and began to count on her fingers as he playfully gave her a love pat on her rear end. "My darling," she said, "be careful what you wish for. You've taught our son to search for God's gifts and to follow his heart. Who knew?"

Lester Grossman enlisted four months after his eighteenth birthday. He had given up the violin for the weight room and devoured military history from Thermopylae to Desert Storm. He was ready. After Basic Training Lester was assigned to a unit charged with the development of a long-range plan outlining options for future weapons systems. While

MANIPULATION

it was true that Lester came to the Army it is also true that the Army came to him. The video games that he loved so much had grown up alongside him to become the platform for a new generation of strategic weapons systems. After several years he found himself on Tiger Team. Lester had found a home. For the first time in his life he felt like he truly belonged to something. The guys on the Tiger Team had embraced him as one of their own. He ate with them, drank with them, trained with them, lived with them twenty-four/seven.....even got laid with them. They laughed together. They even gave him one of the cherished nicknames: 'The Head Man'. "Lester", they said, "you the Man." He loved these guys. They were his family.

At Mack's command Lester began to process information at a staggering rate and he quickly formulated a plan as he came to understand what the enemy was thinking, based upon their weapons capability, manpower, and deployment. He fired up the entire network. "Let's get ready to rumble!" **People were going to die today**.

CHAPTER TWO

The Wall Street Journal American
Sept 12, 2009

The eagerly-anticipated Initial Public Offering of Zybercor Corporation stunned the financial markets yesterday. There was heavy interest at home and abroad for the Kramer Rodgers-led offering of fifty-million shares. Investors fortunate enough to have garnered allotments were gratified with the initial price of $20 per share. By the close of trading, Zybercor crossed the tape at a stratospheric $54 per share.

Zybercor developed the first wearable computer in 1999 and recently won the contract let by the Joint Chiefs of Staff for the Land Force Warrior Program, a $12 billion effort involving the U.S. Army, Marines, and Air Force.

Chief Executive Officer Patrick F. Brady, in a prepared statement, commented "This is a milestone day for Zybercor. The proceeds from today's offering will be used to implement a new generation of patents to supplement our wearable computer product that has provided the basis for the Land Force Warrior Program. We at Zybercor are committed to supporting the U.S. military in its global war on terrorism. It is clear that traditional military methodology is ill-equipped to deal with the challenges of today's terrorist community."

Zybercor has capitalized on a growing notion that intellectual property, including patents, trademarks, methodologies, brands, and corporate secrets are replacing traditional hard assets (bricks and mortar) as the driving force in the creation

MANIPULATION

of market value. *"As the marketplace gains efficiency in its ability to value these intangible assets more and more investment capital will be available to fund research and development," said Johan Erickson, Chief Economist at the Institute for Intellectual Endeavors.*

* * *

Patrick Fortune Brady was having an exceptional day. Enjoying his favorite single malt, the eighteen-year-old Laphroaig, he was relaxing in the back of a stretch limo on the New Jersey Turnpike on his way from New York City to Princeton. Yesterday's IPO had been a smashing success. This morning he rang the bell to open the Exchange. After leaving the downtown offices of Kramer Rodgers, he met with the business press at the University Club on 5th Avenue and 54th Street. The Gestapo-like concierge even let him use his cell phone, verboten in the ornately decorated lobby. He still couldn't believe he pulled it off and right under the noses of the regulators. Never had the notion of national security been so successfully utilized to manipulate the market. Brady played the IPO like a fine instrument in the hands of a skilled musician.

Firstly, his timing was impeccable. He knew Wall Street was ready for the next "big thing". The private-equity surge had peaked and the hedge funds had recently come under heavy scrutiny with new regulations working their way through the political system. Intellectual property and intangible assets would provide the bankers and deal makers with their next round of fees ensuring that the concentration of wealth continued to benefit those fortunate enough to belong to the Lucky Sperm Club. Like the dot-com revolution of the nineties, patented technologies would be bought and sold...capitalized and re-capitalized...and new products and services like risk-linked securities and intellectual property derivatives would fuel the fires of endless greed.

Secondly, he knew that every good deal required a "story" and no one could spin the truth better than Patrick Brady. He carefully kept the "contract" with the Pentagon sealed and out of the public domain under the mantle of national security. He claimed that Zybercor had monopoly-like status with the military due to the strategic nature of their intellectual property. Taking careful notes from the General Electric playbook, Brady buried the facts under layers of operating companies obfuscated by a plethora of confusing footnotes. By the time the information worked its way up into the operating company consolidation it appeared that Zybercor had an unqualified and unending source of revenue backed by the credit of Uncle Sam. The disclosure statement was as exciting as it was vacuous. The company's financial projections exploded off the pages as discounted future cash flows piled up endlessly and Black Shoals navigated cleverly to smooth out the infrequent periods of "lumpy revenue".

Thirdly, and most importantly, Brady knew whom to buy without overpaying. Nobody played the "I'll lie and you swear to it" game better than he did. The right law firms, accounting firms and PR firms said the right things to the right people at the right time for the right price. The right analysts got the right number of options for issuing buy recommendations at the right time to propel the value of the stock in the right direction. The right auditors looked in all the right places and opined that everything was "all right" notwithstanding the specific caveats (to which they didn't refer) in the contract with the Pentagon that could make the company worthless overnight. For example, there was no mention that the contract specified that, on Nov. 15, 2009, an Armed Forces Review Committee would convene to evaluate the efficacy of the technology before going forward with the subsequent lucrative "production phase". These little details never fazed Patrick Brady. He took great comfort in his self-proclaimed genius for making things happen. He had sixty days to play with, and God only needed seven days to create the world. Brady had plenty of cushion. The Joint Chiefs needed him as much as he needed them. The White House and Congress were demanding that the "breakthrough" in strategic weaponry personified by Land Force Warrior accompany the military redeployment to the Middle East scheduled for early 2010 and Brady was going to make a fortune as a result.

* * *

Fortune was the perfect middle name for a guy born into a lower class family in Trenton, N.J., who never had a pot to piss in. His mother's maiden name was 'Fortuna' and she had prayed mightily that her only child would be blessed with good luck. As of close of market today, Brady's 20 per cent ownership was worth $540,000,000.00. How ironic! He marveled at his good fortune. The record setting IPO yesterday, the Exchange in the morning, the press conference in the afternoon, and tonight.....a 40-year reunion dinner at the Ivy Club at Princeton University. He couldn't wait to spend a lovely evening with the arrogant pricks from his college eating club. He was especially looking forward to sharing some quality time with Avery Johnstone, III. Brady vividly recalled the ball busting administered by Johnstone at Parents' Weekend 40+ years ago when 'Trey' went out of his way to introduce Patrick's lower-class mother and father to the well-dressed, sophisticated scions of the northeast's wealthy aristocracy. Johnstone had deftly steered the conversation to areas that highlighted the enormous gap in education and breeding between Brady's family and the others. He kept Brady's father's glass continually full of the rich Scotch that they didn't pour at Quinn's Bar in the heart of South Trenton. Theresa Fortuna Brady kept her hands on her husband's arm, whispering for him to slow down on the booze. That is....until she got "the look" - that dark violent glare from Liam Conner Brady that she knew so well. Patrick's cheeks still burned from the shame he felt as he and his mother literally carried his dad out through the large wooden door of the Ivy Club, halfway-up Prospect Street, past the liveried chauffeurs, the limos and Mercedes to the senior Brady's well-worn Ford. How the worm has turned. Brady had his five-man security force working overtime the last year focusing on Johnstone, III and several of the other members of the Ivy Club that had made his years at Princeton the most miserable of his life. It's amazing what a high-level government security clearance could accomplish. Access to the many databases was supplemented by the high-tech surveillance assets utilized by his security team to dig into the professional and private lives of the Ivy Club alumni targeted by Brady months before tonight's reunion.

Tony DiStefano, head of his security detail was sitting across the limo from his employer waiting patiently to begin the briefing for tonight's reunion dinner. The last six months had been hectic. He not only had to field surveillance teams for the new targets, but was ordered to constantly update the intel on Avery Johnstone, III whom he had under surveillance ever since Mr. Brady had first approached Johnstone Capital to serve as investment banker and co-underwriter of Zybercor's long anticipated IPO. While several other 'old Ivies' had proved to have a rich array of skeletons clanking around in their closets, none had pleased the boss more than those of Johnstone, III.

The limo had just passed the Vince Lombardi Service Center on the N.J. Turnpike, headed south toward New Brunswick and Route1, and then on into downtown Princeton and Ivy Club on Prospect St.

DiStefano had three files in his lap inside a black leather folder. Brady had taught him that information should be presented with form as well as substance. The quality of the packaging was often as important as the content of the package itself. DiStefano understood that his boss always controlled the agenda, shaping and defining the issues to fit his objectives then building an ironclad case backed up by solid research. In the seven years he worked for Brady he had never seen him unprepared for a meeting....not once.

"Let's see what we've got for tonight, Tony," said Brady, adjusting the gooseneck lamp as DiStefano handed him the leather folder. The files were in priority order the way Brady required them. He expected complete oral retention from all his key managers without the need to have any excess copies. Aides were expected to keep only original file folders so that any notes that the boss made in the margins were exactly as he had written them during the prior review. He always required his people to put their asses on the line in terms of their forecasts and expectations. As a consequence, he started every meeting with a review of events subsequent to the last review and evaluated real results against stated objectives. If there was a gap between reality and his expectations, there better be a detailed scenario to get back on plan.

"As you can see, Boss, Johnstone is wrapped up pretty tightly." Brady expected adverbs to end in 'ly' and was a bear when it came to syntax and grammar. "Our last look into his taxes was fruitful. He overstated his losses in three different transactions so his loss carry forward was substantially over inflated. He already took the set off. The IRS would have a field day once they knew where to look."

Brady scanned the pages with the benefit of his prescription contact lenses. He never wore glasses. "It looks like Avery's sexual frequency is increasing."

"Yeah, he's out of control now. Apparently this is not unusual. Once a guy goes down this road, there is usually an obsessive-compulsive personality disorder driving the process and....well, it gets more and more frequent."

MANIPULATION

God was smiling down on Patrick Brady today. Avery Johnstone, III was truly in the deepest of shit. On the surface he lived a textbook life. He resided in the family home in Brookline, Massachusetts with a lovely wife and three children. He had taken over the family investment firm as President of Johnstone Capital, and had participated in the successful public offering of Brady's company. Avery had it all together: deacon at his church, a four handicap at the prestigious Brookline Country Club, and a member of the Republican National Committee. A loving father and happily married man, Avery Johnstone had been on the 'down low' for several years. Using the Internet, dear Avery had been engaging in one-night stands with male sex partners whom he met every other Wednesday. His rendezvous spot was the private parking lot of a secluded storage facility owned by Johnstone Capital. Only Avery had the code. The facility backed up to railroad tracks and thus was perfectly positioned for his bi-monthly trysts. It was also perfectly placed for DiStefano's surveillance team. The parabolic microphone picked up every sound coming from the back seat of his Mercedes 400 Sedan. The infrared, long-range camera could pick up some interesting shots, but the miniature camera his team had inserted in the overhead light was the real winner, capturing the oral sex and awkward coupling. Oh, how Patrick had longed to go public with the picture and tapes! Unfortunately, it would not have boded well for his company's image if a scandal involving his old friend, advisor, and prospective Board member broke on the eve of his IPO. Besides, Brady was going to need to manipulate Johnstone and the devastating details of his hidden life would provide just the insurance he required to ensure loyalty and support for his agenda. Revenge was definitely a dish best served cold.

Brady shook his head and smiled as the Johnstone review was completed and DiStefano had efficiently answered every question.

"So, Tony, what do the shrinks say about this? I mean, what's the deal here?"

"Same old shit: low self-esteem. Unresolved childhood conflicts. He knows at some level that he's successful because of Daddy. He probably uses the kinky sex to punish himself. You remember the Profumo scandal in England a while back. Powerful members of British parliament in long-term relationships with that prostitute....Christine Keeler, I think her name was. It was the same gig for all of them: S & M..........you know, tied up...humiliation...all that kinky stuff. Avery probably gets off the same way by using men."

"I love these guys that are born on third base and think they hit a triple. They're all fucked up somehow. We're better off doing it the old fashioned way," commented Brady.

Yeah, thought DiStefano, there's no difference between earning it and stealing it as long as you didn't get caught.

"So, are we solid on Johnstone? I'd like to spend some time on the next one.......Jacobs...it's a little more complicated. We need at least ten minutes on the Azzato file. I've got some problems there," said DiStefano.

Brady nodded, made some handwritten notes in the margin and promptly opened the second file, Emory Jacobs, Esq.

"Tony, before we get into this one, I want you to

understand how important he is to me. We're going to need to build up the value of our intellectual property and old Emory's going to need to go way out on a limb."

"Could you explain that a little more clearly so that I understand?" asked DiStefano. You could always get the boss to clarify himself if it resulted in a better understanding of the objective. Brady wanted his people to be committed to his agenda and go through walls. He just wanted to be certain that it was the right wall they went through...so he would take the time to explain.

"Tony, the value of this company and in fact most new technology companies, is more than 70% based upon intellectual property: key executives, patents, copyrights, trademarks, branding.....things that have a somewhat arbitrary valuation."

"So, we're going to need him to put a big number on that so..."

"So we can use it as collateral to get some more liquidity from the market if necessary. We have a very important test of Land Force Warrior on September 18th at White Sands. If things don't play out the way we expect, I'm going to need to get my hands on a lot more cash. In order to do that I've got to establish a higher value for our patents and that's where Jacobs comes in. Emory will need to be a good soldier. Is he going to be a good soldier, Tony?"

"As you say, Boss, if we get him by the balls, his agenda and ours will be in perfect alignment."

Avery Johnstone, III wasn't the only target for the evening. The two other "old Ivies," Emory Jacobs, Esq. and Professor Emeritus Louis Azzato were each in for a big surprise as well. Both were going to be invited onto the Board of Directors of Zybercor Corporation with a boatload of stock options. Professor Azzato was a well-respected authority on foreign relations and carried the pedigree of Princeton's Woodrow Wilson School, as well as appointments at two prestigious think tanks. Most recently, Azzato was appointed co-chairman of The President's Advisory Commission on Middle Eastern Affairs. Emory Jacobs had graduated cum laude from Princeton and had gone on to receive a law degree from Yale. His law firm, Jacobs, Wiley and Weinberg, specialized in intellectual property and patent law. Jacobs was going to make a perfect Board member. If Brady was going to need a new valuation of his intellectual property portfolio, who better to do the valuation than his old club mate, Emory. Emory needed money. Lots of money. Even Emory didn't know how much money he was going to need. You see, his firm had bet the ranch on the sale of a patent that they had literally stolen from a client who couldn't afford to pay their fee after an unsuccessful assertion effort against a firm that had allegedly infringed upon the patent holder's rights in the development of a satellite-based transfer station for a wireless cellular network. While the fact base did not lead to a successful litigation against the wireless operator, the owner of the patent was unaware that the firm of Jacobs, Wiley and Weinberg had discovered that the patent had a dominant position in a completely different sector and was worth far more than anyone had anticipated. Emory Jacobs had become an opportunist. He had complained to his wife many times that one couldn't hit a home run in the personal service business because income was a function of hourly billing. He was rankled by so many of his clients having half his I.Q. and ten times his net worth.

All of this would change with the Geopoint patent. Emory's due diligence team had discovered that senior management at Google, Yahoo, Microsoft, and Sprint had come to the conclusion that cell phone subscribers in America were unwilling to pay additional fees for the myriad of new high tech services about to be rolled out. Then they had all arrived at a further conclusion at the same time, to wit advertising was going to be the vehicle to subsidize the new products. The only problem was how to interconnect the cell phone subscriber with the new products and services using the advertiser as the intermediary. The Geopoint patent protected a methodology that utilized latitude and longitude to deliver a specific message to an individual cell phone user based upon a predetermined affinity.

In order for the Geopoint patent to maximize its value to the giant wireless search engines and software companies, it required a partner patent, an emulator that efficiently transported an enormous volume of data from one modality to the next. Jacobs had convinced his partners to spend $5.2 million to acquire an exclusive license for just such a technology. He was convinced that an auction of the "twinned" technology would generate between $30 and 50 million as a sale price plus ongoing royalties.

The auction was scheduled for October 15th. The firm had closed on the licensing agreement in mid-August. All three partners had signed personally for the bank loan of $5.5 million; $5.2 million for the exclusive license and $.3 million for additional software engineering.

Poor Emory. DiStefano had discovered the larceny when a paralegal from the Jacobs, Wiley and Weinberg team revealed it to her new lover, a Zybercor security specialist who had spiked her Chardonnay with a heavy dose of sodium pentathol. Several days later Brady's general counsel had paid a visit to the former owner of the Geopoint patent, Mr. Brian Kangas, in Belmar, New Jersey and spilled the beans on Jacobs, Wiley and Weinberg. Kangas' anger was substantially mollified when he read the double-spaced wording of the contract with Maison de Meyer, a French company wholly-owned by Zybercor Corporation. The terms were a mystery to Mr. Kangas but the $2.0 million cashier's check cancelled out his curiosity. He signed three documents: one, a letter to the Connecticut Bar Association documenting the misfeasance and malfeasance of the law firm of Jacobs, Wiley and Weinberg; two, a letter assigning all rights to the Geopoint patent to the French firm of Maison de Meyer, its successors or assigns; three, a letter on Kangas' personal stationery to Emory Jacobs, Esq. indicating his intention to go public with the letter to the Bar Association and sue him and his firm for fraud. The documents were securely stored in Brady's office safe.

So on the evening of his 40th reunion dinner at the revered Ivy Club, Jacobs would find out that his $5.5 million dollar loan no longer had any collateral, that he would be sued in criminal and civil courts, and that he would likely be disbarred, depriving him of income so that he couldn't even afford his own defense. Emory was going to be a perfect member of the Board.

"Good job, buddy," said Brady as he freshened up his single malt. "I can't wait to see the look on his face when he finds out he doesn't own the Geopoint patent anymore. Tony, I think we've got his heart and mind in our hands."

"Yes, sir! We appear to be in good shape with both of them, but what if they get together? The file says that they socialize with wives twice a year and do occasional partnership deals as well."

"I wouldn't lose any sleep over that. Guys never tell each other the truth. By the way, who was it that got the information from their paralegal that they were ripping off their client?"

"New guy, name is Thomas Andrews. You haven't met him yet; young, about twenty-eight, maybe twenty-nine. Four years at the Farm down in Langley. Before that, he was undercover cop in New York."

"Give him a bonus, Tony, and put him on my schedule when we get back to Reston. Now what about Lou Azzato? You said you were having a problem."

Louis Azzato was a Midwesterner by birth, spending his early years in St. Louis. An overachiever, Azzato was an All-State football player. At age 17 he was invited to linebacker weekend at Notre Dame. At six feet and one-hundred-ninety pounds, Azzato discovered that he was the shortest, lightest, slowest, and weakest (he could only bench press 275 pounds) of the twenty-five scholarship candidates.

A week later Lou had a new plan. Rather than be a walk-on at Notre Dame, he would accept an offer from Princeton University where he would play football and become a serious student.

Lou's time at Princeton was idyllic. He became President of Ivy Club; the oldest and most prestigious of Princeton's eating clubs. He was selected as a Rhodes Scholar his senior year and while at Oxford met and married the lovely Nancy Merrill from Bath, England. They were married in Bath amid the Roman ruins and medieval streets in the 13th century cathedral and took a carriage up to the Circus and down Brock Street for the reception at the Royal Crescent Hotel. Theirs was a marriage made in heaven.

Thirty-eight years later the Azzatos were still very much in love. God had blessed Lou and Nancy with five beautiful children and Lou was at the pinnacle of his career. DiStefano's team had not been able to find anything that could be used against him and Brady desperately needed Azzato on the Board. He needed Azzato's impeccable credentials and reputation to add credibility to a Board stacked with self-interest. Brady felt he could get him to serve, but without leverage he could never get him to go along with his agenda. During the next few months Brady intended to play fast and loose with the rules and Azzato was not only a Boy Scout, but was smart enough to use his Board position to influence other Directors and restrict Brady's flexibility. Brady instructed DiStefano to set him up. He told him to manufacture something that would grab his old friend by the balls. Brady told him to use the kids.

* * *

MANIPULATION

The reunion dinner that night was the same as all the others on the surface of it, however for Patrick Brady, the scotch and the steak dinner tasted better than ever. He loved the limelight and his successful IPO made him the center of attention. He whispered to Johnstone over cocktails that a national security check had revealed his homosexual trysts; but he, Brady, would see to it that the incriminating material would never see the light of day. Brady made it clear that he would be counting on his old friend's support as a new director, especially during the next few months which would be critical to the company's future. Likewise with Jacobs, Brady promised to keep his law firm's larceny out of the public eye and further committed to return ownership of the Geopoint patent to him after certain conditions of loyalty were met. Jacobs and Johnstone, their dirty little secrets in tow, joined the Board of Directors of Zybercor that night with 300,000 stock options apiece and big fees for their legal and financial advisory work.

Lou Azzato agreed to serve on the Zybercor Board that night as well. Brady had yet to figure out how to secure his ongoing support without leverage, but he trusted DiStefano to handle those details. It was 2:00 am before Brady climbed into his limo. DiStefano had returned to the company's suite at the Four Seasons in New York. Brady instructed his driver to proceed to Sacred Heart Cemetery in Trenton. It was pouring. Brady put Verdi's *Aida* in the CD player, poured himself the ninth scotch of the evening, and sunk into a malaise of morbid reflections on the way to visit his parents' graves.

* * *

Theresa Fortuna's father arrived in America in 1907 from a small agricultural village north of Naples. Lured by the prospect of a new life of opportunity and freedom, Francisco quickly found out that the streets of Uniontown, Pennsylvania were paved, not with gold, but with coal dust, and were lined with grinding poverty.

After a methane explosion killed his brother-in-law in 1923, Francisco, his wife, Colangela, and daughters, Theresa and Yolanda, packed up and moved to Trenton, New Jersey. The Fortunas settled in the predominantly Italian Chambersburg section and Francisco worked in an ice factory by day, doted on his family by night, and played bocce on Sundays after mass.

The Fortuna daughters could not have been more different if they had been born on different continents in different centuries. Yolanda was a born performer, taking to the piano as if the keys were the natural medium connecting her thin fingers to her perfect pitch and beautiful contralto voice. Known locally as a prodigy by the time she was twelve, she was well on her way to a career in opera.

Theresa, on the other hand, divided her time between the kitchen and the church. An average student, she was attentive and dutiful in school, but it was 'la cucina' where she radiated ability and warmth that lovingly found its way into the recipes for lasagna, gnocchi, chicken cacciatore, and other dishes included in the dog-eared notebook containing the family recipes. She was a pretty girl. Dark haired and full bodied by her teens some said Theresa was beautiful when she smiled....and she smiled often. She began going out with Liam Brady when she was sixteen. Prior to her dating Liam her mother and father had speculated upon the possibility that Theresa would become a nun, giving herself completely to the Catholic Church she loved.

In spite of his Irish heritage, the Fortuna's gradually accepted the fact that Theresa and Liam Conner Brady would marry and raise a family. Marriage came a little sooner than they planned, however, when Theresa became pregnant several months after her seventeenth birthday. Patrick was born just five months later. The choosing of his name had ignited a storm of controversy facilitated by the enormous flow of alcohol at a party celebrating the boy's birth held at the Italian-American Sportsman's Club in Trenton. One of the unique attributes of an Irish-Italian relationship is that you don't need a specific issue to generate emotional outbursts when there's a lot of booze present. As a consequence, no one can quite remember exactly what precipitated the confrontation of the new grandparents at the affair. It, however, became manifest in the naming of the baby. The negotiations were heated. It was finally agreed that the middle name would carry forward the name of Fortuna, as Patrick's Italian grandfather, Francisco, was an only son. However, the 'a' would be dropped. Thus, Patrick Fortune Brady was christened on a rainy day in the Church of The Immaculate Conception in the Chambersburg section of Trenton in the year of our Lord, 1949.

* * *

Liam's father, Sean Ryan Brady, sailed to America from County Cork as the Irish civil war came to an end in 1925. It was said that the folks from County Cork regularly posted the highest scores on the Civil Service tests administered by the British government since the turn of the century. Earnest and intelligent, Sean was hired at the American Shipbuilding Company located in Philadelphia. Its Trenton plant built steam fittings and other engine components. As long as the backlog of new ship orders was heavy, work was good, but America hurtled into the Depression and new orders at the shipyard dried up quickly. The plant closed in 1931. The immigrants were the hardest hit because they were the first to go, had the least amount of savings, and were the last to be rehired. Sean became a regular fixture at Warren and John Quinn's Bar, corner of Hancock and Cass, and just down the street from the Trenton State Prison. (Technically it was the 'New Jersey State Prison at Trenton' but had always been called by the shorter name.) Sean had shared space in steerage with the Quinn brothers on the boat from Ireland and they provided him with a steady flow of odd jobs in and around their bar. It wasn't unusual for young Liam to accompany his dad, especially on the weekends when families were welcome at the saloon. Monday through Friday was reserved for the cops, firemen, prison guards, and shift workers at John A. Roebling & Sons, the Trenton Brewery and other nearby factories. During the week Quinn's opened early and closed late to slake the thirst of its blue collar clientele. The proprietors had a large steel safe behind the bar from which they would cash a check on payday, allow that customer one drink, and then insist that he take the remainder of the paycheck home to the 'Missus' before returning to drink in earnest. Other ironclad rules of the premises: No raised voices and no women were allowed to sit at the bar.

Quinn's was at the heart of an Irish immigrant community that was vibrant and family oriented. Recreational and sports activities were planned and organized at the bar and implemented on the playing fields, gyms, and bowling alleys of South Trenton and Chambersburg. It was clear early on that little Liam was a gifted athlete. He began boxing in earnest in the 7th grade under the watchful eye of his uncle, Eddie Kenner, a veteran Trenton cop. "Uncle" was a euphemistic as well as familial term in the Italian and Irish immigrant communities. Eddie Kenner was a second cousin to the Quinn brothers and a loyal customer who became very close to Liam's dad as they took their shots and beers together on a nightly basis. He could often be seen on his knees during the weekends holding his big hands out receiving endless jabs from young Liam. Uncle Eddie wouldn't let him use a roundhouse or combination until he perfected his jab, moving to left and right with equal dexterity. Eddie coached the Irish Boxing Club sponsored by Quinn's Bar during the thirties until the beginning of the war. Competition was keen among the Irish and Italians and the Polish and the Hungarians, but especially fierce between the Dagos and the Micks. Eddie knew talent when he saw it and Liam had talent. He was quick with great hand-eye coordination, stamina, and a passion in his punch that eventually turned to real anger when he was informed that he failed the police exam due to bad eyesight that subsequently disqualified him from military service as well. For years Liam had been brainwashed to believe that the path to success for the Irish was the Civil Service, especially the police. On the force you were respected and you could supplement your salary with special services in the community. Uncle Eddie and the Quinns met at the bar after closing one evening and some money changed hands with their good friend Seamus William O'Reilly. The next day Liam was hired as a guard at Trenton State Prison. Liam was smart, tough, and had a chip on his shoulder. Captain of the guards, 'Big Bill' O'Reilly was an effective manager and had a knack for assigning his men to areas that highlighted their unique skills. As a consequence, Liam found himself in the general prison population where he could showcase his quick temper and iron fists. O'Reilly knew that respect and order in his prison were a direct function of discipline and fear. The inmates feared Brady's temper, respected his fists, and hated the very air he breathed. He exuded an air of superiority and constantly resented having to share space with those he called "the scum of the earth".

Rehabilitation was not a well-developed social goal or strategy in America in the thirties and forties. Many men who went to prison desperate soon became depraved lifetime criminals who fulfilled the prophecy of those who managed their incarceration.

In spite of the inhumane conditions and festering frustrations of his employment, Liam loved his wife, Theresa, and their only child, Patrick. Patrick was ten years old when the Trenton Prison riot made front-page news across the country in 1959.

MANIPULATION

The Eisenhower Administration had introduced the notion of rehabilitation and experimentation and relaxed guidelines superseded the rigid standards of discipline and many of the 'old school screws' took as early a retirement as they could get.

'Big Bill' O'Reilly was replaced by a well-educated advocate of the 'new method' with a Master's Degree in Sociology who was committed to transforming Trenton State Prison into an icon of the new mantra.

No one knew for sure what precipitated the riot. Some speculated that it was just due to the overcrowded conditions and inhumane treatment of the inmates. Others attributed it to the lax security standards accompanying the 'new wave' in rehabilitation. Too hard, too soft, too liberal, too conservative.....it didn't matter to Liam Brady and his family. The riot broke out during an expanded physical fitness program in the yard, a cornerstone of the new rehabilitation program that emphasized personal development and group activities. The rampage lasted two days and Liam's group activity consisted of an endless series of rapes while he was handcuffed face down on a bunk in the solitary confinement section in the cellar of the prison. It wasn't until ten hours after the multi-agency task force restored order that they found Liam. Unfortunately he couldn't positively identify a single one of the thirty-odd offenders. His blood pressure was dangerously low and he was dehydrated and delirious. He had lost three pints of blood and was in the midst of a grand mal seizure as they hurried him to the hospital. Theresa, Patrick, and the Fortuna and Brady clans kept vigil at St. Francis Hospital, changing shifts for a day and a half as

Liam underwent multiple surgeries. Finally, Theresa was allowed into the recovery area accompanied by Father Genovese from Immaculate Conception. They returned to the hospital waiting room twenty minutes later, the priest ashen-faced and Theresa bordering on hysteria. "What have they done to my husband?" she cried as she fell to her knees in agony. Father Genovese led the Fortuna's and Brady's in prayer as he wondered where God had been those two days at Trenton State Prison as the devil ran unobstructed through the soul of Liam Conner Brady.

* * *

Liam Brady was stitched up and put on a desk that processed prisoners out the front door and back into the world after they had 'paid their debt to society'. He recovered physically after two additional surgeries and six months of periodic hospitalizations but he was never the same man again. The twin demons of anger and paranoia combined to smother his psyche in self-loathing and misdirected rage. The pattern became familiar - he medicated at Quinn's and directed his rage at those he loved the most.

Tragically, Theresa and Patrick could have handled the abuse better if Liam had always been a violent man. The change, however, was so dramatic that they were incapable of making any kind of rational adjustment. His personal trauma was devastating and unspeakable. Whispered rumors and sidelong glances drove Liam deeper and deeper into his isolation and psychopathy as the downward spiral of alcohol and self-degradation engulfed first Theresa and then Patrick. Theresa and Liam never made love again after 'the incident'. Sex only came in the form of drunken anger with Theresa forced physically to lie on her stomach as her husband brutally impaled her from behind. When she could no longer succumb to the degradation and pain she sought refuge in the church. From 7:00 until 10:00 every night, Theresa would go to evening mass and then to the church hall kitchens to help prepare the food to feed the hungry the following day. Liam's shift was over at 4:00 but he wouldn't arrive home from Quinn's until half past six. His wife would have his dinner on the table and the beer open when Liam walked in the door. As he sat down, she would hurry out the door to Mass and stay away until he passed out at 10:00. If he was still awake when she returned, Theresa could be in for a long night.

Patrick became, most assuredly, the youngest of the many victims of those two tragic days at the prison. He was too young to understand all that had transpired but he knew for certain that the man who came home from the hospital was not his Daddy. When he was sober he was at work or distant and preoccupied in public. When he was home he was rarely sober and always mean; mean deep down in the soul; a meanness that required a victim to expunge some of the anger that surely would otherwise eat him alive. The human psyche has an endless capacity for rationalization. Determined to make a man of his son, Liam exchanged the affectionate father-son trips to the bowling alley for a small gym in the back of the row house and began to teach Patrick how to box.

Patrick dreaded the ending of the school day. His father demanded that his homework be completed by 7:00 every night and that he be ready for his boxing "lesson;" a euphemism for getting the shit beat out of him under the guise of parental supervision. Liam was relentless...the speed bag, the heavy bag, the rope....and then the required sparring. Father versus son - no holds barred. "All fair and no favor", sneered the old man. At first, the young boy was devastated by the changes at home. He couldn't understand why his loving mother had abandoned him to suffer abuse at the hands of a man whom love had abandoned so completely.

Liam saw himself as a failure as a man and began to focus all his attention on living through his son. He began to combine his unique brand of philosophy with their nightly boxing "lessons." He convinced his son that the world was comprised only of winners and losers. Winners had money and power, and losers, like Brady, had nothing and never would unless he took it. As the years progressed, Patrick became an exceptional boxer, winning the Golden Gloves at three different weight classes. When he was sixteen he could beat his father, and in a moment of hormonal rebellion, refused to participate in anymore "lessons." He was on the honor roll, good-looking and popular at school. He told Liam to "fuck-off". The father grabbed him and spun him around, immediately catching the full force of Patrick's right hook. Liam went down in a heap on the kitchen floor. It was a Friday night and Patrick didn't come home, sleeping at a friend's house.

MANIPULATION

The new "lesson" that was waiting for him at home stayed with him for the rest of his life. Liam had finally found something in which he truly excelled. He was an exceptional teacher. Liam didn't have to say a word. It was not necessary to remind his headstrong son that this was his house.....he paid the bills and he had the power notwithstanding Patrick's prowess with his fists. Patrick understood immediately how it would work from then on and transmitted his new-found knowledge to his ever-developing conception of the workings of the world-at-large. Theresa's left eye had already begun to discolor and she had huge bruises on both arms that were so severe that she had to rest her elbows on the counter as she prepared her husband's breakfast while he sat at the kitchen table staring down his son and opening the first beer of the new day.

* * *

Tonight was the fortieth anniversary of that parents' weekend in Princeton when Avery Johnstone, III had plied Liam Conner Brady with liquor. Patrick's parents had been dead those same forty years. His dad had been adamant about driving home that night and, as usual, his mother relented and got into the passenger seat. Fifteen minutes later Liam wrapped his old Ford around a telephone pole on the southbound lane of Rt. 1 outside Trenton. They were both killed instantly.

Patrick's hatred for Johnstone rose to the surface as he screamed into the dark wet night. **He thought of his mother's torn and battered body as he leaned** two dozen red roses against her headstone and then turned and urinated profusely on his father's grave.

CHAPTER THREE

SEPTEMBER 18, 2009
WHITE SANDS, NM
1500 MOUNTAIN STANDARD TIME

Norm Franks was a full Colonel with a twenty-year career in Special Operations in all corners of the globe. Naturally, over that time he had participated in some pretty hairy scenes. But, in dozens of operations from 'search and destroy' to 'snatch and runs', he had never been this wound up. It drove him crazy that he was a spectator and not a participant in an exercise that held such importance to the future of national security and, equally, to the future of his boss, General Cadman.

Franks had been adjutant to General Walt Cadman since the general had been elevated to the Joint Chiefs of Staff three years ago. There was no one that Franks respected more. In point of fact Franks was responsible for selling the general on Land Force Warrior. This was his baby and here he was in the delivery room sweating through a premature birth. "This is all happening way too fast," he thought, as he glanced at the digital countdown screen showing two minutes to game time.

Franks had discovered a lot about politics and economics the last few years with his deployment inside the Beltway. He had learned that the real job was to follow the money, then follow the power, and then kill the enemy. He should have been conditioned by now but he was still amazed that Land Force Warrior was being subjected to a real-time battlefield test at such short notice. All in the interest of politics.

The political environment was operating at fever pitch. In the midst of drafting a new spending bill, Congress speculated that the US could bring the warring parties in the Middle East to the negotiating table and engineer a truce. Israel was finally ready to deal seriously with all sides and the House and Senate leadership had convinced each other that the time was right to get into the history books with a three-pronged plan that would bring long-term peace to the region.

The logic of the entire strategy was tied to the ability of Land Force Warrior to control borders so as to stem the flow of manpower and material into the hotspots in the Middle East and Africa. The other two prongs of the plan, diplomacy and investment, were predicated on the success of Land Force Warrior. It was the strategic linchpin that facilitated the redeployment and concentration of Special Ops and Infantry to stabilize geopolitical problem areas through the eradication of hostiles with no fear of reinforcement from ideologically compatible state-sponsored neighbors. Once an area was stabilized through the elimination of the hard-core terrorists and well-armed militias, the plan was to bring an end to sectarian violence through diplomacy and investment. The democracy-building process would begin with political co-dependency, uniting Shiite and Sunni (in the case of Iraq, for instance), by giving each equal stakes in the growing economy and huge capital investment in infrastructure and education. Simultaneously, indigenous military forces would expand to provide ongoing security and stabilization.

"So here we are....thirty seconds to kickoff," thought Franks, "and here's this guy Brady with his guard dog, DiStefano. I trust him about as much as I can piss up a rope. It was his idea to keep this so tightly under wraps that only the four of us would have the real-time results. Too late to worry about that crap now."

"Here we go," said Franks, as the digital read-out glowed 1500 hours.

* * *

The 'exercise' had started out well enough. Lester Grossman had sized up the battlefield dynamics perfectly. "I'm not even going to break into a schvetz here," he thought to himself as he issued instructions to implement Queen's Gambit Three, a scenario lifted from a classical 19th century chess strategy and adapted to Tiger Team's unique offensive capabilities. Queen's Gambit Three called for a trilateral deployment of one drone to each of the three enemy positions. The drone launch was accompanied by a simultaneous artillery barrage targeting the mortars and fifty calibers of Alpha Team and the howitzers and helicopters deployed at the opposite end of the valley from Macklin's position. The purpose of the artillery was to create confusion as well as carnage. The purpose of the drones was to use laser-guided missiles to eliminate the most immediate threats to Sergeant Macklin's well-being, those threats being the heavy duty capabilities of howitzer, mortar, choppers, and the stationary fifty caliber machine gun. Lester was less concerned with Beta Team's mobile dune buggies. Macklin was fully capable of disabling their sensitive electrical systems with his pulse cannon and then finishing the job with the laser gunnery apparatus (LGA) attached to his right arm. The choppers were likely to cancel each other out in the early stages of the engagement. That was fine with Lester. The three reserve drones would sneak in behind the German-made copters at the right time and stick air-to-air missiles up their asses, freeing the Apaches to mop up the remnants of Alpha Team, neutralizing Mack's secondary threat and eliminating any intel provided to enemy command and control from the clear line of sight afforded by the troops entrenched in the foothills. While Lester called signals, the satellite infrared telemetry indicated the spooling up of the enemy choppers and the sighting of the howitzers. Lester figured that he had approximately 30 seconds to inflict maximum damage before the enemy was able to process the fact that the entire U.S. ground force was only one man. That was more than enough time for the drones and fixed artillery to do their jobs. Within 12 seconds the drones had downloaded the coordinates from Lightyear and initiated the firing sequences for the air-to-ground missiles. After initiating the air attack Lester switched immediately to the 'ground game'. (While chess parlance was used to establish overall strategy, football terminology was used for tactics.) Only Macklin and Lester could call 'audibles' to check-off tactical maneuvers and redeploy assets. Two-way communication between Mack and Lester was essential. Therefore the first thing Lester did was to launch a smokescreen package from one of the reserve drones to shield Macklin from sniper fire from either side of the valley. The 'visibility interference provider' would continue to pump a thick, almost viscous smoke for up to half an hour. All the war game scenarios suggested that the party would be over in a matter of minutes.....eight to twelve to be somewhat more precise.

The artillery barrage was devastating as 100-pound shells peppered Alpha and Charlie Teams' deployment zones. The drone missiles, launched from a thousand feet, were locked onto the stationary mortar, machine gun and howitzer positions. Mack's eyepiece was designed to see through the smokescreen that shielded him from enemy fire. While Macklin was observing the obliteration of Team Alpha, the Apache attack commenced. He had a clear view of the helos as they headed down the middle of the valley to engage the enemy choppers. Concurrently he ascertained that the howitzers at the tail of the valley and the fifty-caliber had, indeed, already been neutralized. Three drones hovered in reserve at five thousand feet above the southern edge of the valley floor as the Lightyear imagery picked up the mobilization of Beta Team now racing to engage Macklin. Perfect, thought Lester. Everything is going exactly according to the playbook.

* * *

Kalil was deafened and disoriented as the Tiger Team artillery barrage hit his unit with devastating impact. He had seen action in Gaza, Lebanon, and Afghanistan, and was a seasoned, battle-scarred warrior but he had never experienced anything like this. As the artillery shells rained down around Charlie's howitzers, the air-to-ground missile fired from the drone took out the battery in a direct hit that sent shrapnel screaming in all directions, decapitating two of the eight operators and pulverizing the rest. "How could this be happening so fast?" thought Kalil. The engagement was not even 30 seconds old and already he had lost all of his artillery. Praise Allah. At least the helos with their firepower and commando units had gotten off the ground and were heading straight up the valley at 500 feet and 250 miles per hour.

Flanked by the Alpha and Beta Teams on the northern and southern boundaries, the German-made helos, he calculated, should be able to operate against the U.S. ground force with impunity. Any effort to support the ground force with helicopters would be quite costly. Team Alpha had three surface-to-air (SAMS) missile launchers as well as the fifty-caliber and would wreak havoc on the Apaches if they attempted to intercept his choppers in the valley.

With his hand-held radio, he ordered Alpha Team to attack... ... but attack what? His Alpha spotter situated behind the fifty-caliber machine gun was excitedly reporting that only one man had entered the valley when a series of explosions ended any further communication. Kalil looked at his watch and was shocked to see that less than two minutes had elapsed and he had already lost his artillery, Alpha's communications, and possibly the remainder of Team Alpha's capability as well.

Caught up in the moment, and in his own trance-like zone, Lester Grossman was oblivious to the presence of the Task Force watching his every move. The high-resolution screens and satellite imagery showed in graphic detail the events taking place on the battlefield below. This was not Oliver Stone or Steven Spielberg. This was the real deal. Blood and guts and gore were all over the place. And Brady and company were watching this real-time on high definition TV.

As the first two dune buggies from Beta Team entered Mack's line of sight, he blasted them with the pulse cannon, disabling their intricate electrical systems and bringing them to a screeching halt two-thirds of the way up the face of the most massive sand dune. Just as Mack raised his right arm to use his laser to finish the job, he began to take fire from a second group of Beta's mobiles. He pivoted on his left foot and fired his laser gun by pointing his right hand at the fast-moving dune buggies and pulling the hair trigger as if it were a normal pistol. The Widowmaker did not operate like anything resembling normal, however. A blinding ray of light connected Macklin's arm to the first dune buggy milliseconds before it was literally sliced in half by the force of the laser. The wheels and bottom half of the chassis continued moving forward but the upper half, including the three men inside, peeled away from the bottom. Two of the enemy operatives were dismembered at belt level, the driver's feet still exerting pressure on the floorboard pedals activating the thirty-caliber machine guns. The third soldier had been standing instead of sitting. His upper body separated from his lower body just above the knees. He lay screaming in the sand, bleeding profusely amid the charred ruins of the dune buggy and the remains of his comrades. The three Islamic fundamentalists were definitely on their way to Allah, thought Macklin. It was as if they were literally sliced in half with a large scalpel, each half cauterized by the laser and resembling a perfectly cooked sirloin steak done Pittsburgh-style - pink on the inside and charred on the outside.

* * *

As if someone flipped a switch, things began to fall apart quickly. The two Tiger Team Apache helicopters incinerated in mid-air, caught broadside by the Godunov cannon mounted on the stalled dune buggy. While their electrical systems had been fried by the pulse cannon attached to Macklin's left arm, he hadn't completed the job with the laser gun when he was distracted by the second of Beta's mobile teams. As it happened the dune buggies had stalled at such an angle that they had a clear line of sight to fire on the Apaches. They capitalized on that freak occurrence, annihilating both Apaches before Mack sliced and diced them with his laser. Further, to Mack's dismay, the German choppers instinctively fired their nitrous and within sixty seconds had disabled the Tiger Team artillery deployment, killing all twelve Tiger Team members before being taken out, in turn, by the air-to-air missiles from the remaining drones. An eye for an eye......Kalil and Macklin had both lost all of their artillery and air support. Beta Team was engaging Macklin with its last two functioning mobiles when disaster struck in the form of a 7 oz. steel-cased bullet fired by the only member of the Alpha Team that wasn't dead or seriously wounded. Mack had his back to the foothills unconcerned with the remnants of Alpha Team, having gotten the "all clear" sign from Lester; the thermal imaging capability of the Lightyear had indicated that any live nearby combatants were already losing body temperature as they bled to death. But the sniper had hidden in a crevice between two huge boulders that were driven out of the earth in the Early Mesolithic Era by subcutaneous forces too immense to conjure. The satellite and Lester just 'flat out missed him' and his first shot stunned Macklin as 3,000 lbs. of pressure per square inch were instantaneously disbursed throughout the body suit causing such a force that it literally blew Macklin's boots off his feet. Lester reacted immediately sending the remaining reserve drone into action putting a 100 lb. missile right in the crack of the ass of the twin boulders....yet not before the second bullet had hit Macklin's spine just above the coccyx. The suit was still processing the impact of the first round when the second round punched through. The sniper should never have been in play. The artillery and drones should have neutralized Alpha Team as priority number one. The drone should have kept up the smokescreen instead of following the German helicopter through the valley into the Tiger Team artillery position. Could'a.....Should'a..... Would'a......Didn't. Macklin was fucked. Paralyzed from the waist down he propped himself up at the edge of a sand dune and, ever the soldier, took out the remaining dune buggies and their occupants, sending them to the same fate as their comrades. Lucky for Macklin the Medevac Black Hawk was undamaged. It arrived on-site within three minutes and had him aboard and hooked up to the life support

MANIPULATION

apparatus two minutes later.

* * *

Command and Control
White Sands

Around the conference table everyone was stunned for a time, for a long time..... and then began talking all at the same time.

Colonel Franks established order and began a thorough and systematic debriefing, starting with Grossman. They were trained to disengage during a post-mortem but Lester was having a difficult time processing information with his buddies dead and dying. He did, however, put his emotions on hold and mechanically reviewed the battle footage talking into a voice recorder as part of the official review. It was obvious that the engagement was initiated effectively and efficiently until the fluke cannon shots took out the Apaches......couldn't fuckin' happen again in a million years. The dune buggies not only stalled at the perfect angle and the perfect time, but the drivers' lives were spared momentarily while Macklin responded to the more imminent threat posed by another attacking mobile force. It just happened too fast. Lester should have realized how significant a threat they were whether they were disabled or not. He just didn't see it.....and Lester didn't have to remind anyone he was the best. After the Apaches went the process simply cascaded out of control; the smokescreen drone was immediately pulled out of its primary role for a job that appeared more mission-critical but that, in turn, opened up Macklin's flank to a sniper. A fluke. Understandable. But inexcusable. And unforgivable.

It was apparent to those at the table that the consequences of this disaster at White Sands would carry far beyond the boundaries of the Land Force Warrior Program. A Task Force Report produced for the Joint Chiefs of Staff in the fall of 2008 had become a red herring for a debate that continued to rage regarding the use of robotics and Artificial Intelligence in the military. One school of thought supported the use of Artificial Intelligence as a means of maximizing the impact of our vast array of weaponry on an increasingly ubiquitous enemy. Thinking machines, they argued, were capable of learning without the use of a programmer or controller. Emotionless, an information superiority-enabled concept of operations could generate enhanced combat capability by networking sensors, decision-making, and shooting to a greatly-heightened tempo that increased lethality and survivability at the same time. The opponents of AI argued that the traditional laws of war requiring discrimination and proportionality would be obliterated by non-human decision-making. The anti-AI forces pointed to the impact of "unforeseen consequences" of AI-weaponized machines that become vulnerable to enemies hacking into the system using our own assets against us.

Advocates of AI pointed to the systems already at work in the industrial / commercial / academic sectors making good use of the knowledge of hundreds of experts and systems that learn. Through the use of case-based reasoning, AI systems use past experiences to guide diagnosis and fact-finding, creating rules for knowledge-based methodology. Genetic algorithms and adaptive search techniques have broad applications for scheduling, modeling, task setting, planning, execution, monitoring and coordination of activities. AI advocates believed that the transition from information-centric to knowledge-centric was a logical extension of the strategy transforming platform-centric to network-centric, as in the case of Land Force Warrior.

What was clear as a result of this disastrous exercise was that Lester was unable to react quickly enough to the initial loss of Apaches to stop the devastating cascade of events that followed. He could not compare the reality against all viable options with the lightning speed required. Emotion, psychology, whatever – to reduce the tragedy to football jargon Lester just didn't 'read the coverage quickly enough, or scramble out of the pocket fast enough, to avoid the other team's safety blitz'. End of game.

* * *

Brady and DiStefano were having coffee in Albuquerque waiting for the company jet to complete its pre-flight checkup prior to returning to Zybercor headquarters in Reston, Virginia.

"We've delayed our board meeting as long as we can," said Brady as he reflected upon the disastrous events at White Sands. They were certainly a long way from having this technology ready for prime time. "Shit, have we oversold this to the market?" he thought, "And to the Joint Chiefs?"

"I thought your idea to delay the meeting until all the directors had their high level security clearances was brilliant," remarked DiStefano. His boss kept his own directors covered in bullshit, as he pretended to wait impatiently for their special security clearances.

"Right. How long have you been holding them in your desk?" asked Brady with a wry grin.

"They're not dated so they can stay in my desk for as long as you want," replied DiStefano. He knew Brady was processing the recent data and recalibrating his strategy for dealing with his board. The Boss had told him many times that a Board of Directors was a necessary evil in becoming a public company. While the public market provided virtually unlimited access to funds for a company like Zybercor, it also came with a new set of rules and regulations promulgated in the Sarbanes-Oxley statutes passed in the aftermath of the corporate scandals of the late 1990's. DiStefano often wondered whether the new millennium ushered in some sort of cosmic era in which perception and reality separated at an ever-increasing rate. The perception was that these new rules actually created an ethical framework for conducting business. The reality was that lies and deceit, begotten on Wall Street, were raised and nourished in the inner sanctums of public companies all across the country, Sarbanes-Oxley be damned.

Brady was always at his best under pressure, focusing relentlessly on obstacles in the belief that they represented the true heart of opportunity. Realizing that it would be impossible to keep the White Sands "live-fire exercise" results from leaking to the full Joint Chiefs, Brady honed in on both the substance and the 'spin' issues. Substantively, he determined that the man/machine mix was suboptimal and needed adjustment. He would instruct the technical team to shift the mix to a closer form of Artificial Intelligence without going so far as to provoke dissent from the anti-AI forces within the Pentagon. The 'spin' would involve refocusing the human factors to essentially "book end" the AI between pre-planned controls to "tune the system" to specific military objectives within the framework of political realities, and, most importantly, implementing "cease fire" to provide proportionality.

As for the operations, he was now convinced that the effectiveness and efficiency of the smart automated brain would produce significantly better results than the human controller. There were simply too many factors at work in the matrix of weapons system options and tactical considerations. The array and pace of the technology simply overwhelm human processing capability.

Brady had acquired an option for an exclusive licensing agreement with Neurogenics, a high-tech spin-off from MIT, for $15 million that he now planned to exercise. The licensing agreement would allow him to quickly merge his technology onto a second generation Artificial Intelligence system. However, and this was a substantial concern, he was going to need to get his hands on a lot more cash given the tight time frames now confronting him.

"Here's what I want to do," said Brady. "We'll call a special Board meeting for early next week. Remind me to have the staff call Huron Lodge. That would be a good venue. We'll create an agenda that gives me the authority to raise additional monies and we'll beef up the resources to get this technology ready for deployment. I'll pretend to be pissed off at you for the delays in security clearances and you can mumble something about 'next week.' Our principal objective will be for the board to grant me a unanimous consent to raise and spend money. Now that we have Jacobs in place, we'll have him increase the value of the intellectual property and go back to the market for some additional cash. We'll play the national defense and shareholder value cards to the max. If we move fast we can ram it through." Brady paused and seemed to go into a trance of sorts. That fingertip-light, sexually-transmitted flutter in the pit of the stomach produced by a dopamine/serotonin cocktail remains, without a doubt, one of the true blessings of humanness. Brady was one of the fortunate few able to experience the 'fantastic flutter' during occasions uninfluenced by the opposite or same sex, depending upon one's individual preference. Brady got the same rush when he had a great idea and he was starting to experience the familiar surge of warmth and butterfly wings that accompany an epiphany. His custom was to speak out loud as he allowed himself to get into the zone, that special place where you could focus on the pure logic, and, if the truth be told, extend the rush of feelings as long as possible because it felt sooooo good. "Wait. Wait just a minute. Why would I pay another $55 million for a license when I could buy the whole company for a little over $100 million? We're the only ones who know what happened today. The rest of the world could be made to believe that we're acquiring Artificial Intelligence to deepen the relationship with the Pentagon and

MANIPULATION

Joint Chiefs of Staff. Hell, we'll swap a little stock with the seller of the AI, give them the impression that we're going to hit a home run. They'll take their 'fuck-you' money and run and fantasize that there's going to be some upside for them. If we time this right we can get their technical support down to the R + D facility in Charleston right away while we work out the details of the acquisition. A couple of good press releases and we should bump our stock a good $10 a share. Is America a great country or what?"

DiStefano had seen this happen before and knew that his job was to shut up and take notes.

Brady continued with his eyes closed, "Now that we own Jacobs and Johnstone we can produce documentation that raises the value of the current intellectual property portfolio in combination with our acquisition of Neurogenics allowing us to go right back to the market for more dough."

DiStefano's sphincter tightened because he knew this ritual either ended up with a brilliant strategy or a pissed off boss grumbling about the one that got away.

"The reason we're going back to the market so soon is to solidify our position... ...our 'monopoly-like' position with the Pentagon through the acquisition of a highly-regarded Artificial Intelligence System incubated in the MIT Brain Trust." Brady allowed himself to relax as he succumbed to a big smile and opened his eyes. "The market will be jazzed by our use of capital, we'll raise cheap money and promote the hell out of our own stock. Hell, we have enough analysts on the payroll to generate tons of buy orders. While we work out the closing details, we'll get Neurogenic's AI system down to

Charleston with some of their technical people and do a quick conversion to our command and control and have a chance at getting everything ready for the Nov. Review."

DiStefano could feel the hair rising on the back of his neck. Brady had this effect on people. He was so damned convincing, almost as if he was communing with a higher source, or lower one for that matter, depending upon your view of things.

Brady looked at DiStefano and regretted that he didn't have a bigger audience for such a world-class performance. "What do you think?"

"Perfect," responded DiStefano. "Damn that's smart," he thought. Brady gets the unanimous consent to raise and spend money and simultaneously keeps his directors in the dark about the status of the technology. The boss loves control, says it's the keystone of flexibility.

"Listen Tony, Kalil can't walk away from this, you know that. You need to see that there are no obvious loose ends here. That means Macklin, if he's able, and Grossman both need to be part of the effort down in Charleston to get the technology ready for the November 15th Review."

"What happens if they don't see things the same way we do?" asked DiStefano, anticipating Brady's response.

"If they're on board, they'll be our guests and part of the payday. If not, they'll be reluctant guests and then loose ends. Either way we have to suck out their brains to speed up the conversion process to Artificial Intelligence. Given our time pressure, they're indispensable."

"The plane's ready, Boss. Let's get the hell out of here and back to civilization," said DiStefano as he picked up both bags and ushered Brady out the double glass doors to the noisy, blistering tarmac.

* * *

    Walt Cadman and Norm Franks had worked together since Vietnam. Franks' Marine squad had been ambushed and had their chestnuts pulled out of the fire by elements of the Army's 75th Battalion led by… …you guessed it, Major Walter Cadman. As if it wasn't embarrassing enough for a Marine to rely upon the Army to bail you out, Cadman continued to bust his balls over the years. They developed a close personal friendship and Cadman looked to Franks as his Chief of Staff when his career finally brought him to the Joint Chiefs. Cadman was a bear of a man with the physique of an NFL lineman – a retired lineman, of course, but formidable nonetheless. He was old school with a buzz cut high and tight. With his lumbering gait and easy smile he looked like he could have been teaching high school in the Midwest instead of running one of the world's most complex organizations. DiStefano had prepared a detailed dossier on Cadman months ago for Brady accompanied by the recommendation that he not be underestimated. Endemic to his national origin, Cadman was a throwback to the ancient Celtic warrior-poets. He spoke four languages fluently, loved fine wines, lectured at the War College and Sandhurst, collected Greek and Roman artifacts, and was a decorated war hero from the dark ages of Vietnam. Franks could not have been more different. Balding since his early twenties, his five foot seven inch frame looked as if it was chiseled out of granite in spite of his sixty-two years of age and great fondness for cold beer, cheeseburgers, and ball park hot dogs. They were bound together, however, by core values that were anchored by a love of their country, tested under fire, and molded by the hot flames of high command.

They were still at White Sands waiting for transportation. Cadman was on his way to visit installations on the West Coast and Franks was heading back to D.C.

"How's Macklin?" asked the General, as he interrupted Franks' cell phone conversation with a black coffee. He knew that Franks was heavily invested in Terrel Macklin, both professionally and personally.

"Not good, Sir," replied Franks. "He's stable but paralyzed from the waist down with severe spinal chord injury. Lumbar 12 was hit. He may never walk again."

"Keep me posted," replied Cadman. He knew what Franks was thinking. "Norm, we lost a lot of good men today and I know you wanted to delay the exercise but events have overtaken us. Congress is flexing its muscles on funding and they're not all wrong in this instance."

"Sir, we should have never gone through with this. We just weren't ready. We didn't even arm the new artillery with its self-defense mechanism. Our guys were sitting ducks when their choppers blew through the Apaches. And Macklin's body armor wasn't ready. We're still adapting the 'Reptile Skin' to the wearable computer fabric and it's obviously not seamless yet. That's why Mack's a paraplegic.

For Christ's sakes Walt, we're just a few weeks from having our gear ready and now we have to deal with the whole decision support system. Our critics are going to have a field day if today's results are discovered."

"Norm, we've got to deal with reality. Our armed forces are past the breaking point. I mean the rubber band has snapped. If the general public knew how bad things were, I tell you, nobody would get a good night's sleep. We had hell to pay putting 10,000 troops into Somalia. We just don't have the manpower, Norm, and I don't see anything else in the hopper other than the Land Force Warrior Program. Whether we like it or not we are stuck with Brady and Zybercor, and he knows it. It's not just the wearable computer stuff, it's the 'integration software' that ties together all the bits and pieces in these new smart weapons systems, and their laser application is way ahead of the field."

"The 'smart technology' didn't look too fucking smart today," snarled Franks. He was truly pissed off but recognized that Walt was right. The political timetable was driving the process.

"Norm, what needs to be done to get this thing ready by November 15th?"

"Why November 15th?" asked Franks. "Shit," he thought, "that's two months away."

"That's the key tripwire in our contract with Zybercor. I can't keep a bubble around the project after that date. There's an intra-service review scheduled and you can be sure Congress is going to demand to be briefed. Hell, they're already all over me for a status report."

"What happens if we're not ready by then?" asked Franks as the acid in his stomach reacted to the bitter coffee.

"Nothing good happens, if that's what you mean. Most likely, the Zybercor contract would be put on hold pending a review. I doubt that Brady could hold it together if the problem became public. The shit will roll down hill so hard and fast that our grandchildren will be covered up to their eyeballs."

"Shit," said Franks.

"Shit is right my friend," said Cadman. "Here's a copy of the Pentagon contract with Zybercor. I've highlighted the drop-dead conditions for the review on November 15th. I don't have to remind your sorry ass that you got me into this mess. I assume you're going to bail me out."

"On one condition," said Franks as Cadman looked at him with a gaze that could penetrate body armor. "When we pass that review board I want you to promise me I'll never have to listen to you tell me how you pulled me out of the jungle again. I mean it. Never."

"Done deal. I've got to go. Norm, keep me informed."

"Yes sir."

* * *

Kalil was surrounded by heavily-armed soldiers. He and four other survivors were herded into a truck with canvas on the sides and top. Their captors were stonily silent with that thousand-yard stare that comes when comrades die in battle. These guys had been Tiger Team Two. They were Tiger Team One now.

MANIPULATION

As the truck carried Kalil and the rest to what was most assuredly their deaths, he reflected back to the time after he was wounded in a firefight in the Takhar province. The long and circuitous road to Guantanamo was a slice of hell. Kalil endured four days in a lorry much like this one with guards much like these. He never could understand these Americans. As a society theirs had little character.

The American culture was greedy and corrupt. It was all about money. Devoid of spirituality or purpose they were addicted to drugs….and oil…… and completely controlled by the Jews. Interestingly enough they were very different when you talked to them one on one. They hadn't been happy fighting in 'god-forsaken Afghanistan' yet they went about their business with a quiet dignity and childlike innocence. They never lacked for anything….food, clothing, shelter, education. They had everything, even it seems, the dark ones……while we have nothing but our faith. More than enough, Allah be praised.

The lorries in Afghanistan had been crowded, with no ventilation, traveling over the worst roads imaginable……and carrying comrades with pleas and prayers and putrefying flesh wounds. Hope, despair, the rattle of death. When the caravan stopped at Mazar-e Sharif for refueling and provisioning an American Army doctor amputated my right arm above the elbow. I could tell that he hated me for disturbing his perfect life with his perfect wife, his house, cars, kids….all safe and secure in his 'gated community'. Not anymore, my officious American doctor friend. Not after the two attacks. Now you must come halfway around the world to do battle with us here to keep us from raping your wife and daughters in your perfect bedroom. Those were my last thoughts before I lapsed into delirium and then a coma. I came to in that hellhole called Guantanamo.

And now here, being driven to my death.

As the lorry came to a halt we were unloaded at gunpoint. I asked the officer in charge if we could complete our prayers. **His eye twitched with guilt as he pointed his weapon and fired**.

CHAPTER FOUR

September 25, 2009
Near Lake George
Adirondacks

Brady had anticipated that events at White Sands would provide the momentum to catapult him through the Armed Forces Review Committee on November 15th into the meaty parts of the Pentagon contract where big bucks began to flow. Unfortunately, in order to pass muster on the all-important review date Brady was going to have to bring a more sophisticated decision support system to bear on the oversight of combat operations for the Land Force Warrior...and that meant a commitment to Artificial Intelligence. Personally, he was determined to acquire Neurogenics, a spin-off founded by some MIT professors who fantasized that, like their Stanford counterparts, they were on their way to the next Cisco. Brady usually insisted on complete control of his business, but this technical bullshit surrounding corporate governance convinced him that it would be more politically expedient to tell his newly-formed Board that he was simply exercising his option for an exclusive licensing agreement. What he really needed was a unanimous consent from his Board to raise and spend money as he saw fit for the next forty-five days. He intended to lean on Emory Jacobs to increase the valuation of his current patents. Simultaneously, he would twist Avery Johnstone's arm to go back to the market for...say, $400,000,000 for use as his personal slush fund. Franks would sing the national anthem on behalf of the Pentagon and the Board would fall into lockstep. Jackson Strawbridge, former U.S. senator and Co-chairman of Zybercor, would smile and nod as he calculated the value of his 450,000 options. Sue Jamieson, Viacom executive and chairman of Zybercor's Audit Committee, would pretend she had some idea of what was being discussed...and then Lou Azzato would kill the whole strategy as he saw through the scam with his X-ray vision. Brady knew that he had to manage Azzato or his billion-dollar plan was going down the tubes.

* * *

Huron Lodge, the brainchild of a brilliant developer, sits on 9,000 private acres. A 45,000 sq. ft. *tour-de-force*, the Lodge itself was built by local labor using indigenous material on the exterior. Massive logs of Douglas fir and Engelmann spruce, with diameters of 24 inches for the horizontal columns and 54 inches for the vertical, provide a serene majesty to the façade. Huge boulders spaced about the grounds, some weighing as much as 20 tons, were leftovers from the last of the fifteen or so glaciers that terminated in the area as the ice cap retreated to the north over 10,000 years ago.

The interior was a masterfully designed collection of large rooms on the ground floor with vaulted ceilings, massive oak timbers, and stone floors. Oriental rugs were generously scattered throughout and oversized sofas and chairs adorned the Great Room and the half-dozen adjoining studies, bars, and alcoves. Museum-grade dioramas and stuffed animals were everywhere... unbelievable specimens brilliantly preserved. The impact was mixed. On one hand, killing such magnificent creatures seemed, well, unseemly, if judged by current standards. On the other hand, here they could be appreciated and admired outside the confines of captivity. Few non-hunters would ever see them in the wild: boar, elk, wolf, cougar, mountain lion, and the magnificent male grizzly which dominated the Great Room. Wolverine, weasel, fox, and other smaller animals found permanent resting places in contiguous smaller rooms. Over the many fireplaces walleye, northern pike, trout, and a variety of bass swam in eternity for all visitors to enjoy. The large interior walls were adorned with American Indian and African artifacts: weapons, masks, baskets and rugs. A vintage Erie Canal barge served as a bar, seating twenty. Two horses that would have pulled the barge in its heyday - huge barrel-chested Percherons, stuffed and impassive, harnessed and seemingly ready to work, were standing on a raised platform behind the bar. They measured nearly eight feet from head to hoof.

All in all, Huron Lodge provided a unique venue for Brady's meeting. The awesome majesty produced just the effect Patrick Fortune Brady sought to achieve.

"Boss, this place is amazing. How did you find it?" DiStefano was overwhelmed by the grandeur and uniqueness of the place, yet, oddly enough, also very much at home as he reclined in an overstuffed chair in front of a huge hand-carved oak coffee table. In a reflex action that betrayed his normal public reserve he had put his feet up on the table.

MANIPULATION

He rationalized that the oak had beckoned and he felt compelled to respond. "I could get very used to this, " he thought to himself. He had been reconnoitering since they had arrived on the corporate Citation several hours earlier. Brady and he were now about to engage in their usual role-playing 'what if' game prior to the next day's meeting.

"I attended a conference here last year. I fell in love with the place. Good to have Board Meetings in different venues. Gets people out of their comfort zones. Always make them travel. Get 'em on your turf and schedule their departures so they'll be really inconvenienced if you don't finish on time. Make 'em think that you're willing and able to stay longer. All you really want to hear from them is 'So moved.'" Brady arched his eyebrows as he stared at DiStefano's feet, propped on the polished table top. "That, Tony, is just not done," Brady said, with a flawless 'Long-Island lockjaw' delivery.

DiStefano couldn't tell whether or not Brady was joking, or jarring him out of a comfort zone, but he quickly removed his feet from the table. He tried to be nonchalant. "I read a biography of Lyndon Johnson. He never felt comfortable before a vote in the Senate unless he had the requisite number of 'peckers in his pocket,'" said DiStefano, stammering just a bit.

"Amen. Speaking of that..."

"I know. Azzato. Listen Patrick, I think you probably shouldn't discuss that one...even with me, O.K? I know what you need. Please trust me on this. The person in question is going to be called home with an emergency during the middle of the meeting tomorrow. We need to have transportation standing by to get him there. I'll take care of that. You need to be prepared to put your arm around him and make sure you get his proxy. The resolutions should all be unanimous in the affirmative tomorrow."

"Why, ah, the intrigue?" asked Brady.

"Because kidnapping is a federal offense. O.K.?"

"Gotcha."

DiStefano took a deep breath before continuing. "You're on a first name basis with the Director of the FBI as I recall. It might be a good idea if you called him on Azzato's behalf tomorrow and got him to commit resources to finding his daughter… you know, the one that will be missing. That way, when she's returned, you'll get some stroke."

"Have I told you lately that I love you?" laughed Brady.

"Yeah, right," said DiStefano. "By the way, we're going to need to stage manage your little hunting trip tomorrow before the Board meeting. I've been working on it long-distance for a couple of days now. Are you sure you want to go through with this?"

"Absolutely. I told you this is all a game. A serious game but a game nevertheless. Nothing symbolizes business in this country more than hunting…it's survival of the fittest…winners and losers. So, what have you got for me?"

"Just this. It's little complicated but I think you're going to like it."

"Nothing is too complicated for me, my good man, or for you. Look at the time. I need my six hours. Come on. Brief me on the way upstairs."

* * *

MANIPULATION

  Brady hated the great outdoors but he relished being seen in hunting garb replete with a Mossberg shotgun, returning with a boar and a turkey that would be cleaned and cooked for dinner. The Great White Hunter feeding his tribe. In reality, DiStefano shot the animals. He had coordinated with the Lodge's staff to ensure that Brady would bring home the trophies. The turkey population was so large that success in killing several of the show birds was virtually assured. The boar, however, was a different matter. They were tough and smart. With toughness and smarts of his own DiStefano had arranged to have one trapped two days earlier. The unfortunate boar was released from a cage mounted in the back of a pick-up truck directly under the sights of DiStefano's shotgun. Voilá, Brady times his return with the gathering of the Board for a late breakfast in advance of their 12:00 meeting.

  Board members were encouraged to arrive the night before and participate in one or more of the many recreational options of Huron Lodge. None did. Several, however, were staying the night after the meeting with intentions to hunt or fish after the anticipated adjournment at 3:00 p.m. Emory Jacobs, in fact, had called his old friend, Avery Johnstone, III to do some deer hunting and spend the night after the Board meeting. Johnstone declined, but Jacobs pressed the matter saying he had something very important that he needed to talk about privately…very privately…and Johnstone reluctantly acceded to his request.

* * *

Brady greeted his new Board on the veranda overlooking the lake. A sumptuous buffet was laid out. One station was given to trout, sturgeon and bass cooked quickly to perfection on a hot grill. Another prepared omelets, griddlecakes, waffles, French toast…. and eggs any way you liked them. An entire table was laden with grain cereals, a dozen different types of bread, cakes and pastries. Another featured a bevy of fruit options along with a large frying pan manned by a local farmer who was well known for his treatment of organically-grown apples with a brown sugar sauce handed down through the generations. The meats, of course, were bountiful…all once on the back of animals raised or imported to the forests of Huron Lodge: venison, elk, boar sausage, and many more..

Brady deliberately avoided eating and drank just a few cups of coffee as his colleagues admired his recent kills. In his practiced manner he regaled them with the story of the raging boar charging from a dense copse of underbrush. He barely managed to get his Mossberg swung around in time to fire before being gored by the ugly sharp tusks, which nonetheless managed to graze his leg producing a tear and cut that still bled a bit. What a man!

Brady excused himself to freshen up for the meeting. In his room he changed into his Savile Row suit. He favored Gieves and Hawkes, the renowned British tailors who had outfitted English generals and statesmen from Wellington to Churchill. "Dress British – Think Yiddish" was Brady's mantra. All of his shirts were from Turnbull and Asser, custom-made and replenished annually. He preferred French cuffs with black onyx cuff links and a matching tie clasp. His tie selection demonstrated his one sartorial stab at individuality. He was partial to the raw silk creations of the legendary Jim Thompson, erstwhile proprietor of the Thai Silk Company, Bangkok, and an Ivy Club member with whom he had no gripe. Unmistakable and unique. He eschewed belts, choosing instead solid colored braces to offset his striped shirts. Brady always had a tan. His natural good looks were enhanced annually at the Swiss clinic near La Reserve on the eastern shore of Lake Geneva. And, even though he was 6'2", he had one-inch elevator soles installed in his hand-crafted Italian shoes. (Taller creating a more favorable impression, according to the data). A little here…a little there; he looked considerably younger than his sixty-one years. No concept too big – no detail too small!

* * *

The meeting was held in the Great Room of Huron Lodge. Brady appeared at exactly 12:00 resplendent in his two-piece charcoal grey suit and convened the Board to order. Brady preferred brevity. He didn't like to have his management team at Board meetings. For that reason there were no in-house executives on the Board and DiStefano was the only non-director in attendance…just the way Brady wanted it. His middle name should have been 'Compartmentalization', not 'Fortune'….or maybe the two hyphenated.

Serving as Secretary, DiStefano called attendance:

"Mr. Strawbridge?"

"Yes."

"Col. Franks?"
    "Here."
"Ms. Jamieson?"
    "Present."
"Mr. Johnstone?"
    "Here."
"Mr. Jacobs?"
    "Yes."
"Dr. Azzato?"
    "Here."
"Mr. Brady?"
    "Absolutely."

"Let the record show that 100 percent of the Directors are in attendance."

"Thank you Mr. DiStefano. I can't tell you how pleased I am that you are all here and have agreed to serve on the Zybercor Board of Directors. We are clearly living in troubled times yet we at Zybercor are privileged to be in a position to help our country strengthen its position in the global war on terror. Several years ago when the Iraqi Commission appointed by President Bush reported its findings to the Senate Foreign Relations Committee, many thought that we had reached a point of diminishing returns relative to the advocacy of democracy worldwide. Those findings provided the rationale for pulling out of Iraq. I think, in hindsight, we were all shocked by the velocity of the Sunni-Shiite civil war and the political ascendancy of Iran. Had we known then what we know now we would never have pulled so many resources out of the region. Now we have to pay the price and reestablish a significant and long-term presence in the Middle East...and this time do it in a way in which we can succeed. That's where Zybercor comes in. The President and the Pentagon are depending upon us to deliver Land Force Warrior as a major part of the redeployment scheduled for the first of the year, and that is exactly what we are going to do. We need to be flexible and nimble if we are going to succeed and I am going to ask you to support me in a series of resolutions that will be presented for your consideration today. I know I will be able to count on your support. While we shoulder a duty to our shareholders, we carry the added burden of supporting the national defense of this great country."

Brady had written this speech two weeks before and rehearsed it every night. He didn't receive the reception he had imagined. The little applause that ensued sounded forlorn, rather than encouraging, in the cavernous room. And a few of those around the table were actually embarrassed by the content and delivery of the message. The Board had never been together before and the chemistry just wasn't there.

Brady was taken aback but nobody would have been able to see the burning of his cheeks under his well-cultivated tan. His response to their lack of appreciation was lightning-quick. Realizing he had miscalculated, Brady's well-honed 'aplomb' mechanism kicked in and he offered his most self-effacing grin, saying "Sorry guys, I am so passionate about our company and technology that sometimes I just get carried away." Well, it broke the ice just as he knew it would. He'd get back at each of the ingrates at a later date. The surveillance camera would catch every nuance and subtlety. He and DiStefano would review it for hours after this absolute waste of time was in his rear view mirror.

* * *

    The Board Meeting adjourned precisely at 3:00 as Brady railroaded an agenda that should have taken weeks of preparation and several days of debate and analysis. In essence, whether they knew it or not…and the level of understanding among the Directors was very different…the Board members had granted Brady absolute authority to acquire the exclusive license for the Artificial Intelligence and raise and spend funds at his sole discretion to "protect our position with the Pentagon and sustain the momentum of the Land Force Warrior Program." Brady accepted the unbridled powers embodied in a unanimous consent with appropriate humility. Johnstone and Jacobs had both performed admirably on Brady's behalf. The juggernaut of Brady, Johnstone, and Jacobs rammed through the Board's resolutions in record time. Debate was limited and objections were steamrolled using the twin rollers of national security and shareholder value. Jacobs presented the new and improved valuation of the intellectual property portfolio and Land Force Warrior patents. He demonstrated that the wearable computer patents alone were worth north of $2 billion. After Jacobs finished with his presentation, Johnstone took over and effectively made the case that the timing was perfect to go back into the market to stockpile funds. "The timing couldn't be better," he opined. "It's always better to have it and not need it than need it and not have it." Further, he argued that the spread on interest rates would actually make the financing a neutral event with the short-term investment strategy he had developed.

Before Brady had opened the floor for any discussion he had called upon Colonel Franks to express the Pentagon perspective on the Land Force Warrior. Even a cynic would have been converted by the eloquent and passionate message delivered by the highly decorated Marine. Having put in his time in Vietnam and Iraq, Franks assured his colleagues that this was not '<u>a</u> program,' but '<u>the</u> program' and was fully supported by the Joint Chiefs of Staff and central to the game plan to combat world terrorism.

In the middle of Franks' presentation, a Huron Lodge bellhop entered the room and slipped DiStefano a note that he, in turn, passed to Brady who immediately called for a brief recess.

Brady pulled Azzato to the side and said, "Lou, this is an emergency message from your wife who told our office to interrupt the meeting. It says here that your daughter, Cindi, may have been abducted. Let's get you a telephone. I'll make arrangements to chopper you to the airport and get you a private plane. I'll be waiting right here. Jesus, Lou, I hope everything's O.K. If there's a real problem I'll get right through to the Director of the FBI. I'm here for you, buddy."

Following a brief phone call, Azzato told Brady, "Nancy is a wreck. She just found out that Cindi didn't make it home last night after a ball game at the University and school security had a report of someone fitting Cindi's description being pulled into a car. Patrick, I think my daughter's been abducted. What can I do?"

Brady put his arm around his old friend's shoulder and, ten minutes later, ushered him outside to the waiting helicopter. "Lou, I'll take care of notifying the Feds and getting you home. I'll make sure you get all possible assistance with this. Don't worry about anything else. Give me your proxy on this Board business and you go take care of your family and give my assurances to Nancy. We'll get Cindi back."

* * *

By 3:45 Brady and DiStefano were aboard the company Citation to Teterboro for a brief meeting, then on to Fort Lauderdale for a couple days of R and R and a session with Washington lobbyist Mark Kauffman.

"How do you think it went, Boss?"

Brady, tie loosened, suit coat and shoes off, with a good slug of scotch in hand, was relaxed and looking forward to a couple of days on board the 'Buona Fortuna,' his 150-foot Hatteras docked in Lauderdale. "I'll tell you Tony, our boys did a good job today. You were right though...about Azzato... we needed to play that card before the discussion and voting. Azzato would never have swallowed all that bullshit about national security....waivers and contract covenants," said Brady. "He's way too sophisticated to have supported a unanimous consent to give me such broad latitude on decision-making and spending. I could see him taking tons of notes during Jacobs' and Johnstone's presentations. As it is, the support was unanimous, with a little help from your friends. Now we can get to work. Is Colonel Franks on his way to Charleston to get our weapon system up to spec?"

"He's going to Washington first to get the General on board with this move to Artificial Intelligence. He's confident that we're on the right track and, with Cadman's support, we should be able to finesse this through the Joint Chiefs. I told him you wanted him to pull out all the stops. He knows that money is no problem. That should keep Cadman off his back. Can he square things?"

"You can fix anything with time and money," replied Brady. " I'm worried about time. Our agreement calls for a November 15th review of the technology benchmarks. That's a drop-dead date. If we can't meet the requirements we're in deep, deep shit."

Brady was all too aware that he was betting everything on the next forty-five days...thirty years of scraping and clawing his way to the top. For what? A public scolding.....a lost contract.....a stock plummet...bankruptcy. He realized that he needed to get outside of the box and build some contingencies into his plan. He couldn't continue to gamble on a one-pronged strategy...that being the Franks-Zybercor team's ability to implement the required modifications. Brady lacked confidence that the Artificial Intelligence could be effectively married to the Zybercor Command and Control System in the time allotted. He had a love-hate relationship with the technology that was at the core of his business. One minute it was like magic and the next minute it was sticking some ineffective hard drive up your ass. He had enough grey hair and scars to realize that you could never bet the whole ranch on an efficient 'interface' anymore than you could bet on a 'marriage made in heaven' in the 21st century. Brady was obsessed with back-up plans and contingencies. While others smelled the roses he smelled the stinking sweat of fear and failure. He needed viable options and needed them fast.

"Tony, we need to explore other distribution channels for our technology. You think this guy Kauffman has access to the international black market?" asked Brady.

"I've spent a lot of time thinking about this," responded DiStefano. And indeed he had. He had already determined what his boss needed. Brady was searching for someplace to unload the technology if everything else went to hell. He wanted to scope out a deal before the November 15th review date in order to maximize the value of a sale prior to any backlash that might follow a poor performance review. He knew his job was to identify the right broker. He had pulled in every IOU he had in the intelligence community…and in the criminal world. All sources pointed to Mark Kauffman.

Kauffman was a modestly successful lobbyist until 2004 when he hit the big time as the hired representative for a consortium of Chinese trading companies based in Hong Kong. It was assumed but not proven that the consortium was a front for the Chinese Intelligence Directorate. It was assumed but not proven that Kauffman was engaged in the illegal transfer of strategic technologies to the Chinese government. It was a tightly held, slow-moving investigation that could take years to complete. In the meantime…

"Kauffman is a direct conduit to the Chinese at a high level. If anyone can get this done, it's him," said DiStefano with confidence.

"If anyone can get this done, it is _he_" repeated Brady. "What else do you know about him?"

"He's a heavy drinker. He parties. He lives the high life. Gives big money to the pols. Wife's a bitch. Two kids. Hell, Patrick, he's a greedy son of a bitch and the size of this deal will capture his full fucking attention. I'm strongly convinced that he's our man." He'd already had two meetings with Kauffman and he knew that the lobbyist would be primed for tomorrow's session on the 'Buona Fortuna'.

"How's he getting to the yacht?" asked Brady.

"We're flying him to Lauderdale on the company plane," replied DiStefano.

"Make sure they have the booze out and available on the flight," said Brady.

"Already handled."

"Let's take a look at your new video," said Brady. He knew that DiStefano had done his homework. Brady needed a man that was thoroughly corrupt and would put loyalty as well as morality aside for the incredible payday that would occur after a successful conclusion to this colossal gamble..

DiStefano put a disc into the DVD player and they watched as the Land Force Warrior Team destroyed three well-armed contingents of Middle Eastern combatants. Brady was stunned that DiStefano had so effectively changed the results of the battle on the doctored video.

"Shit, Tony, how did your guys make this look so real? For a while there I actually was thinking that we won that thing."

DiStefano was watching Brady become

enthralled with his handiwork and replied, "A little computer-generated graphics added to the actual footage…We had enough imagery at the early stage to change the outcome a bit. It's no Lucas but it will convince Kauffman. That's all it's for, right?"

"I wonder…"

"Shit, Boss…let's not get carried away here… this is just a video. The system didn't work. We lost $250,000,000.00 worth of hardware and our best man."

Brady stared at DiStefano as he reflected upon an idea that was fermenting in his mind and replied, "We know that but no one else does. If we hadn't oversold the whole program and then insisted on the White Sands test, we wouldn't be sweating the "bubble technology" and Artificial Intelligence issues. Those shots that took out the Apaches were a fluke. The Chinks don't need to know that. Maybe we could sell them the old System while we add the AI for our guys. How are we looking on time?"

"We'll be wheels down at Teterboro in five minutes," said DiStefano… "an hour on the ground and then we'll be ready to head for Lauderdale. I notice on the schedule that you have a private meeting. Do I need to be involved?"

"No," said Brady; "I had a wild-ass idea a couple of weeks ago and I have a short meeting with this British nerd from Bermuda who's peddling a new form of insurance that transfers risk on intellectual property to the public market through some form of derivative…I really don't know what he's talking about but some smart guys are backing him so…"

"O.K., so you don't need me," said DiStefano. But he made a mental note to find out something about this new angle in insurance. If Brady was investigating it, it was worth keeping an eye on.

Brady knew that his Director of Security was very possessive and needed to know everything that was on the schedule. Sometimes Brady kept him in the dark to keep him off-balance and sometimes simply because he didn't bring anything to the table. This was one of the latter instances.

"No, why don't you follow up with the staff and Azzato. By the way, did you notice Jacobs and Johnstone were staying over?"

DiStefano got the message and immediately shifted his focus to Brady's question. He replied, "We have them bugged. I suspect they're going to whine to each other and get drunk. They're pussies...can't hit major league fastballs. I'll take care of that."

"Cool," said Brady as they buckled up for landing at Teterboro. "By the way, don't forget to get Liz Turney the Board resolutions ASAP. After all, she's our new Board Secretary so let's make her earn her fee."

* * *

Liz Turney had finally grabbed the brass ring and she was going to hang onto it.

Liz's mother was of mixed Chinese and Vietnamese descent. During the last days of American presence in Saigon, she legitimized her year-long affair with Second Lieutenant Ray Turney, an African-American, by way of a quick civil ceremony in the annex of the U.S. Embassy. They celebrated their marriage by boarding one of the last choppers off the ground. The Turneys settled in Los Angeles and their first and only daughter, Elizabeth, named after Ray's mother, arrived by way of a C-section in 1973 about the same time Spiro Agnew was pleading 'nolo contendere' to conspiracy charges while serving as Richard Nixon's Vice President.

Mei-Ming Turney's father had been a wealthy merchant in Saigon and a partner in an import-export company based in Hong Kong. As part of the ruling merchant class, Mei-Ming received a first-class education in one of the coveted French private schools. She was a talented gymnast and a concert pianist. The second child of a family with a first-born son, Mei-Ming was an adornment to her older brother who was the focus of her parents' attention in the manner traditional to her Chinese-dominant culture. While she chafed under the hubris of her older brother, she realized early on that she had to play the hand she was dealt. She vowed that things would be different with her own daughter and thus they were. Liz was taught that there were no limits to her horizons and that there was nothing that she couldn't achieve with education and hard work.

The product of two different worlds, Elizabeth Jane was the recipient of the most attractive features of both. She was blessed with an unusually high I.Q and a vicious work ethic. She flew through her high school and college curricula and took an MBA at Columbia. Due to her looks and maturity she learned early how to manage men. She used them to get what she wanted and she wanted it all. Sometimes it was sex, although she often wondered whether her sex drive was unusually underdeveloped. She liked to think that, in truth, she hadn't found anyone worthy of her undivided attention. Sometimes it was as a stepping-stone to a new level. She made sure, however, that she never left blood on the office floor. Whether it was conscience or expediency, she made sure she never left a legacy of bad feelings. It wasn't always easy but she always made it a point to cover all her bases. Her determination paid off. She got the brass ring. As Patrick Brady's Chief of Staff she was poised for the big leagues. He ran a 'Presidential' management model. As such, the Chief of Staff had an incredibly large range of responsibilities and broad influence. She was Zybercor's Condoleezza Rice….a real Renaissance woman. She was young, educated, beautiful, affluent…and really frustrated. For the first time in her life she was tremendously attracted to a member of the opposite sex. In three years on the job Brady had never come onto her, leaving her confused and uncertain. Liz Turney hated not knowing. His lack of interest surprised and disappointed her. She fantasized waking up in his bed with the *Wall Street Journal* the only thing separating their naked loins…his prodigious member holding the Money section aloft like a circus tent. Yummm. Money and sex in no particular order. Ironically, their professional relationship was unparalleled. He was an incredible mentor. He challenged her constantly while he trained her to understand all facets of his business…all except the R&D, the government contracts, and the deal side. Everything else…the operations, sales, licensing, consulting, finance, and administration came up through Liz in the chain of command. Brady was consistent. He moved her to a new level every sixty days. Recently he involved her more and more in the planning and the high level negotiations with subcontractors and strategic alliances. She didn't know whether she would rather cook his books or cook his breakfast. Vintage Liz….why not both? "I've made lots of headway in one area and no headway in the other," she thought.

Liz learned the lessons of life from her father and discipline and patience from her mother. As a consequence, she possessed both dreams and the means to achieve them. This was America and America is about power and money and then everything else. Mr. Brady had compensated Liz for her relentless determination and her loyalty with both power and money. Mr. Brady had awarded her 150,000 stock options at a strike price based on the end-of-day value of the IPO. Unfortunately, at $54 per share it would be a long time before she was 'in the money'. Speaking of money, her boss had certainly just spent a shit load of it. As she worked through the pile of resolutions with her calculator, she was astonished that so much Board business had been conducted in such a short period of time. Brady had shocked Liz just days ago by informing her over drinks with Tony DiStefano, that she was going to serve as the official Secretary to the Board for an additional annual stipend of $200,000.00. That was the good news…particularly in light of the fact that her options appeared under water. The bad news… she would <u>not</u> be sitting in on the Board meetings. DiStefano would take the notes. She would plan with the two in advance and implement all of the follow-up but not be present at the meeting. She knew better than to question her boss's reasoning.

He respected...and paid for...loyalty and competency above all else. Liz had an unlimited expense account, traveled first class, company BMW, base salary of $450,000, bonus up to 100%, the options and now the additional $ 200,000 for doing what she did in any event. Not bad kiddo.

As she reflected back over the discussion with Brady and DiStefano, it occurred to her that her knowledge in managing Board affairs was sketchy at best. In fact, as she thankfully accepted the job, Liz had suggested that she attend a conference on the 29th and 30th in the District regarding the new amendments to the Sarbanes-Oxley statutes.

'Sarbox' was enacted in the wake of corporate scandals involving Enron, Tyco, WorldCom, Adelphia, and Global Crossing. Sarbanes-Oxley was designed to fundamentally change the way corporations governed themselves. Historically, very often a good ol' boys network ruled the Boardrooms of America. Board appointments were made on the basis of friendship. Since the Chief Executive Officer appointed most members of his Board of Directors, it was expected that they demonstrate their loyalty by supporting the CEO's agenda. Board service was prestigious and lucrative...and in most cases not very demanding...four meetings a year including golf and cocktails for handsome fees and more handsome stock options. As the pressures of public company performance intensified it became common for companies to "cook their books" and use accounting conventions and exotic financing schemes to prop up their quarterly filings. The CEO, the Chief Financial Officer, the Outside Audit Firm, and various Board members were often parties to the obfuscation.

Under the new 'Sarbox' guidelines, it was a felony if a CEO or CFO signed a public disclosure that they knew falsified company performance. In addition, the fiduciary obligations of the Board of Directors were altered, demanding greater independence from the CEO and more responsibility in managing the risk associated with the company's business strategies. All in all it was a very serious bill. Like most federal legislation, it was a rush job designed to make the incumbents look good when they broke for recess. Liz was surprised when both Brady and DiStefano told her that it would be a colossal waste of time to attend the seminar. "Corporate governance was all about common sense," Brady said and DiStefano had agreed. "Besides, look at the quality of people representing the shareholders on our Board of Directors, top-drawer in quality and diversity."

"Well shit," Liz thought aloud. "I'll be here until the wee hours on these resolutions as it is. No sense in over-thinking this, girl."

* * *

Brady was relaxing in the commercial aviation lounge at Teterboro after an interesting meeting with an insurance guru representing one of Lloyd's syndicates. He smiled while listening to DiStefano coordinate activities with Liz Turney by cell phone. Brady preached loyalty as a core value and his employees, sub-contractors, and professional services firms responded with relentless energy and slavish dedication. He had what they wanted and

MANIPULATION

he kept the carrot just out of reach. **"All's fair and no favor in love and war……..and commerce"**, he said to himself in a guarded whisper. Brady Avenue was most definitely a one-way street.

CHAPTER FIVE

Friday
September 26, 2009
Somewhere in the Caribbean

"Captain Bar-Cohen, please review today's schedule," commanded Brady. Parak Bar-Cohen had been hired by DiStefano a year and a half ago to captain the 'Buona Fortuna', ('Good Luck' in Italian), Brady's 150-foot Hatteras. Bar-Cohen had done a five-year stint in the Israeli Navy before joining a recreational yachting company based in Ft. Lauderdale. According to DiStefano the company was owned by several wealthy Jewish Americans who periodically made their floating assets available to high-ranking human assets in the Israeli government. Bar-Cohen and his crew, including Cordon Bleu chef Diane Ben-Shoshon, were skilled security operatives, having spent six months at the famous Mossad School in Ailot. If you wanted safety and luxury this was as good as it gets.

The 'Buona Fortuna' was a custom-designed Hatteras measuring 149.6 feet from bow to stern. Recently the company had moved into the larger luxury vessel business and Brady had jumped at the chance to be one of its first customers. The yacht's hull was a unique combination of the deep V design and the flat bottom that creates less resistance. Brady insisted upon a maximum amount of interior space in order to accommodate an exact duplicate of his office at Zybercor headquarters in Reston, Virginia. He found it impossible to relax without a sophisticated command and control capability on board. The custom design delivered a sharp entry into the water as well as a soft, stable ride that reduced spray while increasing the beam above the water line…ergo, more interior space for the high tech office fit-out and expanded master suite. Brady was willing to sacrifice fuel economy and overall performance for a reduction in cavitations, vibration, and noise.

The 'Buona Fortuna' was an extension of Brady's personality and represented far more than a corporate toy. He was actively engaged in the engineering, design, and interior fit-out, never missing the bi-monthly inspections during the building process. He was bored with the advanced propulsion theories, gear ratios, shaft angles and overall draft features. He was, however, obsessive about the details that mattered to him. He insisted upon rounded corners and the elimination of right angles and sharp edges. Both dining areas (formal and informal) were designed so that his seat was in a commanding position relative to his guests. His custom-designed chairs were a little higher off the deck and larger than the others and he took great care to design backdrops that framed him properly in the center of a composition that inspired respect and admiration for the owner. Dividing Brady's office from the formal dining room was a 300-gallon tropical aquarium with five of the most unique species known to man. Brady had specified a live rock setting, as opposed to coral, and three different lighting systems, including a phosphorescent blue to highlight the fish at night. The overall effect was a dramatic form of "moving art". The rare species appeared like alien holographs floating in space. All of the original artwork complementing the tropical divider was beautifully displayed in custom teak frames with corresponding lighting systems carefully set to achieve maximum effect as the day progressed or the sunlight varied.

Brady had designed his own sound system for the 'Buona Fortuna', spending $250,000 to achieve the perfect blend and resonance. He would select the music for the day over coffee every morning and the staff would dutifully adhere to the maestro's commands.

Brady had been piped aboard the previous night along with Director of Security DiStefano. They were to be joined in the late morning by Mark Kauffman as previously arranged. They would be involved in meetings all day. Then Kauffman would head back to D.C. in the early evening and T. Jackson Strawbridge would join Brady and DiStefano for the remainder of the night.

Captain Bar-Cohen briefed Brady in private. Aboard the Buona Fortuna, everything was on a need-to-know basis. Brady suspected that Bar-Cohen would sidebar with DiStefano and that was O.K. Brady enjoyed teasing information out of DiStefano and liked torturing Bar-Cohen about what DiStefano did or didn't know.

"As you requested sir, breakfast in the main quarterdeck for you and Mr. DiStefano at 0900: juice, coffee, omelet, rye toast, and fruit…oh yes, and Metamucil for Mr. DiStefano."

"At 1300 hrs, you requested the ski boat…single for yourself, sir, and doubles for the other two…uh sir, do Mr. DiStefano and Mr. Kauffman know how to ski?"

"No," Brady replied.

Bar-Cohen reminded his boss that it would most likely be a little choppy to learn today. Brady reminded Bar-Cohen that that was fine. He didn't expect his guests to learn. He wanted them to struggle uncomfortably while he dazzled them on one ski.

"You requested an hour's private time with each gentleman in the afternoon and then a joint conference for two hours during cocktails as we sail into St. Barts at approximately 1900 hrs. You requested that we time Mr. Strawbridge's arrival with Mr. Kauffman's departure at 2200 hrs."

Brady nodded for Bar-Cohen to continue. At 2200 hrs, Kauffman would be taken to the local airport for a return trip to D.C. and T. Jackson Strawbridge would come aboard for dinner and a recreational evening with some 'local talent' arranged by Mr. DiStefano. Dinner would be served buffet-style and all staff would have shore leave until 0900 hrs the next day. Brady needed to be sure that Strawbridge harbored no ill will after the ram-rod Board meeting. He was in it for the money and all Brady needed to do was to remind him that he was tied to the fortunes of the King. All in a day's work.

* * *

Arriving in St. Barts Mark Kauffman was finishing his third Bloody Mary as the landing gear dropped on the Zybercor Citation. This doesn't take long to get used to, thought Kauffman. Brady was a colossal asshole but he sure knew how to do things first class. Limo to Citation. Citation to chopper. Chopper to yacht…and back to D.C. within 24 hours. This was going to be the most important meeting of his 40-year life. The Land Force Warrior Program represented one of a handful of technologies that would affect the balance of world power over the next ten years. Incredible when you thought about it. One highly trained G.I. able to dominate 10 square miles of desert and mountainous terrain. True, the program required a lot of hardware and support personnel but the American public had demonstrated repeatedly that it would bust military budgets and even accept higher taxes as long as kids weren't getting killed...unless, of course, the kids were African.

If the Land Force Warrior technology was as good as its press, the Chinese would move heaven and earth to own it....especially Huan Tsu, Kauffman's handler. The greedy Chink wouldn't believe it. Ha! The inscrutable Oriental wetting his pants, imagining the Land Force Warrior in his hot little hands. An elevator straight to the top floor – the Politburo no less. The military wouldn't want to block him this time. After all, they would be the recipients of LFW. Good for him and good for me. Kauffman reflected back over the past several years since that fateful trip to Hong Kong to pitch his first client from the Far East – the Chinese Department of International Trade. In hindsight, it wasn't like anything out of a Ludlum novel. It was a straightforward business deal. No honey trap or esoteric machinations. It was all about the money. Great suite at the Peninsula. Superb wine and food. In the end it's always about the money. Money transitions beautifully to status in Washington, D.C. So Kauffman traded money for freedom. He understood from the outset that this was about selling out and there was no going back. He was an agent for the Chinese Intelligence Directorate, the spymaster of the Communist Chinese government. All in all, the Chinese paid a lot better and he was proving to be a very special agent. He knew that he had become a priceless asset. He realized that at heart he was a thief...a really good thief. He saw all the angles. He understood value. He never stole crap... just the really good stuff. Most importantly, he knew how to use the vast array of assets made available to him by his well-connected handler. As effective as he had been with political intelligence and privileged information from the Patent Office, his ability to deliver Land Force Warrior would trump them all. He would be set for life. Of course, he would have to drop out of the Beltway, and that would require a massive payday. Land Force Warrior would be the deal of a lifetime. What's good for the Chinese goose is good for the Jewish gander. Huan Tsu has me by the balls so the least I can do is return the favor. The safe deposit box at the new D.C. branch of Bank Leumi — not far from the Chinese Embassy to the U.S.... Kauffman had learned fast. He would take his own pictures as well as tapes and other documentation chronicling his good work for the Chinese. Oh how they hated publicity and this type of espionage would kill careers – literally.

* * *

Brady, DiStefano, and Kauffman had gathered on the upper deck of the 'Buona Fortuna' under a brilliant sun. Brady was sitting on the edge of the shadow cast by the blue umbrella raised in the middle of the teak table. Kauffman was drinking Bombay Sapphire Gin and tonic, DiStefano his standard Budweiser, and Brady fresh-squeezed lemonade. Brady had just shown Kauffman the White Sands video…the DiStefano version. The Land Force Warrior Team had decimated Kalil's forces inside of twelve minutes. Kauffman was stunned with the video and asked for it to be re-played twice.

Brady was lounging in the comfortable chaise with his feet up. "Well, Mark, what do you think of Land Force Warrior?"

"I've never seen anything like it," he replied. "Is it ready for the field now that White Sands is behind you?"

DiStefano answered, "We're making some adjustments in the lab as we speak…and, of course, we have an ongoing improvement process that is, well…endless…but… yes Mark, we're ready to go. Any takers?"

"Are you kidding? I could raise billions for access to that but somehow I don't think your buddies at the Pentagon would appreciate sharing this with, say, the Chinese or North Koreans. Would they?"

Brady and DiStefano had planned for this part of the conversation on the flight from Huron Lodge. They were well aware that Kauffman was owned by the Chinese and believed that they had the dough and the inclination to do the deal. There were two problems. First, how to get the technology to the buyer without the U.S. government knowing, and second, what were the consequences of selling something to the Chinese that doesn't work in the final analysis?

"Theoretically, of course, just for the hell of it,

what kind of value do you think you could get for Land Force?" asked Brady.

Kauffman took a deep pull on his gin and tonic and looked Brady in the eyes. "Three to five billion."

Brady smiled at DiStefano, "I think I'll let you two get to know each other a little better.....I feel like a little water skiing."

* * *

Later that afternoon as the 'Buona Fortuna' cruised toward St. Barts at a steady twenty knots, Brady and DiStefano met in the sitting area of his massive stateroom.

"So what did you learn?" asked Brady.

"I think you figured this right. He thinks he can get somewhere between three and five triple large even though the Chinese have never dug that deep before."

"How much did that son of a bitch drink? Was he still hitting the gin after I left?"

"Yeah. Must have had three more and the co-pilot told me he had three Bloodies between Lauderdale and St. Barts."

"I'll tell you, Tony, never trust an Irishman who doesn't drink.....or a Jew who does. What's the next step?"

"He asked for the tape but I told him no way. I referred him to the public domain information and reminded him that the Chinese have excellent sources in the defense community and they can do their own due diligence. He's contacting his people and thinks he'll have a proposal within a week. What do you want me to do now?"

"If we go this direction we've got to make it look good. Tell Kauffman I want $4 billion for the program….as is. No Artificial Intelligence. As is. That's important. I don't want this coming back to bite me in the ass. The Chinks own half the planet already. Life's too short."

"How do you want to take the money? Not through the company I hope?" asked DiStefano.

"Hell, no." said Brady. "Set up a dummy corp. in the Caymans that we control through a blind proxy and tell Kauffman that the money buys a 30% option in the shell. Make it a single-purpose LLC for research and development."

"You want the Chinese as a partner?"

"Why not? We have no idea how this is all going to play out. Thank God for free agency. Makes it easy to change jerseys. Confirm with Kauffman right now and let's get rid of him as soon as possible. I need some R and R."

"Roger, boss."

* * *

As the Bell chopper carrying Kauffman took off from the aft deck, Brady and DiStefano waited for Strawbridge to come aboard in the dinghy. Strawbridge was a trusted associate and knew how to bend the rules but Brady didn't want him involved in the prior discussion with DiStefano and Kauffman. He had no need to know anything other than the official Zybercor agenda at this point. Brady needed a contingency plan. One he hoped he'd never have to use. Tonight was for team building and relaxation.

* * *

Brady woke up at 0500 hrs. as a rosy-fingered dawn crept through the bay window of the 'Buona Fortunas' massive master suite. Both of his guests were still asleep after a crazy night. The sex had been incredible. Brady was sated. He never felt better than the morning after. He felt...well...himself. Brady quietly took two lines of cocaine from the nightstand to kick-off his morning and clear the cobwebs. Renewed with a jolt of power, Brady showered, shaved, and climbed into cut-off jeans with a Michael Jordan autographed Bulls jersey on top and topsiders below. As he reached the galley he poured himself a steaming cup of black Colombian coffee in his special pewter Zybercor mug, presented to him by his former management team on his 55th birthday. They admonished him that Styrofoam just didn't fit his image. They were right about that but wrong about everything else.

They had been like an anchor tied around his neck. They simply could never see the big picture. Hung up in process and bureaucratic bullshit, Brady had given them their pink slips one by one. The only piece of gold in all that dredge was DiStefano. He was the one that suggested the strategy of a long-term payout tied to a gag order. In addition, Tony's team created just enough documentation to convince each of them that a damaging lawsuit would appear from Zybercor's litigator's safe if any breach in the handsome severance agreement were to occur. Thank God for DiStefano. DiStefano and Brady made a great team. Tony was a Navy Seal for four years before moving to Naval Intelligence. He was still remembered by counter-intelligence staff as a gifted operator who ferreted out dozens of software and hardware black marketeers. The largest of these networks required months of surveillance, wiretapping, and documentation. Tony learned the whole package. Seventy-hour weeks and civil service wages, however, finally combined to take their toll on a marriage already weakened by infidelity. In a moment of sheer madness Tony promised Sally he would do anything to save their marriage, including taking an early-out pension from the Navy and arranging a more lucrative security job in the private sector.

After two years in security consulting Tony finally got the offer he was looking for – Head of Security for a successful private equity firm. His salary was O.K. but the bonus and option package made him a millionaire on paper and Sally went crazy. Before he knew it they had moved into a new house in Westchester County, joined a country club and built their expenses up to forty thousand per month. His salary couldn't handle the burden and the bonus didn't begin to measure up to the commitments made. Hey, welcome to Wall Street. Just because you're paranoid doesn't mean someone's not out to fuck you. You want loyalty, get a dog.

Brady was in serious need of someone with Tony's talents but he never believed when he first hired him that he would become so bloody indispensable. Not only did he perform all the dirty work, keeping Brady at a distance, but he implemented it better than Brady would if he spent all his time doing it. They had the same value system. Trust no one and fuck them before they can fuck you. Brady trusted DiStefano completely, letting him get closer to him than anyone ever had. DiStefano was completely loyal, as well he should be. Brady had made him a multimillionaire over the past few years. He hired DiStefano when no one else would. You see, DiStefano had a skeleton in his closet and Brady loved skeletons. In 2000 Tony had been caught with his hand in the cookie jar.

His boss, the well-known head of the prominent Park Ave. private equity firm, was as averse to scandal and publicity as a dog was to fleas. He simply cut DiStefano loose and told him he had six months to repay 'the loan' or he would have him arrested. Brady heard about the situation and reached out to a desperate DiStefano. He hired him as Head of Security with a substantial six-figure start. Tony and Sally soon divorced and Sally, of course, received a formidable alimony. Unfortunately, she suffered a tragic accident soon thereafter, succumbing to an overdose of barbiturates. Oh well. Six months later Brady brought Liz Turney in as Chief of Staff and the company began its meteoric transformation into a big-time technology and defense contractor.

* * *

Brady took his coffee to his seat out on the bow. Specially made, the seat was carved out of the fiberglass and a foam mold had been installed with armrests and an electrical hookup waterproofed for CD's and top-of-the-line Bose headphones. Today it would be Stevie Wonder's *Songs in the Key of Life* followed by some up-beat opera...maybe *The Mikado*. Among the many gifts from his sainted mother, his love of opera was probably the most cherished.

Brady had a unique ability to detach from the moral and ethical framework that burdened others with the constraints of convention. He was the perfect corporate pirate, as pure a predator as you can find in business...no conscience, no hypocrisy... just the kill. He had already put White Sands in his rear view mirror as he focused like a thin beam of hot light on the issues at hand. His new three-pronged strategy gave him a renewed sense of confidence as he looked out over the next forty days. He would keep the pressure on Franks to adapt the Artificial Intelligence System to Land Force Warrior. DiStefano would monitor that situation on a daily basis to ensure that the team stayed focused on the specific benchmarks that would be subject to review on November 15th. In the meantime, Kauffman would shop the technology overseas. The Chinese would be a perfect buyer. He didn't need reminding that the deal with the Chinese would have to close before November 15th.

There was only one card left to play. The insurance broker from Lloyd's had given him an idea. He suggested that Brady consider an insurance policy that transferred the risk of a catastrophic event impacting Zybercor's technology to Lloyd's... for, of course, a pricey annual premium. In the case of a catastrophic event, Lloyd's would step in and provide the funds necessary for the company to re-establish its intellectual property...thereby protecting the company from a serious loss of market capitalization. "Hell," thought Brady, "I can manufacture a catastrophe as well as anyone." His momma didn't raise no fool. He smiled and relaxed as he contemplated a side trip to Bermuda to start the insurance negotiations. Thirty years of struggle for a forty-day window to either harvest a fortune or go down in flames . . . all or nothing....or as his sainted mother used to say in Italian, "Il reste de niente"...the rest of nothing. There was no way he was going to lose this fight. He had been training for this his whole life.

For two hours Brady sat there drinking coffee as the music soothed his soul...the 'Buona Fortuna' traveling at a smooth twenty knots as the mellow waves of the Caribbean broke over the bow.

* * *

Huron Lodge

Emory Jacobs felt like a jerk in his camouflage gear as he shouldered his overnight kit and awkwardly accepted a rifle that he never intended to shoot and climbed the makeshift ladder to the deer blind situated a mile and a half from Huron Lodge. Avery Johnstone would rather have had hot toothpicks under his fingernails than spend the night in the middle of nowhere in a wooden box thirty feet in the air. He liked Emory. He really did; but there was nothing in the Ivy Club annals that required this proof of friendship. Something was terribly wrong.

The inside of a Huron hunting blind, while not a Four Seasons suite, was warm, comfortable and well appointed with chairs, a refrigerator, dozens of books and, most importantly, a well-stocked bar.

They dumped their gear unceremoniously in a pile and sat down. Before Johnstone's ass hit the cushion, Emory had the vodka out. Before Johnstone could ask what the hell they were doing here, Emory was pouring himself a second shooter and blurting out the reason for their impromptu hunting trip.

"Brady found out that I fucked over a client, and he's blackmailing the shit out of me," said Emory.

Johnstone listened intently as Emory recounted, in detail, the circumstances surrounding the Geopoint patent. By then Johnstone had also done a two-and-a-half gainer into the vodka, and he was starting to feel the full effect of his third drink. While he was listening to his old friend recount how Brady had discovered his larceny, he was thinking about his own dilemma and wondering whether or not to share his troubles.

When Jacobs had completed the litany of events leading up to his bogus valuation of the Zybercor patents, he was well and truly wound up. "So, there it is," he said. "That prick has me by the balls, and he just keeps squeezing. I either go along with the program or face bankruptcy as well as disbarment...maybe even prison." Tears began to stream down Emory Jacobs' face as he looked imploringly into the eyes of his old friend. "What am I going to do? The hole just keeps getting deeper. My partners are up my ass, and my marriage is going down the tubes. I'm losing it, man."

"You've got to calm down so that we can deal

with this rationally," said Avery making the decision to get everything out on the table. "When you're digging yourself into a hole, the first thing to do is put down the shovel. What do you think Brady would do if you called his bluff and threatened to go to...I don't know...the FBI or the Securities and Exchange Commission?" Before revealing his own dirty secrets, he wanted to see how far Jacobs was willing to go.

"Are you kidding? He's got me by the short and curlies. Sure, I reveal him for the lying, blackmailing prick that he is, but where does that leave me?"

"Completely fucked," said Johnstone, "Just like me!"

Over the next three drinks Avery Johnstone told Emory Jacobs about his secret life on the Internet and in the back seat of his Mercedes. His eyes never left the floor as he went back to the first time he had sex with another man. He professed his heterosexuality with great passion, explaining his down-low life as a release of tension and a means of dealing with the everyday stresses of life in the fast lane.

Jacobs put on his most compassionate visage, but deep inside he was thrilled to the bone. Avery was in just as bad shape as he was...maybe worse. After all, he had a lot more to lose.

They spent the rest of the bottle trying to figure a way out of their dilemma with no success. Halfway through the second bottle, they gave up and went to sleep, pledging to pick up the conversation in the morning. Emory feigned sleep immediately and zipped up his sleeping bag to the neck as he glanced nervously at his old, less-than-fully-heterosexual, friend.

A LAND FORCE WARRIOR CHRONICLE

* * *

Washington, D.C.

As Brady planned and played on the 'Buona Fortuna', Norm Franks flew to D.C. to brief General Cadman before continuing on to the Research and Development facility in Charleston to work on the Land Force Warrior technology in preparation for the Review Committee on November 15th. Brady had shared with Col. Franks his strategy to modify the decision-support system of Land Force Warrior. Ironically, Franks agreed with Brady that the proposed shift in the man-machine mix could increase the overall effectiveness and efficiency of the program and, in the final analysis, save more American lives. He was determined to press that theory upon General Cadman and then get to work.

Franks and Cadman met at an Irish pub near Union Station in the District. They both liked their beers cold and their burgers loaded, and they picked a place far from the eyes and ears of the Pentagon, politicians and the press.

"How are June and the kids?" asked the General as they went to work on their first Budweiser of the evening. Cadman was the godfather of Franks' first-born daughter and a close friend of the family. He knew the Land Force Warrior Program had become a jealous mistress and kept Norm away from home a lot more than usual.

"They're good Walt, thanks for asking. June's handicap is down to 15 and mine's up to 18. I haven't been on the golf course for six months now. How's Jeanna?"

"Okay, we just spent our thirty-fifth anniversary in different places. Sounds like we could all use some time away. What say we take the girls to Hawaii after this Review is completed?"

"Do we pack the golf clubs, Sir?"

"That's an order, Colonel."

"Yes, Sir."

They sat in a comfortable silence, put in their order for two more beers, cheeseburgers and fries, and then got down to business.

"How did the Board Meeting go?" asked Cadman. The General had insisted that Franks serve as an ad-hoc Board member of Zybercor as a condition in the contract. He respected Brady's abilities, but he didn't trust him.

"Not bad," replied Franks. "Brady is a real prick, but he knows how to get things done. The Board of Directors gave him a unanimous consent to raise additional monies and spend them at his sole discretion. Hell, the whole thing only took three hours start to finish."

"So, what's the plan?" asked Cadman.

"What if we could alter the decision-making capability of the Land Force Warrior Program by installing Artificial Intelligence to maximize our effectiveness during combat operations without...... however.....triggering an endless debate on A.I.?"

"How the hell can you walk that line without pissing off one side or the other? If we turn this into a policy debate we're dead!"

Norm knew that he had to handle the answer to the General's question with a lot of confidence. If he allowed the conversation to deteriorate into a political debate on A.I. they'd never be ready for the November review.

"I realize that. You need to stay with me on this. The anti-A.I. forces have relied up on a three-part argument. One, they argue that the traditional laws of war require discrimination and proportionality and those notions would be blown away if an emotionless system, or a robot for that matter, was in control of combat operations. O.K., we counter that through the control of the system on the front end and back end of the combat operations. In other words, guys like Grossman are there to "tune" the A.I. system with inputs according to a set of predetermined restraints tailored to specific combat environments. That would deal with the issue of discrimination. As to proportionality, the human controller maintains complete control of the "cease –fire mechanism".

Cadman leaned forward and prepared to interrupt, but Norman put his hand up saying, "Please Walt, let me finish and then you can tear me a new asshole." Cadman leaned back and listened intently.

"O.K., their next argument has to do with the unique requirements of military applications. We all know that Artificial Intelligence has been used effectively in industrial/commercial/academic sectors for years. They refer constantly to the Desert Storm situation, in which five of our guys bought the farm when a missile inadvertently vectored onto their position as opposed to the enemy target coordinates. The investigation proved that the system was rebooting and things just got fucked-up beyond repair. Bottom line…military applications demand higher performances at reduced-cycle times and at less cost than industrial/commercial applications. O.K., we accept that. Here's the kicker. The Zybercor Network Command and Control System, in combination with the new M.I.T. based A.I. systems, Neurogenics, solves those problems...and Brady has already secured an option for exclusive licensing...and now has the dough to exercise the option. Hell, he just got approval from his Board to buy the whole company. We can have their technical people in Charleston the day after tomorrow. The net effect is a multi-domain operations network command system with Artificial Intelligence capability managed by well-trained, professional soldiers."

Norm was on a roll, and Walt knew better than trying to pull rank on his old friend now. So he relaxed, actually enthused thus far, and ready to take the rest of the ride.

"And lastly, you, mon general"... Franks always practiced his pidgin French after a couple of drinks and frequently admonished Cadman with the phrase..."'ne give me any shit pas'. You, mon general, always told me that desperate circumstances have a way of overwhelming ethical dilemmas in Washington, D. C., and we are in a desperate circumstance where political expediency is on our side. The bad news is we don't have any choices that I see. The good news is that we can provide an operations breakthrough with long-term strategic advantage globally. The more challenges we face across the world, the more our limited assets become stressed. An expanded Land Force Warrior capability would allow us to manage multiple fronts at the same time...reduce uncertainty while maximizing coverage."

Norm was so focused on his mission that he failed to notice that Walt had slipped a fresh beer in place of the old one. He could feel the perspiration under his arms as he took a deep breath and sat back in the over-sized booth and waited.

Cadman was, as the Brits would say, "gob-smacked". He had just listened to the most articulate and compelling vision for the future of the U.S. military that he had ever heard…and at a time of great duress.

Six beers and a couple of cheeseburgers later Norm Franks drove home to sleep in the same bed as his wife for the first time in three weeks before heading to Charleston and the most important mission of his career.

CHAPTER SIX

Zybercor Headquarters
Reston, Virginia

Two days after the Huron Board Meeting Zybercor Chief of Staff Liz Turney and her team had still not completed the reams of documentation necessary to implement the sweeping resolutions that had been passed at the initial executive assembly. She had just spoken to Mr. Brady on his yacht and he had instructed her to begin preparations for an offer to buy Neurogenics, the Massachusetts company with the Artificial Intelligence technology, instead of exercising the option as the Board had approved. He also instructed her to 'kick Jacobs and Johnstone in the ass' to get a secondary financing under way for $400,000,000.00. She was cool as a cucumber on the outside but nervous as hell on the inside. Things just weren't adding up. Within days of the IPO Brady was raising more money based upon the new valuation of the intellectual property portfolio by none other than the law firm of Jacobs, Wiley, and Weinberg. The old patent value was carried on the balance sheet at $400 million. The new valuation was over $3 billion. How was that possible in such a short time? General Counsel Mike Chadel had just raised the 'dreaded' conflict of interest issue as they discussed the new valuation over 'mojitos' in the Zybercor dining room/lounge, long after the majority of employees had left for the day. "Unfortunately he's right," thought Liz. "Jacobs has a serious conflict of interest problem here. Not only is he a Director - supposedly an independent - with 300,000 stock options but also an attorney charged with conducting an ethical third-party, objective evaluation of a highly sensitive patent. It's absurd that such a topical, high-profile company would so visibly abuse the law of the land unless it involved a matter of national security. That has to be it. Brady is operating with a wink and a nod from the highest levels of government." "Girl, you've got to make sure his tracks are covered," vowed Liz to herself.

Liz finished her third mojito and called it a night. She took Chadel's arm as they walked to the parking lot. "Mike," she said, "I want you to very discreetly see what you can find out about the Jacobs' patent valuation. We want to make certain that Mr. Brady's interests are being protected here."

* * *

As Liz drove out toward her place in Manassas she replayed in her mind the latest sequence of events at Zybercor. "Why doesn't Patrick allow me to get closer?" She screamed out loud, pounding the steering wheel in frustration. "If he only knew how really good I am." A husky, sultry laugh and a slight shimmy of her shoulders brought a smile to her lips. "If he only knew. If. Big little word. My dad used to say '<u>If</u> Grandma had wheels she'd 'a been a trolley'. If only I understood what was in his mind I could be so much more effective." She flashed back to his recent appearance on *Larry King Live* (Liz had accompanied him to the studio, rehearsing Q & A's en route) as she put the CD in the player to listen to the interview for the umpteenth time.

Larry: "We have with us tonight, Mr. Patrick Brady, CEO of Zybercor Corporation. Last week your initial public offering set a new one-day record for a technology company. To what do you attribute your good fortune?"

Patrick: "Larry, I have a great team of people working in the company. Our scientists and technicians have developed a wonderful technology and our business staff has translated that intellectual property into the Land Force Warrior Program... a breakthrough in the global war on terror."

Larry: "How have you been able to attract such talent? I've read that your turnover has been the lowest in the entire defense sector over the last five years. That includes such giants as Lockheed, Boeing, and Northrop Grumman to name a few."

Patrick: "Larry, we like to hire people with three basic traits... character, intelligence, and a strong work ethic. If we mess up on character, which we do occasionally, we hope they're dumb and lazy. No, seriously, we stress ethics and integrity at Zybercor and we believe in meritocracy.....sharing in the wealth that we create for our shareholders. Every employee has the opportunity to achieve financial independence and, in a number of cases....real wealth."

Larry: "Speaking of real wealth... according to this report, your net worth is now close to $1 billion. How does it feel to be living the American Dream?"

MANIPULATION

Patrick: "Only in America could this happen. I come from a poor working class background. Growing up, we lived paycheck to paycheck. And now we're in a position to help other people who haven't been so fortunate. You know, Larry, this is a magnificent country we live in, but America is in trouble. Since the 2006 elections we have weakened our resolve in the fight against terrorism with disastrous consequences. Our enemy has gotten stronger. Three additional attacks on American soil, two on U.S. embassies, and a hijacking of a cruise ship, all since December of 2008. It is obvious to me that this pattern will continue….and accelerate as long as we keep our heads buried in the sand. We have got to re-engage the enemy on their turf or concede that we will suffer an endless series of attacks. The Land Force Warrior Program will allow us to physically dominate large areas of hostile terrain with maximum use of technology and minimum loss of life."

Larry: "Can you explain to us in layman's terms how this technology works?"

Patrick: "Actually you need to think of Land Force Warrior as a new weapon system using state-of-the-art technologies in satellite imaging, communications, pulse disruption, laser weaponry and guidance, and wearable computers. The LFW system gives the power of an entire battalion to one G.I.…on the ground…acting with real-time information in a highly mobile environment…to direct artillery, missiles, and attack helicopters against enemy positions and hostile terrain. Unfortunately, and for obvious reasons, I can't go into any more details as a matter of national security."

Larry: "Some critics say that this system will lead to a massive deployment of American forces in the Middle East and elsewhere. Can you comment on that?"

Patrick: "Larry, I can only give you one man's opinion. I have great confidence in the President. I believe that he realizes that the heart of global terrorism is the Middle East…an area that, as it happens, still supplies most of the world's fossil fuel energy. These factors, coupled with the political instability in the region, require a physical military presence…not only for the reasons I just mentioned but to protect our allies in Israel <u>and</u> to counterbalance the developing nuclear threat posed by Iran. The Land Force Warrior Program will allow us to control those borders and thereby restrict the flow of Islamic fundamentalist militants and their armaments. This way we can concentrate our special operations people in the hotspots and begin to isolate and eradicate the hostiles…with minimum loss and maximum long-term strategic advantage. Most importantly, we will be dealing from a position of strength which will allow our diplomats to gain the traction they need to negotiate a lasting peace."

Larry: "Well, it seems too good to be true. Surely there are a host of challenges that need to be met to get to the future state that you describe. Can you talk to those challenges?"

Patrick: "Most certainly, Larry. I'd be glad to. I believe the biggest challenge we face as a country is to define our position in the world we live in. Far too much time and energy has been spent dealing with the internal problems of other countries...like Iraq. In the meantime, China and India...China specifically, is eating our lunch....to use a vulgar phrase if I may. We can't continue to export jobs and services and import goods. The tremendous trade deficit with China drains our cash and subsidizes their military and social development. As their middle class grows, our's shrinks. We have fifty million Americans without health care coverage and tens of thousands of kids going to bed hungry. Our public education system is deteriorating faster than even our bridge, highway, and waste treatment infrastructure. We need to focus on a strategy internationally that is consistent with our domestic needs. That is our biggest challenge."

Larry: "Before we run out of time, I want to deal with one more issue that I think is very important to our audience tonight. You are a well-known hawk as it relates to the current debate on how best to deal with the threat of terrorism worldwide. Take a step back and share with us your views and philosophy. I mean, half of the Congress thinks we need to take a more diplomatic than military approach. What would you say to those that want to ride that horse, so to speak?"

Patrick: "That horse has left the barn and jumped the fence already. A little bit of theory if I may. At its essence terrorism management is a public affairs challenge...it's about messaging. Messaging should be about offsetting the risk of being a prime target of terrorism. Because of U.S. geopolitical interests relative to oil and support of Israel the U.S. has made itself the prime target, witness 9/11/2001 and the devastating effects of the Bush Administration's policies in the Middle East."

Larry: "Let's shift gears for a moment. You, Mr. Brady, have been one of the most outspoken critics of the Bush Administration and its handling of the Iraq War yet you are regarded as a 'hawk' in military interventionist circles. Help our viewers understand why you have been so critical of our former President."

Patrick: "By all measures imaginable Iraq was the worst foreign policy blunder in our country's history. The cost was well over half a trillion dollars and 6,000 American lives, and as devastating as those statistics are, that, Larry, is merely the tip of the iceberg. The incompetent leadership this country suffered for eight years set us back decades in the court of world opinion and the Middle East is in shambles. Even our closest allies and trading partners cannot be relied upon to support future initiatives."

Larry: "How could this have gone so wrong and, more, importantly, what are we going to have to do to keep the Middle East from dragging the world into a global conflagration?"

Patrick: "The answer to the first question is simple. Neither Bush nor Cheney nor Rumsfeld understood either the world situation or the realities in Iraq. They were arrogant and stubborn and, instead of putting the shovel down, they kept digging harder and faster. The net effect of their incompetence was to make Iraq a vassal state of Iran and, at the same time, extend Shiite fundamentalism throughout the region. To make matters worse, while Bush was paving the way for Iranian hegemony in the area with his mishandling of Iraq, he alienated Iran with his "Axis of Evil" speech, shut down all communications, and opened the doors for Russia and China to push us out of the way and establish close ties with the ruling clerics. China provided the missile delivery system and Putin delivered the enriched uranium. Bottom line - Iran has the bomb and, on the record, is committed to the destruction of Israel and the control of Middle Eastern oil. That is the Bush legacy, Larry..........and......and that's why the answer to your second question is so complicated."

Larry: "Ladies and gentlemen, there you've heard…"

Liz had drifted off the right side of the road onto the grassy shoulder - the alien sound and feel brought her quickly out of her reverie. "Shit...and me with three mojitos under my belt," she said aloud. Wide awake now, she righted her BMW, made a U-turn and headed back to the office. It was only nine o'clock and she could get a few more hours of work in tonight. She was working for a great man… no, a genius…and he deserved her full attention.

* * *

In virtually any corporation in America it's not uncustomary for certain employees to work on Saturdays, if the matter at hand is important enough. In the Alexandria offices of Greystone Accounting Associates senior partner Gary Davis had summoned manager Stephen Iverson and associate Donna Howard for a senior account review on a brisk Sat. morning at 9:00 sharp. All three had their requisite Starbuck's and were ready to begin.

Davis: "This fairness opinion for Zybercor represents a big opportunity. Who has been doing the work?"

Iverson: "Donna has the point on this and I'm providing oversight as account manager." Iverson knew that Davis was on the warpath for new business lately. It seems like he's been under a lot of pressure. Best not to get sideways with him this close to bonus time, he concluded "How's it look, Donna?"

Donna: "I have a lot of concerns about this new valuation of the patents. It seems over-inflated and, furthermore, I can't figure out why they need to raise so much money so soon."

Davis: "Tell me about the due diligence."

Donna: "The valuation was conducted by a reputable intellectual property firm, but one of the principals is on the board, and…"

Iverson: "He did recuse himself from the actual process didn't he?"

Donna: "Yes, but…"

MANIPULATION

Davis: "Well, what was it based upon?"

Donna: "The paperwork from the Patent Office was in order. The Land Force Warrior patents are surrounded and, according to the chief analyst, a Mr. Nefrin, the language, documentation, and duration are all 'triple A' but…"

Davis: "So what's the problem? Was there an issue with the Pentagon contract?"

Iverson: "Actually I read that with Donna…all 1,100 pages and it was as thorough an evaluation as I've seen…" He saw exactly what Davis wanted from this.

Donna: "But the colonel who conducted it is also on the board and I'm not sure…"

Iverson: "Ad hoc director, Donna, and he has <u>no</u> financial interest in the company. The Pentagon wanted one of their own in the inner sanctum…"

Davis: "How much are we billing here?"

Iverson: "This engagement is $400,000.00."

Davis: "What's our opportunity beyond this…assuming, of course, that we meet their expectations?"

Iverson: "It looks like they'll need someone like us for a secondary and, maybe three or four other pieces of work…maybe five to six million over the next year or so."

Davis: "Let's do this right, shall we? I want you to set up a meeting with Brady at the earliest opportunity. I understand he's a man who appreciates loyalty."

* * *

At the offices of Cal-Ray Communications in the District, senior account executive Barry Sorken was reviewing the latest press release announcing the results of the Zybercor Board Meeting with co-founder Esther Calvin, former Reagan speech writer and Assistant White House Press Secretary under Bush I. Cal-Ray had represented Zybercor for five years and now that their client had made the big leagues they were looking forward to a long and lucrative run.

Esther was tall, thin, and perfectly coiffed….. combining an intelligent visage with a predatory gaze. She read the press release twice, removed and folded her aquamarine reading glasses, and shifted her focus to Sorken.

"Barry, this looks great. A secondary financing to take advantage of expanded opportunities with the Pentagon. Now please tell me again why we're here on a beautiful fall afternoon?"

Sorken cleared his throat a bit uncomfortably and accepted the draft as Esther slid the two pages back across the smooth uncluttered surface of her desk. As the Cal of Cal-Ray, Esther liked the staff to refer to her as Cal.

"Cal, I know how important Zybercor is to you. I've been senior on the account for two years now and I think it's time you re-negotiated our fee structure with Brady." Everyone at Cal-Ray knew that Esther was enthralled with Patrick Brady, but few were aware just how far perception and reality had parted company in the matters of Zybercor's public pronouncements.

"Aren't we at $50,000 per month now?" asked Cal, recalling that Brady's interest in the IPO was north of half a billion dollars.

"Yes, Cal, we are currently at fifty thou."

"Are you spending a lot more time on the account?" she asked.

"No, but I think our risks are not being commensurately rewarded," he said. "I think you should double our fee and increase my salary by ten thousand per month. Sorken put his hands together after folding and pocketing the draft release and patiently waited for a response.

Cal had been reading between the lines in Washington for more than thirty years. "Barry, dear, why don't you draft me a letter to Mr. Brady that contains a reasoned justification for a fee increase. I'll meet with him and give you 20% of whatever our incremental increase turns out to be."

Cal and Barry smiled and shook hands as he went to his office to compose a letter from Esther Calvin to Mr. Patrick Fortune Brady. The price for lying had just doubled.

* * *

Mike Chadel graduated from Georgetown Law and wanted to stay in D.C. His first job was at Freddie Mac during the time that the institution was embattled by the Bush White House, Congress, and a host of alphabet-soup regulators. He learned first-hand the consequences of cavalier corporate governance. During his three years he saw the CEO and half of the Board dragged through the political gristmill. Careers, marriages, and reputations were mud-splattered on the front page of the *Washington Post*. Chadel himself finally got a bullet to the head when the general counsel was fired because he couldn't resolve one of the giant shareholder suits that were feasting on the leftovers from the variety of investigations.

When he was hired at Zybercor he felt that he had turned the tables and transformed a sow's ear into that fabled silk purse. He still couldn't believe that he held the title of General Counsel. At his age and level of experience he would have been thrilled to be Assistant Counsel to a much more experienced corporate lawyer. He was shocked when Patrick Brady offered him the position telling him that he was the kind of young man that could build a company. Mr. Brady told him not to worry about experience. "We can always pay outside counsel to document the details once we make the right business decision." He had worked hard, kept his nose clean, and was in the option pool of the IPO.

* * *

Johnstone and Jacobs were their own worst enemies. They had spent the day in Reston working on the secondary financing. Brady, talking down to them as if they had been junior staffers, had "instructed" them to have $400,000,000.00 in the bank by the end of the month. In the meantime, he and DiStefano were floating around the Caribbean having drinks adorned with those little pink umbrellas. Emory Jacobs loved those umbrella drinks and, unlike Johnstone, who seemed constantly depressed, was well and truly pissed. Complaining constantly, he finished up his bogus valuation of the patent portfolio for dissemination to the group of investors that Johnstone had identified. Liz Turney had just busted their balls passing on instructions...('instructions', again)...from His Highness, Patrick Brady, to get a $110,000,000.00 advance for the acquisition of Neurogenics, as opposed to the option scenario and licensing agreement approved by the Board. When they asked Brady by telephone how the technology fit into the Land Force Warrior Program, Brady blew them off telling them it was way above their pay grade. On top of all this shit Mike Chadel, Zybercor's general counsel, had requested a dinner meeting with Jacobs to discuss the intellectual property valuation prepared by his firm. Shit! Shit! And more shit!

* * *

Chadel had arranged the dinner meeting with Emory Jacobs at Bobby Van's Steakhouse in the District. They were shown to a private booth in the back of the restaurant. Chadel knew he was skating on thin ice and wanted to bond with Jacobs over a couple of martinis and a good steak.

After the drinks were ordered he started the delicate dance that Liz had instructed him to perform.

"Mr. Jacobs, I appreciate you meeting with me on such short…"

"Please, Mike…Mr. Jacobs is my father…call me Emory."

"Great, Emory…I'm part of the team implementing the Board's resolutions from last week's meeting and was hoping that you could help me understand the new valuation of the company's intellectual property portfolio."

"Glad to. Where would you like to start?"

Chadel reminded himself that Jacobs was an old friend of Mr. Brady as well as a Director. He wanted to let Jacobs know that they were on the same team. "You're the expert. I'm just here to dot the I's and cross the T's. My job is to make sure we don't have any exposure and to cover everybody's backside," said Chadel.

Jacobs downed half his martini, smiled and replied, "Hey, just because you're paranoid doesn't mean someone's not out to get you."

"Don't I know? I spent three years fighting with the regulators at Freddie Mac. Corporate governance has become a blood sport. Look at Spitzer in New York. He subpoenas three years of e-mails and brings down giants like AIG and Marsh McLennan. Next thing he's in the Governor's Mansion eyeing the White House."

Jacobs felt a fluttering in his stomach. Why was this twerp raising the Spitzer specter? AIG and Marsh got caught for price fixing and kickbacks to brokers. Jacobs was determined to stay cool and find out what Chadel did and didn't know.

"Mike, I'm delighted that someone like you

is looking over our shoulders. Why don't you play devil's advocate and put me through the ringer?"

"A capital idea. I acted in summer stock during college. I'll be the prickly SEC lawyer and you're the prestigious Director. I like this."

They ordered another round of drinks and Chadel straightened his tie and began the mock interrogation.

"Mr. Jacobs, perhaps you can tell me why there is such a vast difference between your valuation of the Zybercor patents and the prior valuation...that was done...let's see...less than a year ago?"

Emory was determined to play this game out. In fact, he was thinking this could be a good dress rehearsal. Might as well make the best of it.

"Good question, counsel. The market place dictates value. Putting values on patents is a fairly complicated algorithm. We study the language and structure of a patent and first determine how well-protected it is. Then we look at other patents that might be present in the same space. If the space is crowded we analyze the economic value of comparable patents..."

"Do you mind if I interrupt you as we go? This is fascinating stuff."

"Not in the least."

"How do you analyze the economic value of a patent?" continued Chadel.

"Several ways. If the space is crowded, we look at licensing revenue, product development potential, and infringement issues. In other words, is somebody with deep pockets stepping on our hallowed ground? If so, we put a dollar value on a lawsuit. If a patent is unique and in a dominant position, then we evaluate the potential to exploit the space unencumbered by competition. The Zybercor patents have the best of both worlds."

"Interesting. I wonder how Smith Reed et al missed that potential at the time they conducted the valuation last year. Aren't they one of the largest law firms in the country?"

"Good question. And yes, they are a fine firm and one of the best. But at the time they conducted the analysis the Pentagon contract had not been issued. The Land Force Warrior Program wasn't quite ready for prime time."

"How much did they charge the company for their valuation?" asked Chadel, warming to the subject and feeling the effects of his second martini. I could get used to this, he thought.

"I don't recall," said Jacobs. "As you know, I'm the new kid on the block."

Chadel answered his own question, "I believe their fee was approximately $500,000.00. The company paid your firm over $2 million so it stands to reason that you did a much more comprehensive and thorough analysis.....and in half the time."

Where is this guy going? thought Jacobs.

"Yes, time is money and we were given a very short window in which to work. You know Patrick. He was in a big hurry. I had to recuse myself for obvious 'conflict' issues. But I do know it tied up our whole firm 24/7 for a while."

"That was the right thing to do...I mean removing yourself from the analysis. The last thing we need here is a conflict of interest," said Chadel. "Were you privy to the due diligence process your firm used?"

"The same we would use in any case like this. We started at the Patent Office and got documentation from the pertinent case officer. We then interviewed officials at the Pentagon and thoroughly reviewed the contract and then we had an independent accounting firm review the cash projections pursuant. Clean as a whistle."

"I'm satisfied and impressed, quite frankly," said Chadel. "Maybe these options we have are going to be worth something after all, in spite of the strike price."

"Are you in the A or B tranche, Mike?" asked Jacobs.

"I'm in B. My job title, evidently, didn't warrant inclusion in the A group."

"So, your strike price is $54.00."

"That's right. I'm sucking wind right now. The A tranche's strike is what…$30.00?"

"$26.00 to be exact. You know, maybe the Compensation Committee should reassess your options. You seem like you could make a helluva' contribution to the company."

"Well, thank you, Emory. Oh, here are the steaks."

Chadel was loaded and had to call a taxi for the ride home. He left his car in a parking lot equidistant from the restaurant and the strip club where he and Emory Jacobs finished the evening with a couple of after-dinner drinks. After the martinis and a bottle of wine the stingers did him in. He had a good feeling, however, about his meeting. Liz would be satisfied with his report and he thought he now had a friend on the Board who would look out for his interest. He felt rather accomplished, if the truth be told. He liked the big leagues. He was relishing his promising future in the private sector as he nodded off to sleep.

Emory, in the meantime, had sobered up considerably as he headed back to New York on the late night Amtrak. He thought that things had gone well but Chadel was a lightweight and Jacobs' song and dance would never hold up in a shareholder suit or sustained SEC investigation. What the hell had he gotten himself into? More importantly, how was he going to get out of this mess? He dozed fitfully as the train rocketed through Philly on the way to the Big Apple.

* * *

Next morning
Charleston, SC

Colonel Norman Franks tightened his seat belt as the surly stewardess announced that the fifty-seat commuter jet had been cleared to land at Charleston International Airport. It seemed that in-flight personnel had all undergone charisma by-passes in the early nineties when the airlines went through their first round of bankruptcies. Obviously the surgery was irreversible. Franks had gone straight to Washington after the Board meeting to brief General Cadman and assure him that the company had the money and the people to throw at the Land Force Warrior Program to get it up to spec. The LFW Program enjoyed "Brick Bat" status since the President's Inaugural. "Brick Bat" was Pentagon terminology signifying the highest priority awarded a civilian contractor. There were eight levels of priority; the highest being the most recent deployment of a 10,000 man expeditionary force in Somalia. Other than that, a Brick Bat project, such as LFW, took precedence over everything else for access to manpower, materials, and shipping. For example, a C130 could be heading down a runway fully loaded with, say, a priority three cargo and would turn on a dime, unload, reload, and take off for a different destination for a "Brick Bat". Los Alamos, the Manhattan Project, was a "Brick Bat." Franks was instructed by his military and non-military masters to pull out all the stops. He hadn't slept at all the previous night, going through the checklist of things that had to be done. He had tried to prevent himself from mentally scanning the project before trying to get some sleep. But he had a Homeric and unforgiving memory and once he started the scanning he would have to review every detail before nodding off. The procedure had taken six hours from beginning to end. Sleeping pills didn't help any more than the beers he had with the General. As if he needed a pep talk. Shit, what he needed was a miracle. It was too late in the game to break in new people and the current team had been burning the candle at both ends for months. On the plus side, additional technical support would be accompanying the AI from Boston and the Neurogenics personnel would definitely help reinvigorate his team.

    The R&D lab and test facility for Land Force Warrior was located in a Level Three security area in the old Charleston Navy Yard, off Interstate 26 and bordering on the Cooper River. Once one of the largest naval facilities in the country, it had fallen victim to the recommendations of the Base

Closing Committee in the mid-80's. The local press and politicians had fought like hell, projecting a Doomsday scenario of double-digit unemployment and economic disaster. In fact, neither happened. The thousands of skilled workers were absorbed into the growing regional economy and into the robust expansion of the Charleston Port facilities, now third largest in the country.

The Navy base itself became a catch-all. Inside its boundaries were training facilities for law enforcement, storage areas for nuclear material, and an internment "brig" for the most serious "off the battlefield" terrorists like the Shoe Bomber and John Walker Lind. Situated between a dry dock on the dredged banks of the Cooper River and the highest security detention facility was building #F3. A cavernous structure, #F3 contained 125,000 square feet under a fifty-foot ceiling and was home to the Land Force Warrior research and development program.

As Franks drove through the checkpoint he was subjected to the rudimentary security process of I.D. and retinal scan. The young men...and two women...who comprised the security staff were the most recent in a revolving door of personnel. Each time a new training class came in for the month-long course conducted by the U.S. Army Military Police Academy, part of its curriculum was providing security for building #F3. Looking at the fresh-faced kids checking him in, he reflected back to the first month of operation when he insisted upon having a weapons locker located inside the building. God forbid they should ever have to defend themselves! They looked too young to vote, drink, or shave. He didn't trust anybody under 40.....

unless they'd already raised teenagers. Now that was combat training.

The staff meeting had been called for 1100 hours and Franks settled himself at the head of the table with his standard cup of black coffee and his signature pile of 3x5 cards.

"O.K. guys, let's take it from the top on a priority basis. First, and I only want headlines here...no details...what the fuck went wrong at White Sands?"

The six others sitting around the table all knew the drill. Because Franks had a photographic memory he never needed detail. He would assign one 3x5 card for each senior member of the team. He also insisted that the interfaces, or "hand-offs" as he liked to call them, were well understood. If you wanted to really piss off the Colonel put your own agenda ahead of the team's. Those around the table had never done that more than once.

"Fluke. One in a million. A googol occurrence."

"Still rather have Grossman calling the shots than some 'bubble head' technology."

"Priorities changed with the loss of Apaches. Poor adjustment. Artificial Intelligence would not have allowed the cascade to gain momentum."

"Should have hit Alpha Team with napalm to make sure no one survived. The sniper killed us."

More scatter-gun comments followed. Fifteen minutes later each member of the team had made his contribution and gone silent, waiting for Franks to "drill down" into the next layer of questions.

"Let me understand what you geniuses are telling me. One, the exercise turned into a gigantic cluster fuck. Two, the occurrence that precipitated said cluster fuck was an absolute fluke and couldn't happen again in a million years. Three, once the first event occurred the chain of events it precipitated was so rapid that the human mind was incapable of reversing the momentum. Am I right?"

"Yes, sir." In chorus.

"O.K. So let's assume that a form of Artificial Intelligence would improve the efficiency and effectiveness of the whole system...just for a moment... where are we now and what would we need to do to make the whole process fully integrated? Floyd, you start us off."

Floyd Ratliff was a weapons system expert on loan from the Pentagon. Undergrad, Cal Tech..... masters and doctorate, MIT, he was tops in his field... quantum mechanics and computer applications to strategic weapons systems.

"Let's make this simple. The Navy has used a form of Artificial Intelligence for more than twenty years... they call it "Sea Whisk." Basically it interfaces the radar system to the firing system on its big guns. If a foreign object is heading for a destroyer at seven hundred miles an hour the chances are it's unfriendly. The system switches to autopilot and instantaneously begins to fire upon said foreign object without human input. The system doesn't care if it's an airplane or a missile. It's bad so the system kills it as quickly as possible."

"O.K., give me another example," said Franks.

"Yes, sir. The drones we use as part of the LFW system are predicated upon a remote weapons platform. You remember how it used to work. The drones could be operating in Afghanistan with remote 'pilots' sitting behind a cockpit at Offutt Air Force Base in Nebraska. To the pilots it was the world's most exciting video game. To the schmucks on the receiving end it was no fun at all. So, for the last eighteen months, instead of remote pilots, we've baked their intelligence into the drones themselves. Of course, we need to program them before missions to customize the scenarios. But that's good; it allows us to 'tune' the weapons systems to the enemy."

"Bottom line?" demanded Franks.

"Bottom line.....it's a short leap in theory but it's going to take time to simulate the permutations of complex battle scenarios. We have already completed the bulk of the process for AI. Hell, we've been loading experience-based data and raw intelligence for over a year and we're currently at 95% efficiency on the Land Force Warrior Command and Control system."

"O.K., Floyd, while you consider how long it's going to take to convert to AI, Murray, you're going to tell us what the size of the prize is if we get it right. Aren't you, Murray?"

Murray Michaels had one foot in the State Department but his ass (and other foot) were owned by NSA. His expertise was the grey area between the battlefield and the negotiating table.

"Well, we would have great leverage if we could move assets around with impunity, as opposed to the other way around."

"In English, Murray, " said Franks.

"O.K. We can't control the flow of men and arms...especially explosives...across borders. We know Iran and Syria account for the vast majority of IED's in Iraq. IED's account for the majority of deaths and injuries. Reverse the paradigm. Assume that we use Land Force Warrior to secure the borders and also adapt aspects of the technology to urban warfare. We cut off their manpower while we eliminate the existing census of hostiles. We take and hold the streets, gaining geographical and political stability. History doesn't repeat itself... geography does. Now we have a big seat at the negotiating table...you know......leverage. Now, if we added an Artificial Intelligence capability to Land Force Warrior, then we could actually pre-program operating responses to various 'bad guy' scenarios and that would serve as a deterrent. You know...they take a finger...we take a hand, and so on...the 'Chicago Way', so to speak. That, Colonel, becomes real leverage."

"O.K. Big problem but big prize. Who here doesn't understand what you are going to do in the next twenty-four hours?" asked Franks. "Tell 'em, Floyd."

"Sir, we are going to advise you what needs to be done to take a qualitative leap without seeking perfection because, sir, perfection is the enemy of progress and progress is our middle fucking name... sir."

"What would you studs think if you had the opportunity to be the first to marry real Artificial Intelligence to combat operations command and control in a major theatre of operations?"said Franks.

The room became eerily silent as six sets of highly-intelligent eyes searched Franks' face for signs of humor. Seeing none, Ratliff was the first to speak.

"Colonel, is this for real?" he asked quietly.

Franks stood up and leaned forward, both hands on the table. He was only too aware that these men had his career...and much more...in their hands. "If this team can adapt a new generation

MANIPULATION

of Artificial Intelligence to the Land Force Warrior Command and Control System by November 15th, we believe that the Commander-in-Chief will authorize its deployment in the Middle East next year. You men could change the nature of warfare and create a strategic advantage for your country that just might provide some progress toward peace in this crazy world we live in." He finished by reminding them that they were the finest team ever assembled and that their work would save an untold number of American lives as the meeting broke up and his people headed for their workstations.

As Norman Franks walked toward another section of #F3 his thinking turned toward the two soldiers he was about to visit. Initially he had agreed with Patrick Brady's suggestion that Terrel Macklin and Lester Grossman be re-assigned to Charleston. Macklin could get excellent medical help for his rehab and both could be used effectively in upgrading the Land Force Warrior Program. Who knew it better, warts and all? And the re-playing of the exercise would be a good way for them to exorcise the demons. But Franks couldn't allay the queasy feeling he had about the way his boys were being 'handled'. Oh, Macklin was getting top-notch care, sure enough, and Lester's input was gratefully received by the R&D team. What bothered Franks was that his boys were treated more like prisoners than U. S. Army enlisted men.

Building #F3 had originally been organized into four distinct quadrants: the simulator area, which was the largest of the four, the software development and network communications quadrant, the sleeping and living quarters for the fulltime staff of twenty, and the administrative quadrant. After the White Sands exercise a fifth sector was added, a 20 ft. by 20 ft. secure room adjacent to the living quarters. The room was under twenty-four hour guard. Security was provided by two of DiStefano's professional staff - serious guys who were heavily armed and never cracked a smile. Two cameras kept Terrel Macklin and Lester Grossman under surveillance day and night.

Macklin had round-the-clock medical treatment from an Army doc specializing in trauma rehab. His lumbar twelve was seriously damaged and for all practical purposes he was a paraplegic... paralyzed from the waist down. However, he was beginning to have some control over bowel and urinary function, prompting his first smile in weeks.

Franks entered the security alcove staffed by DiStefano's security staff while Macklin was engaged in physical rehabilitation and Grossman was enduring another endless debriefing by the systems analyst who was charged with sucking his brains out. Franks was furious that his boys were under DiStefano's thumb but realized that particular decision was made above his pay grade. He smiled and shook hands all around as he dismissed the doc and systems analyst. He huddled with Macklin and Grossman over by the wheeled bed where they could be seen, but not heard, by the guard detail.

He looked at Macklin and whispered, "How's it goin', son?"

"Just great, Colonel. I could actually feel myself taking a shit yesterday. What say we get my big black ass back in uniform and out of this friggin' hospital gown. Baby blue's just not my color."

O.K., that's good, thought Franks. He's got some attitude back and that's going to be important. "Before we think about the uniform, how about we get you into something a little more mobile than that bed you're lying in? Why don't you convince the good doctor that a wheelchair would be in order? He's pushing mobility, right? So tell him that would help you exercise when he's not around. Mack, make it a real heavy-duty wheelchair. You know, because you're so big. Lester, you suggest that you might even be more helpful here if your big buddy could move around a little and free up some of your time. Do you catch my drift Corporal Grossman?"

"Yes, sir. A wheelchair. A very large sturdy wheelchair. A wheelchair that could get Sergeant Macklin and his friend, Corporal Grossman, the fuck out of here. How long do we have Colonel?"

"I don't know. Right now we're very important because they need us to bring the new decision support system on line. After that I just don't know. These guys play hard ball like I've never seen before and General Cadman's ass is way out there. I was shocked at the call to take out Kalil and his men after White Sands. They could have been changing golf shirts for all the emotion they invested in that decision. My plan is to get you guys out of here at the first opportunity."

"What about you, Colonel?" queried Macklin.

"Don't worry about me, son. This hairy old Marine's ass is covered six ways to Sunday. I know where all the bodies are buried. They don't have the balls to fuck with me....way too many friends. Oh, by the way, make sure your new set of wheels has a flat steel panel on the right arm......you know……just the right size for a modified laser…just in case. I'll catch you boys later. And Lester, don't give them everything at once for Christ's sake. Dribble the information out in little bits and pieces."

* * *

It was late afternoon before Franks could get out of the building. He was truly pissed off that Mack and Lester were essentially under Brady's house arrest and he was damned sure going to do something about it regardless of the consequences. He had one more task to perform before a big steak, a movie, and a clean bed. He had to see an old friend…a retired Marine Corps Captain who had served under him for over a decade. He needed his buddy to jury-rig a pick-up truck to accommodate a large wheelchair during a fast ride. He was going to need a ramp for the physically-challenged and some kind of apparatus to keep Macklin from being slammed around in transit. Might even require some armor plating on the side just in case. **Shit, what are friends for? Semper Fi.**

CHAPTER SEVEN

Brady's three-pronged strategy was now underway in earnest. He was on his way to Bermuda to accelerate discussions with the Lloyd's underwriting team to develop a risk-based policy that would protect the Land Force Warrior technology in the event of a catastrophic event. Franks was in Charleston to spearhead the transition to Artificial Intelligence, and Kauffman had promoted the Land Force Warrior technology to his handler Huan Tsu, Head of the Chinese Intelligence Directorate.

* * *

Beijing, China

Huan Po Tsu was educated at Harvard and Oxford before returning to Beijing to fulfill his destiny as one of the principal architects of China's ascendancy on the world scene. Son of Dr. Suchan Tsu, Visiting Scholar at Georgetown University in the early 70s and friend to President Richard M. Nixon, Huan remembered fondly traveling with his father to the White House on many occasions to discuss the 'opening of China' by the powerful United States President. How typically arrogant of the Americans; his father and colleagues in the bureaucracy had planned for years for just such an occurrence. The old men in the Politburo were no different today than in past iterations of political power in the Middle Kingdom – they were scared to death of a billion, hungry, angry peasants. The Chinese bureaucracy, on the other hand, had been running things in China for several thousand years, from Genghis Khan to Mao Tse-tung. Things were no different today. Names and titles may change but the fundamentals remained the same. The principal difference was the ubiquitous role of the Peoples Liberation Army.

As Acting Head of Chinese Intelligence, Huan Tsu was perfectly positioned to 'ride the tiger' all the way to the top. A small but powerful clique of politically-connected career bureaucrats sought to control the Politburo and steer China into the 21st century. China had leapfrogged to fourth place among the world's economies in 2008, then overtook Germany to occupy the number three spot, and was now trailing only Japan and the US. Due to the endless supply of low-wage workers and seemingly endless influx of foreign investment, China had embarked on an ambitious program to produce high-tech goods to supplement its premier international ranking in agricultural and low-tech factory output. China's traditional target industries were steel, coal, machinery, light industrial products, and textiles. While the technology transfer process from foreign investment had gone a long way to facilitate China's move to high tech, the real gemstones had come through the outright pirating of proprietary, patented technologies from the U.S. Huan Tsu had made his reputation in the all-important area of Chinese intelligence gathering, established to steal the methods necessary to 'break through' and reverse-engineer computers, autos, petrochemicals, machinery, and advanced electronics.

A secret meeting was underway in a private residence a block east of Tiananmen Square just forty-eight hours after Mark Kauffman returned to Washington from his meeting with Brady in the Caribbean. In attendance were three high-ranking Chinese officials: Huan Tsu, representing the Intelligence Directorate, Wei Deng, member of the Politburo, and Shi Wu, number three man in the Chinese military.

Shi Wu: "How far can you trust this man Kauffman?"

Huan Tsu: "He does not know what he does not know. Yet he has seen the Land Force Warrior technology first hand and is a close confidant of Brady."

Shi Wu: "The capability is as your memo portrayed it to be?"

Huan Tsu: "The report is a conservative estimate of its capability. In short, the Land Force Warrior Program will change the face of warfare as we know it. The U.S. will finally align its military capabilities and ambitions with its public temperament... quicker results with much fewer casualties... a potent combination."

Wei Deng: "Your best guess on timing and strategic application?"

Huan Tsu: "According to Mr. Kauffman, and corroborated by our assets in the Pentagon, we expect the first round of deployment in Afghanistan. Then Pakistan, Iraq, Saudi Arabia, and the Lebanese-

Israeli border by the fall, or as required. Negotiations are under way with Russia as we speak. Its application is limitless beyond that."

Wei Deng: "It's all about the oil."

Huan Tsu: "It's all about the oil *and* global terrorism."

Wei Deng: "They go hand in hand."

Huan Tsu: "Perhaps that is why we have no suicide bombings in Beijing."

-Silence-

Shi Wu: "Can either of you imagine the impact this technology would have for our Army? Russia is currently the number two producer of oil in the world behind Saudi Arabia, with a seventh of the world's total reserves. We can support our economic growth through military dominance of the region without getting involved in that Middle East cesspool."

Wei Deng: "And the Russians will what... sit back and allow Chinese hegemony without a nuclear response?"

Huan Tsu: "Putin is sitting on top of enough plutonium to turn Eastern China into a parking lot. What will we do with the remaining 700 million peasants?"

Wei Deng: "We must form a stratagem that will allow us to complete Phase Two of our economic expansion...requiring 40% more oil than we are currently consuming over the next 10 years…without initiating wide spread regional conflict."

Shi Wu: "Impossible."

Huan Tsu: "Possible."

Wei Deng: "Speak."

Huan Tsu: "Iran is the only answer."

Shi Wu: "Ridiculous."

Wei Deng: "Please continue."

Huan Tsu: "Iran has enough oil to supply our needs simply through the exertion of some of their new-found political influence. We have verified that their nuclear capability is sufficient to eradicate Israel and potentially damage the United States, as well as Western Europe. Not only has Iran emerged as the most powerful and aggressively anti-western force in the region, consider in addition that, by 2020, 80% of the world's oil supplies will come from the Middle East. Iran seeks to lead an Islamic empire that stretches across North Africa, through the Middle East, and across South Asia. With oil and missiles, they will be very dangerous."

Shi Wu: "The Americans will never allow them to become the leader of a pan-Islamic world that controls 80% of the world's energy supply. For that matter, neither will we."

Wei Deng: "Unless…"

MANIPULATION

Huan Tsu: "Unless we knew for certain that our domestic supply of oil would be assured through long-term guarantees by Iran."

Shi Wu: "Aren't you missing the force of the 800 pound gorilla? The Americans will bomb Iran back to the Stone Age and continue to bully OPEC and Saudi Arabia with their nuclear capabilities and conventional forces."

Huan Tsu: "They have already missed the window of opportunity to block Iran's uranium enrichment program." Russia has erected roadblocks in the UN Security Council because it is selling Iran nuclear technology and other goods to finance the Russian oligarchs' retirement plans. As the Americans were premature in Iraq... they are too late in Iran... a nuclear stalemate."

Shi Wu: "Under that scenario, they will move to disable Iran using conventional force deployments... particularly the new Land Force Warrior Program."

Huan Tsu: "Not if Iran is in possession of the same technology."

-Silence-

Wei Deng: "If I understand, younger brother is proffering a trade between China and Iran, assuming we have control over the Land Force Warrior technology...a simple matter of supply and demand. We supply the Iranian government with the LFW military system and they meet our demand for oil... that assumes, of course, that the Iranians ascribe a relative value to guns for oil... and of course, we cannot trade what we do not have. How long will it take to replicate the technology of the Land Force Warrior?"

Huan Tsu: "If we had to reverse engineer the process it would take years and billions, so that is out of the question. Instead, I propose that we purchase it for $3.5 billion using Mr. Kauffman as an intermediary. Once our scientists understand all the systems and applications, we license it, so to speak, to the Iranian government and they use it as they see fit in all geographies except Asia. We will continue to make improvements by monitoring the project through our assets in the United States to ensure that the Persians comply with the oil part of the bargain...at say.....50% of the wholesale price per barrel of crude. That's a fair deal considering we will need to provide them with the satellite capability and drone technology."

Wei Deng: "So you see, Shi Wu, by this strategy we avoid direct confrontation with the United States and Russia while we hone our competitive advantage. It is very important that the United States economy stay vibrant for the next ten years. After all, they are kind enough to subsidize the growth of a Chinese middle class through the disassembly of their own. As they continue to outsource manufacturing as well as services, we gain through taxation, stronger domestic consumption as well as in the balance of trade differential."

Huan Tsu was impressed with the old man's

understanding of the global landscape. The United States was strong enough to carry the twin budget deficits of trade imbalance and federal deficit spending for another 10 years. The Chinese would continue to invest its giant cash surplus in U. S. Treasuries creating the win/lose scenario that will bring the United States economy to its knees without firing a shot. In the meantime, China buys its oil at a deep discount, financing the $3.5 billion purchase price for the LFW in less than six months.

Huan Tsu: "Honored father and older brother...shall we proceed?"

Both: "Yes. Yes."

Wei Deng: "With care and haste."

As his bodyguard opened the back door of the nondescript gray sedan, Wei reflected upon the recent conversation. He had become addicted to American poker and watched it constantly on the satellite television in his private flat in the suburbs. He felt confident that he was playing a very strong hand. The United States had become weak through greed and corruption following the same cynic curve of *ascendancy – peak – descent* as Greece, Rome, and Great Britain. He was constantly amazed at the gross negligence exhibited by American leadership. The key to world power historically had been the growth and development of a strong middle class. A middle class creates stability politically and competitive advantage economically. Yet the Americans continued to outsource their precious manufacturing and service jobs to us and India. Once our energy supply was assured with this deal with Iran, we could build the transportation infrastructure to link our growing manufacturing capability. As a national network we will be unstoppable. A car for every peasant. Soon we will be the people living the American dream. He wondered if he would be home in time to catch the World Series of Poker on A&E.

Shi Wu breathed a heavy sigh as he settled into the backseat of his chauffeur-driven Hummer and lighted up a Camel. He felt old and useless. Clearly his "younger brother" from Intelligence stole the meeting out from under him. He wondered listlessly how Huan Tsu could be so well prepared for every meeting, as if the answers appeared before the questions were asked. He sensed the ground slipping out from under the military as the economic war continued to favor the Chinese. Wei had constantly assured him that there was no honor left in the American psyche and that their military was a hapless servant to the greedy and corrupt interests of the corporate and political looters. That must be so if the LFW program could be acquired so cheaply. Still, he said to himself, "If I could get my hands on that technology…"

Huan Tsu relaxed contentedly on the massage table as the strong fingers of the masseuse dug into the stress and tension in his neck and shoulders. He marveled how such a tiny woman had such strength in her small hands. As she worked out the tightness he reflected upon the afternoon meeting with Wei and Shi. Things could not have gone any better. He achieved everything he wanted. "Be careful what you wish for," he thought. Now he had to produce. He thought back upon his telephone conversation with Kauffman on the secure line from Washington. "I kid you not. You've never seen anything like this," said Kauffman, as he reported his session aboard the Buona Fortuna. "It was right out of a Star Wars movie. Lasers, satellites, attack helicopters, drones…"

"Mark, calm down. I can't follow you. You're talking too fast. Please start from the beginning."

"O.K. I'm not on board half an hour when Brady's Director of Security, guy's name is DiStefano… they're joined at the hip……puts on this DVD with a top-secret clearance preamble. It was only about ten minutes long. I couldn't believe it. In about eight minutes I saw their Land Force Warrior Team annihilate three teams of sand monkeys… sorry…Islamic enemy combatants that had been released from Guantanamo Bay…Hell, they had choppers, artillery, mortars, 50 calibers, and these heavily armed…"

"Please slow down."

"O.K. Sorry. Get this, there was only one soldier on the ground. Guy had on this incredible suit with some kind of pulse cannon on his left arm and a laser gun…I kid you not…a laser gun that shot out this beam of light that literally cut armor in two. You should have seen it slice people in half like a hot knife through butter."

Huan had never heard Kauffman talk like this. He wondered if he was inebriated.

"Are you telling me that one man inflicted that much damage on…how many enemy combatants?"

"At least fifty," said Kauffman, "and all armed to

the teeth. I'm serious. They looked to be fairly balanced on helicopter and artillery, but this guy was wired through this computer that literally popped out of this chest plate to a satellite that controlled these drones with air-to-air and air-to-ground missiles. They said the satellite was 'off the shelf' but the whole system was proprietary. The way it all worked together was amazing."

Huan could feel the perspiration drip down his forehead as he processed Kauffman's words. He was fluent in English but he had a tough time comprehending at 100% when the speech was so rapid.

"Mark, what would we need to do to replicate this? Could we reverse engineer this like we have done with so many other proprietary technologies?"

"No way! This is top-secret stuff and it would take years. We're going to need to pay for this and it's going to cost real money."

Huan asked, "How much?"

Kauffman didn't skip a beat as he answered, "Four to five billion dollars."

There was silence on the other end of the phone.

"Listen, I know that's big bucks but this thing is going to change warfare as we know it. This system can manage huge geographical areas. A dog couldn't cross a border without being picked up. They will be able to isolate whole regions, mop up the bad guys and move on while they hold the ground they took." Kauffman had learned to match silence with silence. It seemed to last forever when communicating with Huan.

"Mark, what makes you think they would sell it

to us? How is that possible?"

"Trust me, it's all about the money. This guy, Brady, is a world-class scumbag. Besides, they aren't concerned that you have it. It's not like anyone expects the U.S. and China to be knocking heads. You both have too much to lose and too much to gain. They see this as securing their interests in the Middle East, Afghanistan, maybe Africa. Think of it as a licensing deal," he chuckled.

Huan rolled over on his back with a sigh. There was nothing quite so pleasant as a happy ending.

* * *

Emory Jacobs had been thoroughly spooked after his conversation with Mike Chadel regarding Jacobs' revised valuation of the Zybercor patent portfolio. While he played his role with great bravado, he knew his argument wouldn't hold up under a seasoned interrogation. He was in this mess up to his eyeballs and all he had to show for the risk were his inflated legal fees and 300,000 stock options. And Brady had him by the balls. Unless he could turn the tables on Brady he didn't have a way out. He instructed his secretary to place a call to Avery Johnstone on his secure line. Even though it was Sunday everyone was in high gear.

"Avery, Emory here. I just participated in a very difficult conversation with Chadel, the company's General Counsel. It seems that some of the staff are on to Brady's little scam here." Jacobs was overstating the case but he felt he had to, in order to get Johnstone's attention. Johnstone had been very distracted lately.

"Yes, yes…conflict of interest and Sarbanes-Oxley was used a half-dozen times regarding the two of us…I don't like this one bit, but we need to meet as soon as possible. Dinner tonight at Mario's. See you at eight."

Johnstone, as usual, was working in the New York offices of Jacobs, Wiley, and Weinburg. Brady had insisted that they have a New York presence to supplement their Greenwich home office. Johnstone, instead of working from his Boston headquarters, was busy raising an additional $400 million from the original syndicate that he had put together in conjunction with Kramer Rodgers. Johnstone was feeling like a hired hand. Brady owned him lock, stock, and barrel. He had lapsed into a deep, deep depression. The only emotion he demonstrated since Brady sprung the trap was anger… unbridled anger at the smallest of things… calls not immediately answered… those maddening over-the-counter sleep aids that you couldn't open if you chewed your nails. He hadn't had a good night's sleep in more than two months. His whole existence revolved around Brady's agenda. Nothing seemed to belong to him anymore. He couldn't even achieve an erection. He needed a Viagra prescription to masturbate. He was truly desperate when Jacobs called from Greenwich on the law firm's secure line. He listened to his old friend with a deepening sense of hopelessness… he was down inside the looking glass and things were spiraling past the Cheshire Cat to the ultimate Queen of Spades. Johnstone was seriously considering suicide.

MANIPULATION

Mario's was conveniently located on 56th St. between Fifth and Sixth Avenues across the street from the Chambers, an old-world hotel catering to business travelers with a predilection for highly attentive personal service. Jacobs and Johnstone were seated in the back......across from Carl Icahn's table in a private alcove.

Jacobs: "I think the shit is about ready to hit the fan. Senior staff is reviewing the whistleblower section of the Sarbanes-Oxley bill. Chadel as much as accused me of a conflict of interest in connection with the new valuation of the Land Force patents."

Johnstone: "How did you explain the $3B valuation?"

Jacobs: "I stuck to the party line. I explained that our due diligence covered the Patent Office, the Pentagon, and finally a third-party accounting assessment that addressed the new accounting standards for intellectual property. Our cover is foolproof. We're papered up the ass."

Johnstone: "Then why are you so paranoid?"

Jacobs: "What's the guy's name in the Patent Office...Nefertiti something?

Johnstone: "Pasha Nefrin."

Jacobs: "Right...so didn't DiStefano assure us that he was taken care of?"

Johnstone: "According to DiStefano, his hooker has

him addicted to crack. He has the whole thing on video. He told so many lies, he's into this thing as deep as we are. Fucking DiStefano is amazing."

Jacobs: "The prick."

Johnstone: "So what's the problem? If Nefrin's not, who is? I told you those guys in the accounting firm will do whatever you want. You lie, they'll swear to it."

Jacobs: "I think we're probably o.k. there but this guy Franks is a Boy Scout."

Johnstone: "What do you mean? Emory, you're driving me nuts."

Jacobs: "Not so much a drive as a short putt these days. You look like shit."

Johnstone: "I feel like shit. Let's stay on Franks. The Pentagon documentation is two feet thick. It says the right stuff. He signed it. What's the problem?"

Jacobs: "The problem is this fucking thing may not work according to the specifications of the contract. Rumor at Reston is that things didn't go so well at some top-secret simulation out in New Mexico a couple weeks back. In fact, rumor has it that that's why Brady needs this fresh money…to correct some serious problems with the technology. Under normal circumstances Brady would have returned from White Sands to trumpets and garlands. Instead of the conquering hero he was uncharacteristically silent and withdrawn and so there's rampant speculation concerning the outcome of the test." Even though they were seated in the back of the restaurant, an overflow crowd now forced them to lean forward and speak *sotto voce*.

"What if this thing is a bust? Is it possible that Brady duped the Pentagon?" asked Johnstone. He was starting to perspire under his shirt as a newly-acquired tic affected his left eye.

"I don't think that's possible, even that prick isn't good enough to fool those boys. But think about it – they're under a lot of pressure from the White House, Congress, and the Joint Chiefs to come up with something to throw against the towel heads. So, are the powers-that-be overstating its capability? I'd bet on it." Emory knew that he now had his old friend right where he wanted him. He continued. "And why haven't the Directors gotten their high level security clearances so that we can get behind the smoke and mirrors and touch this vaunted technology. It shouldn't take this long. Do you think this is coincidental? Bullshit, nothing's coincidental where Brady's concerned."

Johnstone was hitting the wine pretty hard and ordered another bottle impatiently.

"So we're like mushrooms...planted in the dark and covered with bullshit while we jump through hoops for the ringmaster. He could cover us all in shit and the whole world would know it. We'd be reading about ourselves in the *Wall Street Journal*. Fuck me."

"No thanks. I'd rather fuck Brady."

"How do we do that?"

"Before we talk about that, let's talk about the feasibility of raising this extra dough Brady wants to raise."

"We are having no problem raising the cash. Zybercor's perceived to be a blue-chip. If they only knew we were a one-trick pony on a broken leg. Shit, my reputation is shot if we don't somehow pull this whole thing off."

Jacobs looked at Johnstone in earnest. "That's what I want to talk about. We're both hung upside down in the town square if this thing goes upside down but we have no real upside if there's a home run."

"The last time I looked Brady had both of us by the balls. Neither of us would be worth the powder to blow us to hell if he pulled the plug on us. What choice do we have? This whole thing is killing me."

"Are you so out of it that you can't count to seven?" Jacobs asked seriously.

"What are you mumbling about?"

"Four out of seven."

"You're really starting to piss me off, Emory."

"So...Avery, now listen up....four votes out of seven Directors is a majority. I think we can take him out if we play our cards right."

"You can't be serious. If we try to take him on he'll release everything he has on us and then what? I look like a faggot and you look like a thief."

"I'm sorry Avery but you are a faggot and I am a thief... but then blackmail is a felony and he won't risk losing everything to expose us."

"I can't take that chance. At the very least, I must protect the money I have... and besides, how do you move against him for something he hasn't yet done?"

"Christ sakes, Avery, we don't take him on for blackmailing us. We take him on for violating a dozen conditions of the Sarbanes-Oxley Bill. We line up two more votes and we steal the company right out from under the lousy bastard."

Johnstone, III and Jacobs, Esq. killed a bottle of Santa Margherita Pinot Grigio, two bottles of Vino di Nobile Montepulciano and half a bottle of Sambuca. They diagrammed the *coup d'état* on the white tablecloth after Mario's staff cleared the halfeaten remains of a fine Italian meal.

Jacobs was closest to Azzato. Now that Cindi, his daughter, had been returned he should be back in the day-to-day. Azzato was key, they figured. Jacobs was going to need to convince him that Brady had been responsible for his daughter's disappearance and miraculous return. Once the three old Ivies were rock solid, they only needed one more vote.

Johnstone would meet with Liz Turney. He would make her a once-in-a-lifetime offer. Then he and Liz would meet with Susan Jamieson. As Chairperson of the Audit Committee she had a lot of exposure if this whole mess exploded and apparently she and Liz had a good relationship.

The plan would be to delegate Azzato to meet one-on-one with Jackson Strawbridge. As Co-Chairman of the Board, Strawbridge was Chairman of the Governance Committee...and charged with being a watchdog of sorts over the CEO. They knew Strawbridge and Brady were good friends but, with four votes in their pockets, he would have no choice but to broker a deal. Assignments clear and straightforward, they paid the bill, leaving an overly generous tip, and returned to their respective hotel rooms. Johnstone hadn't felt this good since before the reunion at Ivy . As soon as he got to his suite he opened his laptop and went on-line.

* * *

Liz Turney had met the Chief of Investigations/Corporate Fraud Division of the Securities and Exchange Commission several weeks before at a cocktail party on the Hill. He was definitely not her type but had been aggressively pursuing her nonetheless. Operating on instinct, she called him and orchestrated a dinner date the very same evening at a quiet French bistro in Georgetown. While he was fantasizing about getting lucky, Liz, in reality, was determined to get up-to-speed on the Sarbanes-Oxley Bill and the nuances of corporate fraud. She would gladly exchange a hand job for an understanding of the hot buttons of an SEC investigation. But why was it she always thought of Patrick Brady when she sat down in front of her mirror, in her sexy underwear, to put on her make-up? **She knew exactly why she always thought of him…….as her nipples began to swell.**

CHAPTER EIGHT

Company Headquarters
Reston, Virginia

Zybercor's headquarters was nestled in a tree-laden office park across from the Hyatt Regency in Reston, Virginia. Brady, tan and rested, hit the office like a tornado at 7:00 a.m. His secretary, Bridie Donaghue, had scheduled him 'bell to bell' at twenty-minute intervals allowing him to cover every aspect of the company in a single day. Bridie was a redoubtable Irish grandmother who in another lifetime had surely been a queen of no small renown. She had been with Patrick Brady for over twenty years and managed his affairs with a passion for detail and a personal commitment to his well-being. Her husband of forty years was retired and a gourmet cook, allowing Bridie to work the requisite sixty-hour weeks which kept the wheels of Zybercor oiled and turning. The entire building was like a tuning fork when Brady was in town. Staff scrambled around getting ready for their meetings with the Boss under the watchful but light-handed touch of Liz Turney. She was confident in Zybercor's staff. They all knew their jobs. She was there to make sure that specific job functions were integrated and knit together so that Mr. Brady got a seamless, well-organized presentation. She'd been through this drill so many times that she could do it in her sleep. Liz was the blossoming princess in the court of Sir Patrick Brady just as surely as Bridie ruled like a dowager empress. The two women were quite fond of each other and worked together seamlessly implementing the complex strategies of His Highness.

MANIPULATION

"Good morning, Bridie my darlin'. Are we ready for a great day altogether?" chimed Brady in an over-the-top Irish brogue. When he was in the office he was like a candidate on the campaign trail. He worked the facility floor by floor and room by room touching all two hundred employees if only with a nod or quick handshake and always with a smile and upbeat countenance. Brady was a big believer in mental toughness and the power of visualization. He believed if you thought like a winner and acted like a winner, well surely, you'd be a winner. He was a disciple of Dr. James Grogan, sports physiologist, author, and mental toughness coach for the three previous U.S. Olympic teams. Over the last two years every employee with managerial responsibility had attended a three-day seminar conducted in Dr. Grogan's facility outside of Orlando. The focus of the entire session was "Managing Energy and Maximizing Performance." Brady had installed a fitness center and fully-staffed kitchen under the stewardship of a fitness guru and a nutritionist, respectively, to implement the program and reinforce the core message of the seminar. It worked. Productivity was up. Less sick time and fewer unplanned absences. A noticeable drop in medical claims. According to the sign in the fitness center the 'fatties' in the company had lost a collective 750 pounds. The bad news was that Brady had to practice what he preached and that meant personal training three times a week, and snacking only on fruits, vegetables, and low-carb energy bars. Not to mention various and sundry vitamins and supplements, all awful, twice a day. "I can't believe I started this shit," he said to himself as Mrs. Donaghue served him some hot tea with dry wheat toast and egg whites.

"Now Mr. Brady, just look at you…so clear-eyed and fit and healthy," she said returning his brogue with a twinkle in her eyes as she slipped him one of her homemade oatmeal and raisin cookies. "You've been one of the most eligible bachelors in America for twenty years. You're still a grand boyo, sure'n you are, but we've now to work a little harder to keep all those gorgeous women drooling."

"Ah, go away with you now, and your ol' chat. But may the Good Lord bless you and keep you, Mavourneen," said Brady as he dunked the cookie into the tea and took the dreamy first bite. "I suppose you've booked me into the gym this afternoon for an hour of unmitigated torture with that sadistic wench."

"Aye, so I have. If this is Monday then you'll be setting the example for all of your loyal subjects at 3:00 as usual. Remember, it all starts at the top, with Patrick Fortune Brady, Himself. And all of us ladies have found that the 'Curves for Women' franchise you installed has done wonders for our figures…… much to the delight of our husbands and boyfriends, I might add."

"As you wish, but Jesus wept, and can you blame him? What's our schedule this morning?"

"Accounting, Marketing, Sales, Operations, and Legal at twenty minute intervals with a half-hour for you to wrap up with Liz. This afternoon, it's New Projects, Research and Development, Corporate Communications, and Investor Relations. Tonight you have three stops in the District: two House member cocktail parties and dinner with Mr. Strawbridge and Secretary Terry at Homeland Security," said Bridie. When discussing business she dropped the brogue and became a professional dynamo.

"What's the deal with the dinner agenda?" He liked an occasional dinner with Strawbridge but Jason Terry was a pompous Texan who was loud-mouthed and tedious.

"According to Mr. Strawbridge, the Secretary wants to explore using Land Force Warrior on the Mexican border."

"Oh, sure…we're going to blow up a truckload of wetbacks sneaking over the border to flip hamburgers and cut grass. Is he out of his mind?"

"Do you want me to cancel?"

"Yes. No. Shit. Tell Strawbridge he owes me one and make sure Terry's office knows I have to be out of there by 8:30. By the way Bridie, I'll be staying at the suite in the Mayflower tonight and I want you to get me over to London just for the day tomorrow. Here's the business card of the guy I'm meeting with. You can put it all together; just make it as efficient as you can."

"Do you want to fly the Citation?"

"No, for London I like British Air First Class. Can't beat that."

"Will do. Accounting's here with Liz…are you ready to get started?"

"Righto. Let's lace 'em up and play ball."

* * *

DiStefano had flown commercial from Lauderdale to LaGuardia while Brady took the company jet back to Dulles. His security detail wanted to see him right away and that usually meant trouble.

He wondered what Jacobs and Johnstone were up to now. His boys were dedicated to keeping them under surveillance 24/7. It pissed him off, though, that they had begun to use secure lines and pay phones. Fucking amateurs.

DiStefano met the head of his Jacobs and Johnstone security detail inside his suite at the Intercontinental on 54th St. Cal Whitfield was DiStefano's best man. Stocky and white-haired, Whitfield was in his mid-fifties and looked it. It was hard to believe that he was a former Green Beret. He had gone from an exciting three-year stint in the field to a long and monotonous assignment behind a desk before taking the 'twenty and out' retirement package and starting a second career in corporate security.

"What's up, Cal? It's not like you to be so circumspect over the phone."

"I felt it was important that you saw this in person," Whitfield said as he unfolded a white tablecloth adorned with a lot of scribbling amidst wine stains and splotches of spaghetti sauce.

"What the hell is that?" said DiStefano as he leaned over to study the tablecloth that Whitfield had spread out on the ottoman.

"This, Mr. D, appears to be the diagram of a plot to take over the company. It seems that Jacobs and Johnstone aren't quite the pussies we thought they were. Either that or all the booze they guzzled gave them a temporary dose of courage."

"How did you get the tablecloth? Don't tell me they left it on the fucking table."

"Hard to believe, isn't it?"

The diagramming on the tablecloth clearly represented a battle plan to oust Brady and reorganize the business. Jacobs and Johnstone had drawn arrows linking their names to various directors and staff members. The stupid assholes had even detailed a redistribution of stock with the lion's share allocated to themselves and Azzato. Strawbridge's name was prominently penned in the center of a circle encompassing all the directors with several large question marks. Obviously they didn't know where he would stand on a vote to oust Brady. Jamieson, on the other hand, appeared under the names of Jacobs, Johnstone, and Azzato. Franks was sitting out on the edge of the circle with an 'X' through his name and Liz Turney had a series of dollar signs next to hers.

"Listen, Cal. I need to get to D.C. right away and share this with Brady. In the meantime I want you guys on these bad boys like horseflies on shit...I mean I want to know everything they do and especially whom they talk to and what is said. Call one of our contractors to double up our detail and get parabolic mikes. I want you to update me every four hours." He looked out the hotel window for a brief moment and then back at his chief field operative. "Are you still here?" he asked as Whitfield hurried from the room.

DiStefano caught the two o'clock Acela to D.C. He liked the high-speed train from N.Y.C. to Union Station in the District. Two and a half hours to sit quietly and think. Jacobs and Johnstone alone didn't trouble him unduly but the possibility of a well-organized effort involving staff and other directors did. Especially now, when there were so many balls in the air. The Boss had always told him the key to good juggling was first to understand which balls were glass and which were rubber. "Always give priority attention to the glass balls…if you drop one of those they break. The rubber ones always come bouncing back," he said. Well, we have a glass ball on our hands here, DiStefano thought as the train rocketed past Princeton Junction toward its next stop at 30th Street Station, Philadelphia.

* * *

Jacobs and Azzato had been friends for 40 years. A Jew and a Catholic, they both were raised in the shadow of The Shrine of Perpetual Guilt. Their personal affinity was tenuous initially, but, as the first semester at Princeton moved on, it became clear that they had more in common with each other than either had with the basic WASP makeup of third and fourth generation 'Tiger legacies'.

Azzato acculturated better than Jacobs, who was withdrawn and introverted and very intense. Azzato's success on the football field and in the classroom appeared to come easily but he was always among the last to turn the lights off at night and the first to rise in the morning. It was not unusual for Azzato and Jacobs to run into each other as they left Firestone Library after hours of studying.

Saturday night was a different matter altogether. Saturday was date night and Azzato had his pick of the female litter, and was always considerate in setting up his buddy with one of the friends of his various ladies. Jacobs was always at his best after a half-dozen scotches when his uptightness turned to lightheartedness and his quiet intensity gave way to a quick wit and demonstrative affection. He would fall in love every weekend and pine endlessly until the process started all over again the following Saturday. When Jacobs called Azzato the morning after his late-night soiree with Johnstone the harried attorney was suffering from a serious hangover.

"Lou, Emory here. Listen, I need to see you right away. It's very important."

"I'm down in Princeton for a few days," said Azzato. "Things have been pretty crazy around here since Cindi's abduction. Nancy's still a nervous wreck. You can't believe this shit can get so close to home. Thanks for asking."

"Shit, I'm sorry, Lou. I heard Cindi was found and was home safe. That was very inconsiderate of me but I've got a lot on my mind. I'm sorry. Is she O.K.?"

"She's fine now but that was the longest twenty-four hours of her life. The police got an anonymous phone call and found her sedated in a cheap motel near campus. She can't remember anything after being pulled into a car."

"Unbelievable. Thank God," said Emory as he waited impatiently to get the conversation back to his agenda.

"Now what's so important that it can't wait a few days?" asked Azzato.

"It's about Zybercor and Brady. There are things going on that you need to know about and I can't get into it over the phone," said Jacobs.

"It's that important?" asked Azzato. He knew Emory could get his knickers in a knot over the smallest issues, and, besides, Patrick Brady had been a prince over the last week, pushing the FBI to make Cindi a priority, and on the phone to Nancy and him every night.

"It's as important as it gets. It's got to be now and it's got to be private," said Jacobs.

"Can you get down to Princeton… say two o'clock at Ivy?"

"Yep. See you there."

Azzato had called the club and reserved the upstairs library for his meeting with Jacobs. He had started smoking again after his daughter's disappearance. Fuck it. There is only so much a guy can take. At this stage you get your medication and stress relief wherever and whenever you can. For the past two hours he had sat spellbound as Jacobs revealed his problems and their friend Avery Johnstone's...and how Patrick Brady…their dear old friend, Patrick Brady…had systematically blackmailed and bribed them into supporting his agenda to manipulate Zybercor to his own benefit. Azzato's first instinct was to immediately confront Brady, but when Jacobs proffered the theory that Brady was responsible for his daughter Cindi's disappearance, he took a long step back and his Italian temper went into overdrive. If, indeed, Brady was the monster that Jacobs described, Azzato was going to have to fight fire with fire and that was going to require a cold, calculated approach.

Jacobs carefully replayed his conversation with Johnstone and did a good job constructing a case that Brady could be brought down. Azzato agreed that the key would be to build a consensus involving key staff and key directors and that Strawbridge was the guy to put it all together. Jacobs and Johnstone were clearly compromised and Azzato admitted to himself that he was out of his element at this level of intrigue and maneuvering. My God,

Avery Johnstone having sexual liaisons with other men. How could Brady have found that out? The situation with Jacobs and the patent fraud. What kind of surveillance capability did Brady have at his disposal to get them under his thumb so effectively? The same kind of capability that could make his daughter disappear. "That miserable son-of-a-bitch. Who does he think he's dealing with? I'll kill him, " he said out loud to the massed photographs of Ivy Club members, arranged by class year, adorning the walls in the second-floor library.

* * *

Brady wanted DiStefano to meet him at a fundraising cocktail party on the Hill as soon as he got off the train. However DiStefano gently resisted, suggesting, instead, that they meet after Brady's dinner, in his rooms at the Mayflower. Brady rather reluctantly agreed. Brady had a sixth sense when there was trouble and DiStefano could tell his antennae were up. One thing was for sure. He had to talk to Kauffman before meeting with his Boss. He knew Mark was planning to go overseas to put the deal together with the Chinese. Kauffman would be ultra-sensitive to the risks of a Board uprising. They were all in the same boat and couldn't afford to spring a leak now. He had some fledgling ideas germinating but needed to talk to Brady before sharing these thoughts with Kauffman. He would need to juggle and tap dance at the same time.

DiStefano was standing at the bar at the Mayflower when Brady strode in, took him by the elbow, ushered him into the elevator and pushed the button for the Penthouse. After withdrawing his security card from the gold-plated slot, Brady looked DiStefano in the eye with a "Now what?"

"We've got some serious problems." He held up the bundled tablecloth and said, "You're going to have to see this to believe it."

The elevator opened and they entered the suite through the large double doors. DiStefano spread the tablecloth on the glass coffee table in the middle of the sitting room and then went to the bar to pour two glasses of scotch…both neat and both large.

Brady took the proffered scotch and sipped thoughtfully as he concentrated on the diagrams and numbers executed in Jacobs' careful script. "I think our boys just grew some hair on their asses, Tony. This isn't such a dumb plan. What do you think? Have you had some time to study it?"

"Yes, on the train. I think these guys could be big trouble now and we have to respond decisively."

"Why does my asshole pucker up every time you use the word 'decisive'?" asked Brady.

"Because somebody always gets hurt," said DiStefano.

"What's the worst case, Tony?"

"O.K. Let's see. Kauffman heads for Europe to cut the deal with the Chinese. According to the timelines on the tablecloth, these chicken shit Benedict Arnolds are going to spend the balance of this week getting legal counsel and lining up Azzato and Liz Turney. So we have a week to act. Do you think Turney will turn on you?"

"Maybe," said Brady. "She's sharp and they'll offer her the moon. She'll pull Chadel into their camp and then go after Jamieson. Sue is way over her head and they'll get a lawyer to scare the shit out of her for signing the disclosure docs. As Audit Chairman she has a lot of liability for the accuracy of the information. We both know its bullshit and she will too. Son of a bitch. They just might pull this off," Brady said with no small amount of admiration in his voice.

"You don't seem very upset, Patrick. What am I missing here?"

"Nothing really. I can't believe that these fools understand the consequences. They don't realize that they're risking everything....and I mean everything. That's bad for them. Risky for us but bad for them. I assume you've covered everybody on this tablecloth with surveillance. We have to know everything that goes on from here on out. That includes Strawbridge and Franks. No surprises from here forward, understood?"

"Understood. It's already been taken care of."

"Let's take a step back for a second. Do you envision them being at the same place at the same time over the next week?" asked Brady.

"Not really. It seems as if they both have their respective assignments and after they have their ducks in a row...see this arrow here...I think that means Azzato would meet with Strawbridge one on one. Hell, I can't make out the dates. For all we know that meeting's already happened."

"No way," said Brady. "I was with Jackson tonight. I'd know it if he was involved. Listen, they'd have to call a special Board meeting if they were going to push for my resignation. Only Strawbridge and I can call a special meeting. What if we controlled the time and place? Wouldn't that give us an edge if we really had to get...how do you say... decisive here?"

"Let me sleep on that," said DiStefano. "In the meantime I'm going to talk with Kauffman before he flies to Europe. I need more details about his meeting. He tells me that Huan Tsu is bringing a third party representing Iranian Intelligence. Kauffman says it's going to be a three-way deal and that's the only way he can get the Chinese to fork over the big bucks. Their end game is oil. Look, Patrick, I don't want to overstep my boundaries here, but to me we're at crunch time and we're going to have to take the gloves off ....all the way off."

"These are our people and they're trying to destroy us," said Brady, "just assuredly as if they had guns in their hands and all their little fingers were on the triggers. This is now a matter of survival. The ball's in your court. I trust you like a brother to do what's necessary here...whatever it takes. What's your agenda with Kauffman tonight?"

"I don't know yet," replied DiStefano. "Maybe we can kill two birds with one stone. He's a greedy and clever man and we're partners here. Right?"

"Righto. While you figure this out I need my beauty sleep. See you for breakfast?" Brady was deeply troubled but maintained a confident air. Never, never let 'em see you sweat.

"Eight o'clock, here?"

Brady nodded. "Good night, Tony."

"Night, Boss."

Brady couldn't sleep. He'd taken two Xanax and still was nervous and on edge. With a possible coup hanging over his head his fears came roaring up from his subconscious and overwhelmed him. When Brady had a panic attack he itched all over and couldn't get into a comfortable position, rolling from side to side in a *danse macabre*. All the usual images cascaded through his consciousness. His father, drunk and very angry, leaning over him in the bed shouting, "Loser, loser....no good fucking little loser." His own father wouldn't lie to him, would he? If they took away his company, he'd lose everything. He'd be a loser just like his Dad said. Brady cried out in the dark and pounded his fists into the pillows. He reached for his phone and hit the speed dial...for a number he only dialed in times of utter distress. Tonight there was only one thing he could do to get his mind right. He knew he was heading for the deep, dark underbelly of the D.C. 'hood.'

Patrick Fortune Brady took a large gulp of Irish whiskey and chased it quickly with a cold, long slug of Harp Lager. He breathed deeply and cleared his mind of everything but the essentials: time, space, speed...a predatory focus on a single objective... the kill. He lifted his weapon of choice and cradled it lovingly in both hands. He and his weapon became one. Body and mind folded into one another creating the perfect platform from which to launch his killing machine. There are many targets to choose from but he saw and felt only one. He knew if he took down the leader the rest were his. He let his breath out slowly and began his attack at last. The moon and sun and stars have aligned in perfect symmetry as he threw his weapon. He glided as he followed through and listened intently as the ball was taken over by the perfect rotation of the spin and picked up speed. Finally, in a moment of pure ecstasy his weapon struck the lead pin viciously in the heart, shattering the entire herd with a thunderous crash. As the pins settled to the alley floor in violent disarray the only sound comes from the hunter himself…a slightly audible…'Yessss'.

The alarm went off in the Mayflower suite at 6:00 a.m., startling Brady awake after just three hours of fitful sleep. Normally, nothing relaxed him more than an empty bowling alley. The only fond memories from his childhood were the rare occasions when his father took him to the bowling alley on Saturday mornings, with the hopes of seeing the legendary Vince Lucci, Trenton's perennial All-Star bowler, practice.

His hangover generated physical and emotional side effects. His head throbbed and his mouth tasted like rotten fish. What made matters worse was the sense of foreboding that had overcome him. He felt alone and defeated and the fight hadn't even started. How could this be? Normally he felt confident and energized when things got tough. That's when he was at his best…training for a fight. This morning, however, he was immobilized and completely sapped of energy…unable to deal even with room service and a hot pot of coffee. He fired off an e-mail to Bridie instructing her to 'cancel his morning' and get him to London later in the day. He turned off the phone and pulled the covers over his head hoping to stop the shaking as chills racked his body relentlessly.

* * *

Liz and Bridie were having coffee and a snack

behind closed doors in the small conference room adjacent to Brady's opulent office overlooking Reston Town Center. Liz and Bridie were very close. From the day Liz first joined the company Bridie had been her biggest fan and most helpful confidant. Liz was everything her own children were not...thoughtful, hard-working, considerate, and purposeful. Liz, alone in the world since the death of her own mother, confided in Bridie and gratefully participated in a relationship that they both allowed to go beyond the boundaries of the office.

"You look troubled, dear. Has our Patrick gone and done something?" asked Bridie, getting straight to the point, as usual.

"It's not something he's done as much as something he hasn't done, and I'm becoming very concerned about him and the company," said Liz. Her dinner with the head of investigations for the SEC had troubled her considerably. Worried at one point that she had gone too far in her line of inquiry with her unwary dinner companion, she had steered his attention away from Zybercor with some intimate fondling under the table that most assuredly put his mind on a totally different path.

"Dear, I've never seen you this upset. Talk to me," said Bridie. Indeed, Liz was always the paragon of calmness with an impenetrable professional demeanor. Bridie sensed there was a real problem brewing.

"I'm not going to bore you with the gory details, Bridie, but, suffice it to say, our Lordship has played fast and loose with the rules...and, I think, if he gets caught...well, we could be reading about ourselves on the front page of the *Post*."

"Is it that serious, Liz?" asked Bridie, losing all of

her natural Irish lilt. "We both know that Patrick has little patience with certain details."

"I'm not talking about certain details, Bridie. I'm talking about gross misrepresentation to the public. Private companies have a lot more leeway than public companies. We're now subject to an entirely different set of rules and Patrick refuses to use outside legal counsel or hire a strong financial officer. We've become a highly visible company so we have a bulls-eye painted on our forehead. Honestly, Bridie, corporate fraud has become a blood sport. I need to meet with Patrick and he hasn't returned any of my calls for two days. He's gone completely dark on me and that just compounds my angst. What's happening?"

"You know about as much as I do," said Bridie. "He's staying at the suite in the Mayflower. He told me that he's working on a deal and that I should cancel his appointments, not forward any calls whatsoever, and get him on a plane to London around noon.. Frankly, he does sound troubled."

"I need the phone number of the suite. I've always respected his privacy…as well as your confidentiality, but I need to talk to him…at a minimum, before he leaves for London."

Somewhat reluctantly Bridie wrote the private number down on a paper napkin, after dusting off crumbs from her delicious Irish brown bread.

Liz returned to her office, closed the door and told her personal assistant to hold all calls. She wanted to compose herself for the call to Patrick. He had instructed her to begin the process of readying the Artificial Intelligence software and its collateral technical support for transmission to

Charleston. That task entailed a wire transfer of fifty-five million dollars. She was positive a transfer of that amount would breach Zybercor's existing bank covenants……until some of the new funds were credited from the secondary financing.

As she was deep in thought her PA timidly stuck her head in the door to say that Avery Johnstone was on the phone for the third time that morning demanding to talk to her regarding a most-urgent matter.

* * *

Brady's sleep was a fractured series of bleak images. Hidden beneath his aura of confident bravado lurked a tortured soul and a complex psychopathy that insatiably gobbled up the fruits of his labor and always needed more. It wasn't the fight itself that provoked such a violent and uncharacteristic response in Brady, but the actual nature of the fight. At a conscious level he knew that there was abundant history to document the futility of fighting a two-front war. Both Napoleon and Hitler had been ruined by multi-front campaigns, their resources squandered and their armies' will broken. At a subconscious level Brady's understanding of his current dilemma was accompanied by the prospect of pending doom. **If fear could be defined as the crippled feelings of the past projected into the future, one could imagine the phantasmagoria of Brady's horrific dreams as the old Ivies merged into the leering madness of Liam Conner Brady.**

CHAPTER NINE

Mayflower Hotel
Washington, D.C.

Brady was awakened again at 10:00 a.m. by the sounds of the vacuum cleaner in the hallway and the knocking by 'housekeeping' at his door. The intrusions to his sleep grated on his sensitive nerve endings like a broken car alarm. His hair was soaked in sweat and his body ached all over. Those years with the gloves on, dedicated to 'the sweet science', had taken their toll as arms and upper torso suffered from the stress and pressure of endless blows given and received. He was convinced that stress aggravated his arthritis and Advil was becoming his ubiquitous companion. God, he hated getting old. The thought of losing everything haunted him and opened the hidden doors of his psyche to the demons of his tortured past. He felt angry and out of control. He knew he had to compose himself but he was isolated and had nowhere to reach for strength and comfort. God had abandoned him as surely as his parents had many years ago. He had no family and no friends. He searched in futility for something to dull the pain.

* * *

Tony was getting more impatient by the minute waiting for Kauffman in the Starbucks at Connecticut and K. He knew he was directing him into deep and murky waters but there were no other options that DiStefano could envision. He had to rely on Kauffman to utilize the Chinese and Iranian Intelligence Services to abort a Board uprising at Zybercor. If Brady was deposed the whole deal would fall apart and they'd be left with their joints in their hands like the rest of us....especially Kauffman.

"Where is that lazy son-of-a-bitch?" DiStefano said to himself as he got in line for another mocha cappuccino.

* * *

Brady had finally pulled himself together sufficiently to finish a pot of coffee and a ham and cheese omelet with rye toast - his ultimate comfort food. He was packed and dressed and waiting for the limo to take him out to Dulles, and then on to London.

DiStefano was right insisting that he act as normal as possible and that meant going to London as planned. He was a liability given his current state of mind, nevertheless the catastrophic risk insurance from Lloyd's was the important third leg of his overall strategy. He would compose himself during the six-hour flight and complete the insurance negotiations. And he'd rely on DiStefano to map out a plan for dealing with the insurrection. He wanted to kill them now. His anger flared red-hot as the ringing telephone jolted him back to reality.

"I thought I told Bridie to hold the damned calls. No one could get this number unless she gave it to them," he said to himself, as his frustration and anger rose a notch. "Hello", he said, a bit cautiously.

"Patrick, this is Liz. I'm really sorry to bother you but we need to talk before you head off to London."

"What's so important?" he responded curtly. He couldn't handle office matters right now. Christ, that's what she's there for.

"I've been giving a lot of thought to the last Board Meeting and the secondary offer that's underway and I would like to talk to you in person," she replied calmly, with more confidence in her voice than she actually felt.

As if he hadn't heard a word he said, "How are you doing with the implementation of the offer for Neurogenics? Has the wire gone out? When are they scheduled to get down to Charleston?"

"I haven't sent the wire yet or completed the documentation. That's one of the reasons I want to see you. I am concerned that we might breach the bank covenants by going into our reserves before the next round of financing is complete...and I'm concerned about the financing as well."

The timing could not possibly have been worse. All of the nightmarish demons and raw emotions that Brady had kept bottled up inside came rushing to the surface as he directed his unbridled rage at the first available target.

"Liz, just do your fucking job and let me worry about the banks. I told you very clearly I wanted the Artificial Intelligence option exercised and a technical team in Charleston tomorrow. If you can't handle that, I'll find someone who can." Brady slammed the phone down and bellowed at the top of his lungs until he ran out of breath, too lightheaded to continue.

MANIPULATION

* * *

Mark Kauffman arrived at Starbucks half an hour late and got a ration of abuse from DiStefano. Then, for a full fifteen minutes he listened to the man across from him outline a tale from the dark side that moved from the absurd to a reality so frightening that, for once in his life, he was totally speechless. DiStefano looked sane. He was well-dressed and calmly sipped his cappuccino with a demeanor consistent with a discussion of yesterday's sports scores. However, the words coming out of his mouth simply did not compute to any algorithm in the world Mark inhabited. Oh, to be sure, he wasn't uncomfortable on the wrong side of the law, and, in fact, had thrown his ethics out the window a long time ago. He regularly used bribery and blackmail as tools of his trade. He could rationalize lying, cheating and even treason. But what DiStefano was proposing was murder, pure and simple. It was more than the fact of the matter that was so stunning. It was the cold dispassionate way that DiStefano told him the way it had to be...the way it was going to be....with or without him.

"Mark, listen, this is really very simple," DiStefano said as he finished his cup and glanced around the room. "You can make a shit load of money and live the good life, or you can get the fuck out of the middle. And I will handle things from now on. The choice is yours. However, make no mistake about this...if you stay in the game, you've got to see this thing all the way through. Your life depends upon it. It's all or nothing. I'll give you until 5:00 to make your decision."

As DiStefano stood up and left the table, he pointed a finger at Kauffman and said, "Don't ever be late again." He then smiled and walked away.

* * *

Strawbridge and Azzato were having coffee at the Princeton Club on West 43rd between Fifth and Sixth Aves. Instead of the Dining Room, they were safely ensconced in comfortable leather chairs in an alcove on the second floor. Azzato had a portfolio open with copious notes.

"I'm sorry to put it so bluntly, Jackson, but our friend Brady has truly screwed the pooch and put himself, us, and the company squarely in the crosshairs of the regulators."

He handed over a one-page, double-spaced sheet of Zybercor stationery. "This is the list of actions that staff believes are in violation of the 202 section of the Sarbanes-Oxley legislation as well as the Code of Ethics at the Big Board. This is the tip of the iceberg. We need to hire outside counsel and throw Brady out."

Strawbridge remained relaxed and commented, "But Lou, this is Patrick's company. He founded it. He did the deal with the Pentagon. For God's sake, he..."

"You of all people should know better...this company belongs to the public...the shareholders...and our job is to make sure that the CEO does things right. Even Liz Turney has seen the light and is working to build a case to remove him." He knew that Johnstone was having drinks with Liz that evening so he stretched the truth in anticipation of her support. They had researched the public documents to see what her overall compensation package entailed and knew they could sway her with a much heftier offer.

"He brought you in as financial advisor and appointed us all to the board with plenty of options. Let's put him in a room and read him the riot act....... but this..."

"Jackson, he had my daughter abducted. He's blackmailing Johnstone and Jacobs. If we go against him on this basis the company will implode, the Pentagon will distance itself, and the shareholders will be left with nothing but lawsuits against us. Don't you get it? We have no choice. None."

Strawbridge was stunned by Azzato's revelations. My God. This couldn't be happening? How could Brady have been so arrogant? Strawbridge needed to buy some time. "Lou, I need to be alone for a while with this. I'll call you in the morning. In the meantime…and I mean this…nobody talks to anyone outside the company. Lou, absolutely no one."

"O.K. but let me leave you with this. One way or another that son of a bitch is going to pay. Don't get between this dog and the bone, Jackson. I like you."

* * *

Jack Strawbridge had sailed since he was a young boy. He always felt closest to God when he was on the water, regardless of the weather.

Today the weather matched his mood perfectly - dark, and angry. How could Brady have put himself in this kind of situation? A former Marine Lt., Strawbridge had served two tours in Vietnam before being seriously wounded below the waistline - every man's nightmare. He knew he would never marry so he threw himself relentlessly into his new career - politics. He returned home to Minnesota and eventually ran for Mayor of Duluth. He held that office for 10 years before running for Congress, where he served admirably for six terms before being elected to the U.S. Senate in 2002. Strawbridge made a name for himself balancing his support for a strong and vibrant military and his predisposition to use diplomacy as the primary tool of U.S. foreign policy. At the top of his influence and popularity he announced that he would not seek reelection and was retiring from politics for personal reasons. He was immediately sought after to serve on boards of public companies including Zybercor. He reflected back to his first meeting with Patrick Brady...soon after the World Trade Center disaster on 9.11.2001. Strawbridge was serving on the House Armed Forces Committee as Brady was testifying at the behest of the Joint Chiefs of Staff.

JS: "Mr. Brady, could you please describe for the committee your theory in connection with the Administration's planned response to Al Qaeda's growing power?"

PFB: "Congressman Strawbridge, we would be making a terrible mistake sending traditional ground forces into Afghanistan and Iraq. If we get embroiled in a land-based occupation in these countries we will only wish we were back in Vietnam."

JS: "Mr. Brady, I served our country in Vietnam and therefore am quite familiar with the good, the bad, and the ugly of that war and frankly I struggle with the notion that Afghanistan and Iraq are Vietnam in disguise."

PFB: "Congressman, everyone in this room is aware of the sacrifices that you have made personally on behalf of our country and the fact that you are so widely admired is why it is important that you speak out so that we avoid a disaster of enormous proportion. Afghanistan and Iraq combined represent 8% of the world's non-aquatic surfaces. Local populations in both instances have been in conflict for centuries. Terrain is hostile. Borders are porous and we are dealing with an enemy that is fanatical and state-funded. Our air power will destroy infrastructure as well as command and control, but to establish an indigenous democracy we will have to depend on ground forces. Our resources are simply inadequate to deal with hostilities, reconstruction, and democratization at the same time. We will be stretched to secure the borders and isolate the pockets of resistance. As a result, we will experience significant casualties and progress will be slow. We run the risk of losing public and political support. We can avoid this if we bite the bullet now and retool our military to fight the new 21st-century enemy."

JS: "And that brings us to the point of today's hearing. I have in front of me a white paper produced by the Joint Chiefs that suggests your company has developed a patented technology that would shift the paradigm in connection with ground strategies and tactics. Now before you explain to us how the Zybercor technologies work, I think that it is only fair to state my very strong personal bias...and it is this... there is simply no alternative to putting soldiers on the ground in the type of battles that will need to be fought. No technology will take the place of a well-trained, well-equipped, motivated soldier... especially in an environment where we need to capture hearts and minds as well as kill bad guys."

PFB: "Congressman, you simply could not be more correct. The key to success resides in our ability to leverage the impact of our soldiers over a wider sphere of influence...using technology and mind-set to establish an entirely new paradigm... a new approach to combat...a new enemy...on new battlefields...with new tactics. We have the ability to..."

In hindsight Brady had been right. Iraq was a disaster and Afghanistan wasn't far behind. We couldn't stop the flow of men and firearms across borders. The oil and poppies provided the currency and Islamic fundamentalism provided the bodies. We've been losing the war on terror just as surely as our economic position in the world deteriorated day by day. Shit, we need the Patrick Bradys of the world to provide the drive and innovation to remain a world power. We can't make things any more. We can't even service our own industries but we continue to outsource back offices to China and India. The only competitive advantage we have is our ability to think...to develop new technologies and approaches...and Brady is the top dog in innovation. He admired Brady. Brady was an incredible man.

The wind began to shift and Strawbridge came about and headed into shore. He was a soldier and was taught to adapt and overcome. God knows he paid the price for that lesson. As the wind picked up the skiff cut through the water and he reflected back to the day that changed his life forever.

Thomas Jackson Strawbridge did not look like a typical soldier - five feet ten, slight of build, he had an almost feminine countenance. His drill sergeant had called him "pretty boy" at OCS. That was until it came to the second half of the program and his incredible mental toughness rose to the surface. He had the heart of a lion, a steel-trap mind, and was a natural at map reading and tactics.

When Strawbridge had informed his father that he was going to enlist, he got advice that probably saved his life. "If you're going into the service you're likely to end up in the infantry." His dad and uncle had both been grunts in World War II, one in the Pacific, and one in the European, theatre. The three of them were drinking cold Union Dortmunder at John and Anne's Bar in downtown Ely, Minnesota.

"Listen son," said Uncle Don. "This is a jungle war and it's in their backyard. You've got two problems with the infantry. One, you never get to really know the guys next to you. They're here. They're gone. The other thing is the officers. These First Lieutenants come out of college, go through OCS and, bam, they're out in the field and they don't know shit."

"Don's right," said Joe Strawbridge. "You get all the possible training you can get before they send you over there. You've got three years of college under your belt. Go to OCS and volunteer for every damned training program in the book; weapons, tactics, logistics, map reading…"

"Especially map reading," said Don. "I had officers that didn't know the difference between north and south. Those guys will flat out get you killed."

"Son, you've been out on these lakes all your life…since you were a kid. You know how to handle yourself. You can shoot a rifle. You can hunt. Hell, you're a better shot than me or your uncle. Go for marksmanship. Try to get affiliated with tough experienced men."

"Go for Sergeant, Jack…don't you think Joe?… get to a place where you can have some control over events…as much as you can in that mess… and shit is it ever going to be a mess. Reminds me of…"

The enemy were hardened North Vietnamese regulars and the Marines' mission was clear…search and destroy…take no prisoners. His seven-man team was comprised of some real bad asses. He sometimes experienced more fear sitting around the fire after a successful ambush than facing the enemy. Some of his guys were truly scary. A daily dose of killing changed a man into something less human…a throwback to an earlier time in which the constraints of civilization were a lot less relevant than the endless parade of mosquitoes and leeches that wreaked havoc on your mind and body twenty-four hours a day. His unit dropped into areas on the trail that were regarded by intel as heavily trafficked. They were an elite unit…thirty days in the bush and two weeks R and R. Not bad. But when they were in, they were in……. deep. They would recon an area

MANIPULATION

for a day and pick a spot for an ambush. Then they would deploy in an "X" formation, with claymores strategically placed along the trail to inflict maximum damage and to simultaneously disperse the enemy into the sweet spot of the kill zone, where machine gun fire and grenades would rip them apart. Each leg of the "X" was approximately sixty yards in length with snipers stationed in the trees at both ends looking for officers and those foolish enough to try and escape using the path on which they arrived. Inexorably the legs of the "X" would close until there were 100% casualties. No prisoners. Typically, they were up against enemy contingents of thirty men with an equal number of the sturdy mountain burrows that were strapped with several hundred pounds of gear. They always ate well after a successful bushwhack.

One of the many reasons that Strawbridge was attracted to the benefits of the Land Force Warrior Program was due to his experience in Vietnam. His unit of hunters was backed up by fast-moving jets loaded with napalm, as well as artillery. Coordinates were called in, to air and ground units, before the trap was set and confirmed as the team went quiet. Each individual had a pre-determined escape route and a rendezvous point for pick-up. Timepieces were coordinated so they knew when to advance and close the arms of the "X" and when to get the hell out of Dodge. Three squelches on the hand-held radio signaled the fixed wing and artillery to release hell. Strawbridge always held the radio. The system worked perfectly. Within six months his unit had more kills than an entire division. They became well known to the North Vietnamese. Bounties were put on each American head......higher for those taken alive.

The day he would never forget started out like all the others…hot, wet, and sticky. They had reconned the area the day before and began to establish their kill zone. According to intel several platoons of regulars with a contingent of Viet Cong were moving heavy machine guns and mortars south along a part of the trail that led to a well-delineated fork bordered by a stagnant patch of water. Strawbridge used the natural flow of the terrain to set up the "X" to drive the enemy to the point of the fork and placed a dozen claymores to push the survivors along the southern fork in the creek bed where he would mop up with the 50 caliber. On most occasions Strawbridge was up in the trees with his sniper rifle. Since he was in constant radio contact with each man through an open frequency he liked the high ground for its clean lines of sight. Better to direct traffic and redeploy asset as needed. You never knew how the enemy was going to react when the shit hit the fan. The biggest risk was being out-flanked. As long as his men directed their fire inward the enemy was taking fire from at least two directions. A successful flanking maneuver, however, would shift the advantage to the enemy with their greater manpower. Strawbridge didn't place a high probability that the enemy would try to escape the ambush using the north fork due to the force and directionality of the claymoors as they sent thousands of ball bearings into their midst at a thousand feet per second. Nevertheless, he had to safeguard against that possibility. So he stationed himself about thirty feet up in the crotch of a banyan tree with a sack full of grenades and his sniper rifle.

MANIPULATION

At 2300 hrs. Strawbridge was advised that the point man of the North Vietnamese supply contingent had entered the plane of the "X." It took twenty minutes for the enemy to congregate fully inside the perimeter of the kill zone.

An unusually large enemy force, it appeared to be almost twice the normal size...well over 50 men. At exactly 2322 hrs. Strawbridge squelched his hand-held and the claymores unleashed a devastating barrage of death into the main body of the enemy. Simultaneously his team opened up with sniper fire, M-16, and machine guns. Even though they were outnumbered nine-to-one, their night vision capability, element of surprise, and devastating hardware all had the desired effect. The survivors from the claymores and first round of fire fled north into the wet ground, according to plan, searching for cover. The fire coordinates had already been called in to Artillery and Air Support. Strawbridge quickly unleashed five grenades at the lead contingent, dissuading any notion that the southern fork in the path offered a safe haven. He squelched three more times on the hand-held signaling his troops to depart along their pre-determined escape routes and beat feet to the LZ, three clicks to the south. Strawbridge never even saw the RPG streak into the Banyan tree approximately ten feet below the branch that he had been straddling. The force of the explosion sent huge splinters up through his groin severing his genitals and blowing him out of the tree critically wounded yet, thankfully, unconscious. Two of his team saw the explosion and watched in horror as their Lieutenant fell over thirty feet to the ground. They retrieved their shattered comrade whose fall had been cushioned by a heavy ground cover of fungus. Strawbridge didn't regain consciousness for three days. When he awoke he was in a private room in a U.S. Army field hospital in Da Nang. A male nurse gently informed him that he would never be the same and he drifted off into a troubled sleep with morphine-induced nightmares that he knew would never end.

* * *

Patrick Brady was seated in the last row of first class, next to the window. Bridie had been prescient enough to purchase the companion seat as well, so that 'Himself' could avoid the hassle of spending six hours listening to a stranger's inane prattle. He had taken a Xanax and was into his second scotch as the jumbo jet gained altitude and the patchwork quilt of Northern Virginia receded below.

* * *

Mark Kauffman, in a stupor, nearly rolled into the aisle attempting to buckle his seat belt as the Air France stewardess instructed the passengers to prepare for landing in Amsterdam. He had a two-hour layover before connecting with his short flight to Nice and then a half-hour taxi ride into the resort town of Juan les Pins. Unfortunately he didn't have time to get into downtown Amsterdam and back again. He could sure use some good weed. He'd have to settle for a few more cocktails and some blackjack in the airport's casino. "Shit, I've been drinking a lot lately," he said to himself. If he hung around with Brady and DiStefano much longer he'd have to check himself into Betty Ford Clinic. He was now convinced that both Brady and DiStefano were insane. If he was right about them, then what did that make him...a gofer for two mad hatters...an errand boy for the Bull Goose Looney... he laughed out loud for no reason at all...just like an old rummy pushing a shopping cart in the lower East Side collecting soda bottles. "Why not a good chuckle?" he thought. Imagine me an accessory to murder. **He wiped the tears away discreetly as the wheels scraped along the runway en route to Terminal D.**

CHAPTER TEN

Liz was furious after Brady hung up on her, having shown such blatant disregard for her position. She nervously packed her briefcase, shouldered her laptop, and was careful to avoid Bridie as she left the office. She sat quietly in her BMW, regaining her composure, and eventually mustered enough self-control to return Avery Johnstone's phone call. He seemed more agitated than depressed as he fumbled along in a one-sided conversation while Liz did her best to concentrate. Without a clue as to what he really wanted to talk about Liz agreed to meet Avery at the Hyatt Regency in Fairfax later in the day. He insisted that they meet in the bar. The only concrete piece of information that Liz was able to derive from the garble was the part when Johnstone blurted that, "Something has to be done about Patrick Brady". "Damned right," she said out loud as she started the car and headed to the spa for a massage and facial..........both on Patrick Brady's corporate account. Screw him, she thought, the Artificial Intelligence deal could wait until tomorrow.

* * *

Situated between Cannes and the old city of Antibes, Juan les Pins has long enjoyed its reputation as a party town on the French Riviera. To honor its largely apocryphal namesake, John of the Pines, hundreds of scarred and hardened woodcutters would descend on this little beach town every

August to blow off steam and make up for eleven months of celibacy and hard labor in the forests of Provence in late 1800's. Modern day 'Juan' still maintained a honky-tonk atmosphere in spite of the five-star hotels, restaurants, casinos, and expensive beach clubs nestled between the coastal roadway and the Mediterranean. Every night at dusk the flea market would spring to life as hundreds of stalls opened up on the broad promenade separating the road from the world's most precious real estate, the shoreline of the Cote d'Azur.

Kauffman had suggested the location for his rendezvous with Huan Tsu and his counterpart from Iranian Intelligence. He knew the town and its restaurants through a half-dozen visits over the years and felt his familiarity with the environs and nightlife would give him an edge in the negotiations. It had finally dawned on him that the nature of the game he was playing was a matter of life and death... ... his. Everyone involved in the deal was a hardball player: Brady, DiStefano, Huan, and now this black-ops bastard from Iran. "Shit, I've never even had a gun in my hand," he said out loud. "We chosen folks have been getting by on our brains and chutzpah for centuries. Why should this be any different? Just keep it simple," he continued. "Money, technology, and oil." Focus on the timing and the mechanics of the deal. Let the other two negotiate the business part during dinner. Once that's done Huan Tsu heads back to Beijing and I can schmooze Rahnajat and talk to him about the side deal that DiStefano laid on me yesterday in D.C.

DiStefano had instructed him, as if Kauffman were merely an errand boy, to orchestrate an armed incursion right smack in the middle of the

Charleston Naval Yard. "Steal the whole program," he said. "And assassinate the Board of Directors and professionals. Everyone wins," he said. "Just fucking do it."

Kauffman had arranged for a private table at the Beau Rivage Restaurant near the Casino at the end of the thoroughfare and just across from the tourist trolley to Antibes. Their booth was set in a corner of the restaurant enclosed in the off-season by glass panes that slid on runners. Rahnajat, the Iranian, Huan Tsu, the Chinaman, and Kauffman, the American...quite a trio, Kauffman thought, as he quickly downed a welcome Kir. The conversation began innocently enough but quickly turned to business.

"The Land Force Warrior Program is of great interest to us but we must be assured that it works as represented," said Rahnajat.

"We are prepared to make that assurance. You will have reps and warranties that are already referenced in the contract in Sections A and B, pages 30 through 35 inclusive. In addition, we will, of course, provide the satellite capability and drone technology. These elements will give you a turnkey solution." Huan Tsu was relaxed in his chinos, with a gray cashmere sweater over a white shirt open at the neck. It was unseasonably warm but the evening was still brisk and breezy. He was confident that he could get a deal inked tonight and hurry back to Beijing to announce his accomplishment at the Politburo meeting the day after tomorrow. He appeared to be cool, calm and collected.

Rahnajat was bearded and overweight and partial to martinis. Kauffman thought he looked like a very dangerous man.......the kind who flew planes into buildings. His eyes never stopped moving. He seemed more a force of nature than human. Kauffman expected him to explode at any moment with the killing force of a suicide bomber. Rahnajat and Huan could not be any more different. The contrast was disconcerting to Kauffman. He desperately wanted to play the role of the deal-making broker but he didn't feel confident enough to insert himself into the middle of any serious discussion.

"We need to be clear on the issue of satellite access. Yes, we need your satellite, but of equal importance is the ability to take out the American satellite surveillance over the Middle East. We know you have refined your satellite-disabling capacity and we need access," said Rahnajat.

"That is patently impossible, my friend. I am operating within limits established by my superiors and under no circumstances can we provoke an American response. That would be out of the question," said Huan.

"That is extremely unfortunate. We would certainly be more inclined to close the gap between bid and asked on the price of oil if we knew that we had that particular edge," countered Rahnajat.

Kauffman saw an opportunity to make a contribution and jumped in. "I think this is a non-issue, gentlemen. The Lightyear satellite that is used to support Land Force Warrior is equipped with a new generation of missile defense capabilities. I don't think you could get to it even if you were so inclined."

Huan and Rahnajat looked at Kauffman and acknowledged his presence for the first time. Good, he thought. I've got my foot in the door - now don't lose it by talking too much. You've made the sale – don't talk yourself out of it.

For the next hour and a half, Huan and Rahnajat danced around the pricing and supply of oil. For the most part the conversation was in English but the intricacies of the crude oil market were a bit beyond Kauffman's ken. So he concentrated on managing a steady flow of appetizers and beverages from the staff.

Eventually Rahnajat and Huan agreed upon the terms and conditions of a long-term oil deal. The algorithm was too complicated for Kauffman but he did understand that the pricing fluctuated with the quote on the spot market, albeit with ceilings and floors based upon volume. In any event, they both seemed content and toasted to their mutual success with a very fine bottle of French champagne.

Huan had requested that they not forget to discuss a closing meeting to take place as soon as possible, so Kauffman jumped in and facilitated that arrangement.

"How long will it take each of you to incorporate the newly-decided deal points into your agreements?" asked Kauffman.

"Within the week," said Huan Tsu.

"Agreed, as well." said Rahnajat.

"O.K. To confirm, my understanding is that these agreements will run for ten years at which point the parties will renegotiate. So, what is now necessary to trigger the agreement is the successful transmission of Land Force Warrior to you, Mr. Rahnajat. Am I correct?"

"Where are we going with this, Mark?" asked Huan, with an impassive look.

"I was just thinking that maybe we could accelerate the process and put some icing on the cake at the same time. What if we could get the technology into Rahnajat's hands directly from the Americans and set their program development back a year or more at the same time? I mean, if we could add some real value to the current agreement through our teamwork and ingenuity, wouldn't it be fair that the three of us share in some of the upside?"

"My government has adapted many of the attributes of the free enterprise system, Mr. Kauffman. However, I doubt that the Politburo would grant me a commission in recognition of some value-added strategy," said Huan.

"I would hope, then, at a minimum, that that would be worth some additional concessions from your Iranian partners." Kauffman was on a roll and he loved it. He knew he could play in the big leagues now. "I believe that I could negotiate a twenty percent commission from Brady against the total sale price at $3.5B. Of course, if we work together to execute the transfer of ownership as I have outlined, then I would be willing to share that commission with the two of you," said Kauffman.

Rahnajat chimed in, echoing Huan's previous sentiments almost exactly. "Indeed, Mr. Kauffman. The mullahs to whom I report would rather eat their young than recognize my efforts with cash. All profits go toward the same goal... ...enriched plutonium.......to fashion the ultimate sword of Islam."

"Gentlemen, I come from a different world. In my world, personal wealth is a function of percentages. The magnitude of this transaction is enormous. Your respective countries are gaining immensely from our labor and ingenuity. Patrick Brady also has a lot to gain and to lose."

"Are you suggesting that Rahnajat mount an effort to steal the software and methodologies directly from the Americans?" asked Huan Tsu. Huan believed he knew where this was going now. If the technology was stolen Brady's ass would be covered. Quite brilliant, he thought.

"Think about it from Brady's point of view. If the technology is stolen by foreign terrorists he doesn't have to explain to the Joint Chiefs how the Land Force Warrior Program got into the enemy's hand," said Kauffman.

"If it is in Mr. Brady's interests then I assume we will have all the cooperation we would need to get in and out of a high security facility with a minimal amount of loss," commented Rahnajat. He had hated the Jews his entire life but this Kauffman was a clever fellow. He was promoting a plan that would fit nicely into Rahnajat's framework of self-interest.

"On the contrary, there would be a significant amount of loss and damage," said Kauffman, "on both sides. Brady has enemies who, obviously, would be anathema to our mutual interests. They would need to be neutralized. But consider the advantages to you both. The destruction of their facility would push the LFW Program back a year for the Americans while you would have the benefits of immediate deployment."

"Twenty percent of $3.5B is seven hundred million dollars," said Rahnajat.

"So it is," said Kauffman. "And if you can stay over for an extra day I can show you some investment real estate and we could work out some of the details relevant to a little armed incursion into the Port of Charleston."

"Things are going well. Don't fuck it up now," thought Kauffman. He looked at Huan and said, "Huan Tsu, you are my honored employer and I would do nothing without your expressed permission, full support and complete participation."

"Assuming that Brady is willing to fund this what do you call it.. ...vig... ...vigorish... ...yes. Assuming that, what would you expect from me for my portion and what would my portion be?" asked Huan.

"Use of a Chinese shipping company to move a very specific container into the Port of Charleston and the use of a Chinese submarine to move very specific items out," said Kauffman "for one hundred million dollars to you in a numbered Cayman Islands account at closing. Of course, I would need a confirmation of your country's commitment for the $3.5B but the official purchase price will be $2.8B as far as Patrick Brady is concerned."

"This capitalism that you practice is very profitable, Mr. Kauffman. What is your position on this, Mr. Rahnajat?" asked Huan. What a pig Kauffman is, he thought. Half a billion dollars for playing a middleman. Absurd!

"I am not averse to an individual retirement plan as long as it does not compromise my country's interest." Rahnajat didn't know where all this was going but he liked the sound of a villa in the South of France. He didn't know how much longer he could stay in the Intelligence game in Iran and there was no easy way out. He'd never known anyone who retired in good health.

"Gentlemen, I must get to Nice for a return flight to Beijing. We have a deal and should proceed to closing within the next two weeks. Mr. Rahnajat, if you would be so kind as to have your attorneys red line the documents, I will turn them around within forty-eight hours of receipt. Mark, I would be honored to host the closing meeting and will get back to you with a recommendation," he said as he rose and shook hands with both Kauffman and Rahnajat.

As Huan Tsu left the restaurant, Kauffman threw a wad of euros on the table and escorted Rahnajat toward a waiting limo. "Meet Michelle, my favorite real estate agent. Let's look at some villas, my friend. Michelle will show you some lovely views," said Kauffman, as Rahnajat squeezed into the back seat with a knowing smile.

* * *

It had taken DiStefano forty-eight hours to find an intelligence operative who could speak English, French, Mandarin, and Farsi. He didn't know whether there would be translators readily available or not. 'Jean Claude' had paid the maitrê d'hotel 1000 euros to wait on Kauffman's table. He had slipped the listening device into the handcrafted vase holding the winter orchids because DiStefano required a detailed recording to supplement 'Jean Claude's' oral report. Now that the dinner was over he would download the audiotape and call Mr. DiStefano on his cell phone. It was still a respectable hour in Washington, D.C.

MANIPULATION

* * *

After a massage, a facial and a brisk workout, Liz took a sauna, showered and drove with the BMW's top down over to the Hyatt Regency in Fairfax. Avery Johnstone was waiting at the bar gazing lovingly at a Beefeater martini, up, with olives. He dispensed with small talk and started right in on Liz.

A.J.: "Liz, there are a goodly number of directors who think that Brady is way out of line and could get us all in a lot of trouble. Those same directors hold you in high regard and believe that you should be more deeply involved in the company's future as an officer... ...something like the Chief Operating Officer... ...with a compensation package much more in line with your new role."

Liz: "I really appreciate your confidence in me," she responded. *What in the hell is going on here?* she thought. *This sounds like it's a fait accompli. Can this really be happening?* "Mr. Johnstone, do you think there is a misunderstanding that could be corrected with, uh...some direct discussion between the parties?"

A.J.: "Truthfully, Liz, we're way beyond the discussion phase here. You know yourself that an SEC investigation would sanction the entire Board and the company as well. Think of all of the value that would be lost for shareholders, let alone the downside to our national interests. Look, I've known Patrick Brady for over 30 years. You know how close we are, but this goes beyond friendship. You and I have duties to perform and Patrick has put us in a bind. We've got to do the right thing. You need to decide tonight."

Liz: "Where does Mr. Strawbridge stand on this? Maybe there is a solution if he could broker a deal between Brady and the dissident directors."

A.J.: "I can assure you that we've got the votes and that's all that I can say for now. Once you've decided to come aboard we'll involve you in all subsequent discussions."

Brady-trained, Liz shifted into mental high gear as she rapidly processed Johnstone's offer. Patrick had treated her like shit that morning and she wanted to reciprocate in kind; however her boss had told her repeatedly to disassociate negotiations from emotions - an emotional negotiation was an oxymoron. Brady was convinced that decision-making was a snap if you thought clearly. Well, if clear thinking made decision-making easy, then her decision here was obvious. She could have it both ways. She would accept Johnstone's offer and get under the tent of the rogue directors so that she would be privy to their plan of attack. If Patrick looked weak in the final analysis, she would benefit from a soft landing with a much-improved financial package. If, on the other hand, Brady looked like a winner, she would shift back to his team, providing valuable information that she would claim was acquired for his Lordship's benefit under the guise of joining the opposition.

Liz: "What kind of package do you envision for the

new COO?"

A.J.: "A $700,000 base with very attractive bonus opportunities plus options on 500,000 shares at a strike price of $30."

Liz: "And a board seat?"

A.J.: "Absolutely."

Liz: "And all the usual perks I assume?"

A.J.: "You assume correctly."

Liz: "We have a deal." In for a penny in for a pound, she thought. If it goes to hell at least I have a two year severance, as she shook hands with Johnstone.

* * *

As Brady checked out of the Dorchester, he was feeling a helluva lot better. "My God, these Brits can drink," he thought, as the doorman opened the door to the limo and put his suitcase in the boot. Brady kept his briefcase with him as it contained a draft binder of an intensely negotiated catastrophic risk insurance policy. He settled into the leather seat and took stock of his situation. His strategy was succeeding better than he would have thought possible a week ago.

Goal one: Get ready for the Armed Service Review Committee on November 15th. Status:

Frank's team was making headway in prepping the command and control system for the new AI module. After tearing Turney a new asshole she had finally executed the documentation and sent the wire. The next week would be of critical importance but at least the pieces were all in place in Charleston.

Goal two: Secure a buyer on the black market for the Land Force Warrior technology "as is" without the benefit of AI. Brady had rationalized this most heinous form of treason as, in essence, a rather harmless transfer of technology that would soon be rendered obsolete by the application of Artificial Intelligence. Why not make a few billion on the side? The Chinese get their oil. He gets his money, and the Iranians get the illusion that they've obtained a technology that shifts the balance of power in the region. Status: Kauffman was optimistic about the deal and DiStefano's recent e-mail confirmed that everything was on track.

Goal three: Implement a catastrophic risk policy that provides protection for the company in the event the Land Force Warrior technology is impaired or underperformed expectations on November 15th. Status: Brady had the draft in hand and would be ready to ink an original currently being prepared by the lead underwriter at Lloyd's Denham-American syndicate. Once he wired the $20M, the policy would be in force, providing the company approximately $1.5B in the event of a meltdown.

Even as he basked in self-satisfaction over his

business strategies he agonized over the chain of events that led to the threatened *coup d'etat*. He blamed himself for underestimating the old Ivies and failing to put protective measures in the corporate bylaws. By God, he swore, how I hate lawyers.

The way out of this mess was completely dependent upon the efficient execution of DiStefano's emerging plan. Brady was less than supremely confident because DiStefano had been keeping the details from him.

The first thing he would do, he promised himself, when he got back, would be to meet with his Director of Security to see how all the pieces dovetailed.

The limo pulled up to the International Terminal at Heathrow and deposited Brady curbside for his return to the States.

Brady awoke as the stewardess announced that they had been cleared for landing at JFK. There he would board the Zybercor Citation for the short hop to Reagan and then on to the Mayflower. He had been dreaming about Liz Turney and was moderately tumescent. He couldn't reconstruct the conversation but they obviously were not talking business. If Liz had been disinclined to support the insurrection initially, he had undoubtedly pushed her into their hands after their untoward telephone encounter. That was a big mistake on his part, for many reasons. He was already beginning to feel a sense of loss that was hard to describe. As he buckled his seat belt for landing, Brady reflected back to the first night he had met Liz Turney, nearly seven years before.

Brady had retained the well-established head-hunting firm, Stuart Spencer, to find him the ideal Chief-of-Staff to take responsibility for Zybercor's day-to-day operations, freeing him up to do deals and grow the company unencumbered by the myriad of details necessary to ensure a smooth-running machine. He insisted that Stuart Spencer conduct the search out of their New York office motivating them by means of a large retainer accompanied by an admonition that he wanted the best candidates possible, as long as they wore pants. He was gratified initially that Wilson Wyatt, Managing Director of the New York office, would be handling the search personally, but became well and truly pissed when Wyatt reported that one of the three final candidates was a woman.

"You've got to be shitting me, Wilson," said Brady as he looked at his cell phone in disbelief. "I thought that I made it perfectly clear that I didn't want a broad as Chief of Staff. What part of that didn't you understand?" He couldn't believe that Wilson Wyatt had not only disregarded his instructions but had the temerity to commit him to a dinner that very evening, in New York no less.

"Listen to me for a moment, Patrick, please," said Wyatt. "You instructed me to find you the best candidate possible and I've done just that. She may not have a penis, but she's got a set of balls that drag on the ground….. to go along with an unbelievable mind and a great work ethic. Trust me. And, by the way, she's a real looker, as well. Perfect for the job. Gotta go. I made reservations for three for tonight at 7:00 at Le Champignon. Brush up on your French. I'll take my leave after cocktails. Ciao."

MANIPULATION

Wyatt disengaged so quickly that he didn't hear Brady's crass parting reference to a vital portion of the male anatomy.

    Wyatt, Brady, and Elizabeth Turney were seated comfortably in a banquette in the back corner of the trendy French restaurant. It was truffle season and the unmistakable odor of the delicacy trumped the aromas of garlic and rich sauces in the smallish dining room. Brady felt awkward trying to match Wyatt's French as he easily ordered wine and conversed fluently with the fawning all-French service staff. Brady had worked on his French over the years but he lacked confidence when the conversation breached the boundaries of simple ordering. What's more, he was finding it very difficult to concentrate because all of his attention was focused on Liz Turney. She was the most stunning woman he had ever seen, and as one of the most eligible bachelors in America, Patrick Brady had met a lot of very attractive women. Everything about her was perfect. Her looks - a magnificent mélange of mulatto/Asian with almond eyes, high cheekbones, and a perfectly-shaped mouth with full lips and the whitest teeth imaginable. Her clothes - perfectly tailored and business/conservative, but with just a slight plunge in the neckline and a barely discernible slit up the leg. 'Less is more' was proving to be provocative as all hell. Her intensity was palpable...
...as if she were a human tuning fork picking up the most minute vibration. Yet she seemed calm, detached from the trivial, and able to focus on the priorities. Quite remarkable, he thought. And perfectly exquisite.

    As planned, Wyatt politely excused himself

after his second glass and left Brady and Liz to get to know each other. Brady struggled through the menu with no help from the arrogant waiter who seemed pleased to make things as difficult as possible for him. Liz sat quietly through the ordeal as Brady ordered for both of them; he then excused himself and beat a hasty retreat to the men's room. As Brady worked his way back to the table he noticed Liz in animated conversation with the maitre d'hotel and their waiter… …in fluent, unaccented and rapid French. He didn't know what was said until he queried the maitre d' at the end of the evening while Liz was visiting the ladies' room. Brady asked him what the conversation entailed and whether it might have had any bearing on the subsequent improved attitude of their waiter. **The maitre d' smiled knowingly and told Brady that Liz had threatened 'to remove the waiter's testicles and add them to the truffle pate if he didn't show her gentleman the respect he deserved'.**

CHAPTER ELEVEN

Azzato, Jacobs and Johnstone arrived together for the 12:00 meeting at the Holiday Inn on Main Street in Alexandria, located directly across from the new Criminal Justice Building. Liz Turney and Mike Chadel were already in the conference room on the second floor. Chadel was 'boarding' some key issues on the flip chart as the 'three amigos' strode into the room carrying briefcases.

"Good afternoon, gentlemen," said Liz while Chadel enthusiastically shook hands all around. She was very businesslike, informing the Directors that Brady was in London regarding some business insurance questions and DiStefano was nowhere in sight. Nonetheless, she told them that she didn't want Mike or herself out of the office at the same time for very long. She suggested they get right to work and attempt to conclude the meeting by 2:00 p.m.

"That's O.K. with us," said Azzato. "Let's cut right to the chase then. What did you learn from the review of the corporate bylaws, Mike?"

"Quite a bit, actually. It appears that Mr. Brady didn't do his homework here. Apparently he didn't think something like this was ever going to happen. The only hitch is that it takes a 2/3 majority to remove him as CEO and Co-chairman. The good news is that 80% of his phantom stock and options are tied to his contract as Chief Executive Officer and we have him in a clear breach."

"What about the two-thirds majority?" asked Jacobs. "Doesn't that present a problem?"

Before Liz could respond, Mike jumped up like a hummingbird on amphetamines and blurted out that he...*not* he and Liz...had figured out how to disqualify Franks from participating in a vote to change Chief Executive Officers. "As an ad-hoc Director Col. Franks will have to recuse himself. With Jamieson and the three of you we'll have our two-thirds; four out of six. Perfecto," said Chadel.

Johnstone and Azzato shared eye contact as Jacobs asked Chadel to cite some specific precedents and case law to back up his theory. Jacobs was in favor of bringing in an experienced outside counsel but Johnstone and Azzato had talked him out of it. They said that Brady had cultivated so many contacts over the years that they couldn't risk involving another attorney. And they were persuasive in arguing that, in order to protect their financial interests in the company, they had to acquire a massive amount of leverage and then use it to force Brady to surrender his position and the vast majority of his Zybercor holdings without a public battle.

Johnstone waited until Jacobs was satisfied with Chadel's analysis and then directed his attention to Liz. "Liz, you met with Sue Jamieson last night... how'd it go?"

Liz took a deep breath while she gathered her thoughts. "Sue was very disappointed with our conversation. On one hand she was reluctant to get involved with something that she regarded as messy. On the other hand, her own instinct after the Board Meeting was that something didn't smell quite right. I explained to her that there were significant misrepresentations in the disclosure statement. Anyhow, here's where we left it. One, I would have Mike brief her as to her fiduciary responsibilities and two, I would set up a meeting with you, Mr. Azzato, to review how things will play out assuming we are successful. And she did insist that I attend all subsequent meetings as well."

"So let's get the cart and horse in sequence here. Can we rely upon her support so that we can go to Strawbridge with a *fait àccompli*?" asked Johnstone.

"I think the worst thing we could do is take her support for granted," countered Liz. She realized very clearly that her own leverage was tied to her ability to deliver Jamieson. She could negotiate better on behalf of Sue and herself if she alone managed the process. The deeper the hole these guys dug for themselves, the more they'd pay to be assured of the crucial fourth vote. She could tell they were reluctant to go to Strawbridge without four votes in their pockets and an airtight opinion to disenfranchise Franks from the vote.

Jacobs stood up abruptly and began pacing nervously. He blurted out, "For Christ's sake, Liz, your job was to bring her to the table. We need her fucking support here or we'll have holy hell to pay."

"Emory, I'm reporting to you…"

"It's Mr. Jacobs, please. I'm a Director here."

"Emory, if you'd like me to leave the meeting I will gladly surrender this assignment to you. More than gladly." Liz began to gather up her notes and looked readily prepared to leave.

Azzato had been watching the exchange intently and decided to take charge of the meeting. "Liz, please sit down. Emory, shut the fuck up and sit down…please, Mr. Jacobs…we're all on the same team here and I'd like you all to consider for a moment just who it is that we're up against. If we're going to bring down Patrick Brady we're going to have to work together and not miss a single step. Do you all realize the stakes here?"

Azzato and Johnstone stared intently at Jacobs. Chadel looked like a deer in the headlights and Turney looked cool and quite resolved to stay or go depending upon the outcome of the confrontation. Liz knew that this exchange was worth millions and she knew she could bluff Jacobs. This is what Brady trained her for...hardball.

Emory Jacobs got the message. He sucked up his gut, managed a stiff upper lip and looked Liz in the eyes, saying, "I apologize for that outburst, Liz. I have all the confidence in the world in you and will do anything possible to support your efforts."

"Thank you. I want you to know that I am as committed to this as anyone. I have a lot to lose and, believe me, I do understand that Jamieson is critical. I'm just asking that you trust me here."

"We're all on the same page. Thank you, Liz. Thank you, Emory. Let's focus on some timelines for a moment." Azzato clearly enjoyed being in charge. He was beginning to think that he might make the perfect replacement for Brady.

Whitfield was sitting in a blue SUV across the street from the Alexandria Holiday Inn. He speed-dialed DiStefano, who sounded very much on edge, as he said, "Talk to me, Cal".

"Good news. We've got Jacobs, Azzato, and Johnstone in the Holiday Inn at Alexandria. Twenty minutes before they arrived Liz Turney and Mike Chadel checked in under false names. They'd reserved a conference room for half a day with a set-up for coffee and sandwiches. Bad news, the room was situated in the interior of the building. We didn't have the time or positioning to pick up the conversation. They were only all together for an hour and a half. Unfortunately we don't know a thing that was said."

"Shit," said DiStefano. He wanted Whitfield to know that he was unhappy but understood that there was nothing he could have done differently. "Cal, are you absolutely sure that there was no one else in the room?"

"I'm sure of it. One of our guys went in to freshen up the coffee. After the meeting broke up, we ran a pencil over the indentation made by the magic markers on the flip chart and we have some scribbling that we can't decipher but might make sense to you…'ad hoc' something. I'll bring it right over."

* * *

Johnstone, Jacobs, and Azzato were sitting in a stretch limousine on the way to Reagan Airport to catch the Delta shuttle back to New York.

"Jesus, Lou, I thought you were going to kiss her ass in there," said Jacobs.

"And……?" responded Azzato.

"And what? What was the point? We need to put her under pressure," countered Jacobs. "And telling me to shut the fuck up, that was humiliating."

"Emory, what's to stop her from going to Brady and getting him to up the ante for her? Why do you think she was willing to call your bluff? She knows that her price tag just went up and as long as we're willing to pay, she'll deliver. Let's not be ridiculous here. We've got more than enough to go around. We can always cut her out at a later date, but not until we get that fourth vote. I don't trust Strawbridge to do what we need him to do unless we already have the four votes we need solidly in our pocket. Do we agree on this?"

"The key to this is speed," said Johnstone. "We've got to get Strawbridge to call a special Board meeting immediately. The longer this goes on the more likely it is that Brady finds out and then what? Then all bets are off."

"Here's what I think we should do," said Azzato. "Strawbridge is in Minnesota visiting family. I'm going to telephone him and get a commitment for a special Board meeting within the next five days. That's more than enough time to get ready. Emory, you work up the agenda and the resolutions with Chadel, and Avery, you stay close to Turney. I'll put a term sheet together and write a proposal as to how everybody shares in the pie. Today's Wednesday. Let's shoot for next week and we'll convene the whole team a day in advance."

It was now evident that Azzato was running interference and taking responsibility for managing Strawbridge. Turney was in the cat bird's seat and Jacobs and Johnstone were making themselves more marginal by the moment. Some things hadn't changed.

* * *

Brady had taken the company jet from JFK to Reagan Airport where he was met by DiStefano. They were soon back at the Mayflower with a calendar and flip chart in the room. Brady had informed Bridie Donaghue that he was working on a deal and would be out of the office for a few days. He instructed her to screen and hold all calls.

They were in complete agreement that a special Board meeting must occur soon. The meeting would need to be held in Charleston at the Land Force Warrior facility. The issues they debated were in connection with the timing and sequence of events. DiStefano briefed Brady about the meeting of the co-conspirators at the Holiday Inn in Alexandria.

"Boss, I just don't think you can be the one to initiate a special meeting. As of now they don't know that we're aware of their little game. That's our edge. We can't give that up," said DiStefano. He was relieved to see Brady in such an upbeat mood. Upbeat meant business as usual with Patrick Fortune Brady.

"The only way that we can control events is if the meeting is prearranged in Charleston. Do you propose we sit around here with our thumbs up our asses waiting for Strawbridge to call me?" protested Brady. He was getting impatient and wanted to become more proactive even though he trusted DiStefano's instincts.

"Not at all," countered DiStefano. "You can count on Strawbridge calling you anytime now. He won't tell you he's calling a meeting for a 'vote of no confidence'. He'll use an excuse…probably something about the state of the technology." DiStefano was sure that by now the Directors realized it was not by accident that they hadn't received their high level security clearances. "If he goes down that path it will be easy for you to respond that the meeting should be held in Charleston so that you can organize a demo. If he doesn't use the technology as an excuse, you can tell him that the security clearances have come in and, bingo, back to Charleston for a demo. This way you get what you want by giving him what he wants..... without tipping our hand."

"I like it, Tony. In the meantime what are we doing about a reception committee for the Board?"

"I've already been in contact with Rahnajat, the top dog at Iranian Intelligence. Guy's a pro. He's already staffed the operation. We communicate through an encrypted e-mail and disposable cell phones. He's not easy to deal with but he's got the resources lined up and our interests are completely in alignment. Just like you taught me, Boss. I've got to get down there today to recon the whole area. Under normal conditions I'd like two to three weeks for this kind of an operation," said DiStefano.

"What are you going to tell Franks?" Brady was willing to put all the planning details in DiStefano's hands but he didn't underestimate Franks.

"I'm not worried about that. He'll think I'm down there at your request to look over his shoulder. I'll tell him he's going to have to perform for a special Board meeting in the next few days and that will keep him occupied."

"Just don't sell him short. He's fond of Macklin and Grossman and I'll bet he can be one tough son-of-a-bitch if you push him too hard." Brady had seen Franks' personnel jacket and it was loaded with battlefield commendations.

"He's just one of a dozen issues that are going to have to be factored in here. I admit I don't have all the answers right now. That's why I need to get down there," said DiStefano.

"O.K., but before you disappear let's review my marching orders...One, I act as if it's business as usual but we tell everyone that I'm working on a deal that I'll present to the Board at the next meeting. Two, I have drinks with Kauffman tonight so that he can tell me lies about his meeting in France. Keep him motivated and relaxed. Anything else you can think of?"

"Yes. Cal Whitfield is picking you up tomorrow morning to take you over to a remote location where you're going to learn how to handle an M16," said DiStefano.

"For Christ's sake, Tony, isn't that a bit much? I don't plan on shooting the bastards myself."

"Please don't fight me on this, Patrick. I can't explain everything right now because I don't have all the pieces wrapped into a nice, neat package, yet. You've got to trust me."

"O.K. O.K. But, listen, I want to hear from you every two hours."

"How about every four hours?"

"Make it three. All's fair and no favor. Good luck."

"See you in a few days. Patrick, stay loose."

"Ciao."

* * *

Azzato was finally ready to reach out to Strawbridge to get his commitment to join the insurgency and take a proactive role. He felt that he was as prepared as he was ever going to be. He would have preferred to have Susan Jamieson's vote in his pocket but felt strongly that Turney controlled her proxy and it would simply be a matter of dollars and cents at the right time. Meanwhile he would infer that he had the four votes necessary as well as an opinion that Franks, as an ad hoc Director, would have to recuse himself due to the nature of the vote. In addition, he had two pages detailing misrepresentations of disclosure statements, Sarbanes-Oxley corporate governance violations, and abuses of the New York Stock Exchange Code of Ethics.

Azzato had never felt so alive. He was into this in a big way, increasingly imagining himself succeeding Brady as Chief Executive Officer and picking up a good chunk of his stock. He thought that Turney would make a good Chief Operating Officer to take care of the day-to-day but Jacobs and Johnstone would definitely have to go. The first order of business would be to reorganize the Board of Directors. That thought brought him full circle, back to Strawbridge. He wanted to negotiate with him from a position of strength. The last thing he wanted to do was to compete, in advance, with Strawbridge for the CEO's job. He figured the reason Strawbridge resigned from public life was to make money. He wondered what his price tag would be to facilitate this transition and then disappear into the sunset. He placed the call, got Strawbridge's voice mail, and left an urgent message for him to call back.

* * *

Susan Jamieson and Liz Turney met at the Starbucks near Tower Center in Reston, Virginia. Armed with their favorite afternoon pick-me-ups they sat comfortably in facing armchairs. The coffee shop was only half-full, but the din was still significant enough so they wouldn't be overheard. Nevertheless, they chose their words carefully as Liz briefed Sue on Wednesday's meeting at the Holiday Inn.

"Azzato is by far the smartest of the three. Jacobs can't control himself and Johnstone looks like he's stoned all the time. They're obviously under a lot of pressure and it shows. Azzato, on the other hand, looks cool and relaxed. He seems to like the battle. I believe we can do business with him," said Liz as she maintained eye contact over the rim of her cappuccino.

"Do you think Azzato understands you're speaking for both of us?" asked Sue.

"Clearly. He knows we're a team and I'm positive he realizes that we're not going to come cheaply." Liz needed to flush out Sue's expectations so that she could negotiate a suitable package for them both at the eleventh hour.

"Are you comfortable with the package they offered you as Chief Operating Officer?" queried Jamieson.

"The salary and bonus numbers are O.K. but they're way light on the stock. I'm going to insist on a three-year, rolling, evergreen contract with escalators and every goody my lawyer can devise. He should have my draft done tonight and then he'll go right to work on yours. Have you considered resigning at Viacom and moving over as Chief Financial Officer?"

MANIPULATION

"I've given it a lot of thought and, frankly, I'm inclined to do it. I think you and I would make a fabulous team. How do you envision my package and how much stock do you think we can corral?"

"We would have more combined clout if you reported directly to the CEO," said Liz. You could handle all the financial matters, public reporting, investor relations…you know, including the administrative functions and I'll handle operations, contract management, and research and development. How's that sound?"

"Great so far," said Sue.

"Let's make it simple. We'll have identical packages and take one percent of the company each, with enough unrestricted stock to get some 'fuck you money' out in the next six months." Liz folded her hands and waited patiently.

"Under the circumstances I don't feel much like going back to work," said Sue. "My condo's only a few miles from here. Why don't we go back to my place and crack open an expensive bottle of champagne to celebrate our new partnership?"

"It would be my pleasure entirely," smiled Liz as she followed Sue out the door and into her green BMW.

* * *

Strawbridge got back to Azzato late Friday afternoon. He listened attentively as Azzato recited the recent litany of events and then responded, rather coolly.

"Lou, you make a strong case that Brady has

played fast and loose with the rules. I appreciate that and there has to be an accounting for those infractions. I was just wondering whether you think the punishment that you envision here fits the crime." Strawbridge needed to get to the bottom of this. What was the real motivation behind the conspiracy and was there any way to head it off or broker a peaceful resolution?

"Actually, I think we may be playing with less of a deck here than we think. There's a lot of skepticism about the status of the technology. Brady's been covering us in bullshit all along. What makes you think he's been telling the truth about Land Force Warrior? Why haven't we been allowed to touch and feel it? Why haven't we gotten our security clearances? Surely this troubles you as much as it does me," countered Azzato.

"I'm very concerned and I don't want you to misunderstand my caution for an unwillingness to act. But I've seen how these kinds of things can get out of control. Think about the field day the media would have if they got hold of this. There's no question in my mind that Zybercor could end up in bankruptcy court if we don't manage this carefully. Remember, the Enron Directors were sued personally and had to come out-of-pocket to satisfy the shareholder suits. Can you afford this kind of a pissing contest, Lou?"

"That's why I'm collaborating with you, Jackson. You have the status and know-how to orchestrate this internally and put the right spin on things. I'm asking you how you feel we should proceed."

"Okay. First, I want to talk to Brady and tell him that the Board is concerned about the technology and tell him we should have a special meeting down in the technical facility...and I mean right away. Look, if he has been lying about the technology then we have a very strong case to demand his resignation. In the meantime, you and your team get your votes and documentation in line and we can convene an executive session. After you make your case I can meet in private with Brady and attempt to negotiate an amicable settlement."

"What if he's unwilling to negotiate?" asked Azzato.

"Then I tell him I'm going to the Securities and Exchange Commission as soon as I issue a public statement and resign."

"You would be willing to do that?"

"If all that you say is true and he is unwilling to bow out, I would have no choice."

"O.K., Jackson...you're calling the shots. Would you get back to me after you've made contact with Brady?"

"Most definitely. But for now please keep a lid on this, Lou. If we put Patrick Brady in a corner with no means of retreat, I think he's the type who would rather die than give in."

"You're not telling me anything I don't already know. Back in college he almost killed a guy twice his size, with his fists, over something stupid. **I honestly believe if Patrick knew what was going on behind his back.....he would be capable of murder.**"

CHAPTER TWELVE

Mark Kauffman was staying at the Madison. He hadn't been home in a week and his wife was bitching constantly. He just couldn't deal with her shit now. He had a hangover and was jet-lagged. He ordered coffee and pancakes from room service and thought back over the last forty-eight hours. Man, was he in over his head. He didn't know who was more dangerous, DiStefano or Rahnajat. He needed to get out of the middle of this mess as soon as possible. He couldn't spend five hundred million dollars if he was dead. At least DiStefano now had the cell phone numbers to speak to Rahnajat directly. Shit, it was 3:00 p.m. already and he was just eating breakfast. He had a couple hours of sleep left before meeting Brady at 6:00......plenty of time to get his story straight.

* * *

Promptly at 6:00 o'clock Cal Whitfield opened the door of Brady's suite at the Mayflower, admitting a raggedy-looking Mark Kauffman. Kauffman had dark circles under his eyes and a pasty complexion. Brady, on the other hand, was photo-op perfect, resplendent in a blue blazer over a striped Turnbull and Asser shirt, with traditional grey slacks and loafers. Brady was feeling particularly cheerful having just spent several hours in the woods of Virginia with Whitfield, familiarizing himself with an M16. My God, what an experience! So light but so incredibly powerful. He couldn't wait to do it again.

It could be addictive, he thought, and wondered what it would be like turning it on another human being.

"Cal, you can call it a day. Mark and I are going to catch up on things and have a few cocktails in the suite," said Brady, as Whitfield quickly took his leave with a perfunctory, "Have a good evening, gentlemen." Brady knew that Whitfield was leading the surveillance effort and up to his eyeballs in work. In addition, DiStefano had said he needed Whitfield in Charleston ASAP.

Brady poured two Bloody Mary's from a pre-mixed pitcher on the bar, unobtrusively adding an extra shot of vodka to Kauffman's glass.

"Well, Marko old fellow, how was your trip to Europe? I want to know all the details," said Brady with unaffected good humor. "Up the republic," he said as he raised his drink.

Kauffman countered with a weak smile and clicked glasses across the coffee table. Brady kicked off his shoes and put his feet up, all the while looking as if he didn't have a care in the world.

"I have to tell you it was one of the most complex and difficult negotiations I've ever conducted. Particularly after DiStefano changed the deal on me the night before I left for France."

"I can't keep up with Tony, either, to tell you the truth, Mark. Let's get right to the bottom line. Did they reach agreement on their oil deal and agree to our price tag?" Brady would not even acknowledge the fact that his team was collaborating with Iranian Intelligence on a black-ops maneuver against his own Board. He never could get in trouble for something he didn't say.

Kauffman had no idea what Brady did or didn't

know about the side deal with Rahnajat and he felt he had nothing to gain by going there. DiStefano had shown no interest regarding the economics so he was sure the deal points would all be new to Brady.

"It took a lot of pushing and shoving to reach an agreement on the pricing for the oil and the ancillary support that the Chinese were going to have to provide the Iranians to fully fit out Land Force Warrior…but they finally got there." Kauffman was starting to sweat. Damn it, he hated when that happened.

"Are you feeling all right, Mark? You're sweating like a race horse. Should I adjust the temperature in here?"

"Oh, it's just the accumulation of travel and stress. I'm feeling a bit under the weather," said Kauffman, "and I'm afraid I have some unfortunate news to report on the price that the Chinese are willing to pay."

"Oh, really," said Brady with arched eyebrows as if he didn't already know every detail of the dinner meeting.

"Yes, the fucking Chinks won't go a dime over $2.8B," said Kauffman sheepishly.

"I confess that's quite surprising," said Brady as he refilled their drinks slipping extra vodka into Kauffman's glass once again. He paused for theatrical effect as he stared directly into Kauffman's eyes. He wanted to make him sweat even more.

"No deal," said Brady.

"What?" Kauffman sat up so fast that he spilled half his drink down the front of his pants.

"Relax, old sport. I'm just kidding. Hell, I'm sure you did your best. If DiStefano tells me everything's

O.K. regarding your side deal, we'll go ahead and close on $2.8B, but I'm afraid we're not going to be able to pay you the commission that we had budgeted at the $4.0B sale price."

"What commission?"

"Didn't Tony tell you? We had you penciled in for a hundred million. At $2.8B, however, we're going to need to cut that back to fifty. I'm sure you'll agree that's fair."

"Very fair," said Kauffman as Brady's cell phone began to chirp.

"Hello Jackson...fine, just fine...I'm finishing up an important meeting. Do you mind if I ring you right back...great......talk to you presently"

"Mark, thanks for coming by. Let's get this unpleasantness behind us and the deal done. Then we'll take some R and R on the boat and talk about the future. You're part of the family now, my friend. Good luck."

Kauffman mumbled good night as Brady closed the door, saying "What a schmuck" to himself as he reached for the phone to match wits with Jackson Strawbridge. No sooner had the door of his suite hit Kauffman in the ass than Brady punched the speed dial returning Strawbridge's call.

"Jackson, it's Patrick...I understand you're back in Minnesota...business or pleasure?" said Brady.

"A little of both actually. I'm afraid my father has taken a turn for the worse and I'm helping him get things in order," replied Strawbridge. He didn't know how to breach this subject subtly. When he was nervous or uncertain he tended to be very blunt. Oftentimes it came out as callous instead of uncomfortable. He'd never learned the art of empathy.

"Patrick, I'm at the American Airlines counter at Duluth Airport. I'm taking the connector from here to Minneapolis and then directly on to D.C. I need to see you immediately."

"What can be so important? Is this personal or business?" asked Brady.

"It's business and I can't get into it over the phone...I won't get into it over the phone. Suffice it to say that you have a major problem on your hands and it's got to be dealt with immediately."

"That sounds very serious," said Brady.

"I know that you know what I'm referring to. I'd appreciate it if you didn't make me feel any more of an ass than I already do. I'll take a taxi from Reagan. I assume you're at the Mayflower."

"Yes."

"I'll be there as soon as I can."

"All right, Jackson. Goodbye."

* * *

DiStefano telephoned promptly at 8:00, exactly four hours after leaving the Mayflower. The company plane put wheels down in Charleston at 6:15 and he was in Building #F3 by 6:30. For the last hour and a half he had Franks escort him on a tour of the facility and the surrounding area. The Naval Base was huge. Building #F3 was situated in the very back of the complex near the banks of the Cooper River. Deserted docks stood guard over berths emptied of the destroyers, carriers, and other various vessels that once called Charleston home. The only active programs in this part of the

Yard were Building #F3, close to the Cooper River, the Law Enforcement Training Center located fifty yards further inland, and the High Security Detention Facility that housed approximately seventy inmates classified as "terrorists." Hundreds of thousands of square feet of deserted administrative space and vacant barracks surrounded the three active facilities. DiStefano was pleased with the tour. Very pleased.

Brady said, "It's about time...I just heard from Strawbridge. He's plenty pissed and on his way to D.C. He'll get in after midnight and plans on coming straight to the suite."

"How do you plan on handling him?" asked DiStefano. He knew that Brady and Strawbridge had a personal relationship that went back several years and sometimes he had even wondered........... but that was another matter.

"How the hell do I know? I need to know the fucking details of the fucking plan first." Brady was starting to feel claustrophobic as the forces assembled against him in a classic squeeze play.....a strategy that he often employed against others. But this wasn't supposed to be happening to him.

"Patrick, we've got to stay calm. We're managing a complex process and things are very fluid, but it's coming together rather nicely down here so we need to remain confident and stay focused."

"Are you running for office or takin' up preaching? Was that speech for you or for me?" asked Brady. He chuckled out loud thinking he had used words similar when giving one of his infrequent pep talks to his Director of Security.

"Both of us, Boss...both of us," said DiStefano with a sigh of relief. This was all going to succeed or fail based upon the ability of the two of them to work together seamlessly.

"O.K. Without getting into any gory details, what are your thoughts about Strawbridge?" Brady repeated.

DiStefano had been forming a plan and he was beginning to feel optimistic that it could be implemented.

"Patrick, if you had to place a bet on who's going to be with us and who's going to be against us, who stands where right now?"

"We've got nobody in our corner. Not one of the bastards. The directors and staff have all figured out that they'll be multi-millionaires once they carve up my interest. They're playing 'chicken' with me. They figure if I take them down, expose them, whatever.....then I'm guilty of various felonies and the company will end up worthless. They're right. They know I'll have to cut a deal and you and I will have to skulk out of town with our tails between our legs while they take over Zybercor."

"I promise I won't let that happen. I just needed to know if we had any friends to worry about," said DiStefano. "It would be difficult to identify and cull out specific individuals from the building. What you're telling me is that we needn't worry about having any survivors, am I right?"

"None at all. It's just you and me and the shareholders," answered Brady. He felt a chill run down his spine as he contemplated what was planned and how that meant the end of Liz Turney. Why was her imminent demise having such an impact on him? After all, she was eminently replaceable.....or was she?

"Then this is the deal with Strawbridge," said

DiStefano. "Bring to bear all your usual charm to try and turn him around. Tell him the technology is perfect and you'll prove it to all of them in the next forty-eight hours. Agree to hold a special Board meeting in Charleston this Wednesday...it's got to be in the late afternoon around 4:00...that's absolutely crucial. Inform him if the Board wants you out after the demonstration you'll negotiate an amicable settlement with him and him alone. Convince him that there's enormous dollar value here and you'll do what's in the best interest of the company, but you aren't going to leave all your stock on the table. Insist that you'll want a fair settlement...your CEO contract paid out in full plus...say.....thirty percent of your options...but you want them unrestricted."

"You figure if I don't try and negotiate hard he'll get suspicious," interrupted Brady.

"Exactly," said DiStefano. "We need all these pricks to think they've got you over a barrel and they're going to take your pants down on Wednesday...Are we together on this?"

"All the way," said Brady.

"Good. Listen, Patrick, I've got to go to dinner with Franks now. You know he's making a lot of headway with the AI conversion and...well, that's another matter...we can save that for later," said Tony.

"Before you go, how are our new best friends?"

"They're on a cruise from Abu Dhabi to Charleston on a Chinese container ship. They should be arriving Tuesday afternoon," said DiStefano.

"Tony, I'll talk to you in three hours."

"Four, Boss."

"Right...four it is," as Brady hung up the phone

and strolled to the bar to pour himself a very large whisky. He smiled slowly as he remembered Eddie Kenner once saying there was no such thing as too large a whisky. He said out loud, "Don't worry yourself at all, Uncle Eddie, I'll be comin' off the ropes and throwin' leather."

* * *

Early hours of the morning
Charleston

It was 3:00 a.m. and Lester Grossman had just finished washing his hands after changing Terrel Macklin's diaper. As time passed the two men had settled into an easy rhythm of shared intimacy. There were certainly no longer any secrets between them. Given Macklin's incapacity, he depended upon Lester for support in ways he never could have imagined. Grossman would do anything to help Mack. He agonized about his injuries and would gladly have traded places. His guilt level was enormous.

"Lester, your hands were a little cold tonight. I wish you'd take my advice and get those hand warmers out of the catalog." Macklin never cracked a smile when he busted Lester's balls.

"Gee, Mack, I'm on a short budget these days but I thought I'd allocate what little I have into some nose plugs, you know."

"Wait a minute, my stink don't shit," said Macklin.

"Yes, your stink do shit…or doesn't…if you want

to drop the Ebonics," replied Grossman.

"Hey Lester, is it true that you Jewish guys get the tip of your pee-pee cut off? Shit, man, that must really hurt. And what's up with those beanies y'all wear...keep your brains from leaking out?"

"You want to start with the mama jokes?" asked Grossman.

"Lester, I miss my Mama and I want to see her again. She's already lost one child. I don't want her to worry about me." Macklin was joking one minute and maudlin the next.

"Mack, I miss my mom too. We're gonna' get out of here, my man. Trust the Colonel to get us out." Lester wasn't going to share his fear that they might not get out of there at all. Mack had enough to deal with without worrying about what he couldn't control. Lester was harboring a 'screamin' case of the red ass' (as they said it in basic training) against Brady and DiStefano. He never thought he'd have been capable of these violent feelings. He could kill them for what they'd done.

"Have you noticed that the pace around here really picked up in the last twenty-four hours?" asked Macklin. He could feel a quickening pulse in all the activity, as if things were building to a crescendo. He was very intuitive and he could gauge in the eyes and cadences of the technicians' voices that the whole facility was under pressure. He still had not come to terms with the magnitude of his disability and the enhanced stress in the atmosphere added to his growing unease.

"Yeah, I know what you mean," responded Lester. "The professional staff is pretty excited about the progress they've made in knitting together the intelligent parts of all the various weapons systems into an integrated 'smart' network. They think the automated signal caller is smarter than me already, and after spending today in the simulator I thing they're right."

Grossman had just spent nine hours in the simulator and was highly impressed with the Artificial Intelligence module. They replayed the White Sands scenario and Lester was stunned that the AI had played the war game so much better than he had. The AI brain had seized the reins of the command and control system as Lester input certain conditions into the tuning mechanism.......the so-called front end of the system manipulated by the human controller. The AI instantaneously took control of the battlefield and installed redundancy scenarios and contingencies as it simultaneously launched a brilliant and devastating attack. Mack was totally protected as the smokescreen provided by the Apache was backed up by a dedicated drone. As a result Mack was never vulnerable to the sniper. The AI had automatically split up the two Apaches; one attacking the mobile vehicles and the other mopping up Team Alpha. The enemy choppers were naked and completely at the mercy of Mack's laser, which, in turn, was complemented by a direct barrage from the howitzer battery. The crossfire was devastating, as concentrated laser beams competed with 155mm shells, in wreaking havoc on targets. It was all over in nine and a half minutes with 100% enemy casualties and not even a scratch on the good guys. The rest of the simulations produced similar results, convincing Lester that the Artificial Intelligence system was a major step forward in operational command and control.

"Fuck the robots. You're still the Head Man. I

got my money on you" snarled Macklin with real conviction in his voice.

"Yeah, well look at you. And look at my other boys," said Grossman as his voice cracked, then broke, with emotion. He sobbed quietly then composed himself.

"If I have to crawl over there and kick your ass, I will," said Mack as he pushed himself off the bed with his elbows. "The shit that went down was due to faulty planning and bad luck...period."

"I can't get it out of my mind. I keep seeing our Team getting hammered and then you going down. How could a sniper bullet get through the suit when it took 9mm at point blank range?"

"Patrick 'Make A Quick Fortune' Brady is the guy who pushed the brass into this exercise. He's gonna' pay little brother. Trust me, he's gonna' pay." Mack's voice got real quiet sometimes and, when it did, Lester felt the hair on the back of his neck start to tingle.

"I need you to stay focused, Lester. I need you to be at 100% or we'll never get out of here. We have a lot of work to do. Do you hear me, soldier?"

"Yeah, Mack, I hear you. I got it."

In the ensuing silence both men were left with their own demons as they each drifted off into an uneasy sleep.

CHAPTER THIRTEEN

An angry and frustrated T. Jackson Strawbridge had phoned Patrick Brady from Minneapolis-St. Paul Regional Airport at 10:45 Saturday night advising him that all planes were grounded until Sunday morning and he was spending the night at the American Airlines VIP Suite. Brady mumbled something inane about the weather, thinking, meanwhile, it must be as cold on the ground as it was between the two of them. He had hoped he could use a little scotch late in the evening to warm up the atmosphere instead of coffee and sandwiches in the cold light of day. In any event, they agreed to meet as soon as Strawbridge got to the Mayflower. He insisted that they meet in the main dining room just across from the elevator bank.

* * *

While Brady, sleepless again, suffered through a long night waiting for Strawbridge to arrive from Minneapolis, Jacobs, Johnstone, and Azzato spent a nervous Saturday evening in their own homes. Nothing drains one's energy like the tension surrounding a hostile deal and this one promised to be hostile with a capital "H." They were on an emotional roller coaster with its concomitant highs and lows - moments of euphoria followed by periods of abject terror. The three cohorts had pledged a vow of silence until after 12:00 noon on Sunday. Right.

MANIPULATION

* * *

Sunday
October 5, 2009
Washington, D.C.

Bridie Donaghue let herself into Brady's suite at the Mayflower with her duplicate key at 6:30 a.m. She activated the hydraulic table in the master bedroom, preparatory to the massage she would give, selected one of Kitaro's early works for the stereo and then ground Brady's favorite Colombian blend. She noticed some lines of cocaine on the bedside table and surmised that 'Himself' must have had a difficult evening. While the coffee percolated she checked the status of his bowling ball and shoes and concluded that he had stayed in the suite last night and was, therefore, likely to be in a fairly shitty mood. This was hardly the first time and unlikely the last time that she would have to deal with the special proclivities of the man she loved like no other. In the twenty-three years that they had been together, Patrick Fortune Brady had changed her and her family's lives in ways that were unfathomable. Having just celebrated her sixty-eighth birthday it was hard to imagine that, when she started to work for Patrick, she and Sonny were living paycheck to paycheck. Life was a bitch. God was a tough taskmaster. They had worked hard like good Irish Catholics did…..they raised five children who were now scattered across the country living lives of their own……that is until they needed to borrow some money. "Ah, go on with you, Bridie, that's what parents are for, don't you know?" she whispered to herself.

When she had interviewed for the Administrative Assistant to the CEO position at Zybercor Corp. in Bethesda, Maryland in 1987, she had gotten Sonny up at 5:30 a.m. to get her to her appointment two hours early.

The office was closed at that early hour as was to be expected. She calmly offered one of her home-made raisin bran muffins and a hot coffee from the diner across the street to the first official-looking person she could find. The security guard had 'Whitman' on his name tag so she set up his breakfast on the grey metal desk in the lobby and asked him if he knew a Mr. Patrick Fortune Brady who owned a company in the office building. It seemed Mr. Whitman hadn't been served anything but legal papers since his wife had left him in July so he was more than grateful for the attention and more than happy to oblige. Bridie knew men as well as any woman. She persuaded 'dear' Ian Whitman to open up the office of Mr. Patrick Brady so that she could start the coffee machine, open the mail, heat up the muffins and be ready to greet her new boss. The ensuing job interview, if you could categorize it as such, lasted less than ten minutes. Bridie simply moved in and took over as if the good Lord had ordained it so. And why not? There was no discussion about salary or job title…there was simply an understanding that from now on Bridie Donaghue served Patrick Brady and Patrick Brady took care of Bridie and her clan. Tribal. Celtic.

The first eight years were difficult at best. The company survived month-to-month as the Boss reinvested every bit of loose change into research and development. Bridie would never forget the day that two gentlemen walked into the office, unannounced, with a contract that changed her life forever.

She'd never forget the date - February 12th, 1996, two days before Valentine's Day and what a gift 'the O'Brady Don' had in store for the Donaghues. Unbeknownst to Bridie, Zybercor had been approached by Lockheed Corporation to deliver a critical technology solution in the fulfillment of a lucrative defense contract. Brady drove a hard bargain ever aware that this sub-contract would allow him to pay off his debts and ramp his company up to a new level. He inked the agreement on the same day, February 12th, and when she opened her Valentine's Day card two days later there was a cashier's check for $100,000.00 made out to Sonny Donaghue. The accompanying note still brought tears to her eyes more than a decade later… "A small token of my gratitude for sharing your special wife with me. Without Bridie I'd be carrying my lunch pail to work on a construction site in Queens. As always, Patrick."

She nudged him gently awake as she held the freshly baked muffin near his nose. "Awake, your Lordship," she said. "You've got a big morning ahead of you. It's time for your breakfast now and a nice massage. Mr. Strawbridge is due around 11:00 and you need to be at your best altogether, now don't you?"

* * *

T. Jackson Strawbridge was still in a foul mood as he entered the Mayflower at 11:35. He walked straight past the front desk, turned into the dining room on the right, and sat down across from Brady who was waiting for him in his usual booth along the back wall.

"Patrick, you've certainly put me in a tough spot. My back's up against the wall." Strawbridge had gotten and stayed mad for twenty-four hours in preparation for his confrontation with Brady. Now that the moment had arrived his resolve was weakening, however. "Why does Patrick have this effect on me?" he thought as he waited for a response.

"Jack, you and I are friends. It hurts me to see you like this and hear the anger in your voice. What have I done to deserve it all of a sudden?"

"What have you done? You've blackmailed your friends. You've abducted their kids. You've lied to the marketplace and broken every rule in the book. Shit, Patrick, I'm afraid to be your friend. If you treat your friends like this, I'd hate to be your enemy."

"Are you?" asked Brady.

"Am I what?"

"Are you my enemy?"

"I hope not. I hope we can reach an amicable solution but that's going to be largely up to you. The Board wants you out," said Strawbridge.

"The Board? You can't seriously envision those lightweights running this company. Think about it for a minute. We're in the middle of a major deal to retool America's military. We have forty thousand shareholders. I built this company and I'm not about to turn it over to those incompetent assholes," said Brady as he stared Strawbridge down.

"These incompetents happen to be your directors and they've got four votes and an opinion that disqualifies Franks from voting due to his 'ad-hoc' status...that's a two-thirds majority even if I voted to support you...which, by the way, I would be hard-pressed to do."

This was going exactly the way DiStefano projected, thought Brady. Now was the time to play his card.

Brady sighed. "Maybe I'm not cut out to be the CEO of a public company after all. In hindsight I suppose I should have kept Zybercor privately held."

"We can't wind the clock back now, Pat. We have to deal with the here and now. How do you want to proceed?"

"There's only one way I'm willing to proceed now without a fight," said Brady.

"I'm listening."

"First, I need to make certain that the company is in good hands and that means you would have to commit to become my successor as CEO."

"Patrick, I..."

"Wait. I'm not finished. It's important that you hear this. I'm not going to negotiate this. I'm offering conditions as an alternative to a public battle. My attorney has advised me that I have the right to put this to a shareholder vote. Second, I want my contract honored and I want to walk away with half my stock. Third, I want to dispel these rumors that the technology is deficient. I want the Board to meet right away down in Charleston and I want to control the press release that is issued announcing the reorganization. The company has got to come out of this in a strong position."

Strawbridge nodded thoughtfully as Brady laid out a scenario that exceeded his headiest expectations. He knew he could manipulate the four votes to agree to this new arrangement. They would realize that half a loaf was better than none. He would take half of Brady's remaining stock, share the balance with Azzato and new management, and give Jacobs and Johnstone a graceful exit.

"I don't know if I could accept the CEO position and I can't speak for the other directors," said Strawbridge.

"That's entirely up to you. I am leaving this meeting to caucus with my attorneys and public relations people. If you cannot respond affirmatively by 3:00 today the gloves are off and I'll see you all in court."

"That is not enough time," said Jackson.

"Bullshit," responded Brady. "You chose to pick this fight. You've put my back against a wall, and you know what kind of a fighter I am. Talk to whomever you have to and let me know your decision. I spoke to our team in Charleston and they can have a demonstration of the technology ready by 4:00 Wednesday afternoon."

"How can I reach you?" asked Strawbridge.

Brady tapped his cell phone as he slid out of the booth, leaving Strawbridge with a tepid cup of coffee and the check.

* * *

As soon as Brady entered his suite he dropped a dime on DiStefano who then informed Colonel Franks, in person, that a special Board meeting had been scheduled in Charleston for this coming

MANIPULATION

Wednesday at 4:00 p.m. Franks was stunned that Brady would allow his Board to see the program in its current state of disarray after all the machinations he had gone through to keep them in the dark.

DiStefano made it clear that the matter was not open to debate and proceeded to give instructions exactly where, when, and how the demo would unfold. Before Franks could respond, DiStefano rushed out the door without another word leaving the colonel with a shit load of details running through his mind. And a lot to ponder.

* * *

Rahnajat had taken a suite at Charleston Place at the corner of Market and Meeting Sts. When DiStefano arrived Rahnajat was studying a map of the Charleston Port and Naval Yard. Since they had spoken previously by phone but had never before met in person DiStefano broke the ice by congratulating him on his meteoric rise through the ranks of Iranian Intelligence – information which DiStefano had gleaned from his extensive international contacts. Rahnajat seemed somewhat pleased by the compliment and then returned to the object of his earlier attention, with DiStefano following.

"We're on for 4:00 p.m. Wednesday," DiStefano said as he looked over Rahnajat's shoulder at the map spread out over the antique coffee table.

"I have some thoughts I'd like to share with you," said Rahnajat as he motioned DiStefano to take a seat in one of the high-backed chairs.

"Look here," said Rahnajat. "There's really just

one road that connects the Zybercor facility to the main access thoroughfare. In fact, the whole back sector that includes our building, the detention center as well as the training facility is isolated. If we planted an IED…here," Rahnajat had drawn a large "X" with a black magic marker at a location approximately two-thirds of the way down the lone road leading to the target area. "If we planted a roadside device here and set the detonator to coincide with the breach of building #F3, we could delay any unwelcome company until we're back in the inflatables and long gone."

DiStefano listened intently as Rahnajat took him through his final checklist concerning the operation. DiStefano was highly impressed with Rahnajat's professionalism. He sure looked like a terrorist, but when he spoke he sounded like a professor of history - calm, educated, and compelling.

Rahnajat had fleshed out the details of the operation and had included a diversionary attack on the detention center, which supposedly housed some well-known off-the-battlefield terrorists. By the time the first responders arrived at the scene and sorted out facts from fiction the Ops Team and the Land Force Warrior Program parts would be safely inside a Chinese sub bound for a rendezvous with an Iranian Intelligence vessel in the Mediterranean.

"I agree with everything you've outlined," said DiStefano as he nodded respectfully. "The IED and the diversion at the detention center will give us plenty of time to do what we need to do."

"I still believe it would be a mistake for you to participate in the operation," said Rahnajat as he looked up from the map.

"We've already been over this and it's useless to

try and talk me out of it. I know all the players and the inside of the facility like the back of my hand; besides, this is the way the Boss wants it."

"Suit yourself," said Rahnajat.

"So everything's all right on your end?" asked DiStefano.

"Yes, surprisingly so," he responded. "I keep looking over my shoulder, as you would say, but everything is on schedule. Preparedness is all."

"Good. Very good. Then please listen. **I need to talk to you about Mark Kauffman and that little deal he offered you and the Chinaman,**" said DiStefano as Rahnajat's eyes grew as wide as the top of his martini glass.

CHAPTER FOURTEEN

Day before the Board Meeting

Azzato, Johnstone and Jacobs met for breakfast at 8:00 a.m. at the Newark Airport Marriott Hotel. They had reservations on a Continental regional jet scheduled to leave at 10:00 a.m. for Charleston. It's fair to say that their mood was buoyant as Azzato informed his two old friends that Charleston was the home of three former Ivy Club Presidents and that provided a little karmic symmetry to the challenge in front of them as they planned Brady's demise. Azzato had contacted one of his predecessors and had arranged accommodations for the team at the Princetonian's plantation house outside of Charleston.

Liz Turney and Sue Jamieson were flying commercial from Dulles on a United Express flight arriving in Charleston at 12:30 p.m.

Mike Chadel was taking the 8:30 a.m. U.S. Airways flight from LaGuardia. Emory Jacobs had finally convinced his co-conspirators that they needed a third-party legal opinion from someone with a little grey hair. Chadel's law school roommate's father was a skilled corporate attorney from White, Lipps, and Trembling. The three of them had had dinner together the previous night in order to critique the game plan. According to Chadel, their case was airtight. He passed on some advice that he received, however, in connection with the proposed succession plan. It was midnight but Jacobs had been waiting expectantly for the feedback.

Chadel was very specific as he recounted, for Jacobs, the advice verbatim. Mike was reading from the copious notes he had taken at the dinner. "If you are not buttoned up on a new corporate governance model before ousting an incumbent Chief Executive, then you're vulnerable to a counter-attack. At a minimum you need to elect a new CEO and embody that person with the power to submit a plan of reorganization with, of course, some attendant credible legal advice."

Mike repeated that to Emory Jacobs twice more than Jacobs needed to hear it and was summarily cut off.

Jacobs waited until the breakfast plates were cleared before sharing with Avery and Lou the second-hand legal advice. Emory had already concluded that he would be the logical person to be nominated as an interim CEO. Given his legal background he believed he would be the perfect choice to manage the transition process and that, in turn, would position him solidly to segue into the permanent position of leading the company. He laid his theory on the table with as much sincerity and 'gravitas' as he could muster.

Azzato and Johnstone sat in stunned silence while Jacobs waited nervously, expectantly, for a response.

* * *

12:52 p.m.
Charleston

As United Express Flight #937 landed at Charleston International Airport at 12:52 p.m., Liz

Turney and Sue Jamieson unbuckled their seatbelts simultaneously and activated their Blackberrys at just about the same time as well. They were sitting in different rows because Turney had made the flight arrangements and deliberately ensured they would not be sitting together. She wanted to be left with her own counsel as they entered the climactic phase of the engagement. She had had an intimate evening with Sue Jamieson and should have been relaxed and confident. But she woke up in the middle of the night with an uneasy feeling that there was something that was just not quite right. It occurred to her that she had not heard from Mr. Brady for forty-eight hours; normally they talked three or four times a day. She had been so focused on her own agenda that she had not noticed that Brady had 'gone dark'. Re-thinking the events of the past week over and over during the flight she abruptly experienced one of those life-changing 'epiphanies' and gasped, nearly out loud, "Patrick F. Brady knows everything that's happening!" Liz had allowed herself to get caught up in the heady game of power-brokering and self-dealing. She had lost sight of the win-win strategy that seduced her into the double agent's role in the first instance. In her euphoria she lost sight of how smart her boss was. She realized that he was planning his moves as they were planning theirs. Undoubtedly, Brady saw her as an enemy now. Suddenly she didn't feel so well. She became nauseated and, despite the protestations of the in-flight personnel, rushed back to the lavatory as the commuter jet pulled abreast of the terminal.

MANIPULATION

* * *

1:45 p.m.
Charleston Naval Yard

Colonel Franks was frantically at work on multiple fronts. The special Board meeting forced him to accelerate his plan to engineer Macklin and Grossman's escape. His staff had done a commendable job adapting the laser technology to the wheelchair arm. The laser gun would slide effortlessly into the flat metal base attached to the right armature. Once the brackets were tightened Macklin would be 'good to go'. Terrel's wheelchair was an electric job that gave off a loud hum that could be heard halfway across the building. But that was the least of Franks' problems as he calculated how to best take advantage of the confusion caused by the Board meeting. Adapt and overcome. He would turn the lemon into lemonade. The good news was that the wheelchair and pick-up truck were ready to go. The challenge would be to distract DiStefano's goons and slip his boys through the containment area and out to the loading dock where their chariot awaited them. "Hit 'em as hard as you can, as fast as you can, where....", he thought out loud and then smiled at the memory.

* * *

Tuesday
October 7, 2009
Myrtle Beach, South Carolina

Brady had taken the corporate Citation to Myrtle Beach, wheels touching down at 12:30 p.m. By now he was certain that the opposition had him under surveillance as well. Past experience in warfare – the corporate kind – had taught him that if you were close enough to have your enemy in your gun sights then they were close enough to have you in theirs.

DiStefano met him at the business aviation center in an early model brown Toyota sedan and they headed south on Rt. 17 for the hour and a half drive to Charleston; plenty of time to discuss the myriad of details that had to be managed by 4:00 p.m. Wednesday when the Board convened in the Zybercor facility at the Naval Yard.

"Who else knows where you are?" asked DiStefano as they pulled out of the airport.

"Just the pilots and Bridie," Brady answered. He had spilled his guts to Bridie on Sunday morning while she administered the best massage he had ever experienced, preparing him for the confrontation with Strawbridge. Nothing surprised her as her soothing voice assured him that all would work out for the best. Her only concern was for the fate of Liz Turney. According to Bridie, Liz had not been herself lately and had inquired daily as to his whereabouts and well-being. Brady knew that they were fond of each other and suspected Bridie secretly fantasized that he and Liz would make a great couple in spite of their age difference. Liz was an amazing woman. If she wasn't such a world-class professional asset he would have bedded her years ago. Brady had always kept his priorities straight…or had he?

"I've reserved a four-room bed and breakfast in the historic district downtown under Whitfield's name. There's a suitable meeting area downstairs and the sole proprietor is enjoying an all-expense paid trip to Savannah for a couple of days," said DiStefano.

"Good enough. Now take me through all the details."

For the balance of the ride DiStefano outlined his plan for the next twenty-four hours and beyond. Brady was more than impressed with the complex scenarios that Tony had synchronized yet was being assaulted by a deepening sense that his life would never be the same.

* * *

Tuesday
October 7, 2009
Wellspring Plantation, Outside Charleston
3:00 p.m.

The plantation house at Wellspring was set back over a mile from a scenic highway, and just a twenty minute drive from downtown Charleston. One of the few privately-held working plantations extant, Wellspring was three hundred and twenty years old and still claimed nine hundred of its original seven thousand acres. While the cotton, indigo, and rice that remained were largely symbolic, the peaches, tomatoes, pumpkins, and strawberries were among the tastiest in the South.

The Harkins family had owned Wellspring since 1949 when Johnathon Harkins' father acquired the estate from a proud and old, but impecunious

Carolina family. The elder Harkins had fallen in love with the three-hundred year old oaks, the early nineteenth century home, the tidal creeks, and the magnificent gardens and outbuildings. Johnathon was twelve years old at the time and later went on to Princeton University where he became President of Ivy in 1958. He was only too pleased to make the house and staff available to an Ivy President successor, Lou Azzato, in mid October, for his Board conference. "Unfortunately," he said, "I'll be out of the country but I'll see to it that there won't be any other guests and the house staff will provide you with the finest in Southern hospitality."

By mid-afternoon the whole team had arrived, checked in, and assembled in the antebellum conference room. The mood was electric as Azzato, Strawbridge, Johnstone, Jacobs, Jamieson, Turney, and Chadel took their seats, shut off cell phones and Blackberrys, and opened folders and note pads.

Liz found herself sitting in the middle of the table across from Sue Jamieson and Avery Johnstone, III. She was sitting between Emory Jacobs and Mike Chadel. Azzato and Strawbridge were sitting at opposite ends of the ten-foot antique table. The Plantation staff had arranged for coffee, tea, finger sandwiches, freshly baked cookies and fresh fruit from the orchard. It was eerily silent as the participants waited for someone to take charge and move the agenda forward. Thankfully the silence was broken as Emory Jacobs blurted, "Well, for Christ's sake, is somebody going to take charge of this meeting or are we going to sit here staring at each other all afternoon?"

Azzato cleared his throat and stared across the

MANIPULATION

table at Jackson Strawbridge.

"Our Co-chairman Mr. Strawbridge had a one-on-one meeting with Patrick Brady Sunday in Washington. He informed me regarding their discussion on Sunday evening and asked that I keep his confidence so that everyone could hear the outcome of that discussion from his lips. I did, however, e-mail all of you on Monday morning suggesting that you retain personal counsel to review your options prior to tomorrow's meeting. I trust you have done so. Jackson, the floor is yours."

For the next ten minutes Strawbridge recounted his meeting with Patrick Brady at the Mayflower virtually word for word from notes that he had taken before leaving the restaurant. He made no attempt to editorialize or embellish the conversation.

Liz was processing the information in her own special way. Brady-trained, she wasn't bogged down by what Strawbridge was saying but what was behind his words. More importantly, what was behind Brady's words to Strawbridge. She had watched Brady negotiate for five years and he never allowed his adversary to know what he was really thinking. Brady's style was to obfuscate his endgame, using misdirection and an Oriental inscrutability. There's no way he's going to walk away and turn his company over to these obvious lightweights, she reasoned. Why had it taken her this long to see so clearly what a serious mistake she was making? As her steel-trap mind was clicking away she noticed that Sue Jamieson was 'engaging' with Strawbridge; hanging on every word, asking inane questions, and overdoing the body language 'thing'.

In spite of her iron self-discipline Liz felt her

mind begin to drift as her gaze turned outside to the moss-covered oak trees randomly clustered together, or sometimes growing in straight lines. She blinked, though, when she noticed, in the middle of the front lawn of the plantation house, a solitary magnificent oak that appeared to be standing with its arms folded......staring into her soul, asking her what she was doing hanging out with these colossal assholes.

* * *

Tuesday
6:00 p.m.
Charleston Naval Base

Norman Franks had concluded his staff meeting and his team was busily organizing the software, preparing the simulator, and laying out the various components for the Board demonstration on Wednesday. DiStefano had insisted that the entire package be laid out so that the directors could closely examine each component: pulse cannons, laser guns, exoskeleton, eye-piece, helmet, flat panel screens, drones...even the network communications gear and integrating software discs. It was clear to Franks that they wanted to put on a real dog-and-pony show for the directors. Obviously there were those who questioned the efficacy of the technology. He wondered if rumors had gotten around based on the specific problems they had experienced at White Sands. If so, why had DiStefano insisted that the new deci-

MANIPULATION

sion support system...the Artificial Intelligence...*not* be included in the demo? In fact, they had made terrific progress in adapting AI to the Land Force Warrior Program over the last week and Floyd was confident that they were getting close. Macklin and Grossman had contributed significant input to the system's analysts and technicians in the preparation of the many scenarios that comprised the current strategic protocols. They ran simulations twice a day and the decision support efficiency score had jumped from 63% to 92%, creating a growing confidence that they were nearing the success rate required to satisfy the Joint Chiefs. He couldn't, therefore, understand DiStefano's reasoning. Not only was he adamant that it not be demonstrated, he even insisted that his security personnel remove the Artificial Intelligence and bubble technology software from the premises. Go figure. He hated politics.

* * *

8:30 p.m.
Lowcountry Bed and Breakfast
Aiken Street
Historic District
Downtown Charleston

Brady, DiStefano, and Whitfield had pored over every detail. There was a definite calm in the high-ceilinged nineteenth century living room as DiStefano poured scotch all around. He and

Whitfield were limiting themselves to two glasses each. They were joining the operating team later in the evening and would be out-of-pocket for the duration. DiStefano and Brady each had disposable cell phones to be used only on an emergency basis.

* * *

At 5:00 p.m. the group of dissidents decided to break until eight o'clock when they would reconvene for a working dinner in the cypress-paneled dining room overlooking the tidal creek where barges once ferried the rice crop into the Port of Charleston for shipment to London. Everyone but Liz beat feet to the old game room in the back of the mansion that housed a heart-pine bar and wine cellar. There was still business to be conducted and all were promoting their own contributions to the soon-to-be-reorganized company as a means of enhancing their pieces of the pie. They were dancing over Patrick Brady's grave as if his funeral were already over, or, at the very least, as if his wake had begun. Liz judged the celebration to be premature, as they hadn't the slightest notion regarding Brady's ability to counterattack. And, most assuredly, her Boss was not going to allow this to unfold as planned. She felt the burning in her cheeks as they railed against Brady, calling him every name in the book. She wondered whether it was too late to get to Patrick. She desperately needed to contact Bridie and confess what she knew. She was running out of time.

MANIPULATION

Craving some fresh air Liz strolled through the sedate and very formal English gardens out to the row of semi-restored slave quarters situated between the massive oaks and the patchwork of cotton and rice fields bordering the tidal creek. It had been a sad day indeed for the natives of West Africa when the Americans learned how to plant and harvest rice. It was a crop that required cheap labor to maximize profits and thus slavery found its way to the Americas. The West Africans understood rice, and sugarcane as well, and were captured and sold to the American South, South America, and, of course, the cane-rich Caribbean. The slave quarters were built using red bricks produced by the slave tenants who had a quota of 12,000 bricks per day at the Wellspring Plantation. According to the plaque adorning one of the old, traditional kilns, these very same bricks were used to build Fort Sumter in the late 1830's.

As Liz Turney wandered around the grounds lost in the history and lore of Wellspring, she noticed an attractive young African-American man dressed in 19th century clothes approaching her from the opposite direction. He greeted her with a warm smile and introduced himself as Thomas, a permanent member of the Wellspring staff, whose job entailed educating visitors and guests about Wellspring's history, in general, and Gullah culture, specifically. He walked with Liz and began to explain some of the historical highlights of Charleston and the development of the local Gullah way of life.

"You see," said Thomas, as he pointed to the residual rice and cotton crops, "the work was done in the fields, but the culture was developed up here in these quarters as African animism, Creole language and customs, and Christianity collided and formed a culture called Gullah."

Liz was captivated as Thomas digressed into the highly animated, lilting and singsong patois of a Gullah storyteller – whose stories, he said, were told to pass along life's lessons to the children of the slaves.

"Thomas, I can't tell you how much I have enjoyed our walk," she said, as they found themselves eventually back in the gardens adjacent to the Plantation house.

"Miss Turney, the pleasure has been all mine," he said with a theatrical bow. "I have a thought. You know, tonight I am conducting a ghost tour of the plantation. Would you care to meet some of Wellspring's ghosts?"

"Ghosts! Thomas, you've got to be kidding me," replied Liz.

"Oh, no ma'am. I couldn't be more serious. I assure you it will be an experience you will never forget."

"What time do these ghosts receive visitors?" asked Liz with a smile. She was beginning to think Thomas had an ulterior motive.

"Only at midnight," he replied…"and it's very important that you don't mention this to any of your colleagues…Wellspring's ghosts get nervous around crowds."

"Oh, I'm sure they do," said Liz. "Well, Thomas, you seem like a gentleman…so I'd be delighted to accompany you on your ghost tour. Where shall I meet you?"

"Right here at midnight sharp, Miss Turney," he replied as he left with a smile and a wave.

MANIPULATION

* * *

During dinner the dynamics had changed dramatically from the afternoon's meeting. It was clear that Azzato and Strawbridge had cut a deal and Azzato had evidently become the CEO-apparent.

Liz calculated to herself that Azzato had played his cards well, convincing Strawbridge that his four votes trumped him regardless of Strawbridge's stance. From that moment on it was all about the money. If she had been the one negotiating with Strawbridge, she would have tied his payout to the effectiveness of his negotiations with Brady.

Sue Jamieson was at Azzato's right, clearly the guest of honor. "I wonder what Azzato promised her," thought Liz. It was obvious that Sue had jettisoned their partnership and was operating strictly in her own best interest. She should have seen this coming.

Once the details of the Board meeting were agreed upon, Liz excused herself, telling the others that she wasn't feeling well. They barely noticed her leaving.

The old Ivies had played her like a violin until she had delivered the fourth vote in the person of Sue Jamieson, and then dropped her like a hot potato. At this point she completely discounted the commitments made to her by Johnstone. "What a fool I've been," she moaned to herself as she flopped on the bed in her upstairs guest room. She really did have a terrible headache and was beginning to feel sick to her stomach. **"What a goddamn fool!" She decided tonight was not going to involve** a ghost tour with Thomas after all, so she took a Valium, turned off the light and fell asleep with her clothes on.

CHAPTER FIFTEEN

12:15 a.m.
The morning of the Special Board Meeting

Soon after the grandfather clock in the foyer of the plantation house struck midnight, Liz was awakened by a tapping on her bedroom window. She was startled, drugged, and disoriented as she jumped out of bed but immediately recognized Thomas's smiling face beckoning to her to open the entrance to the outside balcony. Her adrenaline was outpacing her judgment as she opened the door admitting Thomas into her room. She sure as hell was wide awake now.

"Miss Turney, I'm sorry to have disturbed you but I don't want you to miss your ghost tour," said Thomas, bestowing his highly effective smile.

"I'm terribly sorry but I have to stand you up, Thomas. I'm really not feeling well tonight."

"Miss Turney, our mutual friend, Bridie Donaghue would vouch for me and strongly recommend that you place your trust in me this evening."

Liz was stunned by the realization that Bridie Donaghue had orchestrated this complex charade. "If Bridie is behind this I do trust you and your motives, but I am truly out of sorts and incredibly confused at the moment."

"It so happens I have just the thing," he said as he pulled a reefer out of his shirt pocket explaining that it contained a special Gullah herb guaranteed to create instantaneous attitude adjustment.

In spite of herself Liz smiled as she accepted a hit and took the pungent smoke deep into her lungs.

"Wow," she said as she exhaled. "What was that?"

MANIPULATION

"I told you it's a special Gullah herb," replied Thomas, with a wink. "The spirits are very sensitive and don't show up if the vibes aren't right."

They finished the joint outside on the balcony. Liz couldn't believe how relaxed she was. "Man, did I ever need this," she thought to herself smiling into Thomas's handsome face. "This is definitely the best pot I've ever had," she confided.

Thomas took Liz by the hand and led her to the side of the balcony where he helped her navigate the fifteen-foot drop on a sturdy wooden ladder. He took her by the hand as they retraced their path from earlier that night and began to stroll past the oaks, heading towards the most distant of the restored slave quarters.

"Let me give you a little background about some of our more famous ghosts," said Thomas. He spoke in an uncharacteristically serious tone and Liz hung on every word. The scene was surreal and she was completely stoned, to boot.

"Our most famous Gullah ghost was hung by a mob two years after the end of the Civil War. James Runyon was a freed slave who stayed on at Wellspring as a sharecropper. James was a handsome and engaging chap, much like myself from what I understand. In any event, he was caught with a white woman on a night like this and strung up on that very oak tree." He pointed to a solitary oak near one of the slave quarters off to their right.

In her mind's eye Liz could see James swinging from the heavy low branch as a crowd of white-robed apparitions stood silently by with their torches casting horrible shadows on the acorn-laden ground. She was feeling the immediacy of the surroundings and the story. Goose bumps formed on her arms and neck and chest.

Thomas interrupted her reverie as he led her deeper into the row of slave quarters. As they walked further from the plantation house Liz noticed that there was no moon and she could barely see two steps in front of her. She felt like she was floating as Thomas began to tell her the story of a British general who was poisoned in the original plantation house and left to die in agony in the most remote of the slave quarters. Thomas took her hand and pointed it thirty yards down the path that connected the slave cabins and she saw a torch lighting the inside of the last of the shacks.

According to her guide British General Jonathan Coleridge commandeered Wellspring as his temporary headquarters in 1779 when Cornwallis was fighting his way northward. The General took not only the Wellspring Plantation but the lady of the house as well. Mary Smith Johnson was a beautiful woman, devoted to her husband, currently fighting from the swamps as part of the South Carolina militia. They had been successfully ambushing Cornwallis's supply trains delaying his intended advance. A magnificent example of southern womanhood, Mary Johnson shared her bed with the well-mannered General Coleridge at night and systematically poisoned his tea with the toxic blossom of the oleander during the day.

"So, you see Liz, Wellspring is well-populated by the dead." Liz was completely absorbed as Thomas led her toward the doorway, still backlit by the flickering of a torch. As the shadows danced in the torch's strobe, Liz fantasized that she saw the silhouette of the long-deceased General in his tri-cornered hat and silk waistcoat. Thomas gently

MANIPULATION

pushed her through the doorway as he backed away. Liz's heart nearly stopped beating as she made eye contact with the dead British General who bore an uncanny likeness to Patrick Fortune Brady. He smiled as he opened his arms saying, "The rumors of my death are obviously greatly exaggerated."

* * *

At 2:30 a.m. container #568234, in the hold of a Chinese cargo vessel, was opened by Tony DiStefano and Rahnajat. The inside resembled the bay of a C130 cargo plane. A dozen well-armed, dark-clothed soldiers shared the rectangular space with inflatable rafts, custom-engineered outboard motors, stacks of C4 explosives, small arms, and mobile grenade launchers. Against the back wall of the container a modified life support system was bolted to an aluminum framework. It contained an air supply, circulation system, water cooler, and a portable toilet facility.

A pile of prayer rugs competed with the remnants of a food supply for the little space left after accounting for the benches facing each other across the breadth of the container.

Within five minutes four inflatables were quietly heading north on the Cooper River towards the Charleston Naval Base. On shore, at the appointed hour, Cal Whitfield pulled his hand off the head of a lighted flashlight. He repeated the signal twice. The fast-moving rubber rafts glided to the dock with barely a sound as the operations team efficiently disembarked and moved with purpose towards the vacant barracks across the driveway from building #F3.

* * *

Liz Turney and Patrick Brady sat facing each other on a quilt on the makeshift mattress in the slave quarters of Wellspring Plantation.

"Patrick?"

"Liz?"

"What is happening here?" she asked.

"Circumstances are out of control, Liz. I want you to get out of town this morning," said Brady. This little uprising that my old friends have orchestrated has triggered a series of events that have assumed a life of their own. The genie is out of the bottle."

"You're scaring me, Patrick."

"It's good to be afraid. You have to trust me here. I want you to go back to Reston and run the company. No matter what happens at the Board meeting today the company will have to have strong leadership, and that means you." Brady took her hands in his.

They stared at each other in silence as Liz gave in to her emotions, trusting him completely. Well…….. almost completely.

"What do you want me to do?" she asked. Now that she had caught her breath the wheels in her mind were revolving again and triggering all the tripwires: danger, opportunity, greed…..you name it. Survival of the fittest. She couldn't help it if that was the way she was built. The foundation had always been there. Patrick Brady simply supplied the 'finishing touches'.

"I want you to go back to the office in Reston and wait to hear from me. Bridie has a file for you in my safe that contains instructions," replied Brady.

"You knew in advance how I was going to respond to you, didn't you Patrick?"

"I only knew how I felt. The thought of losing you became too painful to bear. I willed this to happen," he said. "Liz, you have to trust me. Before it gets light we have to get out of here and go our separate ways. Things will happen today that will change our lives forever."

"What will happen to us? I want to be with you. I've never felt like this, Patrick."

"This is new territory for me, Liz, but I love it. I love you."

"I love you, too, Patrick."

Even as she mouthed them, though, Liz was mindful that the same words meant different things to different people.

* * *

9:30 a.m.
Day of Board Meeting

Franks' team had off-loaded the Artificial Intelligence module to a bonded courier service hired by DiStefano for transport to the Zybercor offices in Reston, Virginia. It was six hours until the Board Meeting but everything was ready for the 'big show', so Franks sent half his team home for a couple days of R and R. He was pleased with the progress the team had made over the last few weeks and was confident that they would be in good shape for the all-important review next month. Floyd had done a terrific job interfacing the automated "smart" command module with the Artificial Intelligence. In essence the strategy coordinator for Tiger Team would "tune" the command module in advance of an engagement in conformance with the specific protocols...whether border maintenance, urban clean-up, cross-border incursion, or any of a dozen other applications. From that point forward the automated intelligence would take over unless and until there was an override issued by the Land Force Warrior commander and countersigned by the strategy coordinator.

The simulations had proven very interesting. After the pre-battle tuning had been completed, the impact on the enemy of a coordinated attack or counterattack was devastating. With minor exceptions, human intervention came in the form of a 'cease fire' command. For the first time in months Franks could take a deep breath without chest pain. Since all was ready for the 1600 hrs (4:00 p.m.) Board Meeting he headed for his bunk for some desperately needed shut-eye.

* * *

12:00 noon
Charleston Naval Yard

MANIPULATION

Tony DiStefano awoke with a start as his watch trembled on his wrist signifying that it was noon. The incursion would take place at exactly 5:45 as the workday ended on the Naval Yard. The Board would just be completing the demo and moving into executive session and the security detail for Building #F3 would be completing a shift change. Sunset was scheduled for 6:20 p.m. and the busy traffic pattern would make it difficult to reinforce the building and doubly difficult for first responders. If all went according to plan the operations team would be picked up under the cover of dusk by 7:15 p.m. Rahnajat had decided to suit up for the big game and was hunched over a schematic of Building #F3 with a half dozen men, each with a swarthy complexion and hard eyes.

* * *

Wellspring Plantation
2:30 p.m.
Day of the Board Meeting

Azzato was clearly in charge now as the team of co-conspirators wrapped up their dry run, packed, and enjoyed a late lunch before heading over to the Naval Yard for the Board Meeting. Liz Turney had left an e-mail for Azzato and Jamieson explaining that she was deathly ill and had caught an early flight back to Reston. They barely gave it a thought as they focused on the two principal objectives: one, getting rid of Brady; and two, taking over the company. Management and director agreements, resolutions, and press releases were stacked on one end of the table. Azzato and Strawbridge were huddled in a corner reviewing a spreadsheet while the lawyers put the finishing touches on Brady's separation agreement. "Cry havoc," thought Jacobs, "let slip the dogs of war."

* * *

3:15 p.m.
Downtown Charleston

Thomas Andrews picked up Patrick Brady in a non-descript early model Mercedes sedan. Brady was to arrive exactly at 4:00 p.m. Thomas, in turn, was to return to the bed and breakfast to await further instructions. After he had delivered Liz Turney into Brady's arms the previous night he had joined a security detail at Building #F3 and installed a high-tech camera at a specific location and then encased all but the lens in a lead shield provided by Cal Whitfield. DiStefano had issued the instructions personally. Thomas never asked questions. He was having a wonderful time.

* * *

The Special Board Meeting
Charleston Naval Yard
Building #F3
4:00 p.m.

MANIPULATION

The Board assembled precisely on time. Brady was in top form as he greeted everyone individually with a firm handshake, a winning smile, and knowing eye contact. All but Azzato broke off the greeting with a minimal amount of civility. Azzato matched Brady's grip as the two stared each other down like boxers touching gloves as they tensed for Round One.

"On behalf of Colonel Franks and his team, I'd like to welcome everyone this afternoon," said Brady as the directors took their assigned seats around a conference table placed in front of the area earmarked for demonstration purposes.

Chadel was sitting in a folding chair in the back of the room well removed from the conference table. Brady invited him to join the Board at the table in a gesture that appeared thoughtful and disarming. As Chadel pulled his chair up alongside Jacobs and Johnstone, Brady continued with his remarks.

"I realize that there are serious issues to be discussed in executive session, however, I'm sure that we all are interested in the status of our technology as a matter of primary concern."

"While we may have differences of opinion on who should run the company, we can all agree that the future of Zybercor is dependent on our current contract with the Pentagon. That contract calls for a major review conducted by a joint Armed Services Review Committee on November 15th. Our first order of business, therefore, is a status update..."

Jacobs couldn't help himself and interrupted... "I thought we needed a national security clearance to even be in this building."

Brady, seemingly perfectly relaxed, nodded as he responded, "You'll see in your director's file a copy of your clearances. Mike, you'll notice in your folder a disclaimer that you need to sign before the demonstration begins."

Strawbridge wondered how Brady knew that Chadel would be attending. Azzato noticed that DiStefano was conspicuously absent. Johnstone looked at Jacobs and wondered where the hell Liz Turney was.

Brady continued… "In the interest of time, I am going to turn the meeting over to Colonel Franks and his team. I'm sure I speak for the entire Board when I tell you how much we admire you and your team and appreciate the time and effort that has been expended here………Colonel Franks."

Norm Franks was seated on a folding chair at the front of the room with four members of his staff. He had no idea what was going on but he knew all was not rosy at Camelot. He dutifully got out of his seat and stood behind the lectern as he began the presentation.

"Good afternoon. I would like to direct your attention to the large plasma screen on my left. The visuals that you will see on this screen are identical to what we see in the large simulator in the back of the building. If we have time later you're welcome to sit inside the simulator and experience battlefield conditions."

Colonel Franks methodically took the Board step-by-step through a review of the components of the Land Force Warrior System from satellite to AWAC to artillery to Apache gunship to drone. With the support of his professional staff he pointed out that each modern weapon system component had its own version of "smart" technology. "The problem," he said, "is that they were designed and developed by discrete teams working in a literal vacuum." He reiterated that the role of Zybercor in the Land Force Warrior Program was threefold: one, to provide the wearable computer technology worn by the soldiers who were on the ground; two, to provide the network communications and systems integration that tied all of the components together into a seamless program; and three, to adapt all of the company's breakthrough work in laser technology to military application.

The highlight of the demonstration was Floyd Ratliff. He took the Board through the history of the program's maturation curve, from a 60% to a 90%+ efficiency and effectiveness rating, the threshold level required by the set of matrices imbedded in the Pentagon contract. He digressed, unfortunately, into a monologue on Artificial Intelligence that glazed most eyes but, otherwise, 'dumbed down' the language to a level that was clearly understood by his lay audience.

After Floyd completed his presentation, at Col. Franks' suggestion, he opened the floor to questions as directors refilled their coffee cups and Brady glanced at his watch with an uncharacteristic nervousness.

* * *

At exactly 5:30 p.m. Rahnajat and DiStefano synchronized watches with Cal Whitfield and the dozen other members of the team. The operation was very carefully choreographed to consume no longer than thirty minutes inside the building. The timetable called for the team to be back aboard the inflatables no later than 6:55 p.m., reloaded and heading for a rendezvous with the Chinese sub. Rahnajat realized that there had to be casualties to make room for laptops and gear stolen from the Zybercor lab. He and his two lieutenants had divided up the roster and shared responsibility for the fate of those who were expendable. They slipped out of the building and quickly and quietly made their way out of the barracks and then through the hole in the security fence created by DiStefano's staff.

* * *

As Ratliff fielded questions, Colonel Franks worked his way past the men's head to the room housing Macklin and Grossman. As expected one of DiStefano's security operatives was seated in the alcove viewing the screen that showed Macklin in his wheelchair in deep conversation with Lester Grossman. Franks poured the chloroform over his gloved left hand and efficiently dispatched the guard, carrying him inside once he had activated the button opening the door to the detention chamber. As previously planned, Grossman arranged the sedated guard under the covers of his bed as Franks wheeled Macklin through the alcove and out the back towards the building's loading docks. Grossman caught up as Franks completed the attachment of the mobile laser assembly on the steel plate under the right hand armature. He activated the power pack, patted Macklin on the back, looked at Grossman, smiled, and said, "You're good to go. I'll get back to you men later tonight." The three men exchanged salutes and hurried on their way. The loud humming noise coming from Macklin's wheelchair sounded deafening in the confined space of the loading dock.

* * *

At exactly 5:39 p.m., as DiStefano and Rahnajat prepared to breach Building #F3 through the rear entrance, DiStefano noticed a red pick-up truck driving away from the loading dock with a spray of gravel. The ops team proceeded through the unlocked door fanning out in two directions. Charges of C4 were placed strategically along both sides of the building as the black-clad ghosts worked their way towards the light and noise of the Board meeting. Whitfield personally placed a C4-loaded, timed satchel at the entrance of the sophisticated simulator. As the principal operation commenced, the other two diversionary activities were in place and ready for the signal from Rahnajat. The activation of the IED on the access road would, in turn, prompt two members of Rahnajat's team to launch a grenade attack on the detention center. The combination of those two events would create the chaos and distraction needed to execute the primary mission and extraction.

DiStefano was 'in his zone' and ready to play the supporting role of a lifetime.

CHAPTER SIXTEEN

The Breach

"So far so good", thought Norm Franks as he took a leak in the men's head. He wondered where Liz Turney was as he zipped up. He'd instructed his guys to clean the ladies' room until it sparkled and reminded them to put the fucking lids down when they were finished. Franks and his bride, June, had raised a son and three daughters so he was well trained in the arts of bathroom and table etiquette and could say the requisite 'yes dear' in five different languages. He had been away from home for long, strenuous stretches but this latest project with Land Force Warrior had been the most demanding of his career. He was seriously considering retirement as he headed back toward the meeting and wondered how he would ever be able to explain an early retirement to General Cadman, let alone justify the 'springing' of Macklin and Grossman.

* * *

Patrick Brady's nerves were tingling so furiously he fully expected to see twitches rippling under the surface of his skin. It was all he could do to hold it together as his adrenaline and cotachlorimine careened through his brain, hyper-activating both his nervous and muscular systems. He was thrilled by the intensity of the feelings and he couldn't wait to get an M16 in his hands. He had to consciously will himself not to look at the armament cabinet

MANIPULATION

ten yards to his right as he caressed the keys in the pocket of his custom-tailored suit. The directors were getting ready to take a break before going into executive session as the questions came to an end. Where the hell was DiStefano?

* * *

Azzato felt a sense of control and purpose far greater than anything he had ever experienced in academic life. He couldn't believe what he had been missing all these years. This was the real deal…..serious work…purposeful action. From now on he would play in the big leagues and make a difference. The Land Force Warrior exceeded all his expectations. He reflected with disdain on the endless debates and conversations that had characterized his life in the halls of the Woodrow Wilson School at Princeton University and the hopelessness of trying to impact a public policy that was riddled with corruption and self-interest. "Let's move this party along to executive session," he thought. It's time to retire Patrick Brady…the King is dead…long live the new King Lou. He chuckled as he repeated 'long live Lou' to himself, then assumed a distinguished and concerned look for the benefit of his colleagues. Nancy was going to love the restored colonials in northern Virginia.

* * *

Liz Turney had to connect through Charlotte and finally got back to Reston in the late afternoon. She was in a fugue state as the taxi pulled up in front of the Zybercor offices. The driver had to remind her to take the luggage out of the trunk as she fumbled in her purse to pay the fare. Like a well-coiffed guardian angel descending, Bridie Donaghue was there in a flash, dispatching the driver with two twenties and a "keep the change." She took Liz in one arm and her bag in the other as she steered them up the stairs, through the lobby and into the first available elevator. Bridie put her arms around Liz in a motherly hug as they made their way up to the twelfth floor.

* * *

Building #F3 had originally been built as a perfect rectangle. The south side of the building faced the Cooper River, directly across from the deserted barracks that had become the operations team's home for the last six hours. The road that separated the deserted barracks from Building #F3 had not been used for years. At exactly 5:30 p.m. Rahnajat and DiStefano would lead the main body across the street to initiate the operation at the back of the building, preferring to enter from one of the short legs of the rectangle, the one opposite the end in which the Board Meeting was being held. Upon entering, they would divide into two teams and work their way along the inside edges of the two long sides of the building. The north side of the building faced the balance of the Naval Yard and looked out over the guard post which was located at the entrance to the private parking lot where one could see the detention center and the access road. This direction had caused Rahnajat and DiStefano the greatest concern, and consequently, this was where the diversions would take place. The IED would blow a huge hole in the access road to inhibit first responders and the grenade launch on the detention center would occupy the makeshift security personnel within the Naval Yard, allowing Rahnajat's main group ample time to place their charges, gather all of the pertinent elements of the Land Force Warrior Program, dispose of the personnel, and cover the open area in the back of the building to allow the boarding of the inflatables. According to their best intelligence all of the personnel except Macklin and Grossman and DiStefano's security detail would be concentrated in the front of the building where the Board Meeting was being held. They would not fire the C4 charges until the Land Force Warrior apparatus had been carried out the back and the elimination of all personnel had been completed...and after Brady and DiStefano had been well insulated from the timed blasts that would destroy the building.

* * *

Tony DiStefano's breathing was deep and controlled as he led his team at a relaxed but steady pace, paralleling Rahnajat's squad on their path, along the opposite wall of Building #F3. The AK47 felt different in his hands from the standard M16, but the foreign rifle was not only necessary, but crucial.

* * *

As Franks rounded a corner walking back toward the Board Meeting he saw a group of darkly-clad and heavily-armed men carefully laying explosive charges as they worked their way towards the front of the building along the opposite wall. His brain engaged automatically. He froze even as his eyes picked up the movement of another group moving forward less than thirty yards away from him. He was not in their line of sight as yet, but would be soon if he didn't move. Unfortunately, he could not get to the front of the building without being seen unless he exited through the loading docks and doubled back using the front door. He knew what he had to do immediately. It was too late to get Macklin and Grossman involved as they certainly were off the base by now. He couldn't warn his staff or the Board without exposing himself and he had the key to the arms locker. He somehow had to warn his team, disrupt the intended attack, and then capitalize on the ensuing confusion to get to the arms cabinet. He quickly activated a fire alarm and sprinted across the ten-yard opening. DiStefano and his team, startled by the ringing klaxon, saw him but were too stunned to react. As the Colonel ran forward shielded by steel racks, he was shocked to hear in perfect English, "It's Franks, get him before he reaches the arms cabinet."

MANIPULATION

* * *

The high-security facility was equipped with a fire control system that broadcast the fire alarm internally and externally. The security staff at the building's entrance forwarded the alarm to the Charleston Fire Department, as instructed, several minutes after raising the gate to allow a local plumbing contactor, finishing a routine service call, to drive his red pick-up truck out of the facility. According to the security protocol one of the trainees contacted the duty officer at the Naval Yard; one ran post-haste to the building's front door located forty yards from the front gate; and the remaining guard stayed in the shed to direct the local fire department vehicles.

Seconds after the fire alarm sounded a huge explosion rocked the guard hut and a shock wave of hot air hit the remaining guard full force. Hardly had he recovered when the grenade launchers commenced firing on the detention center. Shit, he thought, there's nothing in the training manual that prepared me for this. He rushed into the shack and hurriedly called the duty officer as he looked around nervously for somebody to shoot.

* * *

Inside Building #F3 chaos reigned. The fire alarm system instantly activated the automated sprinklers in the ceiling sending a heavy spray covering every square foot of floor space. Brady's nervous system literally exploded. The nerve synapses, already highly activated by the surge of adrenaline, were instantaneously assaulted on multiple fronts. The sound of the klaxon was deafening. Water poured from the ceiling. Staff and directors lurched to their feet in alarm as Marine Colonel Norman Franks, breathing heavily and wild-eyed, appeared from behind the demo stage yelling for everyone to "get the hell out of here" as he headed, with reckless abandon, for the arms locker.

* * *

Strawbridge was the only person present, other than Franks, with military training. He immediately took charge and shepherded a very-welcome-to-be-led group of civilians toward the front entrance and the reception area where they had gathered in advance of the meeting. He pushed his herd ahead of him to be sure that everyone was accounted for. When he looked back he noticed that Patrick Brady had not moved from the spot where he had been standing between the conference table and the arms closet. Franks was fumbling for a key while the sound of small arms fire could be heard above the alarm system and bullets ripped through the shelving separating him from DiStefano's advancing team.

Strawbridge went into overdrive, focusing intently on the principal mission to get his charges out of the building to safety. They reached the outside wall just as the moon-faced security guard burst through from the foyer and took a fully-automated cluster of rounds center mass, blowing him back through the door from which he had just entered.

* * *

Once the fire alarm sounded and the water began cascading from above, Rahnajat calmly divided his troops into two groups; one to continue the deployment of demolitions, and the other to follow him and accelerate the attack. He reached the front entrance to the building as an armed security guard hurtled, ahead of him, through the front door. Rahnajat fired an automated burst at a distance of ten yards and then promptly collided with a petrified Mike Chadel, sending them both sprawling on the wet floor in front of the wide open door leading to the reception area.

* * *

It had been twenty years since Tony DiStefano had participated in a hostile live-fire operation; training and instinct took over but things were happening too fast to generate a measured response. Startled by the sounds of the fire alert system and distracted by the full effect of the sprinklers, he was too slow to respond to Franks as the colonel successfully negotiated the ten yards of open space and gained cover behind a wall of steel racks. It wasn't until after he barked the order to take him out that DiStefano realized his mistake and by that time his team was surging forward. Whitfield grabbed him by the arm telling him that they needed to complete the positioning of the C4 charges. Like Rahnajat, DiStefano divided his forces, leaving Whitfield the task of overseeing the demolition mission. As DiStefano rushed forward he was thinking how fucked up this perfectly planned strategy had become.

* * *

Patrick Brady was surprisingly calm as he joined Colonel Franks at the arms cabinet and reached for an M16 and inserted a clip of ammo. The initial surge of adrenaline subsided as he instantaneously adjusted to his new role. Like a skilled method actor, Brady settled into the script as if he was born to it. He remembered everything DiStefano had told him from camera angle to line of fire. O.K., he was going to have to improvise..... but shit happens. This was just like business, he thought. No amount of planning can ensure certainty in human affairs. According to DiStefano's script he was supposed to be alone and standing to the side of the arms cabinet with a clear line of fire facing the north wall of the facility. According to DiStefano's script he was to exchange fire with a team of terrorists who had attacked the building to steal the Land Force Warrior technology...all under the watchful eye of the lead-encased camera installed by Thomas Andrews the night before. According to the script DiStefano would be beside Brady, but just off-camera, stage-managing the action including the very delicate part of putting a clean round from an AK47 through the meaty part of Brady's shoulder at just the right time. As Brady processed the reality of the chaos against the precision of the plan he knew exactly what he needed to do to save the script. He stepped out of the range of the camera's eye and used the butt of the M16 to knock Franks out cold from behind as DiStefano burst through the opening between the steel racks and the outer wall.

* * *

The scene in front of Brady and DiStefano was a maelstrom. While Rahnajat struggled to disengage himself from a frantic Mike Chadel, automatic weapons fire from the other three operatives of the attack team took out the three old Ivies in a spray and splatter of blood and brain matter. America's military lost one of its most talented technical minds as Floyd Ratliff went down in a hail of gunfire along with the balance of Franks' staff. They had worked together for months and died together in seconds. Sue Jamieson threw up her hands a millisecond before being slammed by half a dozen steel-jacketed bullets from an AK-47 and T. Jackson Strawbridge died with a look of absolute disbelief, staring into the eyes of his killer as he ran headlong back towards the conference area. His last conscious thought was that he had certainly picked the wrong team as the image of Patrick Fortune Brady, firing an M16 into his chest, faded into nothingness.

***

DiStefano fired a short burst into Franks' midsection 'off-camera' while the balance of his team loaded two dollies with software, laptops, and prototype apparatus from the demonstration area. They would utilize the manpower from the demolition teams to lug the Land Force Warrior components out the back of the building and down to the inflatables, all in the growing cover of darkness. Whitfield was riding herd on that part of the operation. Meanwhile DiStefano took off his balaclava and replaced it with a grey sports coat that he had hidden earlier. The coat was a match for his black pants and turtleneck. He was scripted to play out the balance of this well-crafted scenario as Brady's trusted Director of Security.

***

Rahnajat gathered the three members of his rifle team before continuing the attack into the demonstration and conference areas. They had put headshots into the remnants of the Board of Directors of Zybercor, the security guard, and Franks' staff. He put a full automated burst into Chadel even though the serrated blade of his knife had finished the job quite effectively while they had struggled to disentangle on the wet floor. He assigned one gunman to watch the foyer and moved out of sight with the remaining two, awaiting DiStefano's message on his hand-held that the operation was ready to move to the next stage. Rahnajat checked his watch and was pleasantly surprised that the operation was right on schedule in spite of the unexpected chaos created by the alarm, sprinklers, and subsequent series of events. His reverie was interrupted as DiStefano's voice came over the walkie-talkie cell phone informing him that the area was cleared and the combined teams were moving the apparatus out the back of the building. This was Rahnajat's signal to order the remnants of his rifle team to rush across the open area to join DiStefano and Brady for what they had been told was a mop-up of the operation. They were hit from the front with M16 fire from Brady as Rahnajat provided insurance with back shots from his pistol. The plan was now for him to place the balance of the C4 against the nearest pillar and a thirty-second, lesser charge, caked in thermite, in the foyer. That charge would block the entrance and simultaneously initiate the timing sequence for the other charges designed to bring down the entire building.

* * *

Brady continued firing for the benefit of the camera after the two members of Rahnajat's rifle team went down in a heap with eyes wide open in shock. DiStefano calmly aimed the AK47 as he mouthed to Brady, "This is going to hurt but remember to keep firing." He clicked off one shot from an angle that represented the direction from which Rahnajat's rifle team would have fired. It hit

Brady perfectly in the meaty part of his left arm. As his Boss spun around with the impact of the bullet, DiStefano checked his watch. They had twenty seconds to go before the series of C4 explosives detonated. That gave another ten to twelve seconds of camera time for Brady and then a quick dash to the cover of the heavily-protected bunker inside a steel container left over from the packing project that had transferred the Artificial Intelligence programs to Reston the day before. The structure of this quadrant of the building should remain unaffected by the strategic placement of the C4, but just in case, he had instructed his security detail to leave an additional steel container four feet wide by ten feet long in the storage area behind the arms closet.

* * *

Brady's arm seared with pain but he recovered his balance and proceeded to empty two additional clips at the phantom enemy. The sight of his own blood gushing from the wound below his shoulder only inspired his performance as he delivered the final seconds of his role with great aplomb.

DiStefano disabled the camera, with eight seconds remaining before the chain of detonations were to trigger, and hurried Brady over to the protective container as first one, and then a series of thunderous explosions, tore Building #F3 to shreds and hammered his eardrums as the sound waves cascaded off the steel inside of the open container. **"Shit," he thought, "you just can't think of everything."**

CHAPTER SEVENTEEN

The first responders were delayed for more than an hour by the tangle of traffic and confusion as Building #F3 burned intensely; the combination of C4, thermite, and construction material caused a withering conflagration. Amidst the chaos rumors were legion. Initially there was speculation that the target of what was perceived as a terrorist assault was the detention center, housing terrorists captured "off the battlefield" including the Shoe Bomber, John Walker Lind and domestic Al Qaeda cells captured in the sweep of 2009. However, it became clear that the attack on the detention center was a diversion and the real target was a top secret facility housing the Land Force Warrior Program, a highly-touted breakthrough in military technology that was to be implemented in the new Middle East deployment scheduled for early 2010. It now appeared as if the Land Force Warrior would be deployed to the Middle East much sooner rather than later.

CNN, Fox, ABC, and NBC arrived thirty minutes after the first responders; camera crews and 'piece-to-camera face men' jockeying for position. Ari Rendel hit the media lottery. He was in Charleston on vacation when he got the call from CNN's programming chief and told to get to the Navy Yard ASAP. While he was getting a touch of make-up, the CNN business people were trading for some early video shot by the local ABC affiliate. CNN was negotiating from a position of real strength. Somehow they had gotten their hands on a security camera from inside the building that captured Zybercor CEO Patrick Brady in a pitched gun battle with black-clad assailants.

"Reporting live from the Naval Yard in Charleston, S.C., I am Ari Rendel and this is CNN. Behind me is a scene we're used to seeing in Baghdad, Beirut, Israel, or the Gaza Strip. Today, however, the Middle East has come to the resort community of Charleston in the form of an attack on a top-secret military installation by a terrorist group claiming to be Al Qaeda. We are awaiting confirmation from FEMA and Homeland Security, but our sources tell us that there have been a significant number of military and civilian casualties including former U.S. Senator T. Jackson Strawbridge, co-chairman of Zybercor Corporation. Apparently the attack occurred during a Zybercor Board meeting as the company was preparing to release its breakthrough technology to the Pentagon for deployment in the Middle East. Concern is becoming widespread that the Land Force Warrior system has gotten into the hands of those against whom it was intended to be used. We will now cut to some footage taken from inside the facility during the attack. The man firing the M16 is Zybercor CEO Patrick Brady."

* * *

DiStefano took full advantage of the noise level inside the Bell helicopter to whisper in Brady's ear, just out of earshot of the trauma docs and EMS personnel.

"I shit my pants when that fucking fire alarm went off," said DiStefano as Brady craned his neck to hear and then grimaced in pain. The shot of morphine had kicked in, however, and he was beginning to function better. He asked DiStefano, "Have you got a read on the media spin, Tony?" Brady knew that his entire plan was contingent upon perceptions created by the media in the first hours of the crisis.

"It looks as if we're in good shape so far," replied DiStefano. "The camera we installed survived the blast and Thomas got it to CNN. It's running every fifteen minutes. You looked like John Wayne out there." DiStefano noticed the dilation in Brady's eyes as he waited for the next question. "What're the headlines?" It was important that people perceived this to be a terrorist attack aimed at disabling a new high-tech military application. Brady made it abundantly clear that the plan had to be perceived as "an act of God." The *'force majeure'* clause triggered a payout under his new insurance policy that was an absolutely crucial ingredient in his overall plan.

"Speculation thus far is just as we anticipated," replied DiStefano. He backed up to allow the doc to start the IV in Brady's arm. He waited patiently as the oxygen mask snapped into place behind his boss's head before leaning forward to continue the conversation. "CNN and Fox are both blaming Al Qaeda. Rahnajat should have planted the same rumor at Al Jazeera by now, so I thing we're good there."

Brady nodded as he sucked in the pure oxygen and the morphine did its work. In truth, he felt great......never better, in fact. He loved it when a plan came together.

"Tony, call Bridie and tell her to give Liz the envelope out of my safe. We need to move fast, now, to take advantage of the environment the media has created for us. Tell Liz I want her to pull out all the stops." In spite of the pain and the effect of the medication Brady was alert and focused and something didn't seem right with Tony. "What's the matter with you? You look worried."

DiStefano had just flashed back to when he called out Franks' name as he ran to the front of the building. He knew better than to withhold that information from Brady. If Franks came out of the coma it could ruin everything.

"Patrick, I think Franks recognized my voice during the attack."

A chill raced through Brady's body and the momentary euphoria of success turned into abject terror.

"He's in a coma now and the doc says he's not going to make it. But you know Franks." DiStefano was truly frantic now that he focused on the ramification of a recovering, lucid Franks.

"Yeah, Tony. I do know Franks and for your sake I hope he doesn't come out of this. He'd be likely to take this personally. Get me into a hospital suite and get Whitfield to manage things here, particularly a secure line to Reston. You've got other priorities right now. I think I'm going to take a little nap."

Brady nodded off as DiStefano felt another surge from his overworked adrenal glands and contemplated yet one more loose end that needed to be tied up.

* * *

Terrel Macklin and Lester Grossman sat in silence

in retired Marine Captain Jeff Stone's living room in his house on James Island, less than eight miles from the scene now dominating national television. Stunned at the events being reported on CNN they couldn't believe that the terrorist attack had occurred as they were making their escape from Building #F3. Captain Stone assured them that he had a friend at the Emergency Room at the Medical University of South Carolina Hospital and would try to get some information on Franks' status. The news report was not encouraging. Macklin prayed. To his righteous God.

* * *

The Chinese submarine was a Jinn class, the newest model in their Navy. Upgraded with the most sophisticated anti-detection devices ever designed, she had slipped in and out of the shipping lanes into Charleston Harbor completely unnoticed. The transfer of men and material took less than ten minutes as Rahnajat cracked the whip over his men and the Chinese sailors who were assisting them. He was starting to de-compress from the 'high' of battle and all he wanted was a dry, warm bed. Once his remaining men were on board and the Land Force Warrior technology and apparatus safely locked in a storage area, he put his head down and before the submarine submerged to its running depth of a thousand meters, fell fast asleep.

MANIPULATION

* * *

Cal Whitfield was on the roof of the MUSC Trauma Center as the Bell chopper carrying Brady and DiStefano landed. Franks had already been taken downstairs and was being prepped for surgery. DiStefano walked with Whitfield as Brady was wheeled down to the VIP suite. The bullet had gone cleanly through the fleshy part of his arm, up near the shoulder. He would have a lot of pain for a couple of days but would recover quickly. In the meantime there was a lot to do.

"Cal, I want you to stay here with the Boss. Get a secure line to Reston and keep this cell on you at all times." DiStefano handed him a disposable cell phone. "I have some things to attend to but I'll be in touch every two hours. We have a film crew coming tomorrow morning to produce a video for shareholders and employees. Try and get a few hours sleep. I'm out of here," said DiStefano as he took the nearest elevator to the lobby.

As DiStefano left the hospital he crossed Calhoun Street and ordered coffee, steak and eggs at the all-night diner. He desperately needed to clear his head and focus. After a couple of hits of the heavy, re-heated black coffee he used the speed dial to get Kauffman on his cell.

"Mark, Tony here. Just listen. I don't have a lot of time. Everything is on plan and on schedule. Rahnajat's technical guy is on the sub. He'll inventory the components of the system and double check everything with Huan's guy, who has set up a test lab, on board, for verification. I want you to go ahead and get the parties together to implement the agreement and transfer the funds. Now. Don't give me any details. Just get it done within the next forty-eight hours. Patrick's counting on you."

He didn't want to answer any questions from Kauffman so he hung up quickly and went to work on the steak and eggs, ordered more coffee, and fought through the bile as he contemplated his next move. For the first time he wondered whether it was all worth it.

* * *

General Walt Cadman had a clusterfuck of monumental proportions on his hands. He had actually hung up on the Secretary of Homeland Security rather than keep the President of the United States waiting. Like everyone else he was getting his information from CNN supplemented, of course, by the various military personnel on the ground in Charleston who, in most instances, were getting their information from CNN as well. Thank God the trauma doc treating Norm Franks was ex-military. While the news wasn't good, he could at least keep June Franks informed and promised to provide her and the kids with hourly updates from the hospital. For the first time in his career he was too shocked to function. It was 2:00 in the morning and the whole world seemed to be awake, except his own executive staff, who stumbled into the office looking like deer caught in the headlights and then, in turn, clustered in front of the television getting their information from CNN.

"General, Sec Def is on one and Senator

MANIPULATION

Kennedy on two...and the Chairman is on three... he's on his way in...and..."

General Cadman slammed his door, put his head in his hands and slumped over his desk as his well-ordered world spiraled into chaos.

* * *

Mark Kauffman hung up from Tony DiStefano, completed the e-checkout from his room at the Madison, packed his bag and took the elevator down to the lobby. He'd catch a cab to Dulles and then on to Cyprus by way of Frankfurt and Athens to meet with Huan and Rahnajat. He had a huge smile on his face as he dropped his divorce papers in the mailbox and climbed into the waiting taxi. This would be the last time he would ever fly commercial and, most assuredly, the last time he would ever grace the seat of a flea-infested cab with his ass of gold.

* * *

Liz had moved into Brady's state-of-the-art office and was using it, under his specific instructions, as the command center for the multi-pronged campaign he had devised. The letter Brady had prepared for Liz was very specific...ten pages of detailed instructions. Her first order of business was to preside at a general staff meeting, including all direct 'reports', the outside law firm, the public relations people, and investor relations. While Bridie was busy organizing the meeting Liz was converting Brady's instructions into specific management initiatives. In order to pull this plan off, the timing and sequence of events had to be perfect. Liz marveled at the brilliantly conceived and complex strategy as she pushed everything out of her mind and focused intently on implementing the job at hand. She was surprised that she was able to push the events in Charleston to the far recesses of her brain; almost as if they happened in a parallel universe where murder and mayhem were daily occurrences. In truth, none of the victims was without blame. They had played a game of high-stakes poker and lost to a far better player. She truly believed that they would have pulled the trigger themselves if they had had the guts. She remembered Patrick telling her that Strawbridge didn't have the balls to take him out and that Strawbridge was the only one with the power to strip him of his position. The more Liz thought about it the more she liked the Machiavellian approach to things. It was sexy and profitable........_if_ you could deliver the goods.

* * *

FBI Building
Washington, D.C.

The members of the hastily-assembled Task Force took their seats promptly at 6:00 a.m. in the counter-terror conference room at the J. Edgar Hoover Building. The President's National Security

MANIPULATION

Advisor, Megan Daniels, had brokered the deal with all the multiple agencies clamoring to control the top spot in the high profile investigation. It was agreed that Matthew Kilmer, FBI liaison to Homeland Security, would lead the investigation. But, in order to save face, the CIA, NSA, and State Department would have big seats around the table that Daniels would chair on behalf of the President. Her opening remarks captured the mood of the President, Congress, and the American people. She made it clear that time was of the essence. People......people on the street as well as people in high places...wanted answers and wanted them fast. She reiterated that Special Agent Kilmer was in charge and that the President would not tolerate turf wars on this one. Daniels sat down thinking she needed to get someone to feed the cats and bring her some fresh clothes. Kilmer took over the meeting wondering how a smart guy like himself could have gotten into this kind of a mess.

* * *

Tony DiStefano finally drifted off to an uneasy sleep, under an assumed name and with corresponding credit card, at the Holiday Inn Express three blocks west of the Medical University Hospital where Patrick Brady was resting quietly under fairly heavy sedation. Exhaustion took over but not before he had come to terms with what he had to do. There was simply no choice. He resigned himself to walking into Colonel Franks' room and injecting air bubbles into his IV with a standard syringe. **The** ensuing pulmonary embolism would take a few seconds; he would call a Code Blue and then get on with the rest of his life. And never, never, never look back.

CHAPTER EIGHTEEN

The Zybercor juggernaut was in high gear. Liz had just approved the 30-second TV spots. She instructed her communications people to rotate them on the Eastern seaboard and the important West coast markets. She was targeting the media, shareholders, analysts and, of course, the politicians both inside and outside of the Beltway. The TV spots were part of a multi-media campaign designed to bolster confidence in the marketplace and capitalize on the momentum created by the national media in the first twenty-four hours following the attack.

The Zybercor website was being updated twice daily and e-mails were being forwarded to the company's 43,000 shareholders. Each shareholder would have three direct communications in the next two days: a personalized auto-pen letter from Patrick Brady, an e-mail, and a video taped at his bedside in the Charleston Trauma Center. The objective was twofold: first, to stabilize the shareholder base and second, to mobilize individuals to contact their elected representatives to show their support for the company and to urge the Pentagon to move forward with the Land Force Warrior Program.

Liz Turney was the queen at the center of the beehive. She controlled the message, she pulled the strings, and she managed the various media. She had divided her legal team into two task forces: one to ride herd on the insurance company to effectuate the cash-in of the policy, and the other to commence the negotiations with the Pentagon to restructure the Land Force Warrior contract. She wanted to put both parties, Lloyd's of London and the Pentagon, on the defensive. Patrick had cautioned her that the worm could turn at any time and they had to move fast while public opinion was in their favor. To that end Liz had scheduled a steady stream of interviews...beginning with the national media's "Bedside with Patrick Brady" starting the next day. Brady would add his spin to the growing sentiment that the brazen attack by Al Qaeda could not go unpunished, and their arrogance had to be met with strength and resolve. His plan was to keep relentless pressure on the Pentagon to force them to restructure the Land Force Warrior contract. The Zybercor legal team was already in negotiations with the lawyers representing the Pentagon and the Joint Chiefs of Staff. They had leaked the vital information that the Artificial Intelligence modules were safely housed in the company headquarters in Reston, Virginia. It was imperative, they argued, that the AI be integrated into the system as soon as possible to create a qualitative advantage over the terrorist community who, even as they spoke, was at work to deploy LFW in the Middle East. They were building a compelling case that only Zybercor was in a position to respond to the crisis. The government attorneys were shocked as Zybercor's lead lawyer made the case that the new contract needed to be sweetened with better payouts and relaxed covenants. Even as they began to push back it was clear that Patrick Brady had them over a barrel. The Pentagon attorneys were desperate and only had one more card to play and they played it for all it was worth. Zybercor, they argued, was in a 'breach' position in connection with the current contract. Even if they were to concede that the terrorist attack was a *"force majeure,"* an act of God, Zybercor simply did not have access to the funding necessary to replace the system and meet the rapid deployment benchmarks. On that note both parties agreed that the negotiations were stalled and they adjourned for a four-hour 'cooling off' period. As the government's legal team withdrew to brief the Joint Chiefs, Zybercor's head lawyer rang Turney to get an update on the insurance negotiations.

* * *

Denham-American had a reputation as one of the most innovative of Lloyd's numerous syndicates. With a conservative one hundred and ten year history behind them, Denham, keeping abreast of the times, had recently begun to venture into the world of intangible asset insurance. They had made a killing in D&O insurance and shifted resources from there to intellectual property risk transfer when D&O pricing began to soften in 2007. By 2009 they had placed billions of dollars of insurance in the high tech, biotech, and computer software sectors and they were raking in the profits. They would **not** make money on Zybercor. Just a week after placing the insurance Denham found themselves at risk for 100% of the 'replacement value' of the Land Force Warrior technology in what was assuredly the most visible case of *'force majeure'* since the World Trade Center disaster in 2001.

Subsequent discussions with the company proved anything but collegial. The two principals working on the case for Denham-American referred to Liz Turney as simply 'the bitch' after only a day and a half of negotiations. They offered $1.2B and Turney held firm at $1.8B. She threatened them with a triple damage lawsuit if the settlement was delayed and Zybercor lost the Pentagon contact due to a lack of liquidity.

They concluded that they wanted 'the bitch' out of their lives as soon as possible so they requested authorization from Denham's Managing Director to prepare a draft for $1.5B payable to Zybercor Corp. and began preparing the final releases. 'The bitch' would take a billion five and like it. Or not.

* * *

Bridie Donaghue was in charge of organizing the vast amount of newspaper coverage as well as the electronic media and Internet. She had five young staffers sitting at workstations in the makeshift command center on the third floor. In between telephone calls from Himself she actually got some work done, providing Liz with hourly summaries.

"Mrs. Donaghue, it's Mr. Brady on the line." The young staffer covered the phone with one hand and continued knowingly…"Again."

"Your Lordship," said Bridie, with as much good humor as she could muster on three hours sleep. "I was getting concerned, your Eminence, that I hadn't heard from you for…let's see here…a full thirty-eight minutes."

"Tell me something good, my darlin' girl," replied Brady, completely oblivious to Bridie's sarcasm. "Liz won't accept my calls unless they're on the hour.

She says I'm driving her nuts."

"Well now, she is an extremely busy young lady, isn't she?" replied Bridie.

"Yes, yes. I know, I know. She seems to have a lot on her mind lately," said Brady. He was well aware that Bridie knew more than she was letting on but chose to keep it all business…at least for the next few days.

"Have we got any new poll results?" asked Brady. He knew that public opinion was critical to the next forty-eight hours. If he continued to drive the agenda, it was unlikely that the political machinery would be able to muster a rebuttal as long as the media spin stayed favorable. Knowing each other as well as they did, Patrick and Bridie sensed intuitively when to switch from 'stage Irish' patter to 'Uptown' no-nonsense English.

"Our on-line tracking update is coming across as we speak," said Bridie. "In the meantime the editorials are running in our favor eight to one. The liberal media is expressing standard rhetorical outrage at the attack but using the opportunity to rail against the redeployment of forces in the Middle East. The mainstream media supports a serious reprisal and the conservative media is demanding a strong, on-going military effort. Pretty much as you expected."

"And how is my image faring?" asked Brady.

"Why, Mr. Patrick 'Fortune Smiled on You' Brady, you could run for President."

"Ah, get away with you, that's a good girl. Gotta go. I have an interview with *60 Minutes*. Don't forget to tape all these interviews and call me back with the survey data."

"Break a leg," said Bridie as she collected

the update for Liz and thought to herself, for the umpteenth time recently, what a strange world she lived in.

* * *

When the government's legal team reassembled in the conference room there was a single piece of paper sitting on the table. In essence it documented the transfer of $1.5B to Zybercor Corporation's operating account at the Bank of America. The lead Zybercor attorney merely smiled and gently pushed his revised draft of a new contract across the table to his amazed adversaries.

* * *

Lester Grossman hated hospitals, blood, and sickness. His father had suffered from colon cancer before his grateful demise after a four year, pain-filled struggle. The odors in the ICU brought back all the memories associated with that difficult period but he relegated them to a far recess of his mind and resolved to focus on the mission Mack had given him. His job was to communicate with the Colonel. Franks was the only person who could shed light on the events at Building #F3 and Mack's intuition had alerted him that something was definitely stinky in Denmark.

Lester was informed that the two-hour surgery resulted in the removal of Franks' spleen and part of his large intestine. There was no additional major organ damage but the descending aorta was nicked and he had lost a lot of blood. Also there was considerable swelling of the brain caused by a blow to the back of the head generating concern among the doctors. Lester had conned his way into the recovery room with the help of the head nurse who was a friend of Captain Jones' wife. The Colonel was into his fourth hour post-op but Lester was prepared to wait for as long as was necessary. He shifted the .38 caliber pistol to his jeans pocket and settled into the chair at the foot of the bed as the heart monitor played its relentless, monotonous, yet life-affirming symphony of beeps.

* * *

Matt Kilmer was having a serious problem with the initial phase of the investigation. He had way too many resources tripping over each other in the cramped quarters of the U.S. Army Military Police Training Center across the street from the remnants of Building #F3. Each agency insisted upon on-site presence as the bureaucracies competed for space, computers, file cabinets, and coffee machines. The Training Center had lost two cadets: one inside the building and the other in the blast, and it seemed like all one hundred and fifty trainees had volunteered their services to the Task Force. He hadn't even been able to convene a staff meeting and he'd been in Charleston for half a day. The Crime Scene Team was bitching because their bags were lost, FEMA personnel were unloading from a van, and Matt was starting to experience the familiar early symptoms of a real ass-kicking migraine.

* * *

Tony DiStefano told Franks' doctors that Mr. Brady was very concerned about the Colonel and had instructed him to find out everything he could and report back immediately. The docs were only too happy to report that the surgery had gone surprisingly well and, though the patient remained in critical condition, they felt hopeful that he had a fighting chance. They showed DiStefano to the cordoned-off recovery room and his heart skipped a beat when he saw Lester Grossman through the glass wall, keeping a vigil at Franks' bedside. As if Grossman had been expecting him, he shifted in his chair, made eye contact with DiStefano, and let the latter see the handle of the pistol sticking out of the front pocket of his jeans.

* * *

Patrick Brady was listening intently as DiStefano relayed the details he had obtained from Franks' doctors and the subsequent sighting of one very alive Lester Grossman standing guard at the Colonel's bedside with a pistol in his pocket.

"You've got to get out of town and let me handle this," said Brady. "Have any of these guys seen Thomas?"

"No, I don't think so," replied DiStefano. He hadn't slept in three days if you didn't count the few restless hours the previous night, and was still heavily fatigued.

"We can take care of two issues at the same time. You take the company plane to Cyprus. I'll sleep a lot better if I know you're there. Kauffman should be arriving tomorrow afternoon to meet with the Chinaman and Rahnajat. You can see to that loose end while Whitfield and Thomas take care of our problems here. Macklin and Grossman have to be operating locally and Franks certainly isn't going anywhere, so we have stationary bait."

"Make sure things go as planned in Cyprus. Get the draft from the Chinese converted to a cashier's check and head straight to the Caymans. The plane will wait. Open the account with the central bank and take your twenty-five mill off the top and wait for me there. Tony, it's time for some R and R. You deserve it and I insist. Send Thomas to me and then get going. Now!"

DiStefano was too tired to argue. The Boss was right. Ten hours of sleep and some good food sounded like heaven.

"Okay, you're the Boss, as always. But are you sure things are O.K. here, Patrick? I feel guilty leaving you with a mess."

"Just a couple of loose ends here. No big thing. Whitfield and Thomas will do nicely. C'mon, these are your guys. Your plan worked to perfection. We won, big time. Now go! Call me from Cyprus."

They shook hands and DiStefano left the hospital room, wondering how Patrick Brady could look so good when he was feeling like shit warmed over.

CHAPTER NINETEEN

Cyprus is the third largest island in the Mediterranean - 65 miles west of Syria, 150 miles north of Egypt and 240 miles from the Greek island of Rhodes. It had been invaded by countless aggressors over 3,000 years due to its strategic location in the ancient trade routes. Modern Cyprus is 80% Greek and 20% Turkish and a very convenient place to meet if your embarkation point is Beijing or Tehran. For Mark Kauffman, however, the trip had been a nightmare. Arriving late in Frankfurt he missed his connection to Athens and had to charter a private plane to Cyprus or risk being late for the most important meeting of his life. He was seriously 'wired' by the time he de-planed at Nicosia Airport in the middle of the island; he then took a taxi the thirty-eight miles to Famagusta on the eastern tip. Huan had decided upon Famagusta for some very important reasons. First, he liked dealing with the Bank of Cyprus because an old friend from Oxford was a senior officer and he didn't want the funds traced to Chinese Intelligence. Second, it was convenient for Rahnajat. And third, he had a very competent operative *in situ* at a local winery and he would require his special talents to consummate the transaction. He instructed his man to arrange for a private residence in the Old Town near Othello's Tower. Huan had arrived the night before and was sipping some Commanderie St. John from the local KEO winery in Kyrenia as the sun crept overhead. Rahnajat and Kauffman would be arriving in several hours to finalize the deal that would guarantee China's oil supply for the next decade and solidify Huan's role as a serious player at the highest level.

MANIPULATION

The air smelled clean and fresh with just a hint of salt in the soft breeze coming in off the lazy blue sea.
It was going to be a beautiful day.

* * *

Liz was on a roll. She had always dreamed of being in the corner office calling the shots, but her imagination had been wholly inadequate compared to the actual feelings that accompanied the real power of her current position. Brady was still the CEO in name, and it was most assuredly his brilliant strategies that were at work, but she had her hands on the steering wheel and her feet on the gas pedal. Something unspoken and very subtle was occurring between her and Patrick Brady. While she couldn't pin it down it seemed more and more that he was transferring power to her on a permanent basis...it felt to her that their relationship was evolving into something more like a partnership than a mentor-protégée...the feelings filled her with a sense of purpose and promise unlike anything she could imagine....like an orgasm of the soul. Her senses were heightened and she was infused with energy when she should rightfully have been reeling from exhaustion. She asked Bridie to hold her calls, shut the door to his.....her office, closed her eyes and allowed herself to savor the essence of these new-found emotions. Lizzie, she thought, you could become quite accustomed to this.

* * *

Brady was completing his final interview of the day. A moment earlier Cal Whitfield had made eye contact and tapped the cell phone – something he wouldn't do unless the call was important. As the interviewer shook hands and the camera crew packed up, Brady took the cell phone and heard the news he had been anxiously awaiting. He closed the phone and motioned Whitfield over to his bedside. While he appeared circumspect he talked just loudly enough for the straining ears of the lingering press to hear the message.

"Cal, get hold of Liz and tell her the Pentagon just agreed to the new contract and we have a billion and a half in new funds in the bank. Tell her I expect a very positive response from the market tomorrow and it's very important we keep this quiet." Brady knew this would be over the wires before his interviewer left the hospital. There was still plenty of time before the market closed.

* * *

Matt Kilmer had finally wrestled the investigation task force into place, after relying on Megan Daniels who had to knock some heads together in Washington that were way above his pay grade. He knew he wasn't going to make any friends in this assignment. As the shit ran downhill in sheets it was obvious that Kilmer was the trigger just as certainly as Daniels was the gun. He clearly let all parties know that there was only one gun at the table and he had all the bullets. In spite of the proliferation of bullshit they were actually getting some work done.

Kilmer was reviewing the first cut of the attack on a software simulator. Massive amounts of data had been loaded into the system overnight. The Crime Scene Team, working with five squads of investigators, processed hundreds of bits of information from in and around the building, including footprints, explosion remnants, and first-hand accounts. The software organized the data and time-sequenced various alternatives, after loading all the architectural blueprints and schematics of Building #F3. The system then prioritized the various options based upon the templates painstakingly developed, using the intelligence provided by the federal counter-terror community. Daniels had 'recommended' that Kilmer view the simulation in private, secure from other eyes. She didn't want any leaks and the best protection was single-source accountability... and that was Kilmer. He was instructed to report to her directly by secure line after his initial review.

Megan Daniels hadn't slept in more than forty hours. She had an amazing capacity to process information but her legendary stamina was waning and she knew she had very little time left before hitting the wall. The President was waiting to be briefed as she willed herself to concentrate on Kilmer's report.

"The attack was well planned and brilliantly executed," said Kilmer as he downed his third OxyContin of the day, desperately trying to delay the onset of a full-blown migraine. "It's astonishing how they pulled this off so quickly. According to the simulator they were in and out in under thirty minutes. The IED was detonated on the access road to create confusion and delay first responders at the same time that the detention center began to take fire. Obviously the Zybercor facility was the real target and we have to assume that they got everything they came for, because it's impossible to re-create any kind of inventory from inside the building."

"Was it a coincidence that the attack occurred at the same time as the Board of Directors' demonstration?" asked Daniels.

"I don't know for sure, but my instinct tells me that the attackers had inside information. It was just too slick." Kilmer had already initiated extensive background checks on the living and the dead with a special focus on the last sixty days. He checked his Day-Timer and noticed he had an interview scheduled with General Walter Cadman in half an hour.

Daniel's pulse quickened as she contemplated the magnitude of this kind of a breach of intelligence - treason at the highest levels. "Matt, do you have any idea how they got in and out so quickly?" she asked.

"Our best guess is by cargo ship. Over a million and a half containers per year come into the Port of Charleston and less than 5% are actually inspected. The Coast Guard and Navy have boarded every outgoing vessel leaving the Port within the last forty-eight hours but it will take the balance of the week to check every container. Don't hold your breath. We won't find anything. My guess is they came in on a cargo ship but left by submarine. It would be simple for a sub to slip in and out of the shipping lanes down here without being detected.

Trust me...these guys are long gone."

"What do you want me to tell the President, Matt?"

"Hell, Megan, I'm just getting started here. Tell him it's vintage Al Qaeda. Professionally planned and implemented to hit us where it hurts the most. I wouldn't talk about a Benedict Arnold yet. Let's wait until we have something more concrete or we'll have a prairie brushfire of damaging speculation and no facts. We run the risk of losing credibility before we even get started."

"All right. Keep me posted." As Megan walked from the Situation Room to the Oval Office she wondered if she could stay awake long enough to do some digging over at the Pentagon.

* * *

Franks had not gained consciousness but the doctors still expressed guarded optimism. DiStefano was on his way to Cyprus. Brady was preparing for the short flight to Washington to attend the State Funeral of his fallen colleagues, and to spend some important one-on-one time with the President. He had a lot on his mind. Thomas was keeping track of Franks' progress and Whitfield was busy trying to locate Macklin. "Too many glass balls in the air," he said out loud as he got Bridie on the secure phone and told her to get the Chinaman on the line. "Too damned many loose ends".

* * *

Three days after the attack on Building #F3, hordes of politicians and media began to arrive for the State Funeral to be held on the grounds of Arlington Cemetery. The surviving family members of those slain met privately with the President at Camp David and were then escorted by the Secret Service to the gravesites for the public memorial service.

The President's remarks were brief as he expressed the condolences of "a grateful nation" for "their ultimate sacrifice" as if their deaths occurred on the battlefield in a foreign war. When questioned by the media afterwards, he explained that, indeed, these men and women had died for their country in a war that had found its way to our shores. He articulated the anger felt by the American people and the outrage of his Administration, tempered only by the solemnity of the occasion and the respect shown for the departed patriots. He was effusive particularly in his praise of former Senator T. Jackson Strawbridge, who had survived two tours in the jungles of Vietnam only to be gunned down by cowards, "as he was laboring in the service of his company's shareholders and enhancing the national security of its citizens".

Standing stoically by the President's side, Patrick Brady finally broke into tears during the Strawbridge eulogy as he bowed his head and gripped his sling-shrouded wounded shoulder with his right hand.

Brady rode with the President as they departed Arlington Cemetery. During the short ride back to the White House he informed the nation's Chief Executive that he was seriously considering stepping down from Zybercor and establishing a foundation dedicated to the development of technologies that could create "an ongoing series of strategic advantages" in the war on terror. After assuring the President that Zybercor was in capable hands, he played his trump card. He promised to allocate the entire proceeds of the sale of his stock holdings in Zybercor to this New Foundation that would bear the President's name. The two men shook hands and made a solemn commitment to one another – henceforth joined at the hip, to dedicate their lives to their country. The President agreed to host an annual fundraiser for their New Foundation and insisted that the press conference announcing the launch be held in the Rose Garden. He was the one that suggested Brady receive the Medal of Freedom, the most prestigious non-military award the country could bestow on a citizen. As they sat in comfortable silence Brady wondered if this would be the right time to discuss the President's intervention with the Securities and Exchange Commission to procure a waiver that would allow Brady, as the sole surviving Board member, to implement the reorganization of Zybercor **and** un-restrict his stock so that he could cash out while the market was hot. **With $3B in cash from the Chinese to fund his personal expenses, the least he could do was dedicate his Zybercor stock proceeds to the New Foundation. What American hero could do less?**

CHAPTER TWENTY

The Buona Fortuna had docked at the Charleston Marina the day after the tragic Board Meeting at the Charleston Naval Yard. Now that Brady was up and about, the more-than-adequately-equipped yacht became his base of operations. His first real taste of the good life in quite a while came in the form of a sunset cruise with Liz Turney the night before the planned reorganization of Zybercor. With a little tweak from the White House the Securities and Exchange Commission issued a corporate governance waiver allowing Brady and the new CEO of Zybercor to initiate a restructuring that included the naming of a new board and a profitable exit for Patrick Fortune Brady. In the aftermath of the terrorist attack the Brady saga played beautifully in the media. The near-death experience, coupled with the loss of so many close associates, had fundamentally altered his world view. He was going to dedicate himself completely to the patriotic duty of making America more secure. To that end his New Foundation, funded entirely from the proceeds generated from the sale of his Zybercor stock, would focus on the development of new technologies and applications that would strengthen American security domestically and internationally.

Far from the prying eyes of the paparazzi and national media that had been covering his every move, Brady relaxed with three fingers of Laphroaig on the upper deck of the Buona Fortuna, waiting for Liz to join him for cocktails before dinner. *Madam Butterfly* set the mood as the sun began its descent.....a perfect time....a perfect place... a perfect day.

"Don't you look as if the whole world is at your feet?" said Liz with a dazzling smile as she came on deck. Brady nodded approvingly. Her beauty stunned him into silence. All those years she had been with him and he'd never seen her like this. It was as though she were evolving before his eyes into an image of the perfect woman: beautiful, smart, sexy, and.......tough. Much tougher than he ever imagined.

"Be careful what you say. Remember what the Greek Gods did to humans who aspired to be one of them," replied Brady, smiling, but thinking also that his wings, as well, could melt if he ventured too close to the sun. There were still a few issues dangling out there but he didn't want to dwell on those tonight. Franks was still in a coma, Whitfield hadn't a clue as to Macklin's whereabouts, and the chief investigator, Matt Kilmer, wanted to meet with him the next day. Well, that was for tomorrow. This was now.

"I suggest you wear something a little less revealing at tomorrow's press conference," he said. "The Zybercor shareholders are fairly conservative, you recall."

"I'll dress for them tomorrow. I thought I'd dress for you, tonight," she said as she helped herself to a glass of champagne and seated herself across from Brady in a lounge.

"Business first, Liz. Remember our deal. How are things looking?" he asked.

"I'm glad you decided to have the media event down here," said Liz. "The President can't wait to attend now. With the Naval Yard as a background, the focus will be on the New Foundation and the business side will merely be ambient noise. Nobody will care about the details. All the questions will be directed to you and the President. I'll get off scot-free as the new CEO and be able to get my 'sea legs', to borrow one of your nautical terms, before having to deal with the business press." She smiled and raised her glass.

"It won't take long for the world to realize that Zybercor will be a big winner under your leadership," he replied. Liz will build the company the right way, he thought.

"So you say. You taught me everything I know but I still don't think you taught me everything you know…..you know? What will I do when I get confused about all those complicated issues? Will you still be available to advise me?" Liz was ready to take this to the next level but she would take her time. Life was really good and there was no need to rush things.

"You do know that part of mental toughness is taking the time to recover. I'd be offended if you didn't take some R and R with me. I hope you'll accept a Board seat on the New Foundation." Brady was an avid fisherman and knew that choosing the right bait and playing the fish was great sport. He also, however, was fully aware that he was playing this fish for the long haul and had no intention of a quick 'catch and release.'

"Getting back to tomorrow…" Liz could play the game as well as Brady. "Your stock was on the block today so you should be cashed out by the end of…"

Brady interrupted her, "At today's price what I unloaded nets me about a billion one, plus or minus.

I'd rather not cash out completely until after the press conference tomorrow; that way I can duck any questions about money."

"O.K., but do you mind if I ask how you're going to sustain this rather lavish lifestyle if all your Zybercor stock proceeds are going to the Foundation?" she asked. Part of the deal they made at Wellspring the night their relationship changed was that Liz would trust him implicitly and not ask any questions. He told her he would explain everything, but later….. when he was ready.

"I've got some 'walking around money' stashed away," he replied, "and besides, the Foundation's going to allow me a decent salary and expense account. I said I'd dedicate my talents to the service of my country……..not become homeless."

Liz was wondering which, of the many possible positions, would put the least amount of pressure on his wounded shoulder, as the sun dipped below the horizon and she moved closer to him, in spite of herself.

* * *

DiStefano arrived in Nicosia shortly after Kauffman and was the last of the four to get to the rendezvous in Famagusta's Old Town. He had hit the proverbial wall in Charleston; the stress and lack of sleep had finally taken its toll. Vince Lombardi was right, he thought…"fatigue makes cowards of us all." He had fallen asleep on take-off, taken a leak at the refueling stop, and awakened upon landing. He was refreshed and optimistic as he headed up the stairs for the meeting. This particular item on the agenda shouldn't take long; then on to the Cayman Islands, twenty-five million dollars richer, and a new life, free of the pressure cooker of Zybercor. Patrick was on top of the world and a multi-billionaire and Tony was thinking that he had never met a billionaire he didn't like. Patrick had promised him an executive position in the Foundation. He didn't exactly know what the future would bring, but with Brady he knew it would be a helluva ride.

The private home rented by Huan's man in Cyprus was a magnificent 19th century villa; and like the island itself, a reflection of Greek and Turkish influences. The four parties were meeting on the third floor in order to catch the cooling afternoon breezes. Off-white pillars supported a slanted tile roof. The spacious room was appointed with comfortable seating, a dining table for eight, and was open on two sides, creating a breezeway with a magnificent view of the harbor and the medieval village. The green awnings kept the men in the shade as they made small talk on the terrace while drinks and a tray of food were served. As soon as they were alone the conversation shifted to the business at hand.

Kauffman had never seen Huan so ebullient as he played the role of charming host with uncharacteristic flair. He segued to the business agenda with a toast of an indigenous liqueur called Commanderie, served in exquisite glasses, blown, then etched by a local craftsman in Lymosel. After the good luck toast Huan asked DiStefano for an update on events in America before getting to the issues surrounding the documents and the transfer of funds. As DiStefano began his recitation of events subsequent to the sortie, Kauffman helped himself to another glass of the fine aged liqueur, all the while complimenting Huan on his good taste and his exquisite choice of settings. Starting over, DiStefano briefed the group on the aftermath of the successful attack on Building #F3. Of course, all present had been closely following the media and had their own sources in D.C. However, they expected DiStefano to embellish their information with nuances and subtleties, 'color commentary' if you will, to which their sources were not privy. He didn't disappoint them as he methodically recapped the public and private events of the last 76 hours, but was careful to omit any reference to the fate of Colonel Franks.

Rahnajat was the first to speak. "Tell me Tony, what is the status of the federal investigation reported in the press and will the Pentagon wait for its results before deciding what to do with the Land Force Warrior Program?" His constituents in Tehran were anxious to know how best to take advantage of the technology from both a military and diplomatic perspective. Al Qaeda was arguing for immediate deployment in Afghanistan in advance of their planned spring Taliban offensive.

DiStefano considered his answer carefully. He didn't want to discuss the new contract which Zybercor had negotiated with the Pentagon in any detail, as that might lead to the issue of Artificial Intelligence and Brady had instructed him to avoid that at all costs. On the other hand, Rahnajat and the Chinaman were up-to-speed on the press coverage and knew fully well that Brady was exiting Zybercor to embark on a new venture.

"As you know, Zybercor was successful in renegotiating with the Pentagon, but it's going to take a year to replace the simulator and recover from all the damage done in Charleston last week. The investigation, in the meantime, looks like a slow-moving clusterfuck. I'll ride herd on that through my contacts in the intelligence community. Patrick's protégée, Liz Turney, will be the new Zybercor CEO. So, for all practical purposes, he's still in control of the company. Not to worry."

"That is very reassuring, Mr. DiStefano," said Huan. "The Chinese-Iranian relationship has progressed considerably in the past week. Both parties are comfortable with the terms and conditions of the agreements so we need not burden today's discussion with those details."

Kauffman was suffused with a sense of euphoria, the likes of which he had never experienced before, as Huan spoke the magic words assuring them that it was time to 'show them the money'. He was, in reality, feeling calmer by the minute as his heart rate slowed down, courtesy of the effect of the synthetic narcotic administered through the fine liqueur. He was feeling its full effect before DiStefano, since Kauffman had taken two glasses to DiStefano's one.

The Chinese Directorate of Intelligence had developed some very effective pharmacological weapons over the last few years. Huan chose a derivative of CX4 - a unique cocktail blending a slow-moving poison with a cousin of Demerol and the chemical equivalent of ecstasy. A massive release of dopamine and serotonin was accompanied by a gradual ramping-down of the heart rates until the victims simply stopped breathing......but with smiles on their faces. Huan had planned on a different exit for Kauffman; however, after Brady's phone call adding DiStefano to the list of the dearly-to-be-departed, he chose a more humane option in consideration of Brady's deep devotion to his Director of Security.

The dosage was calibrated to last 30 minutes before completing its task but Kauffman's insistence on the second drink speeded the process up considerably. Kauffman simply stopped breathing in the middle of a thought as he wondered how his partners were going to get him **his** money with DiStefano sitting in the room. He didn't have a worry in the world, though, because Huan and Rahnajat were really great guys, weren't they? They were really.............great.............g.

"Is he dead?" asked DiStefano as Kauffman's eyes stared straight ahead. Mark had a beatific smile on his face and a single tear dropped from his glazed eyelids as his shoulders settled peacefully into the comfortable armchair.

"Very much so," said Huan. He patiently explained the salutary benefits of CX4 as DiStefano began to feel the calm, warming effects of the initial phase. Even as the powerful narcotic began to dull the workings of the frontal lobe, Tony realized that he, too, had been poisoned and that his time remaining on this earth was measured in minutes. As his heart rate decelerated inexorably he fondly recounted his time with Patrick Fortune Brady and asked them to extend to him his best wishes for a happy and healthy life. He gave Huan and Rahnajat the tail number of the waiting Zybercor jet, as well as the account number for the Central Bank in the Cayman Islands, before nodding off in peace.

Later that very day he would join Kauffman on a sunset cruise to the shark-infested waters outside of Famagusta.

Huan and Rahnajat had no intention of flying to the Cayman Islands in the Zybercor jet. Huan released the wire transfer to Brady's account in the Central Bank in the Cayman Islands through his old friend at the Bank of Cyprus - $3.2B after converting the currency at that day's rate.

"What made you change your mind about the trip to the Caymans?" asked Rahnajat as he helped himself to a bottled water from the ice bucket. His appetite for the liqueur had waned somewhat.

"It appears that it's very unhealthy to be around Patrick Brady these days," replied Huan serving himself another glass of the Commanderie St. John from the bottle to assure Rahnajat that it was safe to imbibe.

"Besides, there is nothing more to accomplish in meeting with him directly. We have made our deal and I am satisfied that Brady will keep his end of the bargain. You and I know too much and there is, perhaps, further business to be done in the future."

Huan and Rahnajat had developed an easy demeanor with one another in spite of their deep cultural differences. Ironically, they found it most efficient to communicate in English. They had aligned their interests and both had prospered politically as a result of the global agreements between their governments. The deal they cut with Brady was satisfactory to both men, principally because they believed it was much safer to secure their compensation indirectly rather than risk detection by 'skimming off the top'. Brady had agreed to pay each man $100,000.00 per month for as long as he, Brady, lived. Brady would sleep better at night knowing that Huan and Rahnajat had an investment in his well-being and he, too, saw the opportunity to develop ongoing business together through his New Foundation. He had already expressed interest in obtaining information from Huan concerning the Chinese satellite-disabling technology. He felt comfortable that the math was right among all the parties. A life expectancy for himself of eighty-five years would translate nicely to approximately $30,000,000.00 for Huan and Rahnajat. Less than 1% each, for a long-term life insurance policy, was a bargain by any standard.

* * *

Matt Kilmer had just gotten his ass chewed by Megan Daniels after a pissy morning with his staff. He told his wife of twenty-two years that they should move to Canada, as there was no way the U.S. intelligence community was ever going to get its act together. Human nature and parochial interest would conspire to override the more vacuous notions of teamwork and national security every time. It would take a ruthless autocrat, with the support of all three branches, to hammer the aggregate of agencies together into one integrated efficient organization and that would never happen.

In the meantime, Kilmer was caught squarely in the middle of some violent and conflicting forces and he was rapidly running out of time. His toolbox of skills left him ill-prepared for the job at hand. He was a talented investigator and security operative, not a politician. Every fiber of his body screamed to him that this entire incident was a setup from the outset, but he couldn't put the pieces together in a logical way. It was like a jigsaw puzzle with pieces that fit nowhere with, in addition, a hole in the middle with no pieces to fill it, either. The pressure from the White House was so intense it felt like the top of his head was scalded. The good news was he hadn't had a migraine in two days. The bad news was that the scalding was worse than the migraine. He feared it would become permanent and remain even as he collected unemployment after his ass was canned at the end of this fiasco.

He had a few hours to focus his attention on the key issues before his all-important meeting with Patrick Brady and Tony DiStefano aboard Brady's yacht that evening. Brady had insisted upon dinner, arguing there was nothing unpatriotic about a little civilization and some fine French cooking. He wondered what the proper protocol would be for interviewing a national hero who was the President's new best friend.

Come on Matt...focus. First, who gained the most as a result of the incident? Obviously the bad guys had the most to gain. Not only did they get away with the Land Force Warrior system, they set back our ability to redeploy it to the Middle East early next year. The only other winner seemed to be Patrick Brady but he almost got killed and, though he cashed out of Zybercor with a ton of dough, he committed to put all that money to work in a new non-profit dedicated to the enhancement of national security. It just didn't add up. How did Al Qaeda know there was a Board Meeting taking place at the facility? How did they know that the components and software programs would be so readily available? How did they get in and out undetected? The impact of the C4 and thermite had made forensics virtually useless. Brady, DiStefano, and Franks were the only survivors and Franks might never regain consciousness.

Daniels had given him twenty-four hours to prepare a written report for the President. By this time tomorrow his ass would be on the line. What the hell was he going to do?

* * *

It was nearing 6:00 p.m. in Charleston Harbor. A small flotilla of sailboats competed for the finish line anchored by the harbormaster's skiff. Drinks and bragging rights were on the line as fantasies of America's Cup propelled the seasoned amateurs just beyond Fort Sumter and then back into the harbor. There were few of the larger yachts this time of year..........most having fled for the more sultry weather of the Caribbean.

Aboard the Buona Fortuna, Diane Ben-Shoshon had been at work preparing a special meal for Mr. Brady and his guest. She had planned, under his direction, a seven-course meal served on the aft deck. The water was calm so Captain Bar-Cohen would cast off at 6:15 and cruise up the Intracoastal Waterway and return to Charleston Harbor on the open sea past the Isle of Palms and Sullivan's Island. The crew was aware that Mr. DiStefano was out of the country, however, they knew better than to ask Mr. Brady why he wanted a third setting at the table.

At 6:00 p.m. sharp Matt Kilmer, briefcase in hand, was welcomed aboard by Patrick Brady. Brady was sporting a crew neck sweater, khakis, and topsiders. His left arm was in a sling but he seemed to be getting around well and reached out his right hand to take Kilmer's case as he motioned him on deck.

"Mr. Matt Kilmer, welcome aboard the Buona Fortuna. I've been looking forward to this. There are lots of questions that need answers and I'm certainly hoping you're the man with the answers." Brady had decided to take the offensive with tonight's meeting. His position was well fortified behind the impregnable ramparts of public opinion and he took comfort that his newfound friends in high places would provide ample insulation from aggressive interrogation. Thomas had presented him with a complete dossier on Mr. Kilmer early this morning. He was an impressive fellow indeed: a New York City boy all the way, including NYU Law School and a Masters from the John Jay School of Criminal Justice. He had gone straight into the Bureau and had risen steadily, becoming the Special Agent in Charge of the New York Office at the very tender age of thirty-six. He could obviously hit major league pitching. After 9/11 he went to Washington where he became the Bureau's 'go-to guy' for interfacing with Homeland Security. Counter-terrorism became his *specialité*. According to the report Kilmer had now hit the ceiling inside the Bureau. Apparently he lacked the skills necessary to survive in the highly politicized world of the modern D.C. bureaucracy. His net worth was circa two mil.......so he obviously had to work. In today's world that was a house with a mortgage, a piddling stock portfolio and a modest 401K...not much to show for a good education and twenty years of busting balls. Brady smelled opportunity.

Brady and Kilmer were enjoying some *foie gras* and a fine sauterne as the Buona Fortuna turned north into the Intracoastal. Kilmer had briefed his host on the process that was utilized to attempt to recreate the attack at the Navy Yard. He had gotten permission from Daniels to share the simulation software with Brady and had his laptop open on the table. Together they traced the operation from beginning to end. Brady peppered Kilmer with an endless stream of questions many answered with a reluctant, "I just don't know."

"Matt, you've seen Al Qaeda's work before. Are they really this good?" asked Brady.

"To tell you the truth, this is not their typical *modus operandi*. Their targets are usually more...I don't know...sedentary. Their planning is long-term and not subject to shifting events and uncertain schedules. I can't figure out how they pulled this off so flawlessly at such short notice."

"Are you suggesting they had someone on the inside?" asked Brady. He had been waiting patiently for this point in the conversation. It was time to prod him to find out what he knew and, more importantly, what he was going to put in his report. Franks had still not regained consciousness and his neurologist had been speculating that a blow to the head had precipitated an edema that could result in amnesia.

Kilmer sipped his wine while the appetizer plates were cleared, then replaced by platters laden with pasta in a lobster cream sauce. A bottle of white burgundy, that would have cost Kilmer a month's salary, was placed just within reach.

"Mr. Brady, I..."

"It's Patrick, please, Matt."

"Patrick, the things I believe I can't prove, and the things I can prove I find hard to believe. The truth of the matter is that I am completely stymied. I was hoping that you and Tony DiStefano could help me finalize my report. The big boss is all over me and I have a deadline end of day tomorrow. By the way, when will Tony be joining us?"

"Matt, I don't think Tony will be joining us. I spoke to him this afternoon and he's having a breakdown of sorts."

Kilmer looked stricken. Only three living witnesses to the attack and one was incommunicado, and another in a coma. "May I ask where he is?"

"Yes. He took the company plane to the Cayman Islands for some rest. Tony took this whole thing very badly. He felt responsible, in a way. I tried to reassure him and get him some help but I wasn't successful. He's divorced and, quite frankly, a bit of a loner. I'm concerned he's seriously traumatized, even borderline suicidal. He's a scuba diver and uses that to relax. I'm going to give him all the time he needs, but frankly, I would be surprised if he ever got back in the game." It was eerily quiet on the aft deck, the only sound coming from the bow of the Buona Fortuna as she cruised out to sea for the return leg.

Brady broke the silence. "But, Matt, I've seen this happen before. Once someone gets their 'fuck-you money', they change. Tony's magic number was always ten mil...then figure a 15% dividend tax and a 5% net cash flow without touching principal. Hell, he's made twice that with me."

MANIPULATION

"Are you telling me your Director of Security has made twenty million dollars?"

"And then some," replied Brady. "This is a big job…lots of responsibility…and, let's face it, this world has become a dangerous place. Information is everything and the water I swim in is full of sharks. Tony was invaluable to me. I don't know how I'm going to replace him."

It was 9:30 p.m. when the Buona Fortuna sailed back into Charleston Harbor. The city's lights were reflecting off the still water under a half moon and flawless sky.

For the first time in a long while, Matt Kilmer was pain-free and relaxed. The report would be submitted to the White House well in advance of tomorrow's deadline. Megan would be relieved and the President could focus all of his prodigious intellect on the elimination of an enemy who had, with impunity, planned and executed an attack on a top-secret facility. As for Matt, he would submit his resignation and move from the government to the private sector.

Kilmer and Brady had negotiated his new compensation package between the *crème brueleé* and a VSOP cognac as Patrick Fortune Brady toasted to 'health and wealth' and congratulated his new Director of Security.

EPILOGUE

Nine Months Later
A Private Island in the Caribbean
Late Afternoon

The construction finally complete, Patrick Fortune Brady was lounging in his favorite hammock on the veranda connecting his office complex to his private residence. Brady had purchased the island and all the buildings from a Dutch couple who had built and managed a magnificent high-end getaway for the rich and famous. Reluctant at first, they succumbed to Brady's charm and a cashier's check for $45,000,000.00. The Michael Graves Architect team based in Princeton oversaw the renovation including the installation of an airstrip on the leeward side of the island.

The manor house exterior was virtually unchanged. Brady had fallen in love with the Mediterranean architecture and the open-air design. The Graves team concentrated, therefore, on the interior and the design/build of an adjacent office complex, housing Brady's New Foundation as well as the hub for his far-flung business interests. In addition, they redesigned a half-dozen guest villas forming a crescent bordering a private beach a quarter mile from the manor house. All other outbuildings and accommodations had been razed and replaced with Bermuda grass.

The recreational facilities were all upgraded and included a nine-hole golf course, two clay tennis courts, stables, a diving facility, and, of course, a permanent docking area for the Buona Fortuna II, now two hundred and five feet long with its own helipad.

MANIPULATION

All in all, the effect was stunning. Earth tones dominated all of Graves' major works and the Tuscan influence was omnipresent in the exterior and interior alike. The landscaping alone had a $2M price tag with palm trees lining an interlocking network of Italian stone walkways rich in trellises abundant with bougainvillaea. Brady's passion for sound and light was translated by a separate team into a fully-integrated system that he controlled with a hand-held digital remote that had the capacity to create up to twenty lighting packages and, of course, an unlimited array of music played through sixty well-placed, customized Wilson speakers. Today was the first day in nine months that Patrick was alone. When the last detail had been completed he peremptorily ordered everyone off the island including architects, contractors, professional staff, groundskeepers, even security.

The Citation was bringing Liz tonight at 9:00. He wanted to be alone and show her every square foot of his self-made paradise with no interruptions. He gazed appreciatively at the beautiful diamond necklace that had been delivered by courier from Harry Winston. He hoped his Liz would understand the serious sentiments it bespoke.

He loved the unique feel and smell of the African hemp hammock as it swayed gently in the breeze. He had chosen Vivaldi for this afternoon. The intricate composition and brilliant melodies seemed to float in the air as if, by magic, the woodwinds, strings, brass, and percussion knew exactly what to do and when to do it. Brady, however, knew that magic had nothing to do with the effect. The music was created by the genius, imagination, and determination of man. If this was Heaven...and it was to Patrick Brady...then this, too, was man-made and he was the creative genius behind it.

He opened the first bottle of champagne of the day and laughed aloud as the top levitated ten feet in the air with a 'pop' that sounded like an angel's fart, was caught by the ever present breeze and carried off the veranda to a resting place near the infinity pool. The world was in perfect harmony. His relationship with Liz had blossomed into something that he defined as love. Zybercor stock was up to $115 per share. The Artificial Intelligence capacity had been successfully installed in the Land Force Warrior Program which spearheaded the redeployment of U.S. military capability in the Middle East. Apparently the Chinese and Iranians were at each other's throats. The honeymoon was definitely over. According to Huan, the Iranians could never get it all together. The advanced generation of Land Force Warrior literally 'blew away' the early edition that they had liberated from the Charleston Naval Yard last fall. In any event, they were back at the negotiating table bickering about the price of oil. In the meantime, Huan and Rahnajat were frequent guests and it was with great pleasure that Brady wired them $100,000 each at the end...not the beginning, mind you...of every month.

Matt Kilmer had proven to be an excellent Director of Security. Of course, no one could ever replace Tony DiStefano, but then every war has its casualties.

The Foundation had proven to be a brilliant idea. Under the cover of national security, Brady had obtained various patents and technologies through the not-for-profit vehicle supported by the President and, in turn, cherry-picked those that had the greatest potential and shifted them to his wholly-owned 'for-profit' company located in the Cayman Islands.

There was only one loose end and Brady had conditioned himself to dismiss it as irrelevant. Franks, Macklin, and Grossman had simply disappeared off the face of the earth. Brady and Kilmer had thrown huge resources into a 'man-hunt' that rivaled a high priority FBI investigation and turned up absolutely zilch.

Cal Whitfield had been dedicated to finding Macklin who was confined to a wheelchair, that, according to the file, was equipped with a laser and sounded like a power generator when it moved. Brady often wondered how they managed to get Franks out of the hospital and elude the dragnet. Two days after Franks' disappearance Whitfield's body had been recovered in some marshland bordering James Island with his throat cut. Since then, *nada*. "Oh well," said Brady out loud as he ruminated about the past…"Life goes on." He was invulnerable.

* * *

After a couple of glasses of fine champagne, Brady dozed in the hammock as the Caribbean sun surrendered to the darkening night. After a brief siesta he felt relaxed, refreshed and ready to party. It was 8:00 already and Liz would be arriving soon. He couldn't believe how quiet the evening was. It was magical. He decided to turn the music off as he programmed the lighting system to the muted 'light blue' package that he treasured. The breeze was scented with bougainvillaea and the soft lapping of the waves created a sense of peace and wonderment that was beyond description. He was truly the king of the world. **The only sound other than the beautiful trill of the Caribbean night sparrows was the obnoxious hum of the over-sized wheelchair and the crunching of gravel as it made its way inexorably up the driveway to the veranda in the back.**

Made in the USA